QUEEN
HEREAFTER

QUEEN
HEREAFTER

A Novel

SUSAN FRASER KING

CROWN

New York

Copyright © 2010 by Susan Fraser King

Published in the United States by Crown Publishers, an imprint of the Crown Publishing Group, a division of Random House, Inc., New York.
www.crownpublishing.com

CROWN and the Crown colophon are registered trademarks of Random House, Inc.

Library of Congress Cataloging-in-Publication Data
King, Susan
Queen hereafter : a novel / Susan Fraser King.—1st ed.
p.   cm.
1. Queens—Scotland—Fiction.   2. Scotland—Fiction. I. Title.
PS3561.I4833Q44 2010
813'.54—dc22   2010012340

ISBN 978-0-307-45279-5

Printed in the United States of America

Design by Chris Welch

Map illustration by Richard Thompson

10 9 8 7 6 5 4 3 2 1

First Edition

FOR SEAN, SO LIKE A SAXON PRINCE

Non Angli sed angeli

Genealogy of Margaret and Malcolm

*Erc of Dal Riada → Generations of Irish, Picts, and Scots → House of Gabhran → *Kenneth mac Alpin → many generations of Scots → *Malcolm I

Cerdic of Wessex → *Egbert → *Aethelwulf → *Alfred the Great → *Edward → *Edmund I → *Edgar → *Aethelred II "The Unready"

*Malcolm I
- Dubh (Duff)
  - *Kenneth III
    - Bodhe of Fife
      - *GRUADH = 1. Gilcomgan 2. *MACBETH
        - *Lulach   (no children)
          - Maelsnechtan Daughter EVA
- *Kenneth II
  - *Malcolm II
    - Donada = Finlach
    - Bethoc = Crinan
      - *Duncan = Sybilla
        - Donal Ban *MALCOLM III = *MARGARET
          (1030–1093)   (1046–1093)

*Aethelred II "The Unready"
- *Edward the Confessor
- *Edmund II "Ironside"
  - Edmund
  - Edward the Exile = Agatha
    - *MARGARET (1046–1093) Cristina Edgar the Aetheling
- Royal House of Kiev

*MALCOLM III = *MARGARET
- Edward
- *Edmund
- *Edgar
- Aethelred
- *Alexander
- *Edith
  - *"Empress" Matilda
- *David
  - Henry
    - *William the Lion
      - *generations of kings of Scots → *Robert Bruce → *the Stewart kings → *Mary Queen of Scots → *James I (Stuart) →
- Mary
  - *Matilda = Stephen

* denotes a king or queen

EVA is a fictitious character

11TH CENTURY
SCOTLAND

ORKNEY

CAITHNESS

NORTH SEA

SUTHERLAND

ROSS

Moray Firth

Dingwall •   Burghead
          • •Pitgaveny
Craig Phadraig •• • Cawdor   Elgin
          Inverness

Loch Ness

MORAY

BUCHAN

Lanfinnan •
Kincardine O'Neil •

SCOTLAND

Dunkeld   • Glamis
*BIRNAM
WOOD* •

ATHOLL   Scone •
      Abernethy •   *Firth of Tay*
               • St Andrews
          FIFE
Loch Leven
Dunfermline •
Queensferry • *Firth of Forth*

Dun Edin •

LOTHIAN   • Berwick

Melrose •   • Carham

STRATHCLYDE

NORTHUMBRIA

Durham •

IRELAND

CUMBRIA

ENGLAND

N

0   20   40

Scale of Miles

I am not what you think I am

but may I be it because you think it.

—*Bishop Turgot to Queen Margaret*,
Vita S. Margaretae (Life of Saint Margaret),
EARLY TWELFTH CENTURY

Eva

ANNO DOMINI 1074

Bring to me the harp of my king
That on it I may shed my grief

—IRISH, THIRTEENTH CENTURY

Caught between two willful queens, I am, and should have taken more care to tread lightly—like crossing a stream over slippery stones when the current is strong and cold. Now that I have stumbled deep, who can say whether my two queens will forgive me or condemn me for what I did at each one's bidding. No servant, I am free to do as I please. Margaret and Gruadh disagree.

I am called Eva the Bard, daughter of a short-lived king. I have been a devoted student of Dermot, once chief bard in Macbeth's court. He trained me in the ways of a *seanchaidh*: a thousand songs, a thousand tales, a thousand heroes keenly remembered through ancient ways of diligence, and more. Though I do not know my fate, I know my calling—to tell the old tales and coax melodies from the harp strings to soothe or excite the spirit. Some now accuse me of scheming, but my aim has ever been my craft, and honor. So say I.

The king and queen would order some monk with ink-stained fingers to record my betrayal on parchment, which would crumble over time; the lady in the north would order the account destroyed much sooner. Yet I would compose a song-poem to tell it whole, then take up my harp and sing it to some, who would teach it to others, so it would never be lost.

One queen might call it treason, the other tradition. But I might call it vengeance.

❊

Dunfermline, Scotland
Autumn 1074

AS THE WOODEN BEAM that crossed the door of her cell was lifted and stowed aside, Eva rose to her feet. Cold and damp penetrated her thin wool tunic as she waited. As the guard opened the door and torch-light bloomed in the gap, Eva blinked, her eyes used to darkness after weeks of incarceration.

Still and wary, she heard the rumbling voices of the guard and the Saxon priest who answered, then mellow, clear notes as a woman spoke. The guard appeared in the doorway and gestured for Eva to approach. Defiant, she did not. He stood back.

The woman crossed the threshold, skirts gathered in long, pale fingers as she stepped down to the deeper floor of the dungeon cell. Behind her, torchlight illuminated the small space. The lady paused, slender and lovely, with a veil as translucent as a halo, like some saint or angel bringing relief and blessings to the prisoner.

"My friend," Margaret said quietly.

"Lady," Eva replied, watching the Queen of Scots. Daughter of a king, a bard in her own right, Eva also had a privileged rank—but the old Scotland was changing, she reminded herself.

Margaret approached, the hem of her blue gown, banded by gold thread embroidery, sweeping across the straw-covered earthen floor. Calmly, she clasped her hands before her. Tall and slim, a mother of three little sons already, the queen looked girlish still. Her face was lovely on a long neck, eyes blue as her gown, golden hair woven into two long braids beneath her veil; perfect, ethereal. Margaret's beauty was as well known as her charitable nature: Scotland's young Saxon queen, at first reviled, now increasingly beloved.

Yet Eva had glimpsed beyond the saintly virtues to the fears and flaws beneath. She knew that Margaret, who could be genuinely good of heart, had a core like stubborn rock. Once decided on a matter, she would not be dissuaded for good or ill.

"Eva, we must talk." There was steely will beneath the gentle voice.

"Say what you will, then leave."

"I came to seek your counsel," Margaret said, while Eva glanced at her in surprise. "My husband the king bids me advise him on your fate. He will make the final decision, but he wants the truth of it."

Dread wrenched within. Eva could not tell all the truth, and give up one she loved. "What does it matter? Others will twist what I say. You know that well."

"I never expected betrayal from you, or hints of witchcraft. I do not know what to believe. But I must make a recommendation."

Eva frowned. Though Margaret sometimes thought herself weak and sinful, she was strong-minded to a fault, and her opinion counted for much with the king. "The accusations are unfounded. Tell Malcolm that I am no witch."

"And the Lady of the North? What does she have to do with this?"

"Very little." What she had agreed to do had seemed right at the time. Now she was entangled in old conflict between Lady Gruadh in the north, her kinswoman, and King Malcolm. Scotland's former queen was wise, though bitter, and Eva would honor what Gruadh had asked of her.

"That is not so easy to believe. There are punishments established by the *witanagemot* for criminals and witches," Margaret went on.

"Malcolm has asked me to consider those laws." Her intonation was flat, cool.

"Saxon law does not apply here," Eva said. Yet over several years, Malcolm had instituted several Saxon practices and punishments, and employed his council like a *witan,* a group of wise advisors to the king. Eva had good reason to fear her fate if accused of witchery. Margaret might be her only hope.

"Recommend that I be judged according to Scottish law, not Saxon," Eva said.

"Such crimes merit severe consequences," the queen responded. "Glowing iron, boiling water, or worse, fire. My ancestor great King Alfred helped devise that system of justice. The king could ask for such trials to find the truth." She spoke calmly, but the knuckles of her hands went white. "If you are innocent, as you claim, all will be well."

"Why will you not believe me? I have done no wrong to you."

The queen looked away. Eva sensed her uncertainty; perhaps Margaret wanted to believe her.

"I could pass any test you give me," Eva said impulsively. Guilty or innocent, who could survive such ordeals? "You are a believer in miracles. You will see."

"Miracles?" Margaret seemed intrigued. "Has your faith improved in the last weeks?"

"Lady," Eva said wearily, "we are both in need of miracles, some days."

Margaret sighed, and for a moment Eva glimpsed the young woman she knew, though the longer Margaret was queen, the more she perfected a cool, haughty side. "In England, they burn witches. Do not let it come to that." She stepped closer. "Pray with greater devotion and ask forgiveness for your sins, and heaven may grant mercy. Convince the king of your loyalty and he will show earthly mercy. You are ever stubborn, Eva, but your very soul is in jeopardy now. I will send a priest to speak with you."

"Which one?" Eva looked at her defiantly. "One who follows the will of the Roman Church over the Celtic? Or the one who follows your will?"

"Tor says naught but good of you," Margaret chided. "I will send a confessor to cleanse the wickedness from your heart and set your foot on a better path."

"Can wickedness be turned in a savage Scot?" Eva felt bitter. "You have not succeeded in turning our faces and hearts entirely toward Rome, though you deserve credit for trying to improve us all."

"You are much like your kinswoman. I see that now."

"I consider that high praise."

"Many would not." Turning, Margaret moved toward the door, then paused. "If the priests agree that you did treason and witchcraft, no one can save you from the fires."

"It is not the custom in Scotland to burn witches."

"I am not Scottish," Margaret said quietly. Gathering her skirts in her hands, she stepped across the threshold. The guard closed the door, shutting out the light.

Eva sank to the floor in the darkness and tucked her head in her arms.

Chapter One

Margaret

ANNO DOMINI 1067

The wind sets from the south
Across the land of the Saxons of mighty shields

—IRISH, ELEVENTH CENTURY

My lady mother was so sure the English king planned to be rid of us the moment we set foot on his Saxon shores that she refused to sail there from Denmark. But we had been journeying for months after leaving Hungary, the lot of us: Papa, Mama, my sister and small brother, and a few servants. We were exhausted and sore in need of a home. Papa said we belonged in England, after all. I heard my parents arguing it at night.

My father, born a prince of England, had been exiled to the kingdom of Hungary as a small boy. Lately King Edward, his royal and childless uncle, had summoned Papa—another Edward—home to England to restore his birthright and name him heir to the throne. Mama groused that while our uncle-king had beckoned, he would not pay our traveling costs, and she feared he might lay claim to the priceless treasures we hauled about in crates and chests. My mother, Agatha, was Russian and Hungarian by birth and blood, and little liked the English. Her warrior husband she excused; he had left England at a young age.

My father was Saxon royalty of the old Wessex line, and so were his children, harking back to wise King Alfred, to unready Aethelred and stubborn Edmund Ironside, my grandfather. Our brighter future lay in England. Lady Agatha would be queen there, according to both Edwards. Dignified if stubborn, she acquiesced.

The year I turned ten, we left Hungary, where my two siblings and I had been born. Traveling with a Magyar escort over high mountains into Russia, carrying heavy packed chests in carts the whole way, we stayed weeks in Kiev with my mother's kin, then sailed northward to winter among the Danes, my father's cousins. That place was dull and smoky indoors, but splendid outside. I saw how much we resembled the Danes and the *Rus,* too, for we were long limbed and golden fair, with taut cheekbones and sky-colored eyes. Only my sister Cristina took after the dark and stocky Magyars, the tough bloodline of our mother's maternal kin; she had a bold temperament, too, outspoken where I was acquiescent, hot and impulsive where I was cool and devout as I tried to emulate my pious mother and grandmother.

We crossed the wide, pitching North Sea, while my mother murmured of impending doom and prayed over her black-beaded rosary. Despite her worrying, the Danish vessel skimmed the waves like a winged dragon and brought us swiftly to English shores.

In London town, we were welcomed by lords who spoke the Saxon language that my father knew and we did not. The king was away, but we were housed by the Archbishop of Canterbury, who spoke German, our preferred tongue, with us. We were dined, entertained, and assessed by a parade of bishops, priests, and notable lords and ladies; servants, too, I suppose. Assured that he would be king eventually, my father gently teased his wife that her fears were unfounded.

A week after our arrival, he fell dead at my feet.

A few of us were walking in the archbishop's gardens after supper with some of England's earls and thanes when my father collapsed on a path. We could not rouse him. To this day, years on, I can recall my disbelief and shock, my father's gray face, my mother's paleness, and the scents of calendula and thyme.

Poison was the rumor, denied and dismissed. The king's physician said Edward Aetheling had a weak heart, though my father had been a lion of a warrior, with spare habits and good health. Tainted food was suggested by others, though no one else had fallen sick that night.

Taint or poison, I alone knew the truth: I had killed him.

At my insistence, he had eaten sweetmeats from a golden tray set on the table before him. At first he had refused, intent on his discussion with a Saxon bishop. But with girlish silliness, I pushed the tray toward him, saying he must obey Princess Margaret. Distracted, smiling, he downed the treats in a fistful or two. Within the half hour, he was dead. Likely there was strong poison in those honeyed almonds and hazelnuts—and my father would not have eaten them that night but for my urging.

Mea culpa, mea culpa, but I never confessed my deed to a priest, only adding to the heinous sin. Fear kept me silent. I wore bruises into my knees praying self-imposed penances, while my lady mother approved my pious grieving, mistaking what moved me so. I could not tell her and hurt her even more.

At court, some whispered of the ambitious men who would have benefitted from the death of Edward the Exile: Harold Godwinson was one, brother of the queen and son of an ambitious Saxon earl, and William of Normandy was another. King Edward, rumor said, had bargained his crown to both men secretly and then gave the heir's right to my father. Whether one of them had ordered Edward the Exile killed or some other had done it, my own hand had aided the killer. I shared the sin.

That gnawed at me, crept into my dreams, perched on my shoulder like a demon.

Overnight we transformed from exalted royal family to the foreign wards of a king who took little interest in us yet would not permit us to return to Hungary. My siblings and I were educated as befitted our status in that formal, refined court. But we were in effect hostages housed as king's wards, our little freedom spent witnessing the hunt, hawking, or taking the short and frequent journey between the London and Winchester palaces. Often my sister and I refused to ride in the canopied van that carried the women, delighting in a chance for the saddle. We had been partly raised by Magyar kin, after all.

At five years old, my brother Edgar was named king's heir in a ceremony, while the other claimants for the English throne remained avid and interested. The year I turned twenty and Edgar thirteen, our aged royal uncle died, leaving Edgar the Aetheling, Harold Godwinson, and William of Normandy each believing in his own right to be king.

Harold was quickly chosen by the *witanagemot* and duly crowned. England needed a warrior-king, not a stripling boy, that year. Had Harold taken hawk's wings to soar over the cliffs of England, he would have seen two threats at once: the Danes sweeping in from the east and the Normans coming from the south.

Within months, in the autumn of anno domini 1066, the mail-clad warriors of Normandy slid their boats, silent and lethal, onto our English shore. Harold died on Hastings field and William took us for his wards—but as soon as we could get away, my kin and I fled.

※

And the Aetheling went back again to Scotland.

—*Anglo-Saxon Chronicle*, ENTRY FOR 1069

England
Autumn 1069

THE THUD OF IRON-HEELED boots in the corridor startled Margaret from sleep. She sat up in the darkness, alarmed, shaking her sister's arm until Cristina woke, too. As the door shoved wide, two men stepped into the room, mail armor glinting in the moonlight that slipped through a small window. The maidservant, Kata, shrieked, leaping up from her straw pallet, while Margaret and Cristina stumbled out of bed, clutching blankets to cover themselves.

Margaret felt a twist of fear—surely these were Normans, she thought, and rude devils to enter a convent by force and moon's glow.

"*Mes desmoiselles,*" one of the men said in French, resting a hand on his sword pommel, "hurry! *Dépêchez-vous!*"

Margaret gathered her younger sister close, aware that Norman knights treated even high-ranking Saxon women with brutal disrespect.

"Hurry!" the knight repeated in French, stepping forward. "We cannot waste time!"

Flinching, Margaret nonetheless lifted her chin. "*Partez ici,*" she replied. "Leave! How do you dare! We are princesses of England."

"Ready yourselves by order of the king, or we will carry you out as you are. Bring their belongings—there are valuables here." The man motioned to his companion, who snatched a linen sheet and began to toss their things onto it. Margaret watched in astonishment as he grabbed her Gospel book from the small table, snatched Cristina's needlework basket, too, and opened a wooden chest to dump its contents—garments, veils, stockings, belts, ribbons, and other items—into the sheet. As he began to tie the clumsy bundle, Margaret stepped toward him.

"Give me the book," she said, grabbing the leather-bound manuscript to tuck it under her arm. The Gospel had been a gift in her childhood from the English queen, and she would not lose it to a Norman.

"*Diebe und Schweine!*" Kata muttered in German, the language they often spoke among themselves. She grabbed cloaks from wall pegs and handed them to the princesses, who shrugged into them. "Thieves and pigs! Will they take what little we have? If we had stayed in Hungary we would be safe."

This had been their nurse's constant refrain ever since they had left Castle Reka years earlier. "There was rebellion in Hungary, too," Cristina snapped.

Margaret shoved bare feet into leather shoes and smoothed her long, tousled golden braids, and though she wanted to appear calm, her hands shook. In grim silence, the two knights grasped the girls' arms to lead them through the door.

"Norman pigs indeed," Cristina said in German. "What does King William want with us now? He shut us in here three years ago, and no word since. But this must be by his orders."

"I hoped we would take vows here and live in peace," Margaret said.

"You can take vows, not me," Cristina said. "You are suited to praying and studying. I want my freedom, but not like this!"

Outside in the thin moonlight, Margaret saw men, horses, and a cart. A few nuns and novices huddled with the abbess, their faces pale as they watched. Looking at the familiar walls of the abbey, Margaret began to panic. The shelter of Romsey had seemed so unassailable.

"*Monsieur chevalier,* where are we going?" Cristina demanded as they walked to the cart.

"Away from here, and quickly," the leader answered.

"Why?" Margaret asked. "It is only fair that we know."

He did not reply as he and another knight lifted the women into the cart. It was lined with straw, humble fittings for royal women. The bundle of their things was tossed in after them.

"Even when William's men brought us here, we were not treated like this!" Cristina said.

"Hush," Margaret warned, wary of her sister's abrasive temper. She forced a calm expression, determined to show regal dignity despite her fear. As she looked around, blond braids sliding over her shoulders, heart pounding, she reminded herself to pray for protection and forgiveness, too—but she was agitated and on the verge of losing her own temper.

More than a dozen riders were ready to depart, tough warriors all, mail armor and weapons gleaming in the moonlight. The cart carrying the girls lurched forward, and the escort rumbled through the gates and out into the chill November night. For one panicked moment, Margaret thought about leaping from the cart and running back to the sanctuary of the chapel, dragging her sister and maid with her. Instead, she watched the abbey fade into the distance and darkness.

Romsey Abbey had been King William's choice for a prison for the two Saxon princesses after his Norman armies had taken southern England. Their younger brother, Edgar, had been hastily crowned king at thirteen years old by dead King Harold's *witanagemot* just after the invasion, but William had then taken the boy to Normandy as a Saxon hostage. Lady Agatha, their mother, had been sent to Wilton Abbey, though she had thought to take much of their family treasure, brought from Hungary years before, with her to keep it from Norman hands.

Margaret had spent eleven years in King Edward's pious and glittering court, and she had seen many Normans there. King Edward had encouraged foreigners, particularly the Norman French, in his court, flattered by their interest—now, after his death, they were all paying the price of his gullibility. The royal Saxons had been captured and confined, and the Saxon people were beaten down but for those who advanced themselves by backing the invaders.

Shut away at Romsey for the past three years, Margaret had discovered unexpected peace amid turmoil. Turning to the solace of prayers, theological studies, and the enjoyments of reading and embroidery, she savored the routine at Romsey. Outside, her sole purpose would have been as a political bride, a living alliance expected to produce heirs. But now no man of rank would want her or Cristina. They were landless, worthless princesses but for their bloodline, thanks to William of Normandy.

Cristina leaned toward her in the lurching cart. "Why do they take us away now, tonight? If they had wanted rape and sport," she said bluntly, "they would have done it."

"I do not know. William cannot easily marry off the sisters of a deposed boy king. But if we had taken vows, he would have no authority over us. We would belong to the Church and would be safe."

"Safety, peace, saintliness—I vow that is all you want, Margaret!"

"I would consider myself fortunate to find that."

Huffing impatiently, Cristina turned toward the knight riding closest to the cart. "You! What is this about? Do you know who we are?" She spoke in French.

"We do," the man said, coming closer. He answered in English. "Of course we know."

"Then tell us where we are going, and why," Margaret demanded in English. Despite years in England, as a child she had spoken Hungarian and German and her slight accent revealed her foreign origins: she sounded like a Byzantine.

"We head for the nearest coast to meet a ship." When he pushed back his mail coif to reveal long gray hair and a mustache worn in the Saxon manner, rather than the clean jaw and shorn, thick-topped hair preferred by most Normans, Margaret frankly gaped at him.

"You are not Norman," she said. "What about the others?"

"Saxons all," he agreed. "We guised as Normans, else the abbess would have sent word to the sheriff straight away." He leaned down. Margaret could smell horse and the tang of metal, and she sensed urgency in his manner and speech. "I am Wilfrid of Bourne. What we do this night is rebellion and treason, and you two are part of it now. Your brother sent us."

"Edgar! What of him?" Margaret had not heard from her brother since he had been taken to Normandy. The latest rumors said he had pledged to William, thus ending hopes of rebellion under the young Saxon king.

"Edgar sent word to us in Lincoln for help. Others have gone to Wilton to fetch your lady mother. We are to meet them and then sail along the coast to meet your brother as well. He plans to take you out of England. With the Saxon rebellion gathering in the north, you two are not safe here any longer."

"But we heard that Edgar is William's sworn man now," Marga-ret said, puzzled. "How do we know you are here by his order rather than by some Norman trick?" Not all Saxons were loyal to the cause rallied around her brother, she knew.

"Edgar bids you return this to him yourself." He unfastened his cloak pin and handed it to her. She saw that the brooch was a silver one that Edgar owned and had taken to Normandy; she had pinned it to his cloak herself in farewell. She sensed that the Saxon knight was sincere, and besides, she had no choice but to trust him. Margaret nodded.

"Good," he said. "We must go swiftly, princess."

"What word do you have of Edgar's friends?" Cristina asked. "What of Morcar of Northumbria and his brother Edwin? And Thor-gaut the Dane and others?"

"Morcar and Edwin are both with Edgar. Thorgaut was impris-oned for two years in William's castle at Lincoln as a king's hostage for the good behavior of his kinsmen. He escaped. Tor is my cousin," he explained, "as is Hereward the outlaw, who has proven so elu-sive. The Normans are determined to catch him."

"We heard about the outlaw at Romsey, too," Margaret said. "And Tor? Will he join us?"

"He sailed for Denmark, they say, but after that I do not know his fate. Hereward is an outright rebel now, with the twelve sheriffs of Lincoln on his tail. But we will sail north along the coast, and away from all this," he added.

So many friends had fled or disappeared in the last three years, Margaret thought. She and her family had met Tor the Dane at King Edward's court years earlier; he had been a fine, intelligent young housecarl interested in becoming a scholar someday, she recalled. "What of your kin, Sir Wilfrid? I pray they are safe."

"My wife and sons were killed when Lincoln was burned," he answered briskly. "Driver, move on. Hurry!"

Margaret sighed with regret as the cart rumbled on. In the dark-ness, a captive of this envoy, she had to trust that Wilfrid and his men were indeed loyal and that soon she and her sister would reunite with Edgar and their mother. If her brother truly was in England actively working toward rebellion, then he had gone against William. Having spent most of his life in England, Edgar was more Saxon than Hungarian in his upbringing, and though he was not a seasoned warrior ready to lead a revolt, he could become a leader for the Saxons one day with the help of others.

Cristina shifted toward the cart's rim. "Sir Wilfrid," she called, waving. "Will we sail to Denmark and go from there to Hungary? That would be safe and wise, I vow. We have heard awful reports that William has burned and ravaged York, that the Danes offered help, came in their ships and then left. We must not sail north!"

Wilfrid slowed his horse to match the pace of the cart. "True, the north is no place for princesses, with William's troops burning much of the region and the Northumbrians rising in rebellion. And now the Scots have rushed in to avail themselves of booty and slaves."

"Good Christ and sweet Mary," Margaret whispered, crossing herself.

"Aye, do pray," Wilfrid muttered. "But your brother will not abandon you here in England. King Malcolm Canmore has offered his support, and your brother is weighing that."

"Scots!" Cristina said contemptuously. "And who would save us from *those* savages?"

"Edgar means to bargain with Malcolm," Wilfrid said. "Rest while we ride, ladies. We will reach the coast by dawn." He urged his horse ahead.

Scotland. Margaret sank back as the cart bumped along. While Cristina murmured with Kata, Margaret crossed herself and whispered a prayer for the safety of their journey, and their lives. But her thoughts were elsewhere. Now she began to deduce Edgar's plan, and it gave her chills.

The Saxons would need help to defend against the Normans, and the strongest and most immediate aid existed in Scotland. Despite the pummelings that Malcolm of Scotland, known for his brutish ways, had given Northumbria over the years, he would not want Normans near his own borders. He would expect a stiff price for his help, Margaret was certain, though the royal Saxons, beleaguered and impoverished by war, had little to bargain in return for assistance from Scotland's roughshod king. Yet Edgar would not beg and Malcolm would not provide for free.

With sinking certainty, Margaret knew why Edgar and his Saxon comrades wanted the princesses brought north to join them, even in dangerous circumstances. The Scottish king, it was widely said, was a widower in need of a wife. And Edgar had sisters of exemplary blood. A northern king of inferior heritage would find that prospect even more desirable than a land dowry, or lack of one, since heirs of that union could claim rights through the mother's bloodline, too.

She recalled seeing Malcolm once, years earlier, when he had come south to Winchester Palace to request England's assistance against the Scots king, Macbeth. At the time, Malcolm was struggling to regain his slain father's throne, and Margaret remembered a huge, wild-haired man with a rumbling voice, who wore furs and oddly patterned garments. Canmore had seemed like a rough beast in the elegant English court, where eloquence, piety, and courtliness were valued. But Edward had thought Macbeth too canny, and therefore a threat; so he had given Malcolm troops, funds, and ships against Macbeth. Margaret remembered the keen excitement in the court at the news that Malcolm had first killed Macbeth and then that man's stepson and successor, a young man with the curious name Lulach, so that Malcolm had fully won Scotland.

Malcolm had proved canny indeed, soon requesting from Edward a Saxon bride: Margaret herself, the king's ward. Lady Agatha had refused, arguing that her daughter was only twelve, too refined for Scotland, and meant for a better royal match someday. Malcolm was nearly thirty, a brute of unimpressive lineage compared to the Saxons', and he could find himself another wife. So Malcolm had married Lulach's Norse widow, and King Edward had been pleased; Scotland's peace with the Vikings would benefit England, too.

Now the Saxons needed Malcolm's help and the Norse queen was dead—and Margaret realized that her brother might try to bargain her away to Malcolm, especially since he had applied for her hand before.

She could not imagine living in a barbaric land, wife to a raiding warrior who could not be trusted to keep any bargain. The Scottish king regularly attacked northern England, and she had heard that his country was a backward place, peopled with superstitious heathens who spoke a strange language no good Saxon would deign to learn.

At Romsey, she had found peace and respite from danger, protected from warmongers and sly self-servers. There, she would have taken vows to expiate sins she otherwise dared not confess. Instead, she rode in a cart rattling northward toward a fate she dreaded.

Chapter Two

❧

Upheaved by the breath of the gale . . . and tossed
in the countless dangers of the deep, [Edgar the
Aetheling and his sisters] were forced to bring up
in Scotland.

—JOHN OF FORDUN, *Chronicles of Scotland,*
FIFTEENTH CENTURY

North Sea
November 1069

C radled in a leather hammock, Margaret grabbed a support rope
as another lurching wave brought the ship high, then low
again. Beside her, Cristina clung to their mother, both women moaning,
while Margaret endured in silence. In a second hammock, Kata sat ter-
rified and wide-eyed beside Hildy, their mother's sturdy Saxon maid.
Even the terrors of the North Sea could not frighten Hildy, Margaret
thought with admiration.

"*Cristofori faciem die quacunque tueris,*" Lady Agatha muttered, taking
out a silver medal from the purse at her belt, "*illa nempe die morte mala
non morieris.*" She displayed the silver face of Saint Christopher to the

other women. "Whosoever regards the face of Christopher shall not die that day an evil death. Remember that in your prayers today."

Margaret understood that her mother was doing her best in the absence of the Benedictine priest, Otto, who rode aboard a second ship carrying additional men, horses, armor, and cargo. The other longboat pitched in the heavy seas, upright as yet. For two days, fierce winds and rain had lashed the ship, tearing the great sail, but somehow they had stayed their course, thanks not only to skilled sailors but to the intercession of saints such as Christopher, Nicholas, the Irishman Brendan, and the Princess Ursula, who had sailed stormy seas with eleven thousand virgin friends to safety—and eventual martyrdom. The sainted ones would watch over those who traveled on water, keeping them safe—or at least Margaret fervently hoped so as she sent up another prayer to that end.

As for her mother, Margaret had nearly forgotten over the past three years how fretful Lady Agatha could be. Descended on one side from Magyars who had swarmed the Carpathian basin and on the other from Russian royalty, her mother had the strong-boned beauty of her combined heritage, yet by nature Lady Agatha was fearful and bitter more than tough. Just now her frantic prayers added such tension that Margaret furtively wished her mother would offer some real comfort to her family. Cristina, cut of similar cloth, was keen to point out their difficulties rather than be strong against them—and though Margaret doubted her own mettle, she would not bemoan her fate. Somehow she would persevere, emulating the example of saints and martyrs who had endured far worse.

A gust of wind slapped open the leather curtain that provided shelter for the women aboard the longship. Rain and seawater drenched Margaret's blue gown, red cloak, and red leather shoes, and she wrung out the hems of the ruined silk. After Romsey, she had been thankful to exchange her plain garments for fine ones, though she knew that her love of bright colors and beautiful fabrics was a sinful vanity, a serious flaw in her character. Now she vowed to improve her lesser qualities if only she and the others could survive this awful voyage safely.

Another heavy tilt of the ship prompted Lady Agatha to pray loudly as she rotated her ebony beads and recited in Latin. Cristina told their mother to hush, bluntly, and was slapped for it.

"I have prayed a year's worth of penances today," Cristina said. "Now I pray we reach Scotland soon so we can get another ship to Denmark and go home to Hungary."

"No one should be on the North Sea this time of year, with the winter storms upon us," Hildy said. "We should have stayed in England."

"But Edgar said William's troops would hunt us there," Lady Agatha said.

"He and his Saxon lords have betrayed William with their rebellion, and we are all declared outlaws. We have lost everything," Cristina added bitterly. "Margaret and I are princesses without land and few goods, and little marriage value. What will become of us?"

"We have our royal heritage," Margaret said. "The rest can be regained."

"At least the Scottish king offered assistance," Lady Agatha said. "Perhaps he will give us some of his goods, in addition to what we were able to bring with us."

"He is a pauper, Mama, so they say. All Scots are savages," Cristina replied. "And Edgar does what the Saxon lords want, so he will strike any bargain with Malcolm. What of us?"

"Edgar will be a fine king," Lady Agatha said blithely, as if she had not even heard. "He reminds me of your father."

Margaret sighed. Her mother was so idealistic where her son was concerned. But the sudden reminder of her father brought her such a heart-tug of guilt and remorse that she could not speak. If only Papa had lived—if only she had not given him the sweetmeats that night . . .

Feeling sick, she jumped up as the ship tilted again and cold sea-water sloshed over her feet. She felt like Jonah inside the whale, which must have been a putrid place indeed. She had to get away. "I need some air," she said. "I will go ask how we are faring."

The ship lurched and she grabbed the curtain while her mother and sister groaned in unison and Kata clung to Hildy. But Margaret was determined to get outside. She, too, felt ill, but she tended to a finicky stomach on the best of days and had fasted to lessen her illness aboard ship. Now, dizzy but well enough, she peered through a gap in the curtain and saw men shouting, rushing about or sitting huddled against the wind and rain, while the captain called to the oarsmen to pull harder, landward.

Land? Beyond the tilting rim of the ship, the gray sea slid beneath heavy clouds, but Margaret could see the faint rim of a shoreline and hills. Had her prayers indeed been granted? She had fingered the strand of prayer beads looped over her belt, counting endless Pater Nosters and Ave Marias upon the small semiprecious stones knotted in tens on silken thread.

Truth be told, her prayers had been fervent despite the weather, for she loathed sea voyaging in any conditions, after the long, exhausting sea journeys in her childhood. Though she had learned to mask her fears with calm, she could not wait to attain land.

Through a haze of rain and sea spray, Margaret walked along the deck toward her brother, who sat with some of the Saxon lords who had fled England with them. The men looked damp and cold, clutching leather cloaks as protection from the elements. Edgar, blond hair straggling, looked young and earnest beside the mature warriors as he listened avidly to their conversation.

She walked carefully on the slippery planking, past oarsmen who pulled hard as the boat cut a swath through surging water. Overhead, the prow was topped by a wooden curl rather than the dragon's head carried by warships, for the ship was a wide, low merchant knorr. Beyond, steel-gray waves peaked white as she saw the second ship heaving on the seas behind the first.

Edgar stood as she approached and the men made room for her to sit. She greeted each in turn: Morcar, grumbling, red-bearded, bitter to have been ousted from Northumbria; his capable brother, Edwin, earl of Mercia; Cospatric, the Saxon cousin of Malcolm Canmore; and Walde, a Northumbrian nobleman whose beauty and courtly eloquence were well known and his Saxon loyalty strong; he had William's favor, and had been offered William's niece Judith in marriage, as a bid to anchor Northumbrian fealties.

This tough, clever Saxon lot had betrayed tyrannical William, infuriating him. With their Saxon army all but decimated, their Danish support almost gone, they now looked for Malcolm Canmore's aid in their rebellion. They supported Edgar's claim to the throne of England, yet Margaret did not entirely trust their influence over her brother, who was too young to lead the rebellion these lords favored. She felt wary on his behalf.

But she smiled as she sat beside Edgar, who drew his leather covering over her head and shoulders. She huddled close, her braids pooling like damp golden ropes in her lap.

"Are we nearing land?" she asked.

"Aye. The oarsmen are heading for it," Edgar replied. "The storm spun us about and the hull may be damaged, but we have hope now."

"Thank the saints." She breathed out in relief.

"We are still in danger of sinking," Morcar said bluntly. "And we do not know if that land is Scotland or England. Go back to your mother, lady, and pray for our souls." Morcar was a sour fellow; she had disliked him even in her uncle's royal court. "We would be better off with the sea monsters than with the Normans."

"If it is Scotland, luck is with us," Edwin said quietly. "We will be safe."

"If we are in Malcolm's territory, aye," Cospatric said. "Farther north, the Highland men who dislike their own king also dislike Saxons."

"Aye, and Malcolm will give us sanctuary . . . for the right fee." Morcar looked at Margaret.

"What price would that be, sir?" She looked at him directly, certain she knew what he meant.

"Lady, go back to your mother and your prayers," Morcar groused.

"Give my sister credit for intelligence, sir," Edgar said. "She is the best scholar in my family, and I vow she could outreason any clergyman on matters of theology and logic. If we are to negotiate—"

"Some women are cleverer than is good for them," Morcar snapped.

Margaret shivered in a chill gust, but Morcar's rudeness made her defiant. She would not leave just yet. "What bargain will you make with Malcolm of Scotland? He expects to meet with Edgar and some rebel lords—but I suspect he will be surprised to see the entire royal Saxon family and their household, all in need of asylum."

"We will negotiate for the safety and benefit of all," Edgar said.

"The Scottish king is unpredictable, they say," she replied. "A savage warlord. We cannot guess what he wants." If they meant to marry her off, she wanted to hear it said out loud, now. They avoided her gaze, even her brother—did that indicate something significant?

"Your sister knows too much and not enough," Morcar said. "We will do what is necessary. Go bid the women be ready for whatever comes—the bottom of the sea, or the teeth of Scots."

UNDER THUNDEROUS SKIES, the Saxons were taken off the foundering ship within the hour by fishermen who appeared as if sent from heaven, having braved the rocking seas in sleek boats to convey the strangers to land. Their saviors were local Scots, Margaret learned, who spoke the native tongue, a lilting language that Cospatric alone understood.

"These are Fife men, loyal to Malcolm," he explained, seated in one of the boats with Margaret and several others. "They say their village is not far from one of Malcolm's royal palaces. They will send word to the king's men and we will shelter with the fishing families tonight. Soon we will be welcomed by King Malcolm."

Shivering in her wet things, Margaret was so grateful to be heading toward blessed land that she almost did not care where it was. Tears stung her eyes as men lifted her from the boat and carried her ashore. Sinking to her knees on the pebbled beach beside her kinswomen and others giving thanks, she closed her eyes in silent prayer.

Never again, she decided, did she want to travel by sea, never again did she care to feel the powerful surge of bottomless water beneath her. In that moment, she made a vow—a holy, impulsive, impassioned vow, promising heaven that she would stay away from water. Instead, she promised the saints in fervent silence, she would help anyone willing to voyage by ship, but she would gladly deprive herself of sea travel. That would free her from experiencing such fear and danger again.

As the Scottish fishermen guided the stranded survivors through the rain toward their own homes, Margaret anticipated the heat of a cozy hearth, the feel of dry clothing, and the safety of humble hospitality. She would not think ahead, she told herself, to meeting the Scottish king.

Turning, she saw Edgar offer to one of the fishermen, a tough and elderly man, a purse of coins. The man shook his head in refusal.

"You are welcome to what we have. It does not matter to us where you come from or who you are. Best we do not know, eh?"

A FIRE BLAZED HOT gold within a ring of stones, the rest of the room in shadow as Margaret and the other women gathered around the low central hearth, grasping blankets around their shoulders. Grateful to be warm and dry, Margaret was glad for the simple shift that she now wore while her wet garments dried by the fire. Her sister and mother had grimaced at the plain clothing they had been lent by the fisherman's wife who had welcomed them to her family's cottage; and they did not seem pleased with their quarters, a dank and humble seaside cottage belonging to the woman introduced as Mother Annot and her husband, the elderly fisherman who had guided the stranded voyagers away from the storm-tossed beach.

"I will itch to death in this," Cristina said to her mother under her breath.

"We are warm and dry and did not drown," Margaret said. "And the woman has made us hot soup. We must be sure to thank her."

"I would if she spoke a civilized tongue," Cristina muttered.

"The generosity of these poor fisher-folk should be praised," Margaret said.

"True." Lady Agatha adjusted her blanket with two fingers as if loath to touch it. "Do you suppose there are fleas in this?"

Mother Annot, their tall and gaunt hostess, came forward with a large bowl and ladle, offering more soup. Margaret's stomach felt ill at ease, but she did not want to refuse the kindness and raised her cup, though the soup smelled both salty and fishy.

Her mother leaned toward her. "No need to eat that. We do not even know what is in it."

"It is fish broth," Cristina said, peering into her cup. "Ugh," she said, scratching under the woolen blanket. "I do not much like Scotland."

Seeing the trusting smile on the Scottish woman's face, Margaret felt embarrassed on behalf of her kinswomen. She sipped her soup and smiled. "Thank you, it's very good."

Mother Annot smiled and filled Margaret's cup yet again.

MORNING LIGHT SEEPED through the chinks in the stone wall as Margaret finished her early prayers. Accustomed at the abbey to rising several times a night to kneel in prayer, she could keep that habit anywhere now, although the others still slept, tucked in blankets on the floor. She slipped past without disturbing them.

Mother Annot cooked flat cakes that smelled buttery and good, sizzling on an iron plate suspended over hot flames. Finding her red shoes and cloak drying by the hearth, Margaret put them on, savoring their warmth. Then she stepped outside, going past the house with its attached animal byre to the enclosed latrine beyond; she ducked into that and later emerged to stand in the misty dawn. A few clustered houses with thatched roofs and stone walls created a small, muddy village that lacked a center, for she saw no obvious church or chapel structure. Each home seemed to be as plain as the one belonging to Annot and her family.

Margaret had seen the homes of the poor in England and in Hungary, too, but she had never been inside one of them, living always in the finest royal quarters. These Scottish folk had little, yet they shared without expecting a reward. She breathed deeply of the moist, salty air and once more felt humbled by the kindness shown to the Saxon fugitives.

She went back into the house, where she and the others were eating hot oatcakes when Edgar and Wilfrid came to the door, having spent the night in another domicile. "The ships are being unloaded now," Wilfrid told them as they escorted the women to the beach.

"And this morning Cospatric rode to the king's royal residence, not far from here. King Malcolm will send an escort for us soon, no doubt," Edgar said.

Farther down the beach, Margaret saw two longboats leaning like whales in the shallows while men waded back and forth with crates and gear. English-bred horses now grazed on fresh grass along the dunes, and wooden boxes were piled on the dry sections of the pebbled beach.

"We must see if our things are safe," Cristina said. "That is all the fortune any of us has now," she added.

"At least we have something," Margaret said, though Cristina ignored her and ran ahead.

Searching with her sister through the boxes as they were opened, Margaret looked in particular for an ebony reliquary that contained a priceless crucifix in gold and gems. The treasured piece housed a precious relic, a sliver of the true cross saved by Saint Helena, on whose feast day Margaret had been born. The Black Rood, as some in England had called the cross, had been coveted by Edward of England, but Lady Agatha had guarded it carefully, hinting to Margaret that it might be part of her dowry someday. Other crates contained gold and silver plates, vessels, cups, and candlesticks; several small chests held thousands of coins, English and foreign, the edges clipped with use yet still valuable for trading or melting down. Their well-being might rest on their ability to pay the Scots king, and so Edgar seemed anxious to locate the coins, while Margaret and the others looked for household goods.

Cristina gave a little cry as she discovered the ebony box packed in damp straw, and then she and Margaret looked eagerly through another box. Soon Edgar returned, having walked off to speak with Wilfrid after finding a few chests of coins. "Thank the saints, we have some means," he said.

Margaret smiled, noticing how tall her brother had grown and how somber he seemed. She felt a surge of love and gratefulness to know that they were all safe. And Edgar, who had so much responsibility on his broadening shoulders, might yet have a chance to reclaim England, so long as the Saxon lords supported him and the Scottish king kept his promises.

"The ships need repair," Edgar now said. "The fishermen will make the arrangements. We needs must be guests in Scotland for a little while."

"You had planned that for you and your men already," Margaret said. "But may we hope that Malcolm will harbor so many Saxon fugitives? With all of us here, the Normans have even more reason to attack Scotland. I do wonder if Malcolm will send us away," she added.

"He hates the Normans and does not care what they want," he replied. "Though he was partly raised in Northumbria, he is king in Scotland, and means to defend its perimeters against invaders. He will have sympathy for our plight," he added, "for he was banished as a child from Scotland when Macbeth killed his father, a king called Duncan."

Sympathy was not a quality she expected from Malcolm of Scotland. "We shall see. If he does offer us respite for a bit, that would be most welcome."

"I hope for more than respite," Edgar replied. "Truly, I believe God's will brought us here with that storm. We have been swept nearly to the king's doorstep. He and I had agreed to meet farther south at a neutral meeting place. To be brought here to his home seems . . . fated."

Her heart raced. "How so?" *Please,* she thought, *do not speak of marriage.*

"For the sake of the rebellion, of course," he said. "His welcome bodes well for the Saxon uprising. With his full support, we can reclaim everything we have lost and more."

"He will want repayment for that support, and we have no land, no titles." But they had royal blood and marriageable princesses, she thought, looking sideways at her brother.

"We can win England back," he said only. "Where else can we go?

No other place will accept us now. Wherever the royal Saxon fugitives flee, the Normans go in pursuit. But the king of Scotland does not fear them. Indeed, by sheltering us, he sends William a message that he will not be intimidated."

"So we must stay here indefinitely?"

"We have no choice. Look there," he went on, gesturing toward the grassy dunes that edged the beach. "Cospatric is back—and Malcolm's men are with him."

Increasingly apprehensive, Margaret stood motionless in the whipping wind off the sea as the riders crested the hill. A few men dismounted to walk toward them, and Cospatric strode forward to speak to Edgar while Wilfrid joined Margaret. Some of the Scotsmen were on horses, others on foot, and some wore good mail armor while others had leather. She noticed that many wore patterned cloaks and tunics of the distinctive wool that the fisher-folk had worn, woven of crisscrossing hues. Most wore iron helmets and carried weaponry.

"Why do they bring weapons to meet shipwreck survivors and women?" she asked Wilfrid.

"Saxons and Scots will never trust each other," he said. "My lady, your brother beckons you to come forward." She did, slowly, Wilfrid walking beside her.

"These are Malcolm's elite housecarls," Cospatric was explaining to Edgar. "The king is not currently at his palace in Dunfermline, as he expected to meet us farther south. We are welcome to wait there for his return."

The leader of the Scottish envoy came forward. "This is Sir Robert De Lauder, head of King Malcolm's elite guard," Cospatric said in introduction.

De Lauder bowed his head, showing fine manners, and Margaret smiled politely. He was shorter than she, and wore a long chain mail hauberk with a dropped hood, revealing his dark hair trimmed close, his face clean shaven in foreign fashion. She narrowed her eyes, suspecting that he was not Scottish; the other men were simply dressed and armored, with rough beards and long hair.

"Welcome to Scotland, sire, my lady," he said in English, but with a marked French accent. "You and your party are welcome here."

"You are Norman?" Margaret asked.

"I am from Normandy, true. I pledged to King Malcolm's service many years ago, well before King William came to England." He turned as a second man joined them. This one was tall and broad, blond and ruddy, in shabby leather over a patterned tunic. His expression was grim and he planted his legs wide, grasping the great sword at his belt. "This is Ranald mac Niall, one of the king's guard," De Lauder explained. "King Malcolm sends word that he is grateful for your safe arrival and he wishes you to stay in his palace of Dunfermline, a few leagues from here. You will enjoy many comforts there until he can return."

"The welcome is appreciated," Edgar said.

"Sir, we have horses for you and a cart fitted for the ladies," De Lauder said.

"We brought horses from England," Edgar said. "Perhaps your king will accept some of that fine stock. We look forward to meeting him."

Word quickly spread that the Saxon party would leave immediately for the king's tower, and Margaret and her kinswomen were escorted to a cushioned wagon. When Cristina, who muttered that she disliked carts, mentioned that she and Margaret would prefer to ride, horses were brought forward for them. De Lauder himself assisted the girls into the wooden saddles, offering his cupped palms as a boost for their feet.

"This is a courteous escort," Cristina said, "and it will be good to stay in the king's palace instead of these old huts. I am glad to leave this dirty village, I vow."

Margaret blushed, hoping Cristina would not be overheard. But she, too, yearned for the comforts of a fine palace. She particularly looked forward to a hot, fragrant bath and the feel of clean linen and silk against her skin. "These people have been kind, though a royal welcome is due our brother," she remarked.

"It is our due as well," Cristina replied with a sniff.

The Scottish horses were smaller than Margaret had seen before, stocky and sturdy, and she adjusted her skirts and cloak in the saddle, waiting while Lady Agatha and the maidservants were settled in the cart. Gently tugging the reins as her horse sidled, Margaret calmed him with soothing words and pats to his neck. She caught the Norman knight's look of surprise.

"You handle the horse quite well," he said.

"*Ce n'est rien*," she answered. "It is nothing. We were raised in Hungary and placed in Magyar saddles when we were still very young. And we rode in England, too," she added.

As the men readied to depart, Margaret saw that some local people still waited on the beach. Mother Annot was with them, waving, and Margaret lifted a hand in return, realizing that there had been no time to properly thank their hosts. Just then, De Lauder rode toward Margaret and Cristina and offered fur-lined cloaks for the journey, as the November air was damp and chilly. Moments later, the escort began to move out.

Looking over her shoulder, Margaret hesitated, drawing back on her horse's reins. She felt a tug of remorse, not having thanked their hosts, who had saved their lives and had been exceedingly kind to them. On impulse, she guided her mount around to ride down the beach, despite shouts of surprise from her sister and others.

Reaching Mother Annot and the cluster of women and men with her, Margaret leaned from the saddle. "Thank you for your hospitality," she said breathlessly. "We do appreciate it."

Mother Annot smiled, nodded, and Margaret realized the woman did not really understand her. But she wanted to show her gratitude somehow. None of the other Saxons had bothered, being in a hurry to leave these people for better circumstances—that troubled her, too.

Shrugging out of the fur cloak that De Lauder had loaned her, she unpinned her own red cloak beneath it, swept it free, and handed it to Mother Annot. The old woman caught it, looking astonished, then shook her head in protest.

Margaret gestured her insistence that the woman keep it, but Annot handed it to a younger woman who stood holding a small child, shivering in the wind's chill. Noticing that Annot and a few of the other women were barefoot despite standing on the wet, cold, stony beach, Margaret reached down and pulled off her red leather shoes, which Annot had cleaned and dried for her overnight. She handed them to the Scotswoman and tucked her stockinged feet under her skirts.

"Thank you, woman." Annot tried English, then switched to Gaelic, shaking her head as if to refuse. One of the fishermen, her husband, came close.

"My wife says she cannot take these things from you, lady. You are too generous."

"I want her to have them. Please tell her they will look very fine on her. I have other cloaks and shoes and can do without these," Margaret added. "Please, say I am happy to do this."

As he translated, Annot grinned with delight and shoved her feet into the shoes, which were too small, but she danced a little while the others laughed. Then she looked up at Margaret. "*Tapadh leibh.* Thank you!"

"Tapah-lev to you," Margaret said, smiling. She then rode back toward the others.

Her mother and sister, her brother, and the men stared at her, but De Lauder rode closer, smiling. "Saint Martin himself gave his red cloak to a beggar, they say, and you did better than that. You made the Scotswoman very happy, eh? You are a fine lady," he murmured. "King Malcolm will want to hear about this."

Margaret felt her cheeks grow hot. She did not want attention—she had only wanted to express her thanks, embarrassed that no one in the Saxon party had done so. She had several cloaks and pairs of shoes packed in chests, and Kata would fetch another pair. Most had not been worn since she had gone to Romsey Abbey three years past.

What no one knew was that she was not as generous as they believed. After soaking in seawater and drying by the fire, the red shoes were very tight and their color was ruined. She would not have worn them again. And she told herself that instead of taking pride in her deed, she ought to pray a penance for selfishness.

THEY RODE AWAY from the sweeping gray sea toward mist-covered hills and forestland, and soon Margaret could see round-shouldered mountains far away, layers of blue and green shapes fading into the distance. The escort followed an earthen track as they passed isolated cottages set on steep hillsides where sheep grazed; one cluster of homes, Ranald mac Niall explained, was a *clachan*, the native word for village. Here and there she saw tall stone crosses on the peaks of a few hills, handsomely carved monuments combining a cross with a circle, large enough to be easily seen across hill and *gleann*, as she learned the valleys were termed.

Finally the escort entered the shadowed coolness of a woodland, the track thick with pine needles crushed to invigorating fragrance by horse hooves and cart wheels. A wide stream flowed beside the path with small waterfalls rushing over boulders.

"It is so beautiful here. Peaceful," Margaret breathed, smiling at Cristina, riding beside her.

Tower walls appeared through the trees: a wooden citadel behind a palisade perched on a hillside. The timber structure was of modest size, and Margaret looked for the king's grand palace in what seemed a wonderland of forest, stream, rocks, and waterfalls.

"That must be the gatehouse," Cristina said. "The palace will be close by."

Robert De Lauder, riding in the lead, paused to wait, and as Margaret and Cristina approached, he swept his arm wide. "*Mes princesses*, welcome to Dunfermline Palace."

"*That* is the king's palace?" Cristina gaped.

"His main residence must be farther on," Margaret said hopefully.

"This is his favorite royal residence," De Lauder said. "Dunfermline Tower."

Visible beyond the palisade, the tower itself was square and plain, a few levels of pitch-treated timber and a slate roof graced by a tilted, rusted weathercock. Narrow chimney spouts emitted thin plumes of smoke.

As they followed the slope toward the fortress, the tower came more clearly into sight and the gates opened. Margaret saw tattered curtains flapping in a few high, narrow windows. A rooster perched on a windowsill, and a cat prowled along a lower ledge. Wooden steps led to a second-story entrance. The yard was muddy and cluttered with smaller thatched-roof structures.

They entered the gates, passing servants who moved about carrying baskets or hurrying from one location to another, pausing to stare at them. Three guards came forward wearing leather hauberks, looking strong and alert to trouble. Dogs and goats wandered about, chickens pecked in random circles, and a shaggy black cow crossed in front of the entering party before a guard shooed it away. Margaret saw a small boy gaping up at the riders until a woman snatched him into her arms and stepped aside.

"The king's tower is a busy place." Margaret forced cheerfulness. "I am sure it has a fine and comfortable interior."

"Aye, where they keep their livestock," Cristina muttered. "We *will* return to England, once Edgar drives William out. We cannot stay here long. We must press Edgar to see to it."

But Margaret knew they might stay indefinitely, as Edgar had said. If England was ever to be reclaimed, Edgar and the rest of the Saxon leaders needed solid support in the form of troops, coinage—and a canny, powerful ally in the king of Scotland.

Yet her first glimpse of the seat of Scottish royalty was hardly reassuring.

Chapter Three

Good they are at man-slaying,
Melodious in the ale-house,
Masterly at making songs,
Skilled at playing chess.

—IRISH, TWELFTH CENTURY
(TRANSLATED BY KUNO MEYER)

I am Dame Agnes, the chatelaine here at the king's palace," a plump woman told them as she greeted the newly arrived Saxons. The tower's interior was as rustic as the exterior, Margaret saw, with timbered rafters and whitewashed plaster walls, and the guests were served ale and soup at trestle tables, where tallow candles glowed in iron holders. Although the evening skies were still pale, the musty interior, smelling of dogs and dampness, was gloomy.

Dame Agnes was plain, too, with thick features and a good smile, and she wore a simple linen headdress along with a brown tunic, bleached linen shift, and sturdy leather boots. "I keep the king's household here with the help of my husband, who is the castle steward. I am the king's cousin," she added proudly. "You will have rooms here and a couple of maidservants, with a groom and a page for the men. I am sure you are used to better in England."

"We are fugitives lately come from convents, and my brother and his men were hostages of the Normans," Margaret said as the chatelaine guided them up wooden steps to small rooms on an upper floor. "And so we are grateful for your good hospitality here."

Margaret was to share a small room with Cristina and Kata, along with a little red-haired maid whose Gaelic name no one could pronounce. "Fionnghuala," the girl repeated more than once, patiently introducing herself. "Fi-NOO-ala is my name."

"Finola," Margaret ventured. "So you speak English?"

"Sassenach, aye," the girl replied—meaning Saxon, Margaret realized, or English—and then indicated the narrow beds crammed into the room. "Sleeping now?"

"Prayers first," Margaret said firmly, pressing her palms together. Finola dropped to her knees beside her, and Margaret led them in a Latin prayer. Finola did not recite hers in Latin but in the airy, incomprehensible language of the northern Scots. Yet the girl prayed earnestly.

"Say the prayers in Latin, if you please." Margaret repeated a few lines in proper fashion.

Finola only whispered in her strange tongue. Margaret sighed. Prayerful devotions marked the hours night and day, and whatever the Church demanded was what heaven itself wanted, Margaret had been taught, finding such wisdom reliable and comforting.

"Prayers must be said in Latin," Cristina pointed out. "She risks her very soul by praying in her heathen tongue."

Margaret leaned toward Finola. "*Ave Maria, gratia plena, Dominus tecum,*" she whispered in an encouraging tone. "Go on. Now you say it."

Finola shook her head shyly. Astonished, Margaret realized the girl did not know Latin.

"What is the state of devotion here in this place," Cristina said later, as they readied for bed, "even worse, the state of Scottish souls, if they pray in a barbaric tongue that God and the saints will not recognize?"

Margaret hesitated. Finola seemed a sweet girl with an innocent nature despite her somewhat savage upbringing. "We will say extra prayers on their behalf," she suggested.

"They should be taught proper Latin, if they have the brainpans for it," Cristina said.

STEADY RAIN KEPT THEM indoors for days, and still the king did not arrive. Margaret and her kinswomen settled into a routine when baskets of needlework were unearthed from one of the wooden crates that had come off the longboat, and Lady Agatha found linen panels that needed finishing. Following morning prayers and a meal, the women gathered in the small bedchamber given Lady Agatha to work, talk, and wait out the days, uncertain what would come next.

Glad to have her embroidery things, for she loved stitchery work and had a deft and delicate hand for it, Margaret was content enough. The silken threads in an array of colors, the feel of the fabric textures, the shush of threads drawn through linen were small joys that soothed her spirit, and she enjoyed watching each piece grow toward its completion. Her work was competent and meticulous, but her sister, Cristina, was a master, the artistry of her needlework surpassing even that of their mother, whose handiwork was always impressive.

That morning, Lady Agatha was couching minute gold filament threads in tight looping stitches to create a border for a priest's vestment; she had finished the fabric in whitework, the application of white silk thread on pale linen to produce elegant and detailed designs. While Margaret was capable in all forms of needlework, she tended to worry over the perfection of her stitches even while wishing for the facile touch of her kinswomen. But she was grateful for the skill that had taught her patience, her fingers nimble, her thoughts focused, her spirit quieted by the demands and the rewards of the work.

Now she set down her fabric, hearing a commotion of horses' hooves and the shouts of men down in the bailey. She stood and ran to the window, peering out just as Cristina joined her. The other women, curious, too, came to look.

"Who are they?" Cristina asked, as they watched dozens of horsemen stream into the yard through the open gates. For a moment Margaret felt a stab of fear, remembering the Norman invaders riding into the yard at Winchester, followed by the arrival of King William—and then the splitting up of the royal family to convents and captivity. Gazing down, she saw with relief that these men were heartily welcomed here.

"The Scottish king!" Cristina said as the women crowded at the window. "See the large man on the black horse, with the bannerman beside him, holding a pole with a blue boar stitched on silk? The blue boar is Malcolm's insigne. I remember seeing it at Winchester Palace, years ago, when he came there."

Margaret looked down. The king was taller and broader than most of the other men, his glossy black horse powerfully muscled. The rider lifted away his helmet to reveal a thatch of dark hair and a full beard, and as he tore off leather gauntlets and tossed them to a groom, Margaret heard him snap a command. The groom ran off as De Lauder approached, bowing.

"Malcolm? Good," Lady Agatha said. "Now we shall learn his intentions for all of us."

Margaret went to her seat in silence and took up her needlework, but stabbed her finger, her hands trembled so. Blood beaded on the linen, and though she rubbed it away, the stain remained.

MARGARET GINGERLY DREW her skirts up and lifted her feet away from the floor, where she sat on the bench at supper. The rushes on the floor were fresh enough, but the layer beneath was old, decayed and fusty. Her eyes stung from the rancid smoke of flickering wall torches in need of changing. The meal was already being served, handed about on platters, but the king had not yet arrived for supper. In the confusion, some of the servants snatched dishes from the tables to bring them back to the kitchen until the king was properly in attendance.

Chaos, Margaret thought, had no place in a king's hall. Watching Dame Agnes, she knew that Lady Agatha and Kata would have made short work of the whole mess. So would she, come to that; while she had never run a household of her own, she was well versed in all domestic matters. As the eldest princess in a royal family, she had been originally intended, and trained, for a significant marriage. The Normans had changed those plans and the peace of Romsey Abbey had changed her mind, but she had more than enough skill and knowledge—and a good measure of practicality—to supervise even the largest household. Seeing what could and should be done with the king's ill-managed palace of Dunfermline, she felt a twinge of frustration. Still, she smiled and sat quietly.

She and the other Saxons occupied benches at a long, broad table with a linen cloth sitting askew, having been tugged by one of the taller dogs. Housecarls and household retainers shared tables along with servants, an arrangement she had never seen before. Some of them were already eating; few took notice that the royal Saxons were there and the king was not.

At Winchester, grand feasts and even everyday suppers had been orderly, formal occasions when elaborate meals were served in several courses, and dishes, cups, and utensils were of the finest materials—brass, pewter, silver and gold, even crystal and glass. At Dunfermline, the dishes were wood or pottery, drinking horns and simple cups were more prevalent than goblets, and implements were ordinary wood and metal. Margaret noticed her mother's disapproval and her sister's disdain, and saw Edgar's puzzled expression, too, as he rubbed at a stain on the tablecloth.

Robert De Lauder walked toward them. "King Malcolm will be here soon. He is in his chamber as yet meeting with his councilors, since he has been away in the south."

"He has royal guests. Such rudeness," Lady Agatha remarked in German to her kinswomen. Margaret saw De Lauder frown.

Dame Agnes's wooden-soled shoes made a clomping sound as she crossed the room toward them. She paused to bark out an order to one of the servants before bowing her head toward the Saxons. "Sire," she addressed Edgar in a broad, rolling accent. "Whatever you need, tell me and you shall have it." He thanked her and she left, never returning to the table, busy as she was.

Servants ran back and forth from the kitchens, spilling food from tilted platters, sloshing wine and ale from jugs, tripping on the dogs, large and small, that seemed constantly underfoot. A musician sat on a stool beside the central fire basket, which blazed and smoked in the middle of the long room. The old man played a harp and sang, though the din in the room did not quiet.

Dame Agnes could be heard shouting in the corridor, and moments later, servants rushed into the hall, carrying platters and bowls as if the hounds of hell were at their heels. As Margaret and the others were served fresh dishes of sliced beef and onions—the food was plain but good—the musician began a new tune, a bright rhythm that Margaret found enjoyable.

"He is a good *jongleur*," she said to Sir Robert, beside her. He nodded.

Ranald, the surly blond warrior in the king's elite guard, leaned forward. "He is adequate for a *Saxon* poet," he said with some emphasis.

"It is surprising to find a Saxon poet in the Scottish court," Edgar said. "Surely he must be very good, to have a patron in the king of Scotland."

"King Malcolm was raised in England from boyhood," De Lauder answered. "He enjoys Saxon poetry as much, perhaps more than Scottish."

"We have much finer here in Scotland," Ranald commented. His adequate English was accented with the softening tones of the Gaelic tongue. "Every mormaer's hall has its *seanchaidh* or bard, for music or stories or both. There is a girl in the north, a harper of uncommon beauty and remarkable talent. Her hands move like a breeze upon the harp strings. It is said that to hear her is to step into heaven."

"A female bard?" Margaret asked with interest. "We had female musicians in the English court, too, though they did not play harp.

They sang and played drums and some of them danced. It was very entertaining."

"I hear it said that the girl-bard of Moray is remarkable." A tall man now approached the table, his voice a deep rumble, his English sounding Northumbrian more than Scottish. He threw his cloak over the back of the high carved chair at the table and seated himself there.

King Malcolm, Margaret realized with a start, arrived at his own feast at last. She saw the Scots at the table react, sitting straighter, looking sideways at one another. Edgar blushed bright, waiting for an introduction that did not immediately come.

"There is no bard like her in all Scotland, so I understand," the king continued. "But she does not leave the north."

As the Saxon guests stood to greet the king, Malcolm dismissed their gesture with a wave. He held out a drinking horn and a servant ran forward to fill it with wine. Malcolm raised the horn high and then took a long swallow.

The formal duty of serving wine to the king and the sharing of a cup by guests, Margaret noted then, rightfully belonged to the highest ranking lady in the room. Either she or her mother should have been invited to do so—but proper manners were not much in evidence in Scotland.

"Let us drink to the Saxons, running from the Normans! The enemies of my friends are my enemies, too," the king added magnanimously, lifting his drinking horn again to gulp from it.

Edgar cleared his throat and courteously expressed the gratitude of his party, then began to introduce his kinswomen and comrades.

"Excellent," Malcolm said, nodding as if barely paying attention. "Hector!" he called to the musician. "Give us something to entertain our guests!"

Hector strummed the harp and began to speak in a singsong voice. Immediately Margaret recognized the poem he recited in the rich, rolling Anglo-Saxon tongue—a tale of a wandering soul lost and lonely at sea. Now and then the poet threw his arms up and stomped his feet for emphasis as he shouted and thrashed, and banged a drum

loudly, as if beating time for the oarsmen. Yet he grew still as he came
to the most poignant part of the verses, lines so familiar to the Saxons
in particular that they paused to listen as if spellbound:

> *Where is the horse, where is the man,*
> *Where is the treasure-giver?*
> *Where are the joys of the hall?*
> *Alas, the bright cup, the mailed warrior!*
> *Alas, the chieftain's splendor! Oh how time has passed!*

Rapt silence filled the hall as the poet recited an elegy of sorts for the
passing of a bright age of warriors. Their world, too, was changing,
Margaret thought as she listened. Proud and ancient ways were lost;
new ways were uncertain. Sensing the mournful tone of the poem, she
observed King Malcolm's stormy expression as he spoke with another
man, although the poet was still performing the verses. As Hector finished with much flinging about of hands, Margaret heard her brother
conversing with the Scots seated nearby.

"Moray's lady bard could likely best that fellow," one of the Scottish
lords remarked. He was a burly warrior with a white beard and hair,
a worn leather hauberk, and a tunic frayed with age. "Sir, I am Angus,
mormaer of Mar," he told Edgar. "We have not met."

"Sir," Edgar replied. "A mormaer is an earl, I believe?"

"It means 'great steward' in the Gaelic tongue. Something akin to a
jarl or an earl."

"What of this lady harper you mentioned?" Cristina asked. "Does
she live near here?"

"She lives in the far north under the protection of her fierce kinswoman," Angus said.

"How fine it would be to hear her play someday," Margaret said. She
had not been impressed by the histrionics of the court poet, who now
took up his harp to begin a strident melody.

"I am curious to hear her music myself," Malcolm said, mouth full as he ate. He licked greasy fingers as he addressed Ranald mac Niall. "How long since we sent a note to Moray?"

"Three months," Ranald replied. "You asked for an accounting of king's portion on some properties there. The lady in the north has not replied."

"That harridan had best send me what is owed," Malcolm said. "And if I order the harper chit here in the spring, her grandmama had best send her, too."

"The winter weather will soon worsen and prevent travel between here and there, sire," Ranald said. "Once the snow fills the passes between the mountains, no parties can easily move into or out of Moray. Even if you were to send for the girl, sire, we would not see her before good weather returns."

"I would be surprised if we see her at all," Angus of Mar muttered. When Malcolm grunted agreement, Margaret noticed how pragmatic he seemed. It was a good quality in a king, she decided, even this rough-edged and provincial one.

"Who is the lady in the north?" she whispered to Robert De Lauder, beside her.

"King Macbeth's widow, the former Queen Gruadh. Now she is regent for her grandson in Moray, a vast province in higher Scotland. She has never given the king her full loyalty, with good reason, and the Moray people are totally loyal to her."

"They are all *my* subjects," Malcolm groused.

"That region is so huge and remote that imposing the rule of the crown is futile," De Lauder explained to the Saxons. "It requires too many men and far too much effort for any king to keep close watch over northern Scotland."

"True enough," Malcolm said, his mouth full as he ate. "Lady Gruadh does as she pleases, or thinks she can. Ladies, welcome to Scotland—where the women are as rebellious as the Highlanders."

Throughout the rest of the meal, Margaret heard parts of the men's conversation as they spoke of Normans, of raids and war, of hunting, even of books. Malcolm was adamant about protecting the Scottish borders from the Normans, and though he mentioned the Saxon resistance in the north, Margaret was not sure if he fully supported the effort or was merely interested in his own claims to Northumbrian land. He ticked off a list of his properties on long, thick fingers and complained that territories should be returned to him—but he did not show much concern for the plight of the Saxon people in the north.

He was a bear of a man, Margaret noted, who had changed little since she had seen him in her uncle's English court. Years had passed since then, and Malcolm was now a tough, mature warrior. Even his plain, unadorned clothing belonged to a warrior more than a king: a red cloak, a brown tunic over trousered legs tied to the knee with thongs. His hair was in need of trimming, his loud voice carried easily, his manners were coarse, his opinions blunt and outspoken.

Yet he spoke English like a Saxon and could switch to rapid Gaelic, then murmur in adequate French to De Lauder. Margaret listened as those two spoke of monks at Durham writing entries in annals based on reports that came via travelers and visitors.

"And where is the book I ordered made for me?" he asked De Lauder. "*C'est finis?*"

"It is not yet completed, sire," De Lauder said in French. "It will take time. You will recall that I rode to meet some monks in the south who could create a very fine book, and I gave your commission to them. They agree that this book should not be produced in the usual scriptoriums where annals are made. By the very nature of its subject it requires discretion."

"True," Malcolm said, spearing some meat with his knife and chewing vigorously.

"You will be pleased with the result, I am sure, when it is done."

"A book, sir?" Margaret asked De Lauder when the king turned to speak to Edgar. She felt encouraged by the warrior king's interest in such matters. "I am very fond of books. May I ask if the king has ordered a new copy of the Gospels, or a psalter, or perhaps a copy of a treatise by one of the holy fathers?"

"None of those," De Lauder said.

"A medical or herbal text, then? We had many beautiful books at our disposal in the library of my uncle, King Edward. Does the king collect many books?"

De Lauder gave her an odd look. "The king does not care over-much for books. He is simply ordering a specific volume, a list of sorts, to be prepared for him by a monk in Lowland Scotland."

"The book would not interest you much, Lady Margaret," Malcolm said abruptly; she realized he had been listening. "No doubt you like pretty little books with precious covers and paintings. This one is a chronology of kings and their deeds. Nothing you would read."

"But I quite like histories," Margaret replied.

"Not this one. We have other books here if you want to read those. Ask Sir Robert to lend you the key to the cupboard where they are kept." The king shifted his attention to Edgar and the others, joining their discussion. He listened intently to what they said and replied with calm authority, which the men welcomed. Margaret was reminded, suddenly, of a priest rather than a warrior-king. Oddly, it did not fit with what else she had seen of the Scottish monarch.

More food was served, but she was not very hungry. In other royal courts she had known, suppers consisted of multiple courses and elaborate dishes, but a Scottish feast was a simple array of fresh but plain foods—boiled mutton, vegetable stew, yellow cheeses. The wines were good, the ale frothy. No bread was offered, which Margaret found strange, although she was served crusty oatcakes, hot and good, such as she had enjoyed at Annot's home. She also nibbled at some vegetables and sipped a red wine, tart but excellent, from a polished wooden cup.

"Do you like the wine, Lady Margaret?" De Lauder asked, beside her. "It is one of the king's favorites, which he regularly imports from France." He lifted his own cup in a half toast as he addressed Margaret and the other Saxons. "This one comes from Bordeaux, where my mother was born. There, the grapes are firm and sweet. A better wine than this cannot be had."

"Indeed." Lady Agatha pursed her lips as she spoke in French. "Does the king prefer all things French, wine and Normans and so on?"

"Not in all matters, lady," he answered tersely. "But he appreciates good wines, and orders a variety of imports from France and the Low Countries as well."

"All very good, but he does not seem to appreciate the state of his household or the properness of his manners," the lady then said in German to her kinfolk.

"*Der König hat keine Königin,*" De Lauder said in easy German, so that Margaret lifted her brows, certain that he could, indeed, understand what they said. "Though the king has no queen, Dame Agnes manages the royal household here at Dunfermline, and does a fine job."

Though grateful for the shelter and sanctuary offered her family, Margaret was anxious to leave the noisy hall as soon as the chance came. Throughout the meal, Malcolm had nearly ignored the royal Saxon women, which would have been a plain insult in England. But she suspected that her kinswomen were too tired to take offense.

Privately she felt relieved to escape the king's attention. Soon she left the room with her kinswomen and went to her prayers and then to bed, exhausted.

THE KING REMAINED at Dunfermline, dining with his Saxon guests and meeting with Edgar and various Scottish and Saxon lords. Beyond formal encounters, Margaret rarely spoke to Malcolm and the king did not seem to notice her much. She did not mind, for his intense, blustery manner unnerved her. No mention was made of marriage, but she sensed the possibility in the air, echoed in oblique remarks and quick glances among the Saxons in particular. But she did not ask, for fear that they would interpret that as a sign of her interest.

Malcolm often went hunting or rode out with his men on patrol, and spent hours with his council or sat in moot court with locals, hearing grievances and giving judgments either in the great hall, in the bailey, or somewhere in the countryside. White-robed brothers and bishops of the Celtic persuasion hastened in and out of the fortress for audiences with the king, but when Margaret remarked one day on the king's piety, De Lauder replied that the Celtic clergy were there to barter rights to rental portions and fees due to the crown or the parishes, and to hint at promotions; the Scottish king appointed bishops himself, he told her.

Tension and turbulence rode the air like dark clouds before a storm. Malcolm Canmore and his men left for days at a time to patrol their borderlands, though rumor said they raided northern England to claim land, booty, and slaves in the wake of William's destruction. Unsure of the truth, Margaret knew only that Edgar and the other Saxons who sometimes rode with Malcolm rarely spoke of what occurred on those journeys.

Following a heated argument with the king loud enough to be heard behind closed doors, Cospatric and Walde departed Dunfermline, taking men and horses to England, saying they would inspect their ravaged Northumbrian properties and help their stranded people after further Norman attacks. Uncomfortably aware of a rift between Malcolm and his cousins, Margaret wondered if the Saxon guests would be asked to leave, but they were not.

Malcolm puzzled her. Sometimes he and his men would sit in the hall in grim, dark moods, guzzling ale or gambling; then Margaret sensed that war deeds and secrets lay heavy upon their shoulders and souls. Other times, when she met Malcolm in the bailey or the tower, he seemed no brute, just a big, clumsy man who lumbered past her, blushing like a boy.

Good day, lady, he would say; or *Greetings, lady—the weather is cold today.* The scents of smoke fire, metal, and horse clung to him, along with hints of sweat and unwashed clothing. His gruff manner and masculine scents seemed compelling and oddly safe, somehow, reminding her of her father, who had been a warrior general under the king of Hungary and would have been a strong monarch for England had fate treated him more kindly.

Sometimes Margaret would stare after Malcolm and feel a longing, a sort of loneliness, stir within. He fascinated her in some ways— blunt and powerful, her clear opposite—then she would dismiss her idle thoughts and move on.

Her kinswomen judged him a dull-witted savage lacking refine-
ment and princely bearing. He had been well educated, but his
casual attention to intellectual matters did not show the training of a
true prince, Margaret thought, compared to princes of the Hungarian
and English courts. As for spiritual matters, Malcolm's fortress had
no decent chapel, and neither did the king go often to the church on
the hill.

Yet he was widely praised as shrewd, powerful, brave, and
even reckless, and the Saxon lords admired his persistence and
purpose. Though he did not behave like a prince of state, though
he was provincial and unsophisticated, he was a clever, ambitious
ruler. Margaret found him intriguing, though she would not have
admitted it.

But her mother and sister, and Kata, too, complained often about
Scotland and spoke of leaving. They pressured Margaret, as the
eldest, to talk to Edgar, who could influence Malcolm to let them go.
Crossing the bailey with her brother one day, Margaret suggested
that Edgar arrange a ship to take her kinswomen away from Scotland.

"It is their fervent wish," she said. "They would prefer to sail to
Denmark and then return to Hungary."

"And you?"

"I would be content to travel by land back to Romsey Abbey. At
any rate, your kinswomen would be safer in religious houses, away
from war and raiding. Mama cannot bear it here."

"I am fostering a rebellion with King Malcolm's support, and so
my family will accept his hospitality for as long as he will offer it.
And at whatever price," Edgar said.

"Choose rebellion and Scottish protection if you will, but let us
leave, and soon."

"We will stay," he answered firmly. "Our only safe haven is here."

EARLY, AFTER PRAYERS in her chamber, Margaret ventured out
into the clear, crisp air with Finola. The girl, perhaps thirteen, could
barely manage English, but she made herself clear enough and was an

eager guide. She led Margaret outside into the wide, enclosed yard to visit the kitchen buildings, where one servant turned cakes on a griddle and another stirred steaming porridge in an iron cauldron and tended to sizzling bacon slabs. The cook gave each girl some porridge in pottery bowls, and Margaret tasted it, not used to much food in the mornings. At Romsey, they had shared dark bread and watery beer after dawn prayers, and at the English court, thin slices of fine white bread and some fruit might be taken. Now she ate the hot, salty porridge with a near sense of guilt, for Lady Agatha always said that showing a good appetite was coarse.

Finola led her to the outer gates, and Margaret was astonished when the guards let the girls leave the bailey, turning away without offering an escort. She held her skirts up, for the hems of her green silk gown and linen chemise, and her yellow silk shoes were mucky from the yard. But she was glad of unexpected freedom after more than a fortnight in the Scottish stronghold, and hastened after Finola, who pointed toward the little glen below the castle mound.

"You are wanting to pray today, lady?" Finola asked.

"In the little church across the glen? Oh, aye!" Margaret had noticed the chapel on the hillside opposite the royal tower. She followed Finola through a wooded glen with quiet paths and waterfalls, and as they walked along the track, she heard barking. Turning, she saw two long-legged dogs, as big as ponies, running after them, tails wagging.

"Dogs of the king," Finola said in halting English, patting the animals, then walking onward.

The plain little church, fieldstone with a timber roof, had an oaken door carved with intertwining vines. She stepped into the cool interior and sighed at the palpable peace, as if the prayers of generations saturated the very air.

The altar was a large block of stone beneath a white cloth, and a wooden cross decorated with spirals hung on the wall behind it. Kneeling to pray, Margaret bowed her head, and Finola did the same. The dogs settled for a nap beside them, apparently used to being allowed inside.

Hearing footsteps, Margaret turned to see a man in the doorway who wore a belted, hooded white tunic. His head was balding in front, his dark hair long behind, and a wooden cross on a string hung from his rope belt. Margaret stood quickly, as did Finola, while the dogs whumped their tails on the floor as if recognizing a friend.

He nodded to Margaret and spoke to Finola in rapid Gaelic. "Ah, Lady Margaret! Welcome," he then said in English. "I am grateful that you and your family were spared from the sea. I am Brother Micheil. I oversee this parish." He bobbed his head and she saw that the front of his scalp was shaved from ear to ear above the forehead.

"Brother, may I ask to which order you belong? I am familiar with the Benedictines."

"I am a monk of the Céli Dé, but most call us the Culdees."

"Ah. I have heard of them but know little about their ways."

"We are of the Celtic church, which was founded in Ireland long ago and celebrated in Scotland as well."

Margaret concealed her surprise. She had learned from the Benedictine priests that Irish monks were radical sorts who mixed pagan practices with religious rites. "I did not expect to find Culdees in the royal seat of Scotland," she said.

"We are all children of God. Heartfelt prayers always reach heaven."

"Indeed," she said. "Brother, do your parishioners understand Latin?" She thought of Finola.

"Most do not, lady," he admitted. "Parishes in Scotland are widespread—we cannot teach the people so easily here."

"Rome only approves prayers spoken in Latin. Do you not worry about the souls of your parishioners?"

"The blessed Columba taught prayers in Gaelic to his flock centuries ago. Was he wrong?" He spoke it like a challenge.

"I know of Columba from a manuscript in the king's library at Winchester, copied from a work of Adomnán of Ireland," she explained. "I am also aware that Rome has tried over time to help the Irish and Scottish church understand its proper laws."

"We are content with our own," Micheil said, smiling. "While you are here, you may like to learn more about Scotland. We have many holy places here that may comfort your doubts, lady, including an important pilgrimage route. I would be happy to escort you or arrange visits to some of our holy sites. How long will you stay?"

"I am not certain." She wondered herself. Thanking him for his offer, she departed with Finola to walk back through the forested glen. The dogs rushed ahead, loping up the hillside toward the tower.

Pausing beside the stream to admire a cascade of small waterfalls, Margaret sat upon a large boulder to rest, taking in the rare and lovely peacefulness of that place. Birdsong and rushing water, the scent of pine, the cool mist and translucent, filtering sunlight—the little glen was perhaps the most beautiful place she had ever seen, except that it was in Scotland, where she did not want to be.

Chapter Four

Eva

I will not yield
To kiss the ground before young Malcolm's feet.

—WILLIAM SHAKESPEARE, *Macbeth*

A sweet blur of memory: I a small girl, watching my mother weaving at her loom while she sang to the shuttle's rhythm. Her dark hair flowed like a raven's wing, and she smiled when I sang with her. In the evenings, she would play her harp for the company gathered in her father's hall. Her clear voice and her music fascinated me. From early days, I wanted to become a harper, and fate and heaven arranged that for me—along with other matters more surprising.

I still have my mother's harp, all carved wood and metal strings, and I have two more of my own, often played. But the wood and strings of my mother's harp retain her gentleness and emanate her songs, and touching them brings back to me the memories of my childhood.

My mother was named Leven for the loch near her birthplace, where she met my father when he visited Fife. I knew he was royal, and I met him for the first time just before his death. Because of her, my first eight years were spent in Fife; because of him, the rest in Moray. I loved both places dearly.

Macduff, the mormaer of Fife, was a traitorous brute to some, but to me an indulgent grandfather. I was born at Abernethy fortress, his keep, where my young and unmarried mother kept my father's name a secret from her father as long as she could; by the time he got the truth from her, he already loved me, and agreed to my protection and education due to my royal blood. When I was little, a priest tutored me in Latin and Gaelic, mathematics and theology. From a Saxon maid in our household I learned capable English, and in thanks, my grandfather gave her a plot of land and a husband.

Leven taught me to embroider, spin, and weave—though the latter was the work of common women, my mother loved its rhythms and results—and she taught me the melodies of loom and spindle, of smooring the hearth and rocking the cradle. I inherited her slight form and her shining black hair, along with her clear voice and love of music. She said I had my father's eyes and smile and, she said, the boldness of a kinswoman I did not know. My grandfather said it was a relief that I combined the best of them; the worst of them was not explained.

My mother died of fever when I was seven, and my grandfather passed of the same soon after. His brother Kenneth became mormaer in the region next, and kept me in his Fife household for a while, wondering what to do with me. There I met my father at last—a fair and slender young man whose guard carried the banner of the king: himself. Startled to learn that, I only believed it once I saw his eyes, a changeable blue like mine, and his dimpled smile, my own.

"I am told you sing well, Eva," the somber young king said when we met.

"I do." Eight years old, I was truthful by nature.

"Will you sing for me?"

I did, standing before him at my uncle's table. King Lulach wept a little and kissed me, and when he departed next day, he left gold coins for my care, along with a ring of silver and crystal for me, and a promise to bring me north to live with him and our Moray kin at his court at Elgin. I was eager, for I would be a princess and would have a family—a father, a stepmother, two half siblings, a grandmother, and cousins—and a home where I truly belonged.

Shortly after his visit to us in Fife, Lulach was killed. We heard this was by done by order of King Malcolm, who ruled in southern Scotland after defeating Macbeth; war had split Scotland, and Lulach held the northern region of Moray and other northern regions that did not support Malcolm. Having scarcely met my father, I now mourned him—the idea of him, I suppose, rather than a father I had known. Shortly after, my Fife uncle told me that the south was no good place for me; I was too young, he said, to know how dangerous it was to be daughter to a dead king. Then he sent me by escort to live with my northern kinfolk.

Lady Gruadh, my Moray grandmother, was a tall, cheekboned beauty, youthful still despite years and strife. Her hair gleamed pale copper, and her eyes were silver-blue. She had been a warrior-queen beside Macbeth, and she had elegance and strength; she had the loyalty of the northerners, too. I was in awe of her—she was vibrant and fierce in her devotion to kin and land.

Gruadh acted as regent for my half brother, Nechtan, who trained at swords but preferred books and studying with priests. My half sister, Ailsa, went to live with cousins to be educated and readied for a good match one day. Quiet Nechtan stayed in Moray as its nominal mormaer; traditionally the leaders of that rich and vast province were like kings in the north. I learned quickly that the high kings of Scotland always tread carefully where Moray is concerned.

Now it is years later and I am grown, and Gruadh is still regarded as a rebel by King Malcolm. He sends occasional messages to cajole or threaten her to behave. She is hospitable to his messengers, and delights in crafting rude replies to the king, despite the pleas of her council.

With her gift of Da Shelladh—"the two sights," or The Sight—my grandmother can gaze into flames or water's sheen and see what is unknown and what will come. She warned her Moray council that King Malcolm will bring even more change to Scotland in future, and told them to beware. Though I lack her knowledge of magic, I learned boldness as well as charm from her. Recognizing my interest in music, she arranged for me to be trained by a bard who had once served Macbeth. For that in particular, I am endless grateful.

And so I was schooled in the songs and tales of the Irish and Scottish bardic traditions, learning them by old methods and diligence. A bard must know a thousand songs, melodies, and tales—one for each day of the year, and more than that to fill rainy afternoons and winter evenings. Someday I might attain the mastery of a *filidh,* a poet-bard, though that needs twelve years of study. Or I could declare myself a harper and court singer, a status I have attained already.

Bard-craft is my joy and calling, and I hunger to know more of that as well as of the greater world. My grandmother would like to keep me in Moray, close and safe, where I have a right as bard and princess to a seat on that council. But life has more for me somewhere. I feel it so.

❦

"IN THE SOUTH, Malcolm struts and rules and calls me witch, and now he wants a favor!" Lady Gruadh paced the floor, clasping the folded page with the king's latest missive. Her hand shook a little as she felt, and hid, her near panic. "He orders Eva to act as a harper in his court because he has guests. What do I care about that? She might never return from that place."

"If she went to court for a few weeks, her visit could be useful to us," Ruari mac Fergus said quietly. "She could be the eyes and ears of Moray in the south." He leaned his hip against a table, arms folded, watching as Gruadh walked the length of the hall and back again with a swirl of skirts.

"I will not allow it," she said bluntly. "Witch, I am told he calls me in private, though here he properly writes 'Lady of Elgin'!" She brandished the page. "Most call me Lady of the North now." Secretly she liked that term. "I will not stand for 'witch' from anyone, especially—"

"You are no witch, Rue. Go easy," he added.

"Malcolm Ceann Mór, Big Head, wants our girl-bard for her talent and renown."

"The letter is polite. I think he fears you a little." Ruari smiled.

"So he should." She handed the page to Ruari. "I do control Moray as regent mormaer for my grandson." She felt calmer. Ruari, once a member of her father's guard and later head of Macbeth's guard, was not only her advisor but her lover now. His steady, imperturbable manner—and private tenderness—soothed her ire. "Malcolm cannot ignore the importance of this vast province with all its resources and seaports."

"And its thousands of warriors not keen on Malcolm," Ruari added with a warrior's spark in his hazel eyes. He had fostered the resistance that still survived in Moray. "The king never knows what we are thinking or doing up here in the north."

"May that uncertainty keep him awake at night." Gruadh folded her arms.

"Lately they say he has a new distraction—the fugitive Saxon royal family, the prince and his pretty sisters and others, who fled the Normans over the North Sea only to be shipwrecked on a beach in Fife. Malcolm gives them sanctuary, no doubt to suit his own ends."

"But what does he want? We have heard the reports of William's attacks in northern England, the loss of Danish support, the hunt for the Saxon royals. And now Canmore goes into Northumbria to thrash the poor Saxons further, even with the Aethelings supping at his own table. Malcolm has always been a brute. Macbeth would never—"

"We cannot know what he would have done to prevent the Normans from gaining Scotland," Ruari pointed out. "Malcolm will protect his borders, yet he also hungers to expand his territory in Northumbria. He still means to reclaim his lands there."

"Why shelter the Saxon royalty in his court? That only invites Norman wrath." Gruadh shook her head. "Malcolm soaks up Sassenach ways and diminishes the Celtic traditions that thrived eons before him, back to the ancestors he and I have in common. And now he harbors a Saxon prince to taunt a Norman king. This is too much risk for Scotland."

"If he lends the Saxon prince his military support against William, thinking to tip the balance and flush the Normans out of the north, it will never happen."

"Once again Malcolm backs the losing cause," Gruadh murmured. "It would be nearly impossible to drive the Normans out now."

"True, but with the young Saxon royalty in his debt, his lands and importance could increase. Perhaps he wants a wife in one of those virgin princesses hiding in his household."

"Hah! Saxon blood in Malcolm's heirs would dilute the Scottish blood of generations!"

"More so than the Viking and Irish blood already in the line?" Ruari nearly smiled. "Besides, Malcolm has needed a queen since Ingebjorg's death."

"She wasted away in that southern priory," Gruadh said. "Her gentle spirit was never suited to the south, or to be Malcolm's queen. That sweet girl should have stayed here as Lulach's widow, mother to his children who needed her. She could have married again, could have—"

"Malcolm claimed victor's rights, just as Macbeth did when he wed you. It is that simple."

She caught her breath at the reminder. Years ago, tragedy had finally led to contentment, and then . . . but she would not think on it. "What has become of the two little sons he got upon Inga? Fostered out already, they say, though they are so young!"

"Your bitterness would best you if not for your tender mother's heart," Ruari murmured. He leaned forward until his shoulder touched hers. She tilted toward him a little. "Forget what is past, Rue. See what has been gained in your life. You have power and respect in Moray, worthy grandchildren, and my unworthy heart if you want it. Let all that change you for the better. Else you will always be snappish as an old hawk," he said wryly.

She sucked in a breath. "Let me linger with my old joys and grievances. When I am ready, I will have done." She paused. "I thought you liked hawks."

"I do." He lifted a brow.

"I do have power and responsibilities here until Nechtan is old enough to take over," she agreed. "And you," she said, resting a hand on his arm, "you are my strength."

"Many in the north will support you for as long as you care to rule here," he murmured.

"My grandson is of an age with that Saxon princeling, not yet a blooded warrior. His sister will make a good marriage someday, and their half sister . . ." She sighed. "Eva is a tricky treasure to protect."

Trapped emotions rose in her chest, beating wings to be free. She turned away to pace the room again, folding her arms tight over her chest. Sometimes she felt a little wise, but today she felt fearful. Malcolm might never let her or her family be.

She thought of the spring day that Drostan, abbot of Loch Leven in Fife, had brought Eva north to Elgin fortress. He had lifted the child down from the horse and Gruadh had led her inside to give her some soup. When the little fledgling had finished, she had smiled, mouth dimpling at one corner. Glimpsing Lulach there in her face, Rue was lost to sudden love. The girl's royal blood was unmistakable—and she was enchanting.

A quicksilver child, Eva wore her grandmother's patience brittle, but jigged and giggled her way into all hearts at Elgin. She showed her paternal grandfather's gifts too: Lulach's father, Gruadh's first husband, Gilcomgan, had been a warrior who should have been a bard. His gifts lived on in his granddaughter.

Ailsa was quiet and pretty, Nechtan sober and studious, and their grandmother loved them deeply. But Eva, older than her half siblings, was like sunlight dissolving shadows, luring her grandmother back from the edge of grief that year, scarcely a twelvemonth after the deaths of Macbeth and then Lulach.

Dermot, the *seanchaidh* who had entertained so often at Macbeth's court, returned to Elgin one winter and, sensing the girl's natural talent for singing and harp playing, offered to stay and teach her. Her little fingers were deft and nimble on the harp strings, and her voice was sweet and strong, even so young. Eva had trained for years with Dermot, entertaining those at Elgin with her gifts. At eighteen, she was now a lovely creature with a shining talent. Visitors came away from Elgin's hall praising the young female bard of the Moray court, a rarity for her gender in that calling, as well as for her uncommon beauty and skillful music.

Gruadh sighed and returned to Ruari, who waited silent and patiently. He was her opposite in some ways and her blessed match in so many others, though she had never told him so. He knew, she felt sure of that. He was strong, brown, and as sturdy as a rock. She needed him. As she approached, he stretched out his hand to her and she took it.

"Some say that Eva, the girl-bard of Moray, plays music with the power to enchant," she said. Ruari inclined his head, listening, waiting. "Not a rumor to encourage, that, though there may be some truth to it."

"So you will send her to court after all?"

"Perhaps. We can delay through the winter." She looked down at the folded letter again. "Eva is young for that fox's den, but she is strong and clever, and as you say, she could be a help to us there. Let Malcolm wait until spring to please his guests. Let us see what else he offers for the privilege of Eva's music."

"Do not think to trust him," Ruari reminded her.

"Only when he was a pup, but after that—never. Ruari, whether or not we obey this order from Malcolm, I want you to send word to the men of Moray to be on guard for a summons from us, should we need their support in arms and might."

He looked at her steadily. "If the Saxon rebellion fails, and Malcolm fails, too, and if the Normans come up into Scotland—we may have to marshal our forces and pull away from lower Scotland."

"Just so," she said quietly. "The day may come when my grand-son will rule the north while another king rules in the south. Macbeth did that for a time—but Malcolm was not content and made sure of his death." She sighed.

"We will spread the word to be ready should the Normans set foot in any part of Scotland. Rue, there is something more to consider. Drostan mentioned a rumor that Malcolm has ordered a history to be written in which Macbeth's rule is described in Malcolm's terms rather than the whole truth of the matter. Drostan does not know which scriptorium has been commissioned to create the book. It was not his own workshop at Loch Leven."

"If Malcolm dictates the contents, neither Macbeth nor Lulach would fare well."

"Nor any of us. But if Eva could learn the whereabouts of that book by going to court, we could find it, even destroy it so that it could never be read or copied, or taken as truth in future."

"If I could but hold that book in my hands, I would correct the entries quick enough myself." Crumpling the king's letter, Gruadh tossed it into the fire basket, where it caught flame, burned bright, vanished.

❀

MARGARET WAS NOT USED to much merriment at Christmastide, which was a string of lighthearted days at Dunfermline. The air was filled with the fragrance of pine swags over doorways for protection from spirits, while music, good food and drink, and cheerful camaraderie swelled in the king's hall.

She laughed once, watching the fun at supper, and was pinched for it by her mother. "It is not seemly," Lady Agatha scolded her. "This is a time of reflection and charity, not a time to act foolish!"

In Hungary, Yuletide had been marked by fasting, prayer, incense, and the sheen of Byzantine gold; King Edward's Christmas court had

been somber despite his queen's generosity with small gifts. In Scotland, Lady Agatha admonished Margaret and her siblings to keep apart
from any pagan folly. They said extra prayers and fasted, while Margaret watched the celebrations with fascination, smiling to herself, bounc-
ing to the music, then sobering if she caught her mother's shrewd gaze.

Winter brought bone-chilling damp, sleet, and snow, and Margaret
sat in bright nooks with the women as they all tucked in to sewing and
stitchery. Suppers were served early due to the failing light, and after
stories—Hector enthralled them with good deliveries of old tales,
such as the long poem of the Geats and Beowulf—and after music
and table games, the court retired to bed.

Peat blocks in fire baskets gave off a sweet, comforting scent,
mingled with pine and fruit woods, and Margaret indulged in more
food in cold weather, the fare enticing and satisfying. But her mother
urged both daughters to mark the season of devotion and gratitude
with fasting. Yet though Lady Agatha kept her royal Saxon offspring
apart and aloof, Margaret felt at home in Dunfermline, where she
enjoyed freedoms she had never known, such as wandering the glens
with a maid and a guard, or strolling the weekly market in the town.
She felt safe there, too, knowing that the Normans were not likely to
pursue them northward so long as Malcolm was their protector.

That winter, she sensed Edgar falling away from the hold of his
kinswomen. Surrounded by warriors and leaders in Scotland who
regarded him as a rightful but banished king, he rode with Malcolm
and hunted, trained at arms, tossed bones and dice, raced horses, and
debated war strategies with his Scottish and Saxon comrades. He grew
taller, roughening into a man, and the changes Margaret saw tugged at
her heart; at times she felt more like his mother than his sister.

Once, when she glimpsed the bright sheen of his golden hair in the
dim great hall, she thought of the crown Edgar would likely never
wear. That pulled at her heartstrings, too.

WHEN SNOWDROPS PUSHED through cold earth, followed by
purple crocus, the King of Scots rode out with an army at his back

and trouble clearly to hand. As Margaret went to pray at dawn in the makeshift chapel the Saxons had set up in the king's tower, she looked through a narrow window along the turning stair and saw the men departing the yard. Silver-pink light sparked over their mesh armor as they rode out. Later she heard that they had met thousands more men waiting along the roads and fields from there to Lothian. Malcolm had sent word to all households within a day's ride for any who owed him knight's service for rent to take up arms or send men on his behalf. Many northern Scots, Margaret heard it said at the supper table, ignored the king's summons. Malcolm Canmore had not conquered the whole of his own kingdom, they said, but seemed bent on riding south to attack and conquer outside Scotland.

"But that cannot be so," Margaret told Wilfrid. "King Malcolm supports the Saxon cause now. Why would he ride into England with an army, except to help the people there?"

"We can only hope it is so, lady." Wilfrid did not sound convinced.

Within the week, Edgar and his own companions rode out, too, giving little explanation beyond saying they would join the Scottish king in England. Robert De Lauder and Ranald remained at Dunfermline to oversee the king's guard and his estates. Soon enough, news came that Malcolm and his army were moving through northern England toward York, passing through areas decimated by the Normans under William's command.

"With all this Scottish help," Cristina said bitterly one day, "Edgar feels pressured to make a stand as a rebel king. That will come to naught—meanwhile, we are stuck in Scotland, prisoners more than guests. Who knows what will become of any of us."

Margaret did not answer; she did not know either. Spending more time on her knees in prayer, she began to wonder if all the daily prayers she and the other ladies spun heavenward on behalf of the Saxons would have any effect at all. Judging by the news, prayers made little difference.

She learned, along with the others, that Malcolm had led his men as far as York not to save Saxons, but to pound hard on them himself.

His lands in Cumbria had been attacked by his cousin Cospatric, and Malcolm had acted in retaliation, pushing farther south in his wrath.

Margaret felt sick to her stomach, at times, aware of what Malcolm was doing, what Edgar was witnessing. How could any decent king—any moral man, she thought—raid an almost devastated land to do more harm to people already reduced to nothing, when their own royal family were in his personal protection? She felt profoundly betrayed, so that prayer could not appease her anger.

One rainy evening a message arrived from Edgar, brought by an exhausted young man. The Saxons and Scottish courtiers gathered in the hall to hear him. "Edgar the Aetheling wishes his lady mother and the princesses to remain in the safety of the Scottish king's household. The prince will head north soon by order of King Malcolm."

Margaret sighed, relieved to hear Edgar was returning, though not pleased to learn that he was following Malcolm's orders so directly. "Edgar is safe, then. What of King Malcolm? When will this end in the south?"

"That I cannot answer for you, Lady Margaret—none of us can," the young man said. "Malcolm still has business in England, due to his cousin's actions. Cospatric, now earl of Northumbria by William's favor, wrecked Malcolm's properties there and retired to his family seat at Bamborough, which he retains through a bargain with King William."

"We heard of Cospatric's betrayal. Where is Malcolm now?" De Lauder asked.

"The king is back in Northumbria. He has been burning churches, killing women and children and—"

"Dear God," Margaret blurted, while her sister and others gasped. Lady Agatha slumped into her seat and crossed herself.

"—and pregnant women and—"

"Christ's mercy!" cried Lady Agatha.

The messenger nodded. "The Scottish king stole treasures away from Durham, and now he is leading innumerable English people northward into servitude in Scotland."

"Slaves! Why must we stay here?" Lady Agatha asked in German. "This man is a monster!"

"The whole of northern England is torn by war, and thick with the smoke of burning homes and crops. The roads are haunted by thieves and desperate men, and lined with corpses, between the dev-astations of the Normans and those of the Scots."

"Stop," Lady Agatha said. "We can hear no more of this!"

"We cannot stay here. Edgar is mad to think so," Cristina said. "We must find some way to leave if he will not arrange it for us."

"Pardon, my lady," De Lauder said, "but you would be hunted wherever you go by Norman troops under William's orders."

"It is true," the messenger said. "Thus, Edgar the Aetheling desires his kinswomen to stay safely in the north." He paused. "He asks that you remember the gratitude and loyalty your party owes to the King of Scots."

Margaret shook her head and nearly protested aloud, then turned away. She could not feel grateful to a man so deceitful and cruel as Malcolm.

THE AIR SMELLED GREEN and earthy in early spring, as crocuses made way for buttery primroses and violets peeked through the grass in shady spots as Margaret, Finola, and Cristina walked back from the hillside chapel. Ahead, Dunfermline's open gates were crowded with men on horseback and what looked like hundreds of people on foot—so many that some of them lingered outside the palisade gates. As she walked up the hill toward the fortress, she saw one of the riders remove his helmet, his hair shining gold in the cool sunlight.

She turned toward Cristina. "Edgar has returned!"

"But who are the others?" her sister asked. Margaret did not answer, picking up her skirt hems to run up the slope.

Making her way through the crowd, Margaret wondered, too, who the people were—they were not foot soldiers, but older men and women and children, all of them looking gaunt, pale, and weary, a ragged, dirty, and woeful lot. But as some of them gazed up at the king's tower, she saw relief on their faces, even hope. That sight near broke her heart.

Then the English language murmured among them told her who they were. "Saxons," she said to Cristina.

"Slaves?" her sister asked as Margaret took her arm, tugging her close as they walked toward the men who were dismounting. Edgar stepped down from his horse, spoke to a groom, and turned to see his sisters. Crying out, Margaret ran forward to hug him, feeling the hard press of steel mesh armor as he embraced her, and then turned to Cristina.

"Mother will be waiting inside for you by now," Cristina said. "Come!"

But Margaret held back, taking Edgar's arm. "These are Saxons with you," she said quietly, looking toward the people in the bailey.

"Aye," he replied. "We brought them out of England—they are some of the captives and slaves Malcolm took."

"So many! What will become of them now?"

"Some will be placed in royal households here and elsewhere, the rest taken to homes throughout the countryside to serve there. This group was much larger when we first set out," he said. "Malcolm's men left one or two at every house we passed, I think. Every little house in Scotland will have its Saxon slave now. It is best," he added.

"Best? They should be in England, in their own homes," Margaret said.

"If it were possible, but it is not."

Seeing Brother Micheil and Father Otto in the bailey blessing those who filled the yard, Margaret stood watching. The Saxon slaves filled the space like a market day crowd, yet they were silent, woebegone, no doubt wondering what would become of them.

She looked up at Edgar. "I wish I could greet each one of them and wipe the dust of the road from their faces. I wish I could give them drinks, supper, a bed for the night—yet I am not the chatelaine in the king's household. But Dame Agnes is here now. She will help."

She indicated the woman moving through the throng, followed by servants carrying full leather bladders of what was probably watered ale. "These poor folk have lost their families and friends, have seen their homes and lands destroyed, have witnessed the ravaging of Northumbria—and now they are slaves."

"At least they are alive." Edgar pressed her shoulder. "Dame Agnes and her servants, the priests, too, have the matter well in hand. Let us go greet our mother."

She walked with him past servants running by with flasks, buckets of water, and plates of oatcakes as Agnes called out for straw pallets and extra blankets to be laid out in the tower, byres, and bailey. The people would share makeshift beds in groups, but each would have a clean place to rest for the night, and something to eat. Margaret lingered, still wanting to help, but Edgar tugged on her arm to bring her away.

Inside the great hall, ale and soup were served to the returning knights. When Cristina and Lady Agatha began to closely question Edgar, Margaret hushed them. But Edgar looked up.

"The king is still in Dun Edin," he answered. "His orders are that the Saxon slaves be portioned out to as many households as possible before he returns here."

"But these are our people, Edgar," Margaret said. "Your people."

He shook his head wearily. "There was no choice. Malcolm ordered this done."

The next day, Edgar brought several young female Saxons to meet his mother and sisters, suggesting that they accept the girls as maidservants. Margaret and the others welcomed them warmly, and Dame Agnes found beds for them in the main tower, assigning a few of them to the royal ladies, the others to work in the household and kitchens.

Margaret fiercely wished that she could set the girls, and the other fugitive Saxons, free to return to England. But she knew that a life of slavery in Scotland was a better fate, even for the girls who seemed well educated, with gentle upbringings. Two of those joined Lady

Agatha's circle as maidservants—Wynne, Margaret learned, was the daughter of a deposed, deceased earl, while Matilda was the widow of a landowning knight. Both quietly accepted their new status, understanding the needs of ladies and the skills of embroidery as well as household tasks.

Walking with Edgar through the upper bailey a few days later, Margaret listened while he described the conditions he had seen in England. She sensed a deeper sobriety in his voice and manner, a new determination in the set of his features.

"The ruination is unimaginable, Margaret," he said. "Homes destroyed—farms burned to the ground. Fields sowed with salt by the Normans at William's order, to make sure nothing can grow there. Corpses—are you strong enough to hear it? Aye, then—corpses stiff by the side of the road as we went past, from injury, disease, or starvation, with no one left to mourn or bury them but strangers. And the stench—" He paused. "It is hellish in northern England now."

"Surely some have survived the brutality and remain there. And what of Malcolm? We thought he went south to help, but now it seems he has only added to the dilemma."

"He wrought his share of the destruction, true. And . . . he took Saxon prisoners as well as slaves."

"Prisoners?" Margaret asked, stunned.

"Saxon knights and Normans, too. He shut away a good number in his fortress at Dun Edin, waiting for the price of their ransom fees," he explained. "It is the nature of war."

"He promised that he would help the Saxon cause," she said, feeling distressed. "Oh, I am so weary of this talk of war and things we cannot change. Tell me instead about Dun Edin—I hear it is a grand town and fortress, the equal of some in Europe. A trading town even nicer than Dunfermline, some say. Though I will admit it is very pleasant here." She tried to smile. Edgar's slumped shoulders and haunted eyes upset her, and she wanted to see him brighten again.

"Dun Edin is an excellent place, a fine citadel on a massive rock high above a town and a busy seaport that seem thriving. Malcolm is rebuilding the fortress in stone, and soon it will rival any Norman castellum, I think. Already he is calling it Edinburgh, after a Saxon model. He does admire many things about England, Margaret."

"It does not seem so," she said, and nearly bit her lip. She had meant to be more cheerful.

"Still, it is a very fine place. You would like it there." He glanced sidelong at her.

"How could I like it, with Saxon prisoners shut within its walls?"

"SURELY MY FATHER had good reason to act the way he did," Lady Juliana said in defense of her father, Cospatric, who had eight offspring; brown-haired, seventeen-year-old Juliana was the daughter of his mistress. Cristina had brought up the subject of the war once again as the ladies sat sewing. Margaret knew that her sister enjoyed airing her grudge toward any circumstance that kept her and her family in Scotland.

"But he attacked Malcolm despite the hospitality shown him, and us," Cristina persisted.

Drawing thread through cloth, Margaret looked up. "We must remember that Cospatric may be only protecting his lands and kinfolk in Northumbria. No doubt he had to come into William's favor or lose all, including his head. We know what William can be like—he took our own brother hostage and shut us away." She glanced at her sister, who scowled.

"Thank you, Lady Margaret." Juliana, the youngest of the ladies at court, had come to Dunfermline as a hostage to ensure Cospatric's loyalty to Malcolm—but now the dispute between her father and Malcolm meant that she might never leave Scotland.

The afternoon sun poured gold through the window of Lady Agatha's bedchamber as the stitching continued, and when a rapid knocking sounded at the door, Finola opened it to admit Lady Gudrun, the young wife of Ranald mac Niall, one of the Scottish thanes.

"The king has returned!" Gudrun was breathless. "There is much excitement below stairs over it. Did you not hear the riders arrive?"

"We did, but thought it a hunting party." Margaret looked up from threading a row of stitches on an altar cloth. "What word comes with the king? Is there peace at last? Did he bring yet more slaves north?"

"Is there news of my father?" Juliana added.

"No slaves, and no news beyond what we already know," Lady Gudrun replied. The Norse-born woman was a sunny vision, hair blond, eyes blue, deep dimples in her cheeks. "But now that Malcolm is back, Scotland's role in this will cease for a while. Tonight there will be a feast in honor of his return." She smiled tentatively.

"Did he bring with him the Saxon knights he has captured?" Margaret asked.

"This is a victor's return, to be celebrated," Gudrun replied. "The king brought slaves and prisoners out of England, true, but it is all part of war. He will earn good income for Scotland's treasury by ransoming those men."

"He will wait years to be paid," Margaret said. "The Saxons have nothing left."

"Hush," Lady Agatha whispered, leaning toward her. "We are guests here, dependent on Malcolm's goodwill. And you, of all of us, must take care."

"Why?" Margaret asked, with dread in her stomach. She waited for her mother to mention marriage negotiations, confirming the fear Margaret had entertained ever since leaving the convent last November. Lady Agatha did not answer, merely turned away to examine Lady Juliana's stitchery, correcting the girl's technique.

Silent, upset, Margaret knotted the last threads while the women chatted about the king. As she used her little silver scissors, she realized that news of the king's deeds left her with such resentment that even daily prayer could not ease it. She held up the stitchery piece to examine it, hearing murmurs of admiration around her.

"Excellent." Her mother peered closely. "But those few stitches are crooked."

Without answer or expression, Margaret began to tear out the flawed threads.

Chapter Five

❦

In the year 1070, King Malcolm wasted England.

—*Chronicle of Melrose,* ELEVENTH CENTURY

D amn the woman," Malcolm muttered at supper a few nights later. "Enough of her games!"

Overhearing that, and the grumbling agreement from the men who sat near the king, Margaret wondered if the king was upset with her or her kinswomen, who had been obvious in their disapproval of Malcolm's manners and rudeness. She had not followed the conversation, for she had been listening to Hector, whose harp tune was too fast and loud for a quiet supper. Fearing that she would be ill if she ate to such noise, she had abandoned her plate.

Now she turned to Ranald, sitting nearest her. "Whom does the king mean?"

He waved fingers greasy from roast fowl. "Lady Gruadh, who was Macbeth's queen. She has a talent for setting the king's teeth on edge."

As she had earlier, Margaret felt a stir of curiosity about the woman. "Do you know her?"

"I have met her. A beauty still," he murmured, "and a woman to admire."

Margaret watched Malcolm lift a horn filled with wine, the liquid sloshing down his arm as he drank. The curved vessels, often beautifully decorated in precious metals, were propped on small stands when full, but many warriors found sport in emptying their drinking horns quickly in long gulps. While that was considered manly, Margaret thought, any sensible woman would have used a practical cup.

"That damned Moray woman," Malcolm groused again. "Now she is gathering troops, they tell me! Have you heard aught of this, Ranald?"

The Highlander shrugged. "All I know is what we have heard most lately, sire. The lady has sent word around to alert any Moray men who owe her a fee of knight service. It could be a reminder of service due in place of rent."

"Or else she means to trot out another army," Malcolm said.

Margaret turned to Brother Micheil, also nearby. "*Another* army?"

"She marched against the king years ago. He bristles over it still," the priest murmured.

"She herself led the army?" Margaret was amazed. Micheil nodded.

"Fancies herself a warlord, but she is just a pest." Malcolm sliced into a chunk of meat on his platter. "She wears sword and shield when she likes, and keeps housecarls around her who have been loyal to her near all their lives." He chewed for a moment. "I sent a request that she send her granddaughter here to play harp for us."

"What became of that, sire?" De Lauder asked. "I do not recall any reply from them."

"She refused. Sent word that she expected to be trapped by snow all winter." He frowned, contemplating the meat on the end of his knife. "I wonder what she plans up there. Likely she means to push her grandson's claim to Moray and all Scotland."

Ranald nodded. "It would make sense."

"That boy has a ferocious grandmama." The king belched. "We

should not have let her play so freely up there with her knights and her trading ships, thinking she would keep busy."

"Not busy enough, sire." De Lauder sat forward. "If we could persuade the lady to disband her armies, that is all we need do to avoid trouble with Moray."

"I am not afraid of that accursed female!" Malcolm nearly shouted. The harper played more loudly, suddenly, and Margaret realized that Hector's increasingly vigorous music served to provide privacy for the discussion at the king's table.

"Gruadh practices witchery, they say," De Lauder pointed out. "She would be arrested and burned if this were England or France, sire."

"Witch?" Margaret gasped as her family members looked at each other with concern.

"Interesting," Malcolm replied. "Scotland does not follow the same laws that King Alfred laid down, but we could apply something similar if we had reason."

"Just a rumor," Ranald said quickly. "The lady knows a little hearth magic, but no more than that. Herbs, smoke, and chants are harmless."

De Lauder rapped his fingers on the tabletop. "Sire, what if you took the Moray lad, this young Nechtan, for fostering in your household? Train him as your ally. Then send him back to Moray to rule in your name. You would have a loyal leader in the north."

"A fosterling can return home," Malcolm said, frowning, "but a hostage must remain under threat until released. Moray's regent-witch would have to obey if we held the boy hostage against her willfulness."

"But Nechtan should not be separated from his family," Margaret said, thinking of Edgar, taken as a young adolescent to Normandy as William's hostage.

Malcolm looked at her then. "My lady, surely you have embroidery to do, or prayers to say."

"Prayers?" At his rude dismissal, her temper flared and her usual cool hold over her behavior slipped. "Shall I pray for this council, flummoxed by a clever woman in the north?"

De Lauder laughed, and a few men smiled. Malcolm slapped his palms flat on the table. "Lady, pray for the woman in the north if you will, but leave us for now," he snarled.

"My lord." Margaret forced a smile. Taught to behave with constant courtesy, she would not be made the fool—that was enough to tip her temper. "I would stay."

"Then we had best talk of nicer matters," he snapped.

"Excellent," she replied tersely. "You said that you invited the lady harper to court to entertain." Anything but Hector's twanging, she thought, as the harper continued a fast rhythm, perhaps to cover any raised voices. "Perhaps a new invitation, nicely composed, will flatter the Lady of the North, who may wish for advancement for her granddaughter at the king's court." Nearby, one or two of the men laughed, though she did not think it so far-fetched an idea.

"Hardly! But the girl would make a good hostage," Malcolm said, nodding.

"Hostage?" Margaret felt stunned. "I did not mean to suggest that."

"All Moray would know that their princess is captive in the royal household, and we would have some control. Good!" He smacked the table, looking pleased.

"Sire . . . it is neither right nor courteous to make a prisoner of a young girl!" Margaret said.

"Girl? She is old enough to be married." Malcolm looked keenly at her, eyes bright with wine and a sort of glee. "Now Lady Gruadh will have no choice! The girl-bard will be hostage for her grand-mama's pretty behavior. And you, Lady Margaret, are canny as a general!"

"BUT I LIKE the little Scottish chapel," Margaret protested one morn-ing by the gate as Father Otto stopped her from leaving the compound. "It is a pleasure to walk through the glen to visit Brother Micheil." Beside her, Finola nodded.

The Benedictine scowled. Margaret knew he did not consider a Cul-dee to be a worthy priest for the royal Saxons. "I conduct morning and evening masses in our chapel room in the tower, in proper Latin form," he reminded her. "The priests of the Scottish Church had better start doing so themselves to bring their flocks under Rome's protection. Otherwise what relief from sin do they offer their parishioners? There will be no redemption on the Day of Atonement for the Scots."

"I understand that, Father. I simply wish to bring Brother Micheil an altar cloth that I have embroidered." She lifted the cloth bundle in her arms.

"Very well. If he offers to confess you and assign penance, decline. I will absolve you later."

As Margaret went with Finola through the little glen, called Pittencrieff by the locals, she saw two horses, a black and a bay, munching grass near the little church. She felt a bit disappointed, for she had looked forward to private, tranquil time to pray while there.

The door of the church opened and she saw De Lauder exit, followed by Malcolm Canmore, who towered over Brother Micheil as they all paused on the front step. The king handed Micheil a pouch, which the brother weighted in his hand as if it held coins. Just then De Lauder saw Margaret and spoke quickly to Malcolm, who turned.

"Good day, Lady Margaret," the Norman called in French. "How nice to meet on such a fine day." Malcolm said nothing to her but continued to speak with the Celtic priest.

"Sir Robert. My lord king," Margaret added in English, bowing her head slightly. "Brother Micheil. We brought a gift for the chapel, if you will allow." She held out the folded cloth.

"This is very fine," Brother Micheil said, accepting it to examine part of the embroidery.

"It is indeed. We will leave you, then. Good day, *ma princesse*," Robert De Lauder said. The king only stared at her oddly, then stepped away with the leader of his guard. As Brother Micheil held the door open, Margaret waved Finola through with him and remained on the step, obeying a sudden impulse.

"Sire," she called. Malcolm turned. "May I speak with you?"

He gestured for De Lauder to wait with the horses. "Aye. What is it?"

"Sire, my family and I are grateful for your hospitality," she began.

"You are welcome. Good day." He began to walk away.

"Sire, may I have permission to speak my mind?" she asked hastily.

He turned back, folded his arms. "You will do so regardless, I sus-pect. Say what you will."

"My brother Edgar is young and has a great burden on his shoulders. But he is sometimes easily influenced by those who could gain from the success of a rebellion in England."

He cocked a brow. "No doubt you think me among them. Go on."

"Edgar sets great store by your example, sire. We are indebted to you, but the recent attacks in Northumbria . . ." She paused. "I some-times wonder at the nature of your loyalty toward my brother's cause."

"Is it the habit of Saxon ladies to concern themselves with such matters?"

"What affects her kinsmen is any woman's concern. If you support my brother's rights as king, then consider supporting his people as well. And please advise my brother wisely—"

"Shall I advise him that his sister coddles him overmuch and he should grow ballocks?"

She drew a sharp breath at his crude reply. "I have watched over Edgar since we were children, after my father's death, when our mother entrusted me with the welfare of my siblings. I do not have the right to speak on his behalf, but it is a habit of my heart."

"You should have children of your own if you feel such a tender calling. I, too, lost my father at an early age, but my brother and I were sent to different kin to be raised separately. Your interest is commendable, in that case. I understand that you are neither wed nor betrothed, Lady Margaret," he added bluntly.

She nearly bristled. Such inquiries should go to her brother. "I feel called to do God's work rather than be married, sire."

"A nun?" He narrowed his eyes. "A waste of a good mind and a good bloodline."

He was distracting her from what she wanted to talk about. "Sire, allow me to speak my mind. You now host the Saxon royalty in your household, yet you have attacked the Saxons of Northumbria."

One brow lifted. "Hearsay only."

"Messengers reported it so. And Edgar brought slaves up from England, driven north by you. How will you be regarded after such deeds by your peers in royalty and authority, the leaders of the Low Countries, of France, the Holy Roman Empire, and others—such as those whose trade routes fill Scotland's larders. The pope himself will hear of your deeds," she added.

"What does it matter to you?" he asked.

"Surely you want the respect due Scotland's king, and do not want to be seen as a mere brute."

He nodded slowly. "You think about more than broidery and prayer, it seems."

She thought he mocked her. "I have been given an education equal to any prince's due to my rank. I was tutored in Greek and Hebrew, in the works of the holy fathers, in the stories of the Greek wars. You generously offered to loan me some of your books, sir," she added. "I would like that. My mind is keen, and I wonder about many things, such as matters of kingship."

"Read whatever you like of my books. I have studied the treatises on laws and some others, but there are some on theology that you might find interesting. Robert the Norman has the cupboard key. As for the leaders of the world—my deeds are no worse than King William's, and possibly better. Is there more you wish to say, Lady Margaret?" He seemed impatient to go.

"I only wish to say that if you can help the Saxon cause, and support Edgar, then please do so sincerely. I believe you are an honorable man."

"Do you?" He inclined his head. "My thanks. Whatever I do, I discuss with my war council. Though I believe you could outreason some of that lot," he added.

She lifted her chin. "One other thing, sire. Whether or not you uphold Edgar's cause, it may be best for my kinswomen and I to return home. These are my own thoughts. I do not speak for Edgar."

"You have no home," he pointed out. "England is not safe and your lands are forfeit there, and Hungary is very far away. I hear the warriors there are almost as savage as the Scots," he said wryly.

"The Magyars are tough as any. Sire, I am not concerned for myself, but for my kin. My mother wishes to return to Hungary where her uncle, good King Stephen, God rest his soul, is likely to be declared a saint. My lady mother could help further his beatification if she could return there. It is a very good cause," she defended as he glowered, brows drawn.

"A saint's cause can be furthered anywhere, given ink and parchment, the price of a messenger, and rank important enough for Rome to notice. As for saints, we have those in Scotland, too. We are Christian, though it may surprise you, with your Roman rules."

"The Scottish Church is worthy, though very different from that of Rome, I have noticed."

"All prayers go heavenward." He pointed his finger straight up. "What difference the feathers that lift the wings?"

"Prayers in accordance with the true Church will get there faster," she countered.

"Gaelic rolls smooth off the tongue like the kiss of the wind," he said. "Perhaps God enjoys hearing that instead of martial Latin all the while."

Intrigued, not expecting a poetic thought from him, she tilted her head. "*Loquerisne Latine?*" Did he speak Latin? She was curious to know.

"*Non modo Latine, sed Anglice, Gallice et alias,*" he answered. Not only Latin, but English, French, Gaelic and others. "Norse, too," he said. "Are you surprised?"

"You were raised as a prince, so a command of languages is expected," she said coolly.

He huffed. "Even from the savage King of Scots?"

She did not falter. "Scotland is a worthy place. I rather like it."

"Yet many Saxons think us all ignorant rascals. My lady, you are safe here, whether or not you believe it. But heed some advice, if you will."

"Sire." She waited, hands folded. Heart pounding, too, for he was formidable to face when he was angered, as he seemed to be now.

"Let your brother decide for himself what to do. He will be a better man for it."

"I am only concerned for the welfare of all my family," she said, flustered.

"He wants your happiness, yet he must defend his rights in England. He is young and earnest, without father or mentor but for a few exiled Saxon lords who have their own grudges. I would keep one or two of those and toss the rest," he muttered. "A goal of rebellion must be shared by all, or it will not succeed."

She had not expected sympathy, and it reassured her. "So you are sincere in your desire to help my brother?"

"God knows the lad needs help. It is a wonder he does not embroider, as flummoxed as he is by womenfolk."

Her cheeks burned to be so chastised. "So you truly think this rebellion has merit?"

"The Saxons could gain back some of their losses, but your Edgar is no match for King William. That one is for me to take on. Good day, lady." Heel grinding gravel, he walked away.

Margaret fisted her hands, watching his back. Right or not, the Scottish king had been rude again, with a brusqueness that seemed part of his nature. But she had been impulsive and outspoken herself. What if the king decided that he need not support the ungrateful Saxons after all? He could throw them out of Scotland entirely. If her family was banished again with nowhere to go, and if the Saxon campaign failed due to loss of Scottish support, the fault would be her own.

Picking up her skirts, admonishing herself for speaking her mind, she entered the cool, dim church. An hour of prayer and meditation would soothe her agitation, but would not erase the blunder she had made.

"*INCIPIT EVANGELIUM SECUNDUM IOHANNES*," Margaret read from a page in her Gospel book that began the words of St. John. "*In principio erat Verbum et Verbum erta apud Deum . . .*"

"In the beginning was the Word," Cristina repeated, drawing threads through linen as she listened. "Go on. *Hoc erat in principio . . .*"

Margaret continued, the afternoon sunlight glinting on the gold-inked letters of the opening phrases. The illustration showed an evangelist with red-gold hair and beard, seated in a grand chair; his blue and green robes draped in folds as he raised one knee, with one foot placed on a stool. Holding a feathered quill in his right hand, he paused in thought, a book propped open on his knee. Overhead a golden arch hung with curtains formed an elegant inner frame for the picture.

The little Gospel book was her most treasured and favorite volume, a collection of evangelical excerpts presented to her by England's Queen Edith on the day Margaret had turned twelve. Her own mother did not acknowledge the anniversary of her September birth, beyond admonishing her to pray to her name saint, Margaret of Antioch, and to Queen Helena, whose feast day it was.

Small and portable, the book was easy to carry with her, tucked into the pocket of a cloak. The Gospel, simple yet beautifully made, had four illustrated pages, one for each evangelist, painted in soft, bright colors and gold ink; the text was carefully lettered in sienna with large initials and some phrases in gold or red. Although it was not nearly as elaborate as other manuscripts she had seen, including her mother's copy of the Apocalypse texts, Margaret's elegant little Gospel was dear to her, with its leather cover so worn that it curled at the corners.

"*Et lux in tenebris lucet,*" she continued, "*et tenebrae eam non comprehenderunt.*"

"And the light shone in the darkness," Cristina said, "and——" She paused as a knock sounded at the door. Finola, who had been sitting sewing in a corner, got up to open it.

Edgar entered with Lady Agatha, and Margaret felt a strange, dreadful turning in her stomach to see a twin grimness in their similar features. She set aside the book and stood. "What is it?"

"Margaret," her brother said, "I was summoned by King Malcolm to discuss an important matter this morning." He paused and glanced at his mother, then at Margaret. "He has made an offer for your hand in marriage."

She stepped back, heart pounding. "What!" She sounded like a dimwit, though she was not surprised—she had been expecting this for weeks. "Surely you told him I do not want to marry, that I intend to take sacred vows in a convent as soon as the chance comes."

"I refused on your behalf," Edgar said. "It is customary to refuse at first, after all. We do not want to seem overeager."

"You will appear more virtuous by refusing at first," Lady Agatha said, "and therefore you will seem even more desirable a wife."

"But my refusal is sincere. I am not playing coy."

"This marriage alliance is imperative," her mother said. Edgar nodded somber agreement.

"The king and I are not suited by temperament," Margaret said.

"That is of no concern," Lady Agatha said, gesturing in dismissal. "As my eldest daughter and the sister to a rightful king, you must consider your family's welfare over your own selfish wishes."

"But I truly feel called to do the good work of a nun," Margaret said quietly, hurt by her mother's harshness.

"The marriage would help all of us, and England, too," Edgar said. "Malcolm is a powerful ally. He would grant us even more support—troops, coin, and the continued strength of a cunning warrior-king to help me reclaim my kingdom."

"Surely he knows that I possess neither land nor dowry," Margaret said bluntly.

"You have a fine dowry, as we saved what we could from William's greed," Lady Agatha said. "He forfeited our English lands, but we have treasures of gold and silver, including the blessed black cross brought by Saint Helena to Hungary, which any king would—"

"Malcolm rarely goes to church," Margaret said. "He does not care about that cross."

"Margaret gets the black rood?" Cristina asked. "What about my dowry?"

Lady Agatha ignored her. "The Scottish king needs a wife. He is a widower with two sons."

"What sons? I have not heard of any," Margaret said. "Why were they not mentioned?"

"They are the young sons of Queen Ingebjorg, fostered elsewhere," Edgar replied. "Malcolm wants more heirs, and Scotland needs a queen. He is satisfied that you are suited to both roles."

"He knows little of me," Margaret said indignantly. The king had young children? She felt a heart-tug thinking of motherless princes whose father did not even mention them to his guests, let alone a prospective bride.

"He says you and he had a conversation just a few days ago," Edgar replied.

"We did not talk of sons," she snapped, remembering that he had mentioned her unmarried state. "Let him find a more willing bride. I will not be a sacrificial lamb for the Saxon cause."

"Margaret," Edgar began.

"Nor can we trust a man who is a brute raider," she went on fiercely.

"He seems smitten with you, and determined. I hoped for this marriage offer. And I thought you would be pleased to have so enchanted a king," Edgar said.

"Enchantment is heresy. Witchcraft," she pointed out.

"The marriage has already been agreed upon," Lady Agatha said.

"You promised this before coming here to me?" Her limbs began to tremble, and she squared her shoulders and fisted her hands in anger. "You knew that I intend myself for the Church. You knew I did not want to marry—you did not discuss this with me but left me to guess!"

"A nun's veil will do naught for the Saxons," Edgar said. "A queen's crown will help them."

Margaret stepped back, skirts and legs meeting the cushioned bench where she had been peacefully reading only minutes before.

She felt frantic, now that the reality of what she had feared had arrived. "Malcolm has proven himself a savage, attacking our own people. Why should we negotiate anything with him?"

"We need this," Edgar said wearily.

Lady Agatha moved closer. "Margaret, if you wish to do good works, do them as wife and queen. Cristina, as younger daughter, will serve as our family's tithe to God and the Church."

"Me!" Cristina said indignantly.

"Margaret's marriage will ensure protection for the family. You can devote yourself to prayers for all our sakes," Lady Agatha answered.

Cristina dropped her mouth open in protest. "Margaret wants to be the one to pray for our sins!"

"It is done," Lady Agatha said firmly. "The marriage will take place soon, by Malcolm's wish."

Margaret lifted her chin. "Then let it be a forced ceremony." She turned away. "Leave me be."

"Margaret," Edgar said quietly, "remember—without this marriage alliance, we will spend our lives in exile, either here or elsewhere."

"Our father lived in exile all his life," she pointed out. "And he did well in Hungary."

"He longed for home always," Lady Agatha said. "That is why he came to England."

And he would still be alive if not for me, Margaret thought, but she could never say that aloud to anyone, ever.

Yet she understood what Edgar meant—her family would suffer, indeed she would, too, with a life of uncertainty, danger, and exile, if she did not agree.

"Let the marriage proceed," she whispered. "Now leave me." Once they had departed the room, she dropped to her knees and folded her hands, breath whispering over fingertips as she pleaded for an answer. Heaven had never answered her directly during prayer, but she often knew what was right by the next day.

But now she had agreed. She might long for a life of peaceful prayer and a precious chance to cleanse her soul of its sins and faults. Instead, she would be a queen.

IN THE HOUR BEFORE dawn, unable to sleep, Margaret rose from bed and dressed hurriedly in a lightweight cloak of mulberry wool over a linen shift, leaving her hair unbraided and uncombed. Pushing feet into kid slippers, she meant to go briefly to the little temporary chapel downstairs to pray in solitude. Sleep eluded her, for she was thinking again how soon she would become a queen, a wife, a different woman than she was now.

When she went through the curtained doorway of the small anteroom off the great hall, she was startled to see Edgar there. He was not alone, for two other men were with him: a stranger she did not know—a large man, grizzled and burly—and the king himself, in candlelight and shadows in a corner of the snug little room.

"Forgive me." She paused, stepped back, began to turn.

"Margaret, wait," Edgar said. "It is fortunate that you are here. You will want to meet the abbot of Abernethy, who arrived last night. Sir, my sister, the Lady Margaret."

"Princess." The stranger came forward. He wore a scarred leather hauberk, sewn with protective iron rings, over a shabby tunic and boots. He looked like a rough warrior more than a cleric, and he glared at her like a field general.

Margaret hesitated. "You are . . . an abbot?" she asked. "Of the Celtic church?"

"In a way, lady. I am Kenneth Macduff, lay abbot of Abernethy, mormaer of Fife. Abbot is a hereditary title in my Fife," he explained when she looked confused. His English was slightly accented.

"I see. Greetings, sir." She glanced at Edgar and avoided Malcolm's stare; he leaned a shoulder against the wall, arms folded. She drew her cloak closer around her. "I came here to pray and did not expect to see anyone. I will leave you to your meeting."

"Stay," Malcolm said, a barked command. She did not look toward him.

"Lady," Macduff said, "we would speak with you about the matter of marriage."

"Let the king address me himself if he has something to say." She lifted her chin.

Malcolm came forward two or three paces to face her directly. "I do have a question for you, Lady Margaret. I understand you refuse to marry me. Why?" he demanded.

She felt an urge to back away, but did not. "I cannot condone your actions in England," she said. "It put my mind off marriage, along with other considerations."

"What I do in wartime is not your concern, and neither should it be part of such a decision."

"Should I be eager to wed a man whose actions are cruel and sinful?"

"The match is imperative for your family, for England, for Scotland, too," Macduff said.

She whirled. "The decision is made. There is no need to revisit it." She turned to leave.

Malcolm reached out, his hand descending on her shoulder, a paw so large she nearly stumbled backwards; yet he was gentle, if firm, in turning her.

"I prefer that truths be known in all matters," he said. "You will learn that of me."

"Then learn me this," she said, facing him now, standing straight, feeling herself fill with an ire that strengthened her backbone, made her bold. "Why were you untruthful about your deeds in the south? You went there to help—yet you created havoc, made slaves, took prisoners."

"You do understand matters of warfare," he said.

"King William marched against the English, not the Scots. What reason did you have to attack Saxons already victimized by Normans? And you with Saxon royalty in your care!"

"I had the right to exact revenge for attacks on my lands."

"Vengeance after wrongdoing has some merit. But raiding a suffering people is heinous. Perhaps you should find yourself another bride. Good day, sir." She began to turn, but he tugged at her arm.

"Shall I defend my suit?"

"It is indefensible, sire."

"So a heinous sinner has no right to claim such a prize as yourself?"

"I do not presume to judge a king," she said, breathing quickly, cheeks hot.

"Yet you do." He stood over her, seemed to dominate the room, even with two other men there. "You wrong me, lady, when I think so well of you."

"How have I wronged you?" Indignant, she glared up at him.

"Tell me this." He leaned close. "What did you think would become of the Northumbrians once William's troops were done burning, wrecking, raping, and slaughtering?"

"Those people needed mercy. They were injured and helpless, deserving of aid—food, shelter, fuel, physicking, and absolution. You brought further attacks."

"I admit, I burned their homes," he said. "I attacked parts of Northumbria, returning my cousin's blow by burning lands in Cumbria. And I took slaves. I admit that, too."

"Thousands of slaves," Margaret insisted.

"Should I have left them to starve?" he asked. "Would that have been more merciful?"

She stared up at him. "What do you mean?"

"We led people out of there and made slaves and prisoners of them. Why would we do that? Did you consider it?" He looked at Edgar and Macduff. "Some of them were forced to eat their own dead, flayed and salted. We saw human shanks hung to dry like beef."

"Dear God," Margaret gasped, setting a hand to her throat.

"They seasoned that meat with salt taken from their own fields—

the Norman troops put it there to ruin the land so nothing would grow there. Did you not listen to the messengers, lady?" he demanded.

"We heard about the devastation. We received slaves here by the hundreds, and gave them what relief we could. But you drove them up here!"

"What else was I to do? We burned their homes to cleanse the villages of disease and to drive out the demons of war and pestilence. If that was a sin, so be it. We brought Saxons north as slaves so that they would have shelter and *food*"—he nearly shouted, face reddening—"and if that is sinful, too, then send me to hell and damn my men with me. It was far worse to leave those people there!" He was breathing like a bull now, red-faced, leaning.

"Dear saints. W-we did not know," Margaret stammered, stunned. "We did not hear that."

"We did not put our reasons about, but only a little logic would see it," Malcolm said. "Death or slavery was the only relief we could give those people. I chose for them. It is my doing."

"Sire," she said, and swallowed, thinking. "I . . . judged you unfairly. I should have seen it as an act of charity. The fault is my own." Now that his actions made such sense, she felt remorseful, humbled. "You were merciful, after all. The saints themselves could not have—"

"I am not one of your blasted saints, woman!" Malcolm roared, looming in the small, candlelit room. Behind her, Edgar and Macduff stood silent. "I avenged my cousin's raid upon my lands in Cumbria by burning his fortress black. I have committed many acts of violence, and I own freely to that. But I do not abuse or slay the helpless. I only do what is necessary."

"I was wrong. I will admit that," she said. "About the marriage—"

"Marry me or not, as you will," Malcolm said. "But give me none of your martyrish sentiment." He pushed past her and shoved through the curtain, leaving the room.

"*Jesu,*" Edgar said under his breath as the king departed. "No man speaks to my sister in such a manner." He stepped forward, but Margaret grabbed his sleeve.

"Stop," she said. "He spoke honestly. Let him be."

"I will have words with him later," Edgar said, his forearm tense under her hand.

"Malcolm does what he must," Macduff said sternly, crossing his arms. "On Judgment Day his soul may be forfeit for his wicked deeds, but he acts with good purpose. And he is a canny man who knows the benefits of this marriage."

"This marriage alliance," she amended. "He wants kinship with the royal Saxon line."

"He needs the marriage as much as the political alliance," Macduff said. "You, Lady Margaret, will bring benefit to him and to Scotland as well, with your good breeding, your good sense and manners. He knows that well."

Margaret looked down at her hands, where golden candlelight pooled. She had thought Malcolm a ruffian with no more intent than to ruckus where he pleased, with no interest in improving his character. She drew a breath. "Sirs, I am chastised and proven wrong. I had condemned the king's deeds and his motives. I have been haughty and unwise."

"This marriage could prove the wisest decision you may ever make," Macduff said.

Margaret sighed, realizing that she must find the courage to accept her fate—she had sought an answer, even a rescue, in her prayers. Now marriage seemed the path she must take.

"Aye, then," she said, turning away. The curtain shushed as the men left the room.

She knelt before the simple altar that her mother had ordered erected from a table and a cloth. Lady Agatha had already placed the cherished black rood, the most precious item in Margaret's dowry, upon it. Bowing her head, hair sweeping down like a golden curtain, she prayed. Yet her thoughts spun and would not quiet.

Having just met Malcolm will for will, not for the first time, she knew now he would challenge her again to match him for wits and stubbornness. She was years younger than he and little experienced in the ways of warriors and the harsh world they inhabited—yet she must somehow prove herself a strong and capable woman, as fearless in her way as he was in his. That, or she would be regarded as no more than the foreign queen, a pawn, the sacrificial lamb she so dreaded being.

Life had whirled her earlier dreams about like leaves in a wind. Once she had planned to spend her days in prayer, study, and good works. Instead, she would be a queen—and so she must be an exemplary one. In all things, she could accept no less than the utmost from herself.

Pride was no stranger to her, for she often fought it. This time, she would grant it freedom.

SHE DREAMED THAT NIGHT that Malcolm came to visit her—in the dream she had a humble cottage, tidy and plain—but he was a giant, so large that he filled the room when he stepped inside. His head and shoulders bowed against the ceiling; his voice was like distant thunder as he greeted her: *Margaret, when you are my queen, we will make so many princes that you will be too busy for prayers!*

She could not get past him to escape through the doorway. Beyond, past the cottage, she saw a sunlit meadow with mountains in the distance. Several small boys and girls played in the field, tumbling and laughing. Suddenly she worried that no one was watching the children and one of them would get hurt in the game, and so she felt an urgent need to protect them.

Malcolm held out his hand for her to go outside with him. *Come with me—we are needed now.* And this time she was on the verge of agreeing, for it seemed her only route to freedom from that confining little house when she longed for sunshine. Then she awoke.

SHE DID NOT SEE the king for days, and received no message of thanks from him accompanied by a gift, as a more worldly prince might have done. When he returned, a quick and plain-spoken betrothal was performed in Dunfermline's great hall, with a midday meal and some awkward merriment. Malcolm did thank her then, in his way, with gruff good wishes, and he provided a good new French wine, pale red and crisp, in celebration of the betrothal. Then he went outside to meet his men, and the group rode off with a clatter of hooves and creak of armor and weaponry. That was his true world, she knew, rather than courting or marriage.

Once again he was gone for a fortnight, while Margaret, with the help of her kinswomen and Dame Agnes, planned the royal wedding for whenever he returned. That the ceremony would be performed in relative haste and therefore could be an embarrassment to the bride did not seem to matter. Impatient by nature, the king saw no reason to wait.

Chapter Six

❦

Oh, my own,
Child of my child,
Gentle, valiant
My heart cries like a blackbird's

—IRISH, TRADITIONAL LAMENT

The sun hung pale and bright over the northern mountains on the morning Lady Gruadh sent Eva south. A day after the lady had decided to obey the king's demands, Eva sat bundled on the back of a garron pony, her harp in a fur-lined leather bag slung on the saddle. A few possessions were contained in pannier baskets on the back of another pony; she had not wanted to take much, but the former queen had given Eva some of her own things.

"My robes are fine enough even for Malcolm's Sassenach court," she told Eva. "I am taller than you, but if you sit with the ladies hemming robes with your fine hand for stitchery, you will hear some of the news at court. Send messages to me about whatever you learn."

"I thought I was to act as bard there," Eva said. "It sounds better than hostage."

Lady Gruadh looked up, an assessing spark in her cool blue gaze. "Then hem the things during the day, and sing at night. Either way, keep your ears keen."

Eva looked away, seeing the men in the yard mounting horses, among them Moray men as well as housecarls sent by the king, who had demanded her presence as a royal hostage, a turn of events that had shocked Eva. "I do not want to go," she told her grandmother.

"I know. This time you must. Even I cannot gainsay the king to this extent, or show my hand in war. Aeife, my girl," Gruadh said fervently, wrapping long, slender fingers over the pommel of Eva's saddle. "You must do this for me, and for Moray. Sing for Malcolm and his new bride. You will be given preference, for you are both princess and bard."

"Hostage," Eva insisted. "Prisoner. I could be thrown into a dungeon."

"Nonsense. Even Malcolm would not do that—he has no reason to punish you, though reason enough to keep you, I admit. Send word of how you fare, and send word of anything that Malcolm would keep from me."

"You want me to be your spy," Eva whispered.

"Just so." Gruadh smiled, a dimple quirking the corner of her mouth, fine wrinkles gathering around her eyes. She was beautiful still, her eyes luminous, skin pale and smooth, cheekbones taut, chin firm and stubborn. Beneath her silken veil, her hair, Eva knew, was the color of copper threaded with silver. She was fierce and gentle all at once; exasperating, too. "I have faith in you," Gruadh went on. "You can do this."

"How can I have faith in you, if you agree to my capture?" Eva felt sullen.

"You are so young," Gruadh said, patting her hand. "It is not a capture. You will not be ill treated. Malcolm has promised so, according to his guards and messengers. Eva, I delayed Malcolm as long as I could, but we have no choice. He sent his own guard to fetch you south. Just know that I would never send you into harm." She smiled, then turned away, her red cloak and gray gown whipping with the whirl, head veils floating lightly over her shoulders as she approached Ruari mac Fergus to speak with him.

The lady, now in her fifth decade, was a half head taller than the leader of her guard, who was as thick and powerful as an oak, a handsome man a little older than Gruadh. Yet they seemed suited as a pair, somehow, shoulders close and heads together as they talked. Eva sighed, waiting. She was relieved that Ruari would accompany her south with the king's men, for he was more an uncle to her than a housecarl or local thane.

As for staying in the king's household, Eva could not imagine how she could ever discover the king's intentions toward Moray, if that was what Lady Gruadh wanted her to do. It seemed preposterous. She pushed out her lower lip, feeling truculent. She ought to refuse. It was hard enough to be a prisoner—but a spy? She could not do it. Would not.

Her horse sidled and snorted, impatient to go, though Eva did not want to leave. Elgin was home and hearth to her. She blinked back tears as her grandmother and Ruari walked toward her, still talking between them.

"Malcolm's new queen is finely bred and will have fussy manners, no doubt," Gruadh said. "Likely she will prove a religious reformer, too, for she is of the Roman faith and they have little patience with the Celtic church. I hear she is a lovely creature—Malcolm no doubt pants after her. If she bears him sons," she added low, "she will have whatsoever she wants."

"We do not know what sort of woman she is, or what sort of queen," Ruari argued.

"A Saxon queen cannot be good for Scotland."

"But the wedding will take place before Eva even arrives, whatever comes of it."

"Malcolm took the ones I loved and now he wants the girl, too. He thinks to keep me obedient this way, but I mean to turn his order to Moray's advantage. Eva," she said as she came closer. "Give the king this letter." She handed the girl a sealed, folded parchment. "I have detailed my expectations for your care. He expects Moray to pay for your keep—a Saxon custom, that," she added with a sneer, "so I will send gold with Ruari. The king's mood will be generous now, for he is enthralled with his Saxon bride."

"You will do well enough. Do not fret," Ruari reassured Eva. Then he turned away to speak to his red-bearded brother, Angus mac Fergus, who came toward them now. Both men were part of the lady's personal phalanx and had been friends with Gruadh since childhood. They were as devoted to her as she was to them, though she held something further in her heart for Ruari mac Fergus.

Eva loved Ruari too, and though his hardened air sent many scuttering out of his way, he had a tenderness to his character that Eva trusted. She would not want him to leave the king's court when the time came for him to return north.

Gruadh stood beside Eva's horse. "My girl, play your harp tunes and be our eyes and ears in the south." She placed a hand on Eva's own, over the pommel. "Your voice is silver and your talent gold. They will fall under your spell in the king's court, and that will be most useful."

"If you would just promise to obey the king, I could stay home," Eva pointed out.

"She has your stubbornness," Ruari remarked drily. "Rue, explain to her why you ask her to listen and watch for you. She should know the truth."

Gruadh sighed. "Very well. I want to know what happened to the ones I loved."

"They were killed, each one," Eva said quickly, hotly. "First Macbeth, then my father the young king, perhaps even Queen Ingebjorg, all by Malcolm."

"There, girl! That is the feeling to hold in your heart—anger. Remember that and let that fire warm you at the king's court. Listen well, and learn the answers to my questions."

"What do you want to know?" Eva asked.

"Just this: Does Malcolm plot to kill my grandson, Nechtan, or even me, so that he can rule Moray himself? What does he intend for Moray—will he let us be, or force us and other regions in the Highlands to take on Saxon customs and Roman ways over the Celtic church? And one more question," Lady Gruadh said, leaning close. "Where is that damnable book?"

"What book?" Eva looked at her, startled.

"Malcolm was commissioned a chronicle in which heinous lies will be recorded about Macbeth and Lulach, even myself and my father, Bodhe. Find it for me. Bring it to me."

"Even if I could, what would you do with it?" Eva asked.

"Fire, water, will take care of books. That part is nothing. Find the thing, for it must not survive," Gruadh said. "Now go, and Ruari with you. You will take your time traveling, even with the king's escort—they will have to go where Ruari leads, and if he intends to stop at every thane's house for rest and news, they will do so, too. I am in no rush to send you there, though I must send you. Eva," she said urgently, reaching for her hand again, grasping it tightly. "Stay safe and strong. Come back to me soon."

"I will," Eva promised, as she took up the reins.

Within moments, the escort filed through the gate. Eva guided her horse to ride alongside Angus and Ruari, with the king's housecarls taking up the rear of the escort. When they reached the moorland below the fortress mound, Eva turned to look back.

Lady Gruadh still stood in the open entrance, a slender pillar in a billowing red cloak.

Chapter Seven

※

A king shall win a queen with goods, beakers, armlets;
Both, from the first, must be free with their gifts.

— *The Exeter Book*, ANGLO-SAXON,
NINTH CENTURY

Rain silvered the sky on the day of the wedding, mist drifting around Margaret as she stood on the steps of the hilltop chapel with her kin and Saxon friends. Nearby stood several of the king's men, along with a few Scottish lords with their wives and daughters. They did not go inside the chapel, but stood waiting for the king to arrive. Malcolm was late again.

Margaret brushed raindrops from her cloak of pale blue wool, over a silken gown of fog gray, its hem now dark with moisture. The chaplet of white flowers that crowned her head dripped rain. Sighing, she tried to look peaceful, though inside she simmered like a kettle over her groom's tardiness.

At last the king and his housecarls arrived, some on foot, the king riding a white horse, a grand entrance that was unnecessary, Margaret thought, considering how annoyed the waiting party was by then. The Scottish guests were not pleased about the wedding either, she knew, for Malcolm's lords had not unanimously agreed with his choice of a Saxon bride. Days ago, De Lauder had reluctantly told Margaret that many Scots were not happy to have a Saxon and, worse, a foreign-born queen, and that she might hear rumors of discontent.

"But remember that Scotland is a wide land and its people are far-flung," he had added. "Likely you will see little direct disapproval. They will soon learn how kind and gracious their new queen is," he had said, smiling. "You will win their hearts, I am certain."

But she had not won them as yet. Her wedding party was a small and grim lot, waiting in silence for the king's arrival. Dismounting now, Malcolm looked tired and pasty, beard scruffy, eyes pinched. He had been up drinking and gambling the night before—she had heard the ruckus belowstairs until late into the night, but still she rose early for her prayers and preparations.

He was a large, fit man, but not handsome, and the excess of drink the previous night did not improve his appearance. At least his clothes were clean, she thought; he wore a brown tunic over woolen trews and a plaid cloak over all, in several colors. His shoulder brooch was a magnificent circlet of gold as big as a plate, detailed with wire and gems. Margaret had to admit that he looked like a king in his striking size, carriage, and sheer presence.

One of his men set a red cloak about his shoulders, edged in bird feathers: a savage touch and well done, Margaret thought. He wore a slender crown of beaten gold, crammed askew over his unruly hair. When he stepped up to join her, she turned expectantly, ready to enter the church.

Fothad, the bishop of the pilgrimage church of Saint Andrews, whom Margaret had met the night before, joined Brother Micheil to welcome them inside the chapel. Dressed in white, he was a small man with long gray hair shaved deep across front and top, the always distinctive mark of a Celtic priest. He stood back to let them enter, for the marriage of a king and a royal princess must be consecrated at the altar rather than on the outer step, as was common for those of lesser rank.

Malcolm crossed the threshold, his boot crushing the silvery hem of Margaret's gown. She set a hand on his arm. "Sirrah," she whispered.

He glanced down at her. His hair and untrimmed beard formed a matted russet thicket that obscured his expression, but she thought he looked chastened. He allowed her to step ahead, and as she did he touched her elbow gently, quickly. Then he strode past her toward the altar. He seemed eager to have this done with; well, so was she, Margaret thought.

She followed with deliberate grace, hands folded, though privately she was sure that a hopping toad could show more manners than the Scottish king. The rest of the party gathered inside the church, and the sound of rain was steady on the chapel walls as Margaret and Malcolm stood before the altar, knelt, prayed, repeated vows.

Lowering her head, she prayed silently for guidance, for now she must be not only a perfect wife and a mother someday but a faultless queen as well. God would expect it of her, as would her mother and their priests—but she would demand more of herself than anyone else, for that was simply her nature. Having agreed to this, she would do it to the utmost of her ability.

As they spoke the vows, the king's Latin was adequate but awkward. Her own was better than the very priest's; but Fothad was, after all, a Scotsman. As the ceremony progressed she noticed that whenever she spoke a word or phrase that Malcolm repeated, his pronunciation improved. He was quick-witted, seeking even during those moments to learn more. Glancing at him again, she saw his hands clench, the knuckles blanched.

Inexplicably, she liked him better for it.

DUNFERMLINE'S GREAT HALL was decorated for the nuptial feast with bleached cloths on the tables, glowing tallow candles, swags of early spring flowers and rowan branches. Fresh herbs and reeds were strewn over the floor, releasing their green fragrances as they were crushed underfoot by the wedding guests and servants gathering inside the hall. Margaret and Malcolm sat beside each other in two chairs on the dais while one person after another wished them good cheer before all were finally seated.

Continuing rain pattered the shuttered windows as the guests ate the feast prepared under Dame Agnes's supervision. Margaret hardly ate, for her stomach was never keen on food when she felt anxious. Beside her, Malcolm delved into steaming sliced beef, mashed turnips, and other dishes with a noisy appetite. Her groom did not suffer from excess politeness.

"My lady." Looking around, she saw Wilfrid of Bourne pause just behind her as if he had an urgent message. "More visitors have arrived." He leaned closer. "The fisher-folk are here to wish you well. They walked all this way to present you with a gift on your wedding day."

Surprised, she set down her linen napkin. "How kind. Do let them in, Wilfrid."

"The king's guards have refused to allow them into the hall, nor will they let the servants bring them trenchers from the feast—although I requested that, thinking you would approve."

"Of course, but—they were refused food from the king's table? That must change." Margaret turned. "My lord husband, I wish to invite more guests into our hall."

"Beggars?" Malcolm waved a hand. "Send them away."

"Sire, we cannot be seen as uncharitable at our own wedding sup-per," Margaret protested. The king did not reply as he stuck his knife into another chunk of meat.

Wilfrid leaned forward. "Sire," he murmured. "Pardon me, but may I say that in my errands to other towns lately, I have heard it said that some are unhappy to have a queen of Saxon blood on the throne of Scotland. It is perhaps wise for the queen to win over the people by whatever means she can. The local fisher-folk are loyal to the new queen, and their work, trading by sea and selling in marketplaces, brings them in touch with others."

"Wilfrid is right," Margaret said. "I will let them in myself." On impulse, she stood.

Malcolm gaped up at her. Juices shone on his beard. "Sit down," he said between his teeth. "At least leave it to the servants. You have not even eaten of your own wedding feast."

"My friends were refused at your door," she pointed out. "How can I eat until they are fed? Many will watch to see what we will do now, as king and consort."

"No one is watching. They are all eating but you. Sit."

"God is watching." She stepped away from the chair. Then, realizing that she could not be seen arguing with her bridegroom at their wedding feast, she held out her hand.

"Sire, if you please. Your . . . generous nature is known to all." She leaned down to whisper. "If some wait hungry outside while we feast in here, be sure that the Benedictine priests in this hall will notice. They will send word to Rome of Scotland's lack of charity."

Malcolm sighed, and stood. "Lady," he boomed for all to hear. She took his arm as they walked the length of the hall, and Malcolm waved a hand. "Open the doors! Our new Lady of Scotland, in her great generosity, wishes to welcome everyone on her wedding day!"

"And she will serve them at the same feast," she said.

"And she will feed them from her own dish and spoon!" he called.

She had not intended that, exactly. But she knew that the king would be quick to find the advantage in any situation. He had the instincts of a pageant performer; a useful quality in a king, she thought.

As Wilfrid walked past her to open the doors, Margaret touched his arm. "Thank you, sir."

He bowed, a grizzled and somber soldier, and pressed his fist to his chest. "In all things, my lady, you may count me your man," he murmured.

As one of the housecarls opened the door, Margaret saw Mother Annot and her fisherman husband, along with others, waiting outside. Smiling, Margaret reached out her hands and beckoned them inside. They crowded through the door, glancing about tentatively.

A servant sent by Dame Agnes came forward with a large dish of the beef and turnips, and another brought bowls and a spoon. Whispering to Wilfrid, Margaret sent him back to fetch the pewter bowl and ivory spoon that sat untouched at her place at the table. When he brought them to her, she waited for a servant to fill the bowl with food, and offered it to Mother Annot.

The old woman shook her head in quiet refusal, and pushed a little boy forward. "The child."

"Lady," her husband said, his English better than his wife's, "we did not come here for charity. But the children are hungry, as children will be."

Margaret nodded, then knelt before the boy standing with Annot. He looked four or five years old, eyes wide, his hair thick and shining over his brow. He hesitated, then took a juicy bit of the beef she offered. Margaret felt grateful for that—if the child had refused her offer, too, she would have felt humiliated indeed.

In English villages and towns, she had seen poor folk readily accept charity, and the Hungarians would have dropped to their knees and praised such a gesture as saintly. Prideful Scots, she was learning, would sooner decline what was desperately needed than allow charity. But the child ate, wiping his mouth on his sleeve, and when a small girl stepped forward, Margaret offered her a spoonful. The girl accepted it with an impish smile, and Margaret laughed with delight. A few other children in the group edged closer, so she fed them, too.

She turned toward Dame Agnes. "Order another trestle table set up for our guests, and see that they are all served supper. Everyone is welcome here," she told the group.

Mother Annot smiled, and Malcolm spoke a greeting in Gaelic, while a young woman came forward. Draped over her arm was a thick folded cloth in a handsome pattern of crisscrossed stripes of red, green, and yellow.

"Lady, this is for you," she said, and then spoke in Gaelic. Margaret smiled, not understanding, but Malcolm translated smoothly and quietly.

"She says she wove the cloth herself and it will make a fine blanket or cloak. It is a gift to honor our wedding and to welcome you as the new queen."

Thanking her, Margaret took the handsome wool. "I hope to be worthy of such a fine gift."

"She says that the king does not make mistakes," Malcolm translated. "And she is right," he added.

As he escorted her back to their chairs, Margaret hoped even part of that was true.

HER HAIR COMBED OUT to the sheen of spun gold, Margaret sat against a bank of pillows, wearing only a shift of lightweight linen over her bare skin and racing heart. She had not wanted to think about the wedding night; even her mother had avoided discussing of the role of a dutiful wife. But Kata drew her aside to whisper of secret marital obligations.

"The man mounts, the woman abides, and heaven's will be done," she had told Margaret the evening before the wedding. "Marriage is a sacred state. It is not unpleasant," she added.

Margaret stared. "But—how will I know what is sacred, and what is sin?"

"You will know," Kata replied. She had been married and widowed years before. "The private concord between husband and wife is one of God's gifts to mankind. The creating of a child within a marriage is not a sin. Do not fret."

"What if there is no child?"

Kata had laughed. "Then try again!"

Now the merry crowd still celebrated in the bedchamber, spilling out into the corridor beyond. Malcolm seemed fairly drunk by then, standing just inside the doorway with some of his men, who continually slapped each other on backs and shoulders in felicitation.

Someone was ringing a square bronze bell while a few women circled the room singing behind two young girls who giggled as they scattered juniper and flowers on the floor. Margaret did not understand the Gaelic words or the customs, but she knew they brought blessings of good luck to the marriage, and to the mating about to occur. She clenched her fists.

Dame Agnes handed her a glazed clay cup containing hot wine with a hint of herbs, which tasted strong and sweet. She drank, wishing they would all go away. Then Malcolm, apparently tired of the follies, too, ordered the guests to leave. He shut the door, barred it, blew out the candles, then came toward the bed and began removing his garments, tossing them aside. Margaret looked away in the darkness. When he sat, the feather-stuffed mattress and rope-slung frame sagged under his weight. Yanking the curtains shut, he settled beside Margaret.

Both were silent. After a while, he patted her fisted hand on the bed-covers. Nothing followed, and she scarcely dared breathe—perhaps he was tired enough, drunk enough, for sleep. But then he turned, the bed heaving, his breath smelling of wine. His hand, warm and heavy, found her shoulder, and she quailed, but tried to recall what Kata had said. Her heart pounded like a drum.

But when he began to caress her, she startled only a little—and as the heady wine and herbs took over, she found the drowsiness of the drink and even his touch surprisingly pleasant, even coaxing. She allowed more, then more still, in the silent, dark, curtained haven of the bed. A curious warmth rose in her, strangely similar to moments during prayer, when trust and grace flowed through her heart like honey. Yet this physical encounter felt delicious, too, its very nature secret, forbidden, and enticing.

Easy enough in darkness, she found, to endure, to allow and even enjoy. Despite his brusque manner otherwise, Malcolm proved capable of tenderness, and relished all of it greatly himself, from what she could tell. Caressing, covering, a sudden thrusting that rocked her; she felt like weeping at the astonishing sweetness of it. But she with-

held expression—though being touched so, held so, was unexpectedly comforting. She would have permitted more, feeling curious and
aroused, but the encounter was over quickly, and her bridegroom
rolled away to subside into snores.

She lay awake in the darkness, breathless and changed in some
way she could not define beyond the obvious. Then she remembered
to whisper a prayer as the day, the wine, the exhaustion, took her
down, too, into sleep.

At first light, she awoke alone, later than was usual for her. Malcolm was gone, having slipped away without disturbing her. She
slid from the bed and fell to her knees in prayer, seeking forgiveness
for the wantonness of the previous night. Cringing, she knew she
ought to burn with shame—and yet part of her did not regret it, felt
no remorse for such willingness. Intimate, tender physical love was
permitted in marriage—and she had enjoyed it.

Still, she did not look forward to facing others who would surely
know what she and Malcolm had done. Dressing herself without calling for a maidservant, she pulled on a finely woven blue woolen
gown and tied its side laces over her linen shift. Then she knotted the
leather ties on her narrow slippers of green silk, and stood, adjusting
her skirts. When a knocking sounded on the door, she drew a breath
and glided forward, admitting Lady Agatha, Kata, and Hildy.

"We have come to wrap your head and shoulders in the veil of a
married woman, as is always done the morning after a wedding," her
mother explained.

Margaret nodded and stood quietly while Kata combed and braided
her hair. Then Lady Agatha brought out a rectangle of pale, lightweight silk, neatly hemmed and embroidered in her finest stitchery,
white on white.

Wrapping the fabric over the crown of Margaret's head and under
her chin, Lady Agatha draped the rest over her daughter's shoulders
and pinned it here and there; Margaret's long golden braids hung
past her hips. Then her mother presented her with a belt of enam-
eled disks and silver links. The belt was an elegant fit, low on the

hips, and Margaret took a moment to slide the loops of her small embroidered purse, containing silver scissors, thimbles, and a string of rosary beads, over the handsome girdle.

"There." Lady Agatha cupped her face. "I am proud of you," she said. "Queen Margaret. You will be a perfect Lady of Scotland, behaving as an example on earth of the Blessed Mary, Queen of Heaven. It pleases me to be your mother."

Margaret widened her eyes. Her mother's praise had always been faint, and now the model Lady Agatha declared for her was nearly unattainable. Yet some powerful, irresistible force within demanded that she match that—she must, in order to atone and do penance for the most secret of all her sins, her father's death. Her own mother, widowed by that deed, had just shown her the way. Although heaven had diverted her from the religious life she had wanted and had sent her to Scotland, she could seek forgiveness through her work as queen.

"I will do my best, Mama," she whispered. "I have no choice."

MALCOLM WENT OUT often on early patrols or away for days at a time, and Margaret fell into a routine of household duties. Wondering when the king would return, she reminded herself sternly that her husband had many responsibilities and did not mean to deliberately overlook her. But she felt forgotten when she wanted to feel cherished, and told herself it was vanity in her new status. So she made certain to smile whenever she joined her kinswomen and the Saxon and Scottish ladies to sit in a sunny corner of the great hall with their ongoing embroidery work. The women made casual conversation about the weather, their children, the salty porridge, the knotty quality of the thread. Margaret sensed more deference in their responses toward her and more willingness to please her. Their little circle of tentative friendships now began to center on her as their queen. And she was a new bride as well, with the mystique of that still bright upon her, at least in the eyes of others.

Often she looked toward the door or through the window, anxious for Malcolm's return, eager to see him again, anticipating their time alone later. The pleasurable mysteries of the nights when they were together haunted her in curious and lovely ways. Surely her feelings were not lustful, she convinced herself; these were natural feelings for a new bride, even an ignored one, even a queen who must be a model of behavior. Still, she blushed to the roots of her hair, hidden beneath the new silken veil, and took care to assign herself extra prayers, like a coolant remedy for fever.

The ladies who gathered around her included Lady Juliana and Lady Edith, Cospatric's legitimate wife, lately come to Dunfermline as another hostage for her husband's behavior, along with her youngest son, Dolfin, a sturdy, tempestuous cherub whose young nurse frequently chased him up and down the hall. Ranald's wife, Gudrun, joined them, too, as did Margaret's mother and sister and a few of the Scottish ladies whom Margaret did not know very well.

Most days the women drew their stools and benches into a circle with her, their skirts draping on the floor in rainbow folds. Margaret grew to love them all for their protectiveness toward her, and because they never remarked on how often her bridegroom abandoned his bride to find her own way in his household. He would send messages to De Lauder, who would then inform her that, regrettably, the king was once again distracted by matters in his kingdom.

On the nights that Malcolm was not there to retire to bed with her, she sometimes opened the shutter to gaze at the star-sparkled sky. Uncertain where he might be, she hoped he was safe, and wondered if he thought of her. Then she would go to her knees to pray, for she could never sleep without following the track of her prayer beads, like a necklace for her soul.

"THE WHOLE OF THE HOUSEHOLD and all of its concerns now lie within your domain as wife and queen," Dame Agnes told her as Margaret joined the housekeeper and De Lauder in the great hall in the days following the wedding. "You are no longer a guest here, but chatelaine of the king's households."

"But you are Dunfermline's chatelaine, Dame," she answered.

"I answer to you now, Lady," Agnes replied. "Whatever you ask is what will be done for this and all the royal households. There are several—Dunfermline, Dun Edin, Scone, and Kincardine are among the king's favorites."

Margaret caught her breath. How would she learn all that was expected of her—and however would she communicate her wishes to households that followed foreign customs and spoke the native Gaelic? "I—I will do my best," she said, feeling a little overwhelmed, even as she smiled.

"My lady," Robert De Lauder said, "we will take you around the tower and the fortress to consider all the features of your new domain. This way," he said, gesturing.

As they toured the bailey and exterior buildings, they stopped to greet servants and to discuss the various tasks and needs of the royal household; they spoke with the cook and kitchen servants, the stable grooms and horse master, the falconers, smiths, yard servants, and pages in turn, and then stopped to greet some housecarls training at arms in the lower yard.

Returning to the tower after that, Margaret was greeted by a gathering of grooms and servants, including her own maidservants and ladies. Her kinswomen, the Saxons, and the Benedictines also stood with them to welcome her as queen. No one mentioned that the king was not present. Margaret did her best to appear composed and confident, though she wondered what they thought—and she doubted her own capableness.

Her head spun with the names of servants, the needs of the household, the contents of storage rooms, niches, cupboards, and chests. All would be hers to supervise with one exception, De Lauder explained. The king's treasure room, a small locked chamber tucked behind the king's bedchamber—where she and her husband shared a bed—was accessed by a hidden stair. Only Malcolm had the keys to the great iron lock on the door and the locked chests within.

Throughout, she told herself that she must learn to be a perfect queen and wife. Somehow she must become the heart and soul of all the king's homes. What was expected of her was challenging enough, but to be a foreign queen new to her husband's kingdom was more than daunting.

"The king will take you on progress to visit his other households, no doubt," De Lauder said when she paused with him in the corridor outside the great hall. Moments earlier, Dame Agnes had left them with a tight and uncertain smile. The woman had long supervised Dunfermline, but Margaret sensed that Agnes did not have great faith in the new young queen, especially one raised outside of Scotland. Dismayed, Margaret knew that she would have to prove herself to many at Dunfermline, even those who should support her most closely. And what the king himself thought of her potential as queen, she could not guess.

Now she turned her attention to De Lauder; he was the king's valued friend and advisor, and so she desperately needed his approval, even his friendship.

"My husband has not mentioned going on progress, or moving households. He may wish me to stay here in Dunfermline. The previous queen, I believe, did not go about much."

"Queen Ingebjorg rarely visited Dunfermline," he replied. "She preferred to live at Kincardine, and kept to herself." He studied her for a moment. "She was a gentle lady and a lovely one, true. She was more captive than queen."

"What do you mean?" Margaret asked. "Please, Robert, I must know the truth," she added. "Few have mentioned more than her existence, though we heard rumors before we came to Scotland—awful accusations, and I do not want to believe—" She stopped.

"That Malcolm did away with her? Of course it is not so," he replied impatiently. "She fell ill after the birth of their second son, and he moved her to a hospital in a religious house near the border at Melrose. Her northern kin had no access to her there—and so they say the king was unkind to her, and those rumors have traveled far. She lived almost two years in that place, and died peacefully. She never really acted as Scotland's queen."

"Saints bless her for her suffering," Margaret murmured. "Thank you for your truthfulness. What of her two sons, the princes? They must be young."

"Nine and five, I think. They are fostered elsewhere. The king visits them occasionally."

"Will he bring them here, now that he . . . has married again?"

"That is for the king to decide." He inclined his head curtly, indicating that he did not wish to discuss it further.

She nodded. "Sir, I appreciate your advice and help. I will do my best to understand my new responsibilities."

He smiled. "My lady, I think you will bring to this court what King Malcolm needs most."

"A wife?" she asked. "A family someday?"

"More. Scotland's king should behave, and be perceived, in keeping with his rank," he said. "Less the roaring warlord and more the worldly king. It is imperative if Scotland is to flourish in the wider world. But who will teach him what he needs to know? You, my lady. You will."

"Sir Robert, you have been an excellent influence on the king yourself. And he had an excellent and princely education." She did not want to agree outright that the king lacked manners, even if it was so.

"His education was not as good as one might think—more warring than studying, I gather. And in most matters, he does as he pleases without much regard to what is proper." He shook his head. "Many wait to see what will become of Britain now, with William in the south and Malcolm in the north. The Scottish king must be seen by others as powerful, but also wise and sophisticated, if his country is to gain support from the countries that trade in Scottish harbors."

"I see," Margaret said. "England is already suffering lost trade and exchanges, and will suffer worse if Scotland's king submits to tyranny."

"*Exactement, ma reine*," he said. "William must weigh carefully before coming up here."

"But with the support of Rome and Mother Church," she said thoughtfully, "Scotland can flourish spiritually and earn favor, too. Some practices would have to change for that to happen."

"A great ambition for a new bride," he said. "But perhaps necessary. Indeed, you may be the very helpmeet that King Malcolm needs. You are exemplary in many ways, my lady, and you will be a good influence on the king. Scotland, too."

Margaret looked at him, surprised. "Thank you, sir—but I cannot meet such high expectations."

"*Certainement,* you can and you must, *ma reine,*" he said quietly. "I believe it is your very nature to have a good effect on those around you. I think the king sees this, too. He seems the barbarian to some, but he knows just what Scotland needs."

"I value your advice, Sir Robert." Her thoughts whirled. "Thank you."

"*Ma reine.*" He bowed his head and walked away.

Alone in the corridor, Margaret sighed with dismay. Truly, she did not know how to be a queen in a place like Scotland. She had been trained to run a royal household—but far more than that was needed here.

De Lauder was right. Malcolm Canmore was a sharp-witted king and a tough warrior, but he needed tutoring in proper manners—and even more, he needed to be perceived as a worthy and civilized king. That, along with a Roman-centered faith, would gain him much respect—and that support could even help save Scotland from the Norman threat.

To be sure, she thought, De Lauder had greater faith in her training and example than she did herself. But if she could influence rough-edged Malcolm Canmore for the better, let alone his rowdy court and his backward country, she would do well to try.

And she would have to begin somewhere. Pushing aside the curtain that draped the doorway, she entered the great hall. The floor rushes would have to go, for a start, she decided, and the floor planking scrubbed. Then all the tables should be scraped raw and scrubbed clean.

"And the table linens must be bleached until they are as white as snow," she told Dame Agnes once she had given the new orders. The woman lifted her eyebrows in astonishment. "Send word into town, as well, to the merchants there. We will need several ells of linen, bleached and hemmed. At every meal, the tables are to be set with the very best. Dishes of pewter and gold, silver spoons, glass goblets, and serving dishes, too——"

"And where are we to get all *that*? Begging pardon, Lady," Dame Agnes said hastily.

"From my dower chests," Margaret replied. "We will purchase the rest from merchant ships."

"And how will we pay for all of it?" the woman went on. "If I may ask."

"I have some coin of my own, to do with as I will," Margaret replied. "Dunfermline is a king's hall, not a garrison, and from now on it must look like one. Have the pieces on the wall taken down as well," she said, pointing upward.

"Lady, I do not know what the king will say to that. Those swords and shields belonged to his father and grandfather and others."

"And I vow they still have dirt and blood on them. Let them be cleaned, then, and stored. The more handsome pieces, perhaps, could be hung on the wall near the doorway. In my dower boxes are some very fine embroidered tapestries that once hung in the courts of Hungary and England. They should be aired and pegged up on the walls. And those shabby door curtains should be replaced with good oaken doors." She gestured as she spoke, feeling relief in taking some decisive action.

"My husband will find a carpenter for the task, and he will see to some of the rest as well. We will do whatever you wish, Lady." Now Dame Agnes looked excited, her eyes bright, cheeks flushed. "I will have the walls whitewashed before the tapestries are hung. And the floors should be scrubbed with apple vinegar and lightly oiled before fresh rushes are laid down."

"Good! Then we must consider the other rooms, beginning with the king's bedchamber. And I shall need a solar, where my ladies and I can gather during the day."

"There is much work to be done, I suppose," Dame Agnes said. "But well worth it if Dunfermline is to be a suitable king's residence, as you say. I have suggested changes before, but the king was never agreeable to it."

"He will have to agree to it, if it is done before he returns," she replied, and Agnes smiled suddenly. "I wonder," Margaret mused, looking up, "if we might find an artist to decorate the walls and ceiling rafters."

"Ah! I have heard that the finest palaces in England have such decorations," Agnes said.

"So they do," Margaret replied. "And we will have the same here in Scotland."

Chapter Eight

I have not heard of music ever such as your frame makes
since the time of the fairy people . . . gentle, powerful, glorious.

—"THE HARP OF CNOC I CHOSGAIR,"
IRISH, FOURTEENTH CENTURY

Eva and her escort followed the king's housecarls through the
bailey of Dunfermline tower, aware of the curious gazes of warriors, servants, and nobles, Saxon and Scottish alike. As they climbed
the steps to the royal tower, Eva turned toward Ruari beside her.

"Surely enough Highlanders come to Dunfermline that we are no
novelty," she said in Gaelic.

"Hah! Moray visitors to Malcolm's tower are rare," he replied wryly.

The men led them to a small anteroom fitted like a chapel, with a
cloth-draped table that held a cross and golden vessels. Eva wondered
if they would be expected to pray, for piety was the reputation of the
queen's household, but she soon realized the room had a double func-
tion, for a servant brought them ale in cups and merely asked them to

wait. After that, a knight came to see them, introducing himself as Robert De Lauder.

"The king has gone hunting for the day," he said. "I will tell the queen of your arrival."

"That one," Ruari murmured when the man left, "is a Norman in the king's court." He was clearly not pleased.

Yet Eva sighed with relief, for she had dreaded meeting Malcolm Canmore, her host, captor and murderer of her kinsmen. She was weary besides, as were the others in her party. They had traveled for weeks, crossing the mountains that separated Moray from the provinces south of its boundaries, not because of distance—the journey could be made in a few days when need arose—but because they had stopped at the homes of a few thanes and chieftains, as well as the mormaers of Buchan and the Mearns. While Ruari discussed with the men matters to do with Moray and Scotland—*rebellion* was never said aloud, but it suffused the air at times—Eva had played and sang in return for hospitality. Finally her escort, including the king's housecarls, rode to the sea to board a longship that carried them along the coast and into a wide firth, where they resumed on horseback and rode until they came to the fortress of Dunfermline.

She closed her eyes, wishing she could escape now with her escort following her all the way back to Moray. Instead, the servant came to bring them to the king's great hall.

Walking into the larger room, Eva turned to see her companions pausing to surrender their weapons—dirks and good broadswords—into the keeping of two royal guards. Confiscation was custom in every household, especially the king's own. Ruari lifted a brow, and after a moment, Eva took the dirk sheathed at her own belt and gave it up to the guard, who blinked in surprise.

She turned. The room was long and spacious, and nearly deserted. A servant or two moved about carrying benches from one side of the room to the other; two housecarls sat at a table, heads bent over a board game, and a group of women were clustered on cushioned benches beneath a sunny window, absorbed in sewing and chatting. A wooden dais held two fine, carved chairs, but they were empty.

The queen was not there, Eva thought, as she stepped forward with Ruari when the servant beckoned. She looked about, curious to see the king's house. Her home at Elgin fortress was finer than most—her grandmother had been a queen, after all—but Dunfermline tower, though of modest size, was very well appointed, freshly painted and polished, altogether a prosperous household. Elgin seemed plain by comparison.

Underfoot, thick rushes carpeted the planked floor, and the timbered ceiling overhead was painted with bright designs. Oak tables gleamed, carved chairs and benches were fitted with red and blue pillows, brass candlesticks sparkled, and the jugs and cups set out for wine were of silver and even gold. Embroidered panels draped the whitewashed walls, and a tall iron basket anchored in the middle of the floor glowed with peat bricks and licking flames. Maidservants were spreading white cloths over tables, and two leggy gray wolfhounds approached the visitors, though a servant hastened them toward the door. One of the hounds came to Eva, and she reached out to pat its head, thankful for the eager, panting welcome.

The servants did not seem to be in attendance on anyone in particular, and the women who sat working on stitchery pieces spoke quietly among themselves, watching the visitors. Eva looked uncertainly toward Ruari. "We should come back later if the queen is not here," she told him.

One of the women stood then, speaking softly to the others. They sat on cushioned benches, their gowns bright splashes of color in the sunlight at the far end of the room. A small child huddled at the women's feet beside another large dog. Now and again, the toddler pounded on the dog's haunch, and though the tail flapped, the animal seemed unbothered.

"Dolfin, stop," one of the women said in English. "Leave the hound be."

The young woman who had stood now walked toward Eva and

Ruari. Dressed in a sky blue gown with a translucent, creamy veil, she was tall and graceful, her long skirts trailing on the floor, her pointed green slippers showing as she moved. Beneath the veil, her golden hair hung down in long, thick plaits woven with ribbons. Coming closer, she smiled, and her eyes, very blue, sparkled.

"This must be one of the queen's ladies," Eva murmured to Ruari in Gaelic, "welcoming us in her mistress's absence." All the women appeared to be Saxon, judging by the English they spoke, and by the elegant foreign cut of their gowns, the drape of their veils, and their braided and beribboned hair. Eva lifted a hand to her own unruly black hair, worn loose, and she smoothed, however futile, the skirt of her tunic, its brown linen suited to hard traveling, but not to meeting Saxon ladies. She had not thought to change, and owned nothing so fine as these women wore.

"Welcome!" the woman in blue said in English. Her slight, distinctive accent was not French, Eva realized, but perhaps eastern; she had heard some accents among the merchants and visitors who came to Moray, and she recognized the foreign cadence. "You must be Lady Eva. I understand that the Lady of the North sent you here to perform for us. How kind of her."

"I am Eva. And I come here as a royal hostage," she said bluntly. "We were told the king is absent and that the queen would meet us. Shall we come back later for an audience?"

"Please stay." The woman reached out to take Eva's hand in hers, then kissed one cheek and the other, drawing back. "I look forward to meeting your Lady Gruadh someday, in the spirit of peace. I am sure I could learn much from her about queenship."

"Queen?" Eva gasped, realizing, as the young woman smiled. "Oh!"

Ruari bowed his head. "Lady of Scotland," he said formally, "I am Ruari mac Fergus, thane of Cawdor. And this is Princess Eva." He nudged Eva's shoulder.

She had rarely been called princess, but inclined her head. "I am properly called Aeife inghean Lulach mac Gilcomgan, daughter of the late King Lulach."

"Ay-fa," Margaret attempted. "Eva. Please meet my sister, Princess Cristina." She turned as another young woman came toward them. Unlike tall, golden Margaret, Cristina was dark-haired and stocky, though they shared similar high cheekbones and deep-set eyes. Cristina wore no veil and so was unmarried; a yellow ribbon rounded her brow above brown eyes. Her red gown flattered her sturdy figure, and her fingers glinted with rings. Both women wore slippers of green silk, which Eva thought impractical but fetching; she curled her toes inside her own thick woolen hose and sturdy leather shoes. Margaret and Cristina even carried about them the lovely fragrance of oil of lavender and blossoms. Undoubtedly Eva smelled of horses, damp wool, and too many days' traveling.

"Welcome, Lady Eva," Cristina said in accented English also. A quick frown as she took in Eva's appearance indicated that she was unimpressed. Eva drew her cloak close; at least her plaid was very fine, she knew, patterned in muted purple, blue, and twilight colors, edged with wolf fur, and cinched by a round silver brooch set with crystals. Her earlobes were pierced by a pair of golden circlets set with emeralds, brought from the exotic east by a Viking jarl for her grandmother, who gifted Eva in return. She lifted her head and shook back her hair to subtly show them. Grasping her cloak, her hands showed the callused fingertips and long nails of a harper, and her fingers were slim and strong.

"We thank you for your welcome," she said in English. Her voice carried smoothly in the room, a result of her bard's training. "King Malcolm invited me here under particular terms, as I am sure you know, Lady."

"I am aware," Margaret said. She was very pretty, Eva thought, tall and slender, with delicate features, a long neck, lovely hands. Her hair was thick, striated gold, and her skin was pale, as if she rarely saw the sun. Whether still or in motion, she had a natural grace about her.

"Lady Gruadh sends her compliments on your wedding," Eva

said. "She bids me sing at the king's hearth and tell the old tales of heroes and adventures, and serve in all ways that I can as a *seanchaidh* in the king's household."

"Shawnkhey." Margaret tilted her head. "We have one of those already, I think, old Hector, who sings and plays for us. I have heard of your talent, Lady Eva. Tell me, is it usual for Scottish princesses to do such common work?"

"Common?" Eva blinked. "What do you mean?"

"The singing," Cristina explained. "Do you dance as well?"

Eva stared at her, then looked at the queen. "I am a harper."

"We know. We look forward to something new. The old man who sings for the court is quite dull," Cristina said. "At our uncle the king's court there was a *conteur* who danced and sang, and tossed balls in the air."

"*Conteur?*" Eva asked, uncertain of the word.

"A storyteller. Sometimes a jester, very lively. He told amusing jests, some quite bold," Cristina went on. "His daughters danced with ribbons, and there was a dwarf, too, who did clever imitations of the courtiers. He was a little rude, but it was very entertaining. We laughed often."

"I do not imitate others," Eva said, growing tense. Beside her, Ruari was silent. "I play harp. I sing. I tell stories. Bards are accorded rank in any Scottish household." *I have trained for eleven years,* she wanted to say; *I am nearly a filidh, which in the old days was revered as just below a king's rank.* But such a claim would be wasted on these Sassenach women.

Margaret seemed a bit bewildered. "We look forward to your performance at supper."

"Are you one of the players in the troupe?" the princess in red asked Ruari.

"We are not a Christmas pageant," Ruari said stiffly.

Eva felt her pride and temper rise up like a banner in a high wind. She turned on her heel suddenly and walked toward the door.

Though she heard Ruari excuse himself to hasten after her, Eva did not look back, but shoved through the embroidered curtain and left the hall.

Ruari caught her arm. "Stop."

She shook him off. "I will never," she said through her teeth, "sing or dance like a poppet on a stick, and this Saxon queen will have to beg me on her *knees*," she went on fiercely, "to have even one of the old Irish tales from me. Her sister, too. Their ignorance makes them unworthy of what any *seanchaidh* offers. We are leaving, Ruari mac Fergus. Gather the men."

"That is not your decision," he answered, gripping her arm. "Nor can you leave this court."

"The king is not even here to see us, and I a princess, a bard, too. And the queen is . . . a *needleworker*," she said. "What does she know of what I do? We will go home tonight."

"We will stay, and you will do your mistress's bidding."

"Which mistress?" she snapped.

"Both," he said, leaning close, hand gripping above her elbow. The guards in the corridor watched them, hands resting on sheathed swords. Ruari spoke low so that they would not hear if indeed they spoke Gaelic at all, which Eva doubted.

"Lady Gruadh is right—this Saxon queen does not belong in Scotland. She is weak and shallow, and knows nothing of our ways, to speak of bardic tradition as if it were a bore. You heard what she said of 'old Hector,' whose name I know. The position of king's bard is not to be belittled, yet the queen gives the tradition little credence."

"Then teach her." Ruari gave her a little push back toward the curtain. "Show her what a true *seanchaidh* does."

"I do not toss balls," Eva said.

"You can learn," he growled, "if it serves the purposes of both your queens."

A NARROW WOODEN BED with a good mattress, stuffed with feathers and lavender, was Eva's own in the small bedchamber she was to share with two maidservants. She stood back as two of her Scots escort carried her basket of belongings and her harp—she would trust its care to no one but herself—into the room. The maidservants entered, too, and Eva turned to greet them.

They were Saxon and spoke only English. Wynne, with messy golden curls and a quick smile, and dark-haired Matilda both welcomed her, insisting that they would share the other bed and blankets. Nodding, Eva reminded herself that since she was given two maids and her own bed, she was not being treated like a prisoner, at least so far.

"The king's tower is not large and has few beds to spare, so you are indeed fortunate," Wynne further assured her. "The royal Saxons and their household have taken most of the beds in the tower and in the guest buildings in the bailey. Your Scotsmen will have to find space on the garrison floor while they are here."

"Above our little room is the queen's solar," Matilda said, pointing up. "There is a stair in the corner beside our door. The queen and her ladies work at stitchery there each day for hours, though sometimes they sit in the great hall, too. The queen expects you to join her circle, and we have been told to bring you to her as soon as you are settled here."

Dreading the prospect of stitchery and gossip for hours each day with Sassenach women she did not even know, Eva smiled tightly. "I am a bard," she explained, "and my first duty is to my craft. I must tune my harp, and spend some time daily with the remembering of melodies, songs, and stories. Please tell the queen that I will join her when I am able." If she did not establish her status as a bard and princess early, she thought, she would be relegated to far less.

Her grandmother might chide her for haughtiness if she were here, Eva thought, but pride seemed necessary to her very survival at Dunfermline. And besides, she had learned that pride from Lady Gruadh herself, who had thrust her into this predicament.

"Your first duty is to the queen," Matilda told her. "It is the king's decision for you, so Dame Agnes says."

Eva realized then that needlework was better than a prison cell, for she had best not trust Malcolm to honor his agreement with Gruadh.

"Allow me to rest after my journey. Perhaps tomorrow or the next day I will join the queen's circle."

"Very well," Wynne said. "The queen wishes you and your men to attend supper this evening, and she hopes you will perform."

"I will do that," Eva said. But she would not be dancing about with ribbons, she thought.

When they had gone, Eva removed her harp from its leather and fur wrapping. She rubbed the instrument with a soft cloth, sweeping over the carved willow and oak soundbox, the graceful neck and forepillar. After the jostling journey, the brass strings required careful tuning; the two gold wire strings at the center, tuned to the same note, were extremely sensitive to motion, damp, and climate. Using a little ivory key to turn the pins that held each string in place, she closed her eyes, listening for the resonance of each plucked string, matching that with the perfect sounds in her memory. Finally she swept her fingers over the strings, producing harmonies. Then she played a tune, bowing her head as she surrendered her thoughts—and her rising fears—to the sound.

CANDLES AND WALL TORCHES had been lit against the gloom, and a rainstorm pattered the walls and window shutters as Eva and her Scottish escort entered the great hall. The queen was there, but the king was late, as apparently was his habit, or so Wynne and Matilda had explained. They also pointed out Prince Edgar, the blond young man who sat beside the queen. The Scottish party waited with the others, and the hall had filled with the residents of Dunfermline tower by the time Malcolm finally strode through the hall, three dogs loping at his heels, to take his seat beside his wife.

"We have guests from Moray this evening, sire," Queen Margaret said. Her voice, though quiet, carried well. "They arrived today while you were gone."

"So I heard. Bring them forward, Sir Robert," Malcolm told the Norman, gesturing impatiently.

De Lauder bowed and beckoned to Eva and Ruari, who stood wait-

ing in the shadows. As they walked forward, many of those who stood
or sat in the hall turned to watch with interest.

Seeing the very fine garments worn by the queen and the other ladies
clustered near the dais, Eva was glad that she had taken care with her
appearance after resting that afternoon. Wynne had brought her a large
bucketful of hot water, a fragrant soft lump of soap, and linen; she had
bathed and then freshened her clothing. Now her long black hair was
combed out in supple waves over her shoulders, snugged with a blue
ribbon around her brow, and she held her head high, shoulders square,
carriage proud. She wore a simply cut tunic gown of pale gray over a
white shift, with a patterned cloak of pale colors pinned with a large,
round silver brooch. Her slippers were of brown leather—she owned
no narrow colored slippers such as those the queen and the other
ladies wore—but her accessories were worthy of any royalty. Her
low-slung belt was of hammered silver links, and now her earlobes
held twisted silver wires, and she wore a necklace of bright pearls on
a black cord. Seeing curiosity among the crowd, she lifted her chin
higher. Let them think the Highlands produced rustic Scotswomen
closer to fishwives than queens, she thought; she would show them
otherwise.

Distant thunder rolled outside, and the flames flickered in a draft.
Eva felt a quick chill, as if she had walked into a moment of great
import in her life. She heard a few soft murmurs and whispers as she
crossed the length of the room. Ruari walked beside her, strong and
quiet, neither a step ahead nor a step behind, as it should be.

The queen smiled, and King Malcolm sat forward with keen interest. To Margaret's left, Prince Edgar ceased his conversation with
Princess Cristina and straightened. "Who is this?" he asked, his
voice so clear that Eva suddenly realized how very quiet the hall had
become. "She is lovely."

"The Moray princess," Margaret's sister said.

"King Malcolm," De Lauder said, "allow me to present Princess
Eva of Moray and the leader of her escort, Sir Ruari mac Fergus of
Cawdor."

Eva and Ruari stepped forward and the king straightened, alert, his dark eyes narrowing.

Malcolm Big Head, Eva observed, was neither the biggest nor the most ferocious-looking man she had ever seen. Many of the Vikings in her grandmother's service were larger and fiercer, though Malcolm Ceann Mór could have stood equal with some. But among Lowlanders, Saxons, and foreigners, he would seem huge, she told herself.

Queen Margaret sat to Malcolm's left, slender and fair, golden braids spilling beneath her shoulder-draped silken veil. Her appearance was nearly angelic beside the king and the rough warriors seated nearby. Two older women sat with her, along with the princess Cristina and Prince Edgar.

So here was the landless renegade Saxon royal family rescued by Malcolm, Eva realized. Beautiful but stiff-necked, each of them, like painted tomb sculptures. She stood in silence before them, hands folded, waiting, heart pounding. Heat emanating from the fire basket a few feet behind her burned off the damp chill in the room and gave her a sense of comfort as she faced these cold strangers.

"So Gruadh sent you at last," Malcolm said. "Aeife inghean Lulach mac Gilcomgan, welcome," he continued, in Gaelic. His voice was deep, growling. He had bushy, untamed auburn hair and beard, thick features, dark, snapping eyes. Eva did not like him on sight; she did not want to like him.

"My king," she said flatly. "Mael Coluim Ceann Mór, Rí Alban." She gave the words a formal, dramatic impact. "I am come from Moray at your request. Let me present the head of my escort, Ruari mac Fergus, now thane of Cawdor."

"Ah, Lady Gruadh's loyal housecarl," Malcolm said. "I know your name, sir."

Ruari nodded. "The Lady of the North sends her regards and bids me convey a message."

The king laughed. "Any greeting from her will have thorns hidden in it somewhere."

"Sire," Ruari said, "the lady sends congratulations on your marriage, and recommends to you and your bride the Lady Eva, her beloved granddaughter and household bard. She entrusts Lady Eva to your temporary guardianship. May you and your court enjoy her music, and may she be given the rights and privileges due her as a bard and a princess of royal blood."

"Well enough. Lady Eva, no harm in granting you the privilege of your rank while you are here in our court," he said in English, so that the others could understand, "under our watchful protection."

Eva regarded him solemnly. He had murdered her kinsmen, which she would not let herself forget. And she was no guest here, no matter how nicely her arrival was colored for the court. "My rank? Do you mean my status as a hostage?" she asked.

His nostrils flared. "My agreement with Lady Gruadh states that you will remain here until I decide otherwise. You speak the Sassenach tongue well for one raised in the Highlands."

"We are hardly ignorant in the north, sire." Her heart beat fast. Behind her, she heard someone whisper about her boldness. Well, she would not be subservient to this man and risk having scant respect here, where the Southrons outnumbered the Gaels. As for boldness, she did not care what a murdering king and a horde of Saxons thought of her.

"Even in the south we have heard of your beauty and talent," Malcolm said. "Clearly the one is true, and we will be happy to test the other in this hall."

"Neither is wanting," Eva said.

Malcolm huffed. "You have your grandmother's arrogance. Are you as skilled as they say?"

"As you see, I have the right to wear five colors in my cloak." She lifted an arm with the drape of plaid wool to display its soft colors—pale blue and green, mulberry, cream, brown. "According to Brehon law, the ancient Irish laws which holy Adomnán recorded long ago, and which we honor in Scotland, too, a king may wear seven colors, including the rare purple, in his cloak. A bard may wear six colors, chiefs and thanes, five. A female bard may wear five colors as well. All others must wear no more than four colors by ancient law. Surely you are aware of that, being King of Scots."

"I am." Malcolm sat forward. Eva heard a thrum of voices as some glanced around the hall; though many of the Scots there wore Highland patterns, none had more than five colors, including her own men. King Malcolm himself wore a cloak of solid red—like a Lowlander or, worse, a Saxon, Eva thought.

He held up a hand for quiet. "You, a young girl, are a full bard?"

She nodded. "I am." She was playing a little at being bold, but she was determined to prove herself early on in Malcolm's court. As the daughter of a murdered enemy and the granddaughter of a continued rebel, she could not let him sense any weakness in her.

The king listened as Margaret whispered in his ear. He nodded, and Eva noticed that he was calm and patient with his foreign bride, translating the conversation, which had been partly in Gaelic.

"Lady Eva," Malcolm said, "where we go, you will go, as a watched guest of this court. The queen is willing to accept you as one of her ladies, and you will perform for her and for the court when requested."

Eva nodded. "I have no desire to replace Dunfermline's own bard." She indicated the old man seated on a stool placed to one side of the dais. A lower stool held a harp, so his role was clear. He cast a dark look toward her when she looked at him.

"Hector is our court poet, trained in storytelling and music. He has a permanent place here."

"He is a true *seanchaidh*?" She frowned, for the bard wore a dull brown cloak rather than a plaid of six colors, which his courtly rank dictated.

"Hector is a *scrop*—a Saxon poet," Malcolm answered.

"A Saxon bard in a Scottish court?" Beside her, she knew Ruari tensed in warning.

"My court honors both Saxon and Scottish ways," Malcolm growled low. "Had you been raised by other than Gruadh of the North, you would understand that."

"I was born in the household of Macduff of Fife," she said. "Later my grandmother raised me as a princess of the Gaels. I know Scotland. Not England. Sire," she added.

"Moray Gaels are not known for humility," Malcolm remarked. "Well, Hector will not mind another harper in this court." He gestured toward the poet. But Eva could see that Hector minded indeed, for the old man's brow sank in a frown. "You will play for us later, Lady Eva," Malcolm said in dismissal.

Ruari took her arm and Eva inclined her head regally, stepping back. The queen's steward, Sir Wilfrid, led them to one side of the room. When he directed a servant to bring wine for the Scots and to find them seats together for supper, Eva thanked him.

"You are very welcome, Lady Eva." He smiled down at her. Gaunt, broad-shouldered Wilfrid had the look of a weathered warrior but was dressed like a fine courtier in silver-trimmed green wool. His fingers twitched on his leather belt as if used to finding a sword pommel there.

Sipping the tart red wine that the servant had poured into cups, Eva sat with her escort and watched as Malcolm spoke with others who approached the dais, until servants entered carrying platters of meat and bowls filled with steaming soups. When most had eaten, Hector returned to the stool on the dais and took up his harp to play.

His wire-string harp was larger than Eva's own, the resonance loud, even brash as he played a tune unfamiliar to her. She liked the droning, tight harmony of the melody and the steady rhythm that he produced with clever fingering patterns, and she leaned to watch closely. Some of the courtiers stamped their heels in time to the music, and Hector began to sing verses that told of a sailor over the sea, evoking the rhythm of oars in the plucking patterns.

Malcolm spoke with others throughout the performance, while Margaret smiled, if a bit stiffly. When Hector finished, they applauded, and Malcolm pointed toward Eva.

"Now the lass will play," he said.

"Princess Eva," the queen corrected him gently.

Eva drew a breath and stood. She had brought her harp to the hall, expecting to play, and now one of her Moray companions carried it forward. Eva took Hector's place, sitting down and propping the base of her harp on the lower stool.

She tipped the instrument so that it rested in the hollow of her left shoulder, and lifted her hands to the strings. She had tuned the metal strings earlier, and now she tested, hearing a slight dissonance, which she corrected, twisting the upper pegs that held the strings by using the ivory key, which she kept in a leather pouch slung from her belt.

Malcolm continued a low discussion with some of his men. The queen waited, hands folded calmly. Eva paused, deciding between two songs she had considered for her introduction at court, and then she moved her fingers rapidly over the strings, brass and gold shimmering.

She loved the moment whenever a melody began. A song might be ancient, its origins lost to memory, but a harper could spark the music to life again and join the present and the past. She plucked the strings: two together, one and two; three together, three and four. Her left hand repeated a rhythm in a lower register while the fingers of her right hand flashed like quickfire along upper and lower strings, creating delicate traceries of sound.

Tilting her head forward slightly, she listened and concentrated. Her hair draped over her shoulders, shielding her, so that she was aware of only the harp, the music.

Then she lifted her head and began to sing in Gaelic. Her voice was strong, its natural clarity a little husky from the strain of her journey. The song told of a mermaid sunning upon a rock, and its rhythm and lilting melody were captivating. She deliberately chose the song for its enchanting sort of charm—had she given the court a song of loss or bitterness first, they would credit her with the same from the start. Better this, in a place where she needed friends.

Hill o ro, huill o ro
'S mis 'a chunn-aic!
Hill o ro, huill o ro
Ah, what I saw!
Shining like silver on a rock of the sea
A marvelous sight one morning early
She raised her head and she changed before me
To a seal, a gray seal,.and she cleaved the sea

The verses and refrain went on, lively and charming, and she saw smiles, nods, engaged attention around the room. On the last note, she let the sound fade to silence, lowered her hands, and looked up. Clapping began, caught, and grew. Queen Margaret was smiling, still in that cool, perfect way. She had not understood the words of the song, Eva realized.

Malcolm nodded curtly. "Good. Hector, now you."

Unsure if the king had enjoyed her music or was annoyed, Eva tilted her harp and stood. As she began to move the instrument, a young man crossed the dais toward her. She looked up to see the Saxon prince, lanky blond Edgar, who lifted her harp from the stool before she could.

"That was excellent, Lady Eva," he said. "May I carry this for you?" His hands were long and nimble, and he supported her harp so gently that she smiled, relieved, for she was particular about who handled it.

"Thank you. But one of my men will take it. You need not trouble."

"I do not mind." He carried the harp as they left the dais, and then handed it carefully to one of Ruari's men. "I hope we will have more songs from you soon, my lady." He nodded, golden hair swinging, and smiled before he walked away.

Blushing at his kind and unexpected attention, Eva sat again with the Moray men and accepted a fresh cup of wine from Ruari. As she sipped, Hector, who had already taken up his own harp, began to play and sing.

His voice was nasal, but deep and powerful. Eva recognized the tune as a Welsh one that Dermot had taught her. The lyrics, sung in English, were those of a bard praising his beloved harp as if it were a desirable woman without equal. No earthly woman could match the harp's mellow tone or her exquisite form and timeless beauty, Hector sang. The bard gave his heart only to his loyal, exquisite harp—flesh-and-blood women were nothing to him, claimed the verses.

Just then Hector sent Eva a cold glance across the room, as if daring her to equal him or to try to take his place.

She smiled, giving no hint that she felt the cool reception of the incumbent bard as well as the king. Soon she leaned toward Ruari. "I am tired and would go to my chamber now." What did she care if she seemed rude for it, being all but a prisoner here? When Hector finished one song and adjusted the tuning for the next, she stood and left the hall.

Chapter Nine

❦

Loveliness shone around her like light,
Her steps were the music of songs.

—SCOTTISH TRADITIONAL,
FROM ALEXANDER CARMICHAEL,
Carmina Gadelica

At dawn, roused by the maidservants and urged to dress quickly, Eva barely had a moment to use the chamber pot in a curtained corner before the girls hurried her from the room. They joined a few other women silently descending the stairs by the light of oil lamps carried by their maids.

Eva followed them into the anteroom beside the great hall, where a golden and jet cross and silver vessels gleamed in candlelight. The queen knelt before it, hands pressed in prayer, pale hair rippling down her back, a simple white veil covering her bowed head. Her ladies gathered behind her, each kneeling to pray.

Kneeling, too, for she had been taught to honor a daily routine of prayer, Eva was surprised to see Margaret pray with the fervor of a nun, murmuring in Latin, hands clasped, for most of an hour. Sometimes the queen led her women in a recitation, and Eva kept pace, familiar with the Latin. Once she saw tears gleam on the queen's cheeks before the golden head bowed again, hair sweeping down to conceal her face.

Gasping softly, Eva felt her sympathy caught. What could trouble this beautiful, fortunate young queen so deeply that she cried as if making some heartfelt appeal? Eva could not imagine Margaret responsible for any wrongdoing that might require forgiveness and atonement. She seemed humble, gentle, perfect. But to pray as she did seemed beyond the norm.

When the ladies got to their feet to file out, Margaret passed Eva, silk and linen shushing. She turned. "Lady Eva, your Latin is very good."

"My thanks. I learned from monks. My grandfather insisted on my good education."

"Your grandfather?" Margaret arched fine blond brows. "Do you mean Macbeth?"

"I speak of my mother's father, who was mormaer in Fife, where I spent my childhood."

"I have met Kenneth Macduff of Fife, who sometimes comes here to see the king."

"That one is my great-uncle, though I have not seen him for a long while. He sent me north to Moray when I was eight to live with my grandmother. She made sure my tutoring continued." She did not add that her great-uncle had not inquired about her after bidding her a gruff farewell. Matters between Fife and Moray were not as congenial as they had been in past generations.

"Well done to your family. Royal women should be learned and astute in some matters."

"In Scotland, learning is considered valuable for girls of any rank," Eva said. "King Macbeth wanted tutors and schools provided in every parish and province, but he did not have time to see it done in the warring years before his death. My father might have done so, too, had he lived."

"I see," Margaret said thoughtfully. She turned to the wife of Ranald mac Niall, whom Eva had met only recently. "Lady Gudrun, do you also find this true in Scotland?"

"Aye, Lady, many Scots believe education is important for all. Girls are tutored with their brothers when possible, but it does not apply to all families. Many say that Macbeth and his queen wanted to establish this across the land someday, but it was never completed."

"In Moray," Eva said, "even the poorest families send their daughters and sons to the parish priests for basic lessons. And what of King Malcolm?" she asked. "Will he order more education for the Scottish people at the expense of the crown, after the wisdom of his predecessors?"

"I do not know, but I will ask," Margaret said. "If I am blessed with daughters I would hire tutors for them, but I had not thought of girls in other situations . . . I do like the notion. I have benefitted so from my tutoring." She smiled. "Lady Eva, you surprise me, I vow."

"How so, Lady?" Eva wondered if it was her education, but dreaded it was her boldness.

Margaret shook her head, then, and would not say, though her eyes twinkled as if she was pleased. "Never mind. Only this—I would like you to accompany me when I go to chapel."

"If you wish," Eva said, puzzled. "But your ladies accompany you to prayers every morning. I will be there, too."

"You and I will go together at other times. Sometimes I prefer to be alone, but a queen must always have at least one lady with her. One who prays as prettily as you do would be a good companion."

Eva did not think of herself as devout. "I am not certain that I—"

"As a Scot, you will set a fine example for others who are not so . . . adept in Latin devotions as you are. I will send for you when I feel the need to go alone to my prayers."

"Lady," Eva said. As the queen moved away with her kinswomen, Eva turned quickly to Wynne. "Am I expected to pray with her every morning, so early?" she whispered.

"She prays even more often than that. Usually a group of us go to chapel with her at dawn, and again in the afternoon or the evening," Wynne said.

"But when she wants to go there by herself, she may summon you at any time. Most likely in the middle of the night," Matilda said.

Eva hesitated. She did not want to spend hours in prayer when she should practice her bardic work, but she saw a chance to learn whatever she could of this queen, this court. She nodded.

"Be flattered by her request," Wynne said. "The Lady worries for the souls of the Scots who lack proper Latin. She will be glad your soul is safe and you can be glad of her favor."

Lady Gruadh's household was free of such poperies, Eva thought. Latin or Gaelic was fine, and prayers were said often enough to keep one in good stead with heaven and the priests.

"Queen Margaret was raised in an exotic court called Hungary, and in England, too," Matilda told Eva. "With such a proper and strict upbringing, she wishes to see similar improvements in Scotland."

Later, Matilda and Wynne brought a meal for her at midday, along with a verbal message reminding her to join the queen in her solar when she was rested from her long journey. Without answering that, Eva offered to share the cheese, oatcakes, and pot of frothy ale with Wynne and Matilda, who eagerly accepted.

While she sliced yellow cheese and crumbled the cakes into equal bits, Eva asked the maidservants how they had come to serve in the household of the King of Scots, for she felt sure that both had been gently raised and were not born to servitude. They willingly explained that each of them had escaped the Norman attacks in northern England, and had met while wandering, trying to avoid capture by Normans or Scots, both of whom were raiding the land.

Wynne, who chattered like a magpie when she relaxed, was the daughter of a slain Saxon earl, while reserved Matilda was the widow of a thane. Neither knew if their kin now lived or had died, and both were grateful for their friendship, which seemed sisterlike and devoted. Eva smiled, glad she had found them. She had no friends in Dunfermline beyond her own escort, about to leave—and she had more than a few enemies here.

Though the girls gave few details about their ordeals, Eva realized that they had seen atrocities, had lost dearly loved families and good, prosperous homes. Starving and without hope, they had both been plucked from the roadside by Edgar the Aetheling, who had taken them under the protection of his own patrol. Without question, they both adored, even revered young Edgar, who Wynne pointed out would have been their king in better times. Any good fortune they had, including their positions in Dunfermline's household, they attributed to Edgar. The sainted Edgar, Eva thought wryly—as perfect as his sister.

Curious to know more, she encouraged them. "This Edgar must have proven himself a fine prince and a warrior," she said. "I hear he has the full support of Malcolm against William."

"True, they are trying to build support for a Saxon rebellion, from what we hear," Matilda agreed. "Edgar is just our age, but he will gather a great army to rise up against William. He intends to win back his rightful crown—he is David against the Norman Goliath."

"With Malcolm's help, Edgar will regain England for the Saxons," Wynne said confidently.

"Far better to be Scotland's friend than its enemy," Eva said. "But the Saxon rebels will need an extraordinary leader if they hope to defeat the Normans. Is he that, this Edgar?"

"If he is meant to be king, he will be," Matilda said blithely.

"Ah," Eva said, keeping her doubts to herself. "Tell me about the queen."

"Prayerful and devout," Matilda said. "Saintly."

"Temperamental and demanding," Wynne said in the same moment. Eva raised her brows in surprise. "She is a very kind soul," Wynne amended, "but asks a good deal of others and expects even more from herself. Everything must be perfectly done, or she is distressed and displeased. I grant she is an intelligent and strong-willed woman, with a good and charitable nature."

"She was raised to be a queen, and before her marriage wanted to be a nun," Matilda said.

"And now she is both," Eva concluded wryly.

"In a way," Wynne replied. "You will soon learn for yourself what she is like."

Eva knew she could not avoid joining the ladies much longer. Besides, her grandmother expected news about the king's court soon, which she could not learn if she kept to her room. Soon the Moray men would leave for the north, and Eva should send back with them some word of the king's court to Elgin's lady.

�֍

"HMPH," LADY AGATHA SAID. "She has refused yet again to join your circle? That is a very presumptuous girl!"

Margaret looked up from her needlework. A full week had passed since the Moray princess had arrived, and still she had not come to the solar with the other ladies. Wynne—whose brassy curls, Margaret thought, needed taming again—had said that the northern princess practiced daily on her harp, and for that reason she had no time to honor the queen's invitation.

"Lady Eva does not mean to offend," Wynne said. "She says bards must work for hours each day, and nothing must interfere with that."

"Even a queen's command?" Lady Agatha sniffed.

"Only a Scot would ignore a queen's summons," Cristina put in, and Margaret noticed the two Scottish ladies in the group bristling at her sister's bluntness.

"Her harp music is very good," Margaret said. "It is nearly angelic." And so much nicer than listening to Hector, she thought. Now and then she could hear the sounds of Eva's faint, clear voice over the chime of harpstrings from below, for the girls' bedchamber was located directly beneath the solar. "Leave her to her practice. It is a worthy use of her time, and pleases her."

"Does she think she is better than others because she is a princess? Her blood is not as royal as ours," Cristina pointed out. "I hear her father was not a rightful king, and she is illegitimate, besides. She needs to be educated on the importance of rank and proper behavior at court."

"Leave her be," Margaret repeated firmly. Cristina pursed her lips and resumed her work.

Troubled, Margaret returned to her needlework, aware that her sister grew more disagreeable the longer she stayed in Scotland. Her mother and brother still maintained that Cristina would enter a convent, preferably an English one, as soon it was safe for her to do so. Cristina was as much a sacrificial offering to the Church as Margaret had been in her marriage. Most English dioceses would vie for the privilege and prestige of housing a Saxon princess, for that could attract extra benefits from the Mother Church in Rome.

She understood her sister's snappish resentments, for Cristina wanted a more exciting life, while Margaret was the one who would have gladly entered a convent. That irony was clear, but Margaret was determined to make the best of whatever heaven and fate placed before her.

Yet she wanted more purpose, a greater path for her life. Ordering fine plates for the tables and teaching manners to a boorish king was not enough, but was all she had for now. A need for much more nagged at her, a vague dissatisfaction that she could not ignore.

The Moray princess, she realized then, led a life with an almost wild freedom, even adventure. That made Margaret curious; the contrast to her own life and desires intrigued her.

Drawing a long tail of green thread through unbleached linen, Margaret focused on her work in silence. Eva of Moray was so different from the other ladies at court—she was not refined in the usual sense, though she was intelligent and apparently well educated. Though the girl skipped embroidery sessions, she appeared at morning prayers, and her Latin was impeccable.

And she dared to defy a queen, which earned Margaret's curiosity, even her respect. Lady Eva had proven forthright and quick-tempered, sharing a headstrong nature with Malcolm and Lady Gruadh, too. Perhaps it was the royal Gaelic blood they had in common, Margaret thought. She would not question the girl's lineage, being no expert in Scottish genealogy; Lulach had been a crowned king, and Lady Gruadh, it was said, had more royal blood than Malcolm himself.

Besides, Margaret herself struggled with a quick temper and strong opinions. She understood the heat of the heart, for she strove to quell it in herself nearly every day.

Knotting the moss green thread, she began a line of stitches in ochre to fill in a vine border. She wanted to know more about Lady Eva and her grandmother. From the girl she could learn more about Scotland and its traditions; from the other, valuable lessons in queenship.

We three are like a triad of pride, she thought: *the harper, the Lady of the North, and the foreign queen.* But she doubted the other two, with their prideful tempers, would agree.

❦

ON A SUNNY MORNING, Eva held the door to the great hall open—the oak so new that its oils were pungent—for Lady Juliana, a young Saxon woman whose father, Eva had learned, had betrayed Malcolm by bargaining with King William for lands in England. A hostage in the Scottish court on account of her father's behavior, Juliana, as an illegitimate daughter of a significant man, understood Eva's situation—and vice versa—better than most.

"We are birds in a pretty cage, you and I," auburn-haired Juliana had whispered to Eva one day. "We have luxury and privilege here, but no right to our own freedom."

As they entered the hall with Queen Margaret and her ladies to break their fast after prayers, Eva saw Margaret seated with her foreign maidservant, her sister, and some others. The queen ate little, although Eva knew that Margaret had not eaten yet that day, and she was pallid, refusing most of what Kata, her maidservant, urged on her. Finally the queen tasted a little plain porridge and sipped a shallow cup of hot milk. Then while others ate, she sat discussing household matters with Dame Agnes. Sir Wilfrid brought an account roll for her review, mentioning the queen's royal properties in Scotland, which Eva now heard had been granted to her by Malcolm in honor of their marriage. Finally Margaret rose from her chair and motioned for the ladies to follow her from the hall.

"Where are we going?" Eva asked as she and Juliana walked with Lady Edith, the wife of Juliana's father. The two women got along well, despite the odd nature of their relationship.

"To the chapel across the glen to pray," the older lady answered.

"But we prayed for an hour, not two hours ago," Eva said.

"Hardly enough time to sin again," Juliana agreed wryly.

"The queen insists that daily devotions keep our souls in good repair," Lady Edith replied.

"My soul does not need so much repair," Eva muttered, and Juliana laughed.

She kept to herself that the queen had requested her to sometimes go alone with her to prayers. Truly she preferred harp music over prayer for cleansing one's soul, but thought better of saying so. For her, playing music felt as inspired and healing as prayer, but that sentiment might be considered heretical here.

Eva found a place near the door of the anteroom chapel with Juliana while the queen knelt, folding her hands in prayer. Sometimes, as now, Margaret had such grace and purity that Eva would not have been surprised to see a halo around the queen's head rather than mere sunlight filtering through the little window.

She sighed, wishing she could get away to practice her harp, when Juliana nudged her. "I need to work on my embroidery," the girl whispered. "I pray that my work will be passable today. The queen has an unforgiving eye. Let us go," she urged. "Come, I will show you the solar."

Eva nodded, and they tiptoed from the chapel. Looking back, she saw the queen turn her head slightly as they departed. The Saxon woman missed nothing, Eva realized.

In the sunlit room at the height of the tower above Eva's bedchamber, Eva was sitting with Juliana when the ladies returned to resume their stitching. The queen welcomed Eva and took up her work from a painted basket. Not sure what was expected of her, Eva was glad when Lady Agatha brought her a folded green woolen gown that she said belonged to the queen, and showed her that part of the hem had come loose and needed repair.

"Did you learn stitchery skills in the north country?" the woman asked in her heavy accent.

"Of course," Eva said, biting back further comment—stitchery was one of the earliest skills a girl could learn, north or south.

Silently she began to work, looping the thread snugly as she fixed the torn hem. The gown was neatly made of moss green wool lined in pale silk, with flowers embroidered at the hem, on the sleeves, and on the front of the skirt, and she admired the artistry of that handiwork, turning it to examine the inside.

She was glad that she had worn her good dark blue gown that day and had taken time to neatly plait her black hair with red ribbons. The ladies of the queen's circle wore handsome gowns of linen, wool, and silk in an array of colors, and their hair was smoothly arranged, whether covered by a veil or left loose or braided. Eva had noticed from the first that the queen preferred plenty of color in her own wardrobe, often wearing several bright colors at once in gown, shift, shoes, and cloak. Margaret also had a taste for the finest fabrics and exquisite embroidery with touches of gold and silver threads, seed pearls, and even small inset semiprecious stones in the bandwork. Indeed, her garments draped gracefully along her slim curves, and both bright and soft colors flattered her fair coloring—and Eva had the feeling Margaret knew that quite well, indicating that the foreign queen had a certain vanity mingled with her better qualities.

Wynne had already mentioned to Eva that the queen encouraged her ladies to dress well, as befit their station as her companions. If they did not own or could not afford such things, Margaret helped them by purchasing ells of cloth in the local market and hiring seamstresses in the town to sew the gowns, which the ladies then embroidered. If the queen offered to improve her wardrobe, Eva thought, she would refuse; her own things, though plainer than most, were fine.

"The king, too, now dresses handsomely in things chosen by the queen," Wynne had said. "And the Lady scissor-trims his hair and beard herself. He looks like a Saxon now, with long hair and mustache. You should have seen him before—like a bear," she added with a laugh.

Eva worked on the green gown, silk and wool rustling under her fingers. After a while Queen Margaret rose and circled the little room, speaking to each woman, praising here, gently correcting a technique there. She paused by Eva.

"Neatly done," she said. "Though you might prefer to play harp rather than do stitchery, is it so?" Eva smiled and the queen touched her shoulder and moved on.

Moments later, as Margaret paused by Juliana, she took the piece the girl was working on to examine it. With a quick, impatient huff, Margaret grabbed a set of silver scissors and ripped out a section of colorful stitches that had been sewn with tiny seed pearls. Eva gaped, seeing Juliana's look of dismay as the pearls scattered over the floor.

"This work is uneven," Margaret said. "Only the finest embroidery will do for a priest's vestment, especially if it comes from the queen's circle. Do it again, Juliana. It must be flawless."

Juliana flushed. "I beg your pardon, my lady."

"Only the best, do you understand? I ask the same of myself. Only the best, ever." Margaret returned to her own chair, her cheeks pink as she sat to resume her own needlework.

The queen's stern words hung in the air. Eva saw the other women working earnestly, all of them silent, while the maidservant Finola dropped to her knees to gather up the pearls. Over her head, Eva caught Juliana's gaze. The girl lifted a brow in clear, silent comment. Then she went back to picking loose threads out of the cloth in her hands.

Margaret embroidered a new line of stitches steadily, her expression so calm that Eva wondered if she felt any remorse. The queen had a ruthless side as Juliana had said, and a startling temper out of keeping with her otherwise exemplary manners.

"Lady Juliana," Margaret said a little while later, leaning forward to look. "Those new stitches are nicely done."

"Thank you, my lady," Juliana murmured.

"Do you do much embroidery, Lady Eva?" the queen asked after another stretch of silence.

"I do," Eva answered, and showed the sleeves of her gown, where she had trimmed the blue wool in a looping pattern of yellow and green thread, matching the band she had sewn along the hem. Under the gown, she wore a shift of creamy linen embroidered with blue flowers.

The queen admired the work, smoothing slender fingers over it as she discussed the technique Eva had used. Others peered over her shoulder, including Lady Agatha, who exclaimed and reached out to touch Eva's sleeve. Princess Cristina did, as well.

Cristina gave the work close scrutiny, pointing out missed stitches and stating what would have fixed them. For a moment, Eva felt overwhelmed by a chatter of compliments in various languages; she understood English, Gaelic, and Latin only, and she was impressed by how easily the Saxon women changed languages, even in the midst of a conversation, a necessary skill in most royal courts, she realized, particularly when the queen and her kin were foreigners.

Lady Agatha held out a piece of cloth embroidered with an elaborate design and insets of gold wire, minutely wrapped with the silken stitches. The piece was a priest's stole, Eva saw.

"Take this," Lady Agatha told her. "Trim and finish the back, then line it with that piece of silk and hem it. Your stitches are good enough for that. We have much work to do here, since we are making things for the church as well as for my daughter's household. We will teach you new stitches, and you will learn much."

Taking up a little pair of scissors, Eva snipped loose threads as she had been assigned. She did not want to do this, she thought, and would far rather be elsewhere, away from this earnest little workshop with its busy, productive, unquestioning ladies—but for the Lady Juliana—and its demanding mistress. She needed to tend to her own work of harp playing and bardcraft. But she could not play harp for the queen and her circle unless Margaret asked her, and so the only strings she handled in the queen's solar were of silk and cloth.

But she was a *seanchaidh*, not a seamstress. How long must she be a hostage in Malcolm's court—and worse, in a ladies' stitchery circle?

EVA STOOD IN THE cool morning air watching Ruari and the other men of Moray readying to depart. She wrapped her arms around herself, suddenly and desperately lonely, wanting to ride away with them. While Ruari paused to check his horse's harness, she ran toward him.

"Take me with you," she blurted. "We have been here a month. Do not leave me here."

He smoothed the blanket under the saddle. "We have no choice; you know that. And Lady Rue expects you to do as she has asked."

"Spy for her?" Eva hissed.

A muscle pulsed in his cheek. "Listen and learn while you are here. Send word when you have something to share. Take this"—he handed her a small leather pouch jingling with coins—"and use it to pay messengers and purchase ink and parchment. Send your sealed letters to Abbot Drostan at Loch Leven. He will see to the rest."

Pocketing the coins, pouting like a child, Eva knew she could not win the argument. "Then give this to my grandmother. I wrote down all I have learned here so far," she said, handing him a folded parchment on which she had inked all the news she had. "I have heard of no designs on Moray," she spoke softly. "The queen is lovely and kind, does needlework, and prays a good deal. She has a temper—but so does Lady Gruadh. I have heard no mention of a secret book, but the queen's own books are prettily painted and she reads to us daily. I am asked to play harp and to sew stitches. Though a hostage and a *spy*," she added in a fierce whisper, "I hear nothing of any use to Moray. Tell her there is no need for spying here. Tell her I wish to come home."

"Watch your words," Ruari whispered, glancing around. "Very well, I will give her this. She will cherish it and wait for more—not for secrets, but because it comes from you."

Tears sprang to her eyes. Impulsively, Eva stood on her toes to hug Ruari and kiss his cheek, while he patted her back. "Be safe," he said gruffly.

Nodding, she stepped back and hastened away. She lacked her grandmother's strength to stand and watch while they left her alone here.

❧

THUNDERSTORMS RUMBLED OVERHEAD one afternoon as Margaret sat at a table in the great hall playing a game of chess with Malcolm, who had been surprised when she had suggested it. He and De Lauder had returned a little earlier with several hares brought down by their hawks before the rain swept through, and his hair was still damp, though he had changed to dry clothing. He sipped ale with one beefy hand wrapped around a wooden cup, and he picked at a dish of sweetmeats, which he now offered to Margaret.

She shook her head, for she never indulged in the honey-crusted almonds and hazelnuts. As Malcolm popped one handful after another into his mouth, she thought of her father and had to resist reaching out to stop her husband, who did not know quite how her father had died. Sweetmeats always made her feel ill—but her stomach had been very uneasy of late, so that she could tolerate only small helpings and mild dishes. Besides, a queen should not show too healthy an appetite in front of others, and she had always been taught to eat delicately. Malcolm ate with noisy abandon, even though his manners were improving.

He moved another piece on the board, and Margaret contemplated in silence, hands folded calmly. Nearby, Hector played his harp, while Lady Eva sat at the other end of the table, talking quietly with a Lowland thane, one of the guests who had been hunting with Malcolm that day. Margaret could not recall his name, but remembered that he owned property along the English border. He was also a leering old man who pressed closer to Eva while the girl leaned away.

Margaret beckoned to Wilfrid. "Bid Lady Eva come sit by me," she said, "and tell her that we would like her to grace us with a song or two." As Wilfrid delivered the message, Margaret saw the relief on Eva's face. Within moments, she joined Margaret and the king, though she sat on a stool near them and watched the board game in silence. Malcolm kept glancing at the Moray girl as if he was deeply curious about her, but he said nothing to her, nor she to him. Margaret sensed a cold barrier between them like a wall, and knew there must be anger on both sides.

She turned her attention back to the board. She had not yet demonstrated her skill at chess, which she had learned from her father, and had perfected with various opponents in King Edward's court. Soon she trounced Malcolm with ease and a little thrill of pleasure.

"Aha! Excellent," he allowed. "I did not expect that from a lady who once wished to enter a convent." He grinned.

"Should I know only prayers and devotional quotations? I am well schooled, and chess is a scholarly game. Besides, chess skills are quite useful for a queen of Scotland."

"Queen of Scots," he corrected. "In Scotland we rule people, not land."

"I have not been crowned, so I am only a consort," she pointed out.

"Aye, but you would wear any title and crown well," he replied, watching her for a moment, so that she felt a little thrill that had nothing to do with her chess victory. Then he rose from his seat, ignoring Lady Eva, grabbed the dish of sweetmeats, and walked over to join a few housecarls who were seated at another table, drinking wine and rolling dice.

Margaret began putting the chess pieces away in a leather bag, and Eva came to help, plucking up the pieces from the board.

"A queen should not have to do this." Eva smiled and dropped the two queens into the sack.

"My husband reminds me that I do not even know my own title." Margaret sighed.

"No matter. You won the game and showed the king your worth."

"A queen cannot be found wanting in chess, or anything else."

"Aye?" Eva glanced up. "But losing a chess game is no flaw. Many cannot play at all."

"A queen must be exemplary in all she does." Margaret took the bag from Eva and hung its cord on a little hook attached to the chess table where the heavy stone board rested. "Thank you. Will you give us a song?"

"Gladly, unless you think Hector would be offended. I am found wanting in his eyes, I think." She rose to her feet. "Perhaps a lively song would help on such a dreary day."

When Eva smiled, her lovely face turned winsome and dimpled, and lit her like a candle from within. Margaret smiled and sat back to wait as Eva walked away to speak quietly with Hector. He nodded and left the dais, and Eva took the stool and settled with her harp, which had been perched on another stool.

As the dulcet notes floated outward and filled the room, gradually the others paused to listen, smiling, turning their attention to the bard. Margaret felt the music all through her, a sense of gentle warmth like a soft cloak covering her. The next melody was exquisite and enticing, and Margaret closed her eyes for a moment as the music poured over her, cascading from the brass and golden strings of the beautiful harp.

The girl was skillful and very sure of her music, which flowed outward, entrancing. Then Margaret sat straighter, suddenly afraid to be lured in, as if the girl spun some old form of magic that might enchant those who listened. So Margaret sat stiffly, appearing impervious, smiling coolly, and though the music's beauty made her burn with a sort of impulsive joy, she would not fold against it, but clasped her hands and kept perfectly still.

Chapter Ten

*To the hand of her lord, the first cup of all
Straightaway she shall give.*

—*The Exeter Book*, ANGLO-SAXON,
NINTH CENTURY

The king came blustering into the hall one rainy afternoon after another absence of more than a fortnight, accompanied by a dozen men and the dogs who were always excited to see the men return. The day's mist seemed to blow inside with them, along with the chaos and noise that often surrounded Malcolm like a whirlwind. Margaret looked up from where she sat at the table with Dame Agnes and a few of her ladies, counting neatly folded linens and newly polished pewter and glass goblets. As the brawny king came toward her, she realized that since their wedding a few months earlier, she had spent more time with the courtiers and servants than with her own husband.

Well enough, she thought, for there was always much work for her to do at Dunfermline, and she had been busy of late supervising more improvements. Malcolm stopped in the middle of the room and looked about the hall, with its whitewashed walls hung with embroidered panels, its freshly swept floors and rearranged furnishings, and she saw him note further changes since the last time he had been at home. Glowering, he spun about.

"Margaret!" he thundered.

"I'm here, my lord." Smiling, she stood as he came toward her. On the table beside her were some goblets that were now kept available for the king's male guests, rather than the drinking horns normally used— glass goblets banded in silver, made in Germany, that were part of Margaret's dowry. Choosing a stemmed chalice, she filled it from a leather bladder of Rhenish wine and held it out for her husband.

Ever since the day De Lauder had spoken to her about her purpose in Scotland, she had given her role careful thought as she made changes to the king's tower. Now she saw another way to improve the tone of courtesy at the Scottish court.

"My lord king," she said, extending the full cup toward Malcolm. "Welcome home."

"Lady." Malcolm looked surprised, tipping his head, but he took the cup from her hands and swallowed a few times, handing it back to her with a low rumble of thanks. He shoved down the mailed hood of his mesh hauberk and began to turn away.

Margaret set a hand on his arm, cool woven steel under her fingers. "Sire, take the cup and share it round with the others. It is a *poculum caritatis.*"

"A what?" He cocked a thick eyebrow. "A love cup? What the devil—"

"It is a loving cup when shared before a meal, and a grace cup when shared afterward." She handed the goblet back to him. "It was a tradition much honored in King Edward's court," she said.

"Aye?" Instantly he looked interested. Whatever a Saxon king had done, Malcolm cared to do also, Margaret knew. The king's own ambition would facilitate her self-appointed task of improving Malcolm's manners and household.

"Please, sire, pass it along to the next man. Let it go from lip to lip and back again to us, as our gesture of welcome when guests come to our hall."

Malcolm snugged his brows together like a child determined to master something new as he took the cup and passed it to Angus, the mormaer of Mar, who stood within arm's reach. The man was as heavily armored, sweaty, and muddy as the king and the others, but he took the cup, looking slightly puzzled as well.

"Drink and give it to the next man," Malcolm urged.

The cup went from man to man, and once it was returned to her, Margaret drained the last few drops of wine and set the cup down. She caught De Lauder's gaze as he nodded approval.

"Welcome home to Dunfermline, sire, and everyone," she said, offering her arm to Malcolm. Looking pleased, he led her toward the dais and the two high-backed carved chairs there.

The hour was too early for supper, so the trestle tables were not yet set up. The amber glow of a lingering sunset poured through narrow open windows, and some of the housecarls and courtiers who had business with the king entered the hall. Margaret looked at Malcolm.

"Sire, did my brother return with you?" she asked, for she had not seen him.

"Edgar is riding with Ranald mac Niall and others, not far behind us. They will arrive before midnight, I think." He glanced around the room. "You have changed things again, and for the better. But—Margaret—where the devil are my grandfather's swords?"

"I had those moved, sire. I did not think they should hang here, over our heads."

"Ah," he murmured. "You could be right. The improvements are. . . good, my dear."

She smiled, a little surprised by that. Then she noticed that some of those gathered in the hall now looked toward her as if waiting for her to signal what would come next, whether audiences or a meal. Malcolm, too, looked toward her expectantly.

With sudden clarity, she realized that she was truly regarded as a wife and a queen now. That status had not begun with the wedding,

or on the marital night, or with the assigning of household responsibilities. Rather it seemed to have taken hold just moments ago, when
she had acted deliberately as both chatelaine and queen. She felt a
little stirring of purpose, an elation similar to praying, and far more
than rote responsibility. That revelation filled her like a light.

MALCOLM AND HIS MEN rode out almost daily and otherwise
remained closeted with his council, a group that included Edgar and the
Saxons, most of whom came and went from Dunfermline now, having
renewed ties in England with their journeys south; they included Morcar,
his brother Edwin, and others. Margaret was glad to see the Saxons' influence over Edgar lessening as he spent more time in Malcolm's company;
the king was now his brother by law and so Edgar turned to him for
advice and tutoring in leadership. Relieved somewhat in her natural worry
over Edgar, she still fretted for his safety and because of his gullibility.

When the men gathered with the king, whether Scots or Saxons, a
cleric wrote out documents to which Margaret was rarely privy, for the
matters were either Scottish or, if Saxon, highly secret. Priests and bishops arrived, too, though more often than not, Malcolm discussed taxes
and laws, judicial rights, and legal disputes in meetings that at times
went deep into the night.

Debates would grow so hot, particularly if Normans were mentioned, that Margaret could hear the men shouting either from the anteroom that also served as a chapel, or in the king's bedchamber, or in the
great hall, where they gathered late at night. In the small hours when
she rose for prayers, she could hear voices still rumbling like thunder.

She usually slipped from bed to take to her knees in the bedchamber,
whether alone or if Malcolm slept beside her. When she felt a need for a
deeper, more fervent appeal, she would send a maid to fetch Lady Eva.
The Scottish girl would come bleary-eyed and uncomplaining from bed,
a plaid wrapped around her shoulders, her raven gloss hair mussed, her
cheeks pink, so lovely even in that state——and so unaware of it——that
Margaret tried to avoid the men who might wander out of the intense
meetings with the king. Eva of Moray could be temptation for a man,

Margaret knew, and so she decided to cast a watchful eye over her newest lady, summoning her into her company more often. Besides, she enjoyed the girl's forthrightness as much as her harp music.

Daily, Margaret attended to managing the royal household, ordering changes, and reviewing written records that Dame Agnes and Wilfrid, too, presented for the accounting of the so-called queen's gold, the income from properties in Scotland now assigned to her keeping. She received individuals and small groups who arrived at Dunfermline to request the queen's mercy and generosity, and she continually relied on the advice and the company of her expanding circle of ladies. More women had arrived at court since the wedding, and they were often invaluable in helping with Margaret's responsibilities in reviewing storage rooms and evaluating linens and blankets, dishes, and household items. Gradually, with the help of Dame Agnes, her women, and Agnes's husband, Arthur, a stern and acerbic steward who rarely spoke, Margaret was becoming familiar with the contents of every room, chest, and cupboard in the king's tower. And Malcolm had made it clear that he did not much care what changes and decisions she made, so long as the needs of court and king were satisfied.

"I believe," she told her ladies one day, "that Dunfermline needs more elegance. Finer plate for table and hall, more tapestries and cushions, and new furnishings to suit a royal household."

"We still have things packed away in chests," Cristina reminded her. "There is gold and silver plate wrapped up, along with cups and dishes and sacred vessels."

"We will need those," Margaret said. "And I will order more from the trade ships."

"With so many poor in Scotland, perhaps you should not be seen to indulge your whims by purchasing new goods," Cristina said.

"I understand that there are poor folk in the king's realm, but even so, a king's house must reflect his status. It helps reassure the people. A threadbare king will not make his people feel secure, especially in time of war."

For the comfort of the growing circle of ladies, Margaret requested more chairs and benches, for they worked diligently at their needle-work. Some, such as Edith and Gudrun, had small children, so a little nursery grew at Dunfermline, too, even without royal children.

"That is your most important duty," Lady Agatha reminded her one day as Margaret held Dolfin, Edith's youngest, in her lap. "You must allow the king his privileges, but for the time each month that he must leave you be. Hopefully those days will soon end for you," she said meaningfully, "when you find yourself with child. When you have produced an heir or two, perhaps a daughter as well, then you may refuse him. You may even request your own bedchamber and a separate household if you wish. It is often done." She smiled tightly.

"We have been married but a few months. You never separated yourself from your own husband," Margaret pointed out.

"My marriage was agreeable, thank the saints. Your father, God rest him, was a considerate man. But many women live apart from their husbands once they do what is expected of them. You may find it better to . . . keep apart from such a savage Scot," she whispered.

Lady Edith, seated beside Lady Agatha, laughed. "It is not so bad as your mother suggests, dear queen. How you blush!"

Let them think what they would, Margaret decided. She would not disclose that she found the marriage bed more than pleasant. Nei-ther would she tell them what she already suspected: that she was with child, and had been since nearly the first, a suspicion that each passing day confirmed. She had kept it from her women, but soon enough Kata would realize it, and then they would all know.

And the more she lay with Malcolm, the more she savored secret touches and silent permissions, and the unexpected comfort of his warm, strong form beside her. The physical act was usually quickly done, sometimes leaving her strangely yearning, uncertain of the rem-edy except that she wanted to allow more. By the time Malcolm was snoring, she would sleep a little, or she would rise in the dark to pray at the hours of matins and lauds. She woke regularly to pray at the canonical hours, and did not want to lose that discipline, certain that her soul would suffer if she grew lazy and too comfortable.

But that curtained bed offered a darkened *hortus conclusus*, hiding what her husband offered and she willingly allowed. Giving him all his will so that she could conceive a child, she felt something of his passion echo through her, a hot joy that was powerful and compelling—but she would not give that rein. He touched, he savored with expressive groans and whispers, while she enjoyed, breathless but craving in silence—and did not refuse, though it cost her in prayers later.

She wished desperately for a child to prove to herself that what they did was not sinful.

Time told soon enough, and now she was well along with child. She had been feeling ill in the mornings and sometimes at night, she had a taut thickening in her lower belly, and her breasts were full, tender. And she was yawning, pale, and even less inclined to eat.

Gathering courage, she went to her mother and told her. Lady Agatha seemed pleased—she rarely saw her mother smile and saw only a glimmer of that now—and said that Margaret must not let her husband mount her any longer. But she liked the comfort he gave her, and she did not tell him yet.

Soon the other women knew, too, excited but discreet. Lady Eva said little, but one day brought her harp to the solar and played and sang what she said was an old Gaelic lullaby. The exquisite melody brought tears to Margaret's eyes, and she asked to hear it again, wanting to learn the song to sing to her own little one.

"My dear," Lady Agatha cautioned one day, "remember that a woman must not express too much joy or anticipation over a child until it is born healthy and thrives."

Lady Edith brought little Dolfin to the queen's circle. Willful and affectionate, prone to messy kisses and stubborn demands, he climbed into Margaret's lap and seemed content in her company. That gave her joy, and she began to look forward to her own child, hoping that her babe would be healthy, despite the fears her mother introduced.

She prayed daily for its protection, and she asked Eva again for the lullaby, which she learned to sing softly.

WHEN MARGARET FELT the delicate fluttering that meant the child was healthy and vigorous within her, she knew she must tell Malcolm what she had withheld. That night when he rolled toward her, his hands hot and eager, she told him the reason he should not, could not now.

He upped on an elbow in the darkness. "So! Good! Are you well?"

"I am. The babe will come at the end of the year or just after, I believe."

"A son," he said, rolling back on the pillows. She could hear the grin. "A strong son!"

"The babe could be female," she pointed out.

"God gives me sons. I have three or four already, and we will have more."

Now she sat up. "Several? I have heard of two."

"Duncan and Donald, aye. Ingebjorg's sons. I have another two—or it is three?" He grinned.

"What! You should know!" Margaret burst out. He did not answer, and she wondered if he kept a mistress, even now, with a new bride. "Where are your sons? How old are they?"

"Inga's sons are nine, I think, and five. Old enough to be fostered out, as is the custom here, though it is early for the youngest, but we arranged it. Angus of Mar keeps Donald, the youngest, and my brother, Donal, mormaer of the Isles, has Duncan, the elder. I have two other sons elsewhere, grown men, housecarls in Atholl, northwest of here. I do not see them much. As bastards, they will inherit property from me, but no throne. Good young warriors," he admitted with a grunt.

"Bring Ingebjorg's sons to court. I am a stepmother and soon to be a mother, and I will have our children know one another. Then they may not be rivals in the future if questions arise over who shall be king and who shall be less than that. I have asked this before, sire."

He sighed. "True. I see that Margaret's sons will have an ambitious mother," he teased.

"I would defend any of them," she said, not laughing. "I want to meet Inga's sons."

"Very well, I will have them brought here. They are good lads, handsome and dark as their mother. And more spirited."

"Well, they are young boys," she said pragmatically. "What was their mother like?"

"Loved God and despised me," he said. "I killed her husband, with whom she had a heart match. Lulach was a fine warrior, but he called himself king when Scotland belonged to me."

"A heart match," Margaret repeated softly. She and Malcolm did not have such—very few noble couples did. For a moment she yearned . . . then gathered her wits. What use wasting good thoughts on unattainable things? "Why did you kill Lulach?" She shuddered. "The life that some men lead, as warlords reckoning hard with each other so that death is incidental rather than a heinous sin to regret all one's life—it is not easy to understand."

"It was a necessity. Killing in war is waived by the Church, I understand, with certain penances. Never bothered much with those," he said. "No time for such fuss. I will take my chances with hell."

Margaret stared, hardly knowing how to answer. "What of Lulach?"

"I had the right to be king. My great-grandfather, also called Malcolm, and my father, Duncan, ruled Scotland one after the other. Macbeth bested Duncan, hand to hand, and took the crown, so when I was old enough—my kinsmen made sure of it—I pursued Macbeth for his treachery and finally took him down as he deserved. Lulach claimed the throne that was mine, with the backing of the northern leaders. I took him down, too, and claimed his queen as my right, and got two princes upon her." He seemed proud of that, puffed up by it.

"Poor Ingebjorg, to be taken from her home and married against her will," she said, feeling wholly sympathetic.

"She was treated well, and we made a certain peace between us. She bore a third child, but lost it and took ill, and asked to retire to a convent. I sent her to Northumbria. She did not last long after that," he added, nearly a mutter.

"God rest her. She was Norse?"

"Aye, the daughter of a jarl of Orkney. Thorfin was his name."

"Were you fond of her?" Truly, she wanted to know.

"She gave me sons," he said, as if that explained it all. "She was a gentle girl. When she was ill, she asked me—" He stopped. "She wanted news of her two children with Lulach, a boy and a girl, but their kin had hidden them away in the north. I would not help her find them."

"That was harsh," Margaret said quickly. "Where are they now?"

"With Lady Gruadh, their grandmother, as far as I know. Nechtan is the son."

"Of course! So they are Eva's half siblings? Did she know Queen Ingebjorg?"

"I cannot say. Her grandmother would like to stir rebellion on behalf of Nechtan mac Lulach. He would be about fifteen now, I think."

"A little younger than Edgar." Her heart ached for Ingebjorg's children. "Send for your sons, the two little princes. They are young enough to need a stepmother rather than fostering, and they should know their father. I want your promise that they will be brought here soon."

Malcolm chuckled. "You will be a lioness of a mother, I think."

DUNCAN AND DONALD arrived within a week of each other, when late summer bloomed lush and the sky glowed pale violet well into the night. The younger, Donald, came with his foster father, Angus of Mar, whose daughter was one of Margaret's ladies and whose eldest son was among Malcolm's guards. At five, Donald looked about with great dark eyes, brave but wary, and showed keener interest in the wolfhound's pups than anything else.

Duncan, the elder at nearly ten, arrived a week later with a party of Highlanders led by his uncle, Donal Ban. Malcolm's older son had his father's curling red-brown hair, stubborn jaw, and broad build. He responded politely to Margaret, but his gaze followed Malcolm. He had no interest in a stepmother when his father was a warrior-king.

With relief, Margaret noted that Eva took time to show the boys a kind welcome, speaking to them in their native language, for both princes were fostered in Gaelic-speaking households. Eva explained to the queen that the boys were kin to her Moray family, for they shared a mother with her half siblings. Margaret relied on Eva's help as translator as she got to know her husband's sons.

Their uncle, Donal Ban, stayed a fortnight, and Margaret never wished so hard that someone would leave her home. Malcolm and Donal argued at every turn, in council, at supper, in the training yard, despite their claims that they supported each other as king and noble. A mormaer in the western isles, Donal was as large as his brother, though blond, and the ire in his brown eyes was so formidable that Margaret avoided him.

"Ban means 'fair one,' " Malcolm told her. "And he might be fair where I am ugly—but I am king, and he is not." He laughed bitterly. Years of separation after the death of their father, King Duncan, when Donal was raised in the Hebrides and Malcolm in Northumbria, had not fostered brotherhood. But both knew the value of their alliance.

Margaret became so determined that her child and Malcolm's offspring would be close brothers that she assigned Duncan and Donald a small bedchamber with one manservant between them and requested that Father Otto tutor them together. And she asked Malcolm to order his swordmaster and housecarls to train the boys at weapons together as well.

"They are of different ages and skills," he argued. "Duncan is ready for more challenge."

"They must learn to protect each other. And I want them to stay here until our child is born, and as long as they can after that. Promise me." The more the swell of her belly showed, the more she discovered that Malcolm was prone to grant her requests.

"Very well, but you must not coddle and spoil them. They should be allies as men, true, for one day the eldest will be king and his brothers must support him."

"I hoped that one of our sons would be king someday," Margaret said.

"My older sons were born of a legitimate queen. My father and grandfather fought to establish primogeniture—the right of firstborn to inherit the throne—in Scotland, when the Celtic system of alternating kinsmen was the tradition. And so we follow primogeniture now."

"Our son's blood will be the more royal," she said, "with the kings of Scotland and Ireland on your side and kings of Wessex, Hungary, and Russia on mine."

"They will all be worthy kings, Margaret," he said. "Each one has a right. Let God determine some of this, eh?"

But she felt an irresistible urge to protect her unborn child, an undeniable ambition on its behalf. Her heart quickened with that, even as her child turned and grew within.

FOCUSED ON THE INTRICATE fingering of a melody on the harp, Eva tried not to think about the loneliness she felt, the yearning for home that had not cleared as quickly as she had hoped. With the king away again, the queen was hosting a small supper for her kinfolk and ladies and a few others. When her song ended, Eva sat at the table with the queen and the rest, nodding thanks at compliments, and sipped a little wine. She ate some hot soup, too, a beef stock thick with onions, as conversations went on around her. Listening, she was poised to remember anything of interest for her kin in the north. She disliked the assignment, but it was hers to do.

Margaret spoke with the Benedictine priest and the Celtic priest about theological matters that Eva did not completely follow. The queen showed impressive knowledge, even wisdom, for one so young, quoting scripture and flowing easily from Latin to English. When Brother Micheil's English failed him in a complex answer, he turned to Eva.

"Please," he said in Gaelic, "explain, for I do not have the English for it, that we Scots do not disrespect Rome, as this Benedictine thinks, simply because we do not follow the Roman rite. Tell them clear as you can that we have the Irish rite, the Scottish, the Welsh, and so on. What we practice in Scotland began in Ireland hundreds of years ago, nurtured by Patrick and Columba and conveyed to Scotland. Remind the priest, and the queen, too, that we are very far away from Rome, and so our tenets support the Gaels as well as Mother Church. Tell them," he urged.

"I will," Eva agreed, and patiently translated what he had said. The queen nodded and was about to reply when Father Otto, who also listened, interrupted.

"*Scottorum toti mundo contrarii, moribus Romanis inimici, non solum in misa sed in tonsura etiam,*" the priest said. "Scots are contrary to the whole world, so said the good Gildas, who also cautioned that the Scots go against the Roman rite in many of their practices."

"Who is Gildas?" Eva asked.

"A learned scholar who lived long ago," Margaret answered. "I have read his history. He had little praise for the Celtic style of worship. Yet I do see the worth in many of the Irish and Scottish rites, and I want to know more."

"We should all be concerned," Father Otto said, holding up a lecturing finger, "about the danger to the souls of the Celtic people if they do not follow proper forms determined by Rome. On the final Day of Judgment, they will wish they had obeyed. And the Scots must change their ways for political reasons, too, if they want the support and respect of the rest of the world."

Brother Micheil sat straight. "Our tenets are spiritual and worthy," he argued.

"They are," Margaret said hastily. "The differences are small, yet significant."

"What differences?" Eva asked, intrigued.

"The calculation of the date of Easter each year, which changes, is one dispute," Margaret told her. "The day Lent begins is another. The fast must be forty days according to the Church, but from what I understand, the Celtic calculation comes out to thirty-five days, as they do not count Sundays and begin on Thursday rather than Ash Wednesday."

"Does that matter so much, if the intent is clear?" Eva asked.

"Christ did not take Sundays off from fasting in the wilderness," Father Otto said crisply. "Also, the Celtic monks shave their heads from ear to ear and do not look like monks. The Scottish church differs in the rite of baptism, too. And it is quite shocking to see men and women sharing monasteries here, with women allowed positions of authority over men. Not to mention," he said, "the prayers in Gaelic."

Eva frowned. "Can we not delight in our differences and learn from each other for the good of all?"

Margaret raised her brows, looking thoughtful. But Father Otto waved a hand as if Eva had spoken pure babble. "There are some barbarian practices in parts of Scotland that should be corrected for the good of all."

"Our church is not barbarian, but dedicated to deepening our knowledge and to celebrating the beauty in all aspects of holy studies and traditions," Micheil said.

"Outdoor masses are spoken beneath stone crosses carved with pagan symbols," Father Otto said. "Surely you can understand why some of these things must be changed."

"Beauty and artistry are considered close to God here, and we honor the ancient traditions of the Gaels by blending the new form with the old," Eva argued. "And we pray in our own beautiful language, for that is closer to our hearts, and adds to the teachings of the Church."

"Truly, it is a lovely thought," Margaret told Father Otto.

"Beauty is a luxury and vanity. We must turn our thoughts to proper worship."

As the discussion continued, Eva thought of the leather writing case that Lady Gruadh had given her, along with parchment scraps, a little pot of ink, sealing wax, and feather quills with sharp nibs. Her grand-mother wanted news: perhaps Eva could tell her of this. But though it might be loyal to tell Gruadh what she heard, it also felt like a betrayal of the young queen, who had shown her kindness.

Besides, she told herself, her grandmother awaited a report with sub-stance: fuel for rebellion. Sending any news of the court was a risk, but so far, Eva could say little more than that the foreign queen was beauti-ful, educated, and intelligent; that she could debate with learned priests and was gentle and charitable; she was strict about fasting and prayer; and that she was quick and healthy with a child. Still, Lady Gruadh would relish knowing that her successor was sometimes temperamental and demanding, or that she knew no Gaelic, and insisted that the king wash regularly and wear nicer garments.

There was little to report of Malcolm, beyond that he rode off fre-quently with the prince of England and a host of men, going south to play havoc and to skirmish with Normans. Eva had seen some evidence in support of Lady Gruadh's belief that Margaret plotted a religious and cultural reform, but not to Scotland's ruin. Margaret seemed inter-ested only in improving the Scots' chances in heaven and reputation in the earthly world. And it was all talk, so far as she could see. The only true changes were domestic improvements to the king's tower and household.

News of Ingebjorg's two little sons by Malcolm would interest Gruadh, she decided. The two little boys remained at Dunfermline, smart lads being tutored up for leadership, and plans were for them to stay with their father and stepmother at least until Margaret's winter confinement and probably longer. Margaret, who had quickly become fond of the boys, knew the value of family not only for the children but for Malcolm's image as king, too. Gruadh had worried some about Ingebjorg's sons, so news of their well-being would be worth precious ink and parchment.

As for the manuscript Malcolm had commissioned, Eva had heard nothing about it. Yet she had been at court for months, and must send word of what she knew, fulfilling at least some part of her promise.

Keeping a late hour that night while Wynne and Matilda slept soundly on their cots, Eva wrote out all she knew for Gruadh. The nib of her quill whispered over the parchment piece, and at last she sanded it, blowing gently, folded it, and sealed it with a blob of wax, into which she pressed part of her cloak brooch. Her grandmother would recognize the pattern in the curve as belonging to Eva.

The next day during breakfast, Eva stood pouring some warm, greatly diluted spiced wine into cups for Lady Juliana and another of the ladies. She looked up just as a man entered the hall to speak with Sir Wilfrid and Robert De Lauder. Early that morning she had noticed several men arriving in the courtyard, dismounting to walk toward the tower for a meeting with the king, but she thought little of it. Now she looked more closely at the older man, a fierce warrior, gray and past his prime yet still powerfully built.

And she gasped, suddenly recognizing her great-uncle, Kenneth Macduff, mormaer of Fife. When Wilfrid pointed toward the other end of the room where Eva stood, Macduff nodded and crossed the space with a sure and heavy stride.

Eva stepped away from the other women to greet him more privately in the open middle of the great room. Years had passed since she had last seen him. He had sent her out of Fife and to Moray when she was eight years old and orphaned, and had not inquired after her since. Given that dubious gesture of affection, she was not sure what to say to him now.

Nodding, Macduff paused a few feet away, for all his brawn and natural authority looking oddly like a sheepish boy afraid to come closer. Eva crossed her hands calmly in front of her. She had learned a little grace from Queen Margaret already, she thought, lifting her head.

"Uncle," she said quietly.

"Eva, it is good to see you again," he said in Gaelic, his voice rumbling low. "You have grown to beauty. You are . . . so like your mother." He smiled a bit sadly.

"And my father," she amended, not meaning her reply to sound quite as sharp as it did. "You did not send greetings when I arrived here in court. Perhaps you did not know." Surely he did, she thought, if he was free to ride into the yard just after dawn and be accepted straightaway for an audience with the king. He knew the king's business.

"I heard so, but I was not free to travel to Dunfermline until now. I came as soon as I could. Eva, I have the king's promise that you will be well treated in his custody."

"You know my circumstances, then?" She felt a flush brightening her cheeks.

"I do. And I support his decision. Your grandmother has played the thorn in Malcolm's side too often. All of Moray will take care with you in the king's keeping. You do understand that."

"Partly," she said. "The greater part of me just wants to go home." Saying the words suddenly made her feel like weeping; her breath caught. "Can you speak to the king about that?"

He shook his head. "This is necessary."

"You were never much inclined to watch over me," she answered flatly.

"I knew you would do well in Moray. It was a good place for you to grow." He smiled a little. "You would not have become such a renowned harper without your grandmother's coddling."

"My mother was the first to teach me," she pointed out. Macduff looked away at that, and an awkward silence filled the space between them.

"Eva," he said then. "I sent you to Moray to protect you . . . from him." He tilted his head toward the door, as if to indicate the lord of the house, the king. "At the time, I feared for you, as the only one of Lulach's pups within reach."

"I never knew," she said, watching him intently then, with a sort of hunger to hear more. "Why did you not tell me?"

"Tell a small girl that the king might harm her? I gave you up. It was necessary."

Now it was her turn for silence, for glancing away. "Thank you."

"I sent word," he said. "I sent gifts. Did you like them? The black pup, the dappled pony?"

"I never knew they were from you," she said, astonished. The hound and the pony were at Elgin still, favorite companions since her child-hood.

He nodded once, curtly. "I am not surprised. Well." He blew out a breath. "Eva, I would like to hear you play for the king's company this evening, but I have some business elsewhere." He reached out a hand, broad and weathered.

She slid her fingers into his and felt a grip that was strong, warm, rough. Protective somehow, she thought. "Thank you, Uncle."

"No need. I come to court now and then. We will visit again."

"I am certain to be here," she said, "at least for a while." He smiled a little, and turned to leave.

Before the ladies left the great hall, Eva saw Sir Wilfrid speaking to a young messenger, handing him some rolled documents that Margaret had signed. Minutes later, Eva hurried out to the bailey to walk alone, desperately in need of a little air for an aching head, she had told the queen's ladies. Seeing the messenger about to mount his horse, she crossed toward him.

"Sir," she said, knowing that would flatter him, for he was that young, though old enough to messenger alone. He turned to look at her. "Do you ride north?"

"I do," he said. "I am to carry messages from the queen to her tenant farmers."

Eva had hoped that would be the case. "I have another note for you to carry," she said, showing him her parchment, folded into a tight, thick square. "It must go to Loch Leven, to the monastery there. Do you know it?"

"Of course I know it. Saint Serf's." He took the packet. "I need more than the usual fee, as I must pay the ferryman to cross over. Unless you wish the ferryman to deliver it to the gate."

"You take it in directly," she said urgently, certain that so far no one had noticed a young woman talking to a young man on that bright, cool morning, as the servants and housecarls were busy with their various tasks. The horse sidestepped, its flank further hiding Eva from sight.

"This must go into the hands of the abbot of Saint Serf's, and only him. Drostan is his name."

The boy frowned. "I will do nothing devious. What is this?" He turned the parchment over.

"It concerns myself, my religious mentor, and God. Will you read a list of my sins, when the abbot of Saint Serf's himself waits for it?" At least part of that was true, she thought.

"I cannot read. This will cost you the riding fee and the ferry."

She pressed silver into his palm, the coins chinking. "Please tell the abbot that I am doing my very best here in all ways." She turned and fled, crossing the bailey to arrive in the corridor as Margaret and her ladies were leaving the great hall.

"Eva! Your cheeks are pink and your eyes are so bright!" Margaret smiled. "The high color suits you. Come, walk with me. I want to hear more about the Gaelic north, and you are the perfect person to tell me. If I can learn a little more about their history and their customs, I can better understand the Scots and their church, too. And I do so want to understand." She smiled and tucked her hand into Eva's arm, drawing her along. "I heard your uncle was here today. Did you enjoy a good reunion?"

"We did," Eva said, and left it at that.

Chapter Eleven

※

There is one from whom I would love a long look
For whom I would give the whole world

—Irish, seventh century

Autumn overtook summer's bloom, and Malcolm's sons stayed on. Donal Ban rode off before harvest time after a dispute so loud, with fists pounding tables, that Margaret winced as she heard it above stairs. She breathed a sigh of relief to see Donal gone, and though Malcolm stormed about, he calmed after a few days, saying that the boys would remain with him until the new one was born at year's end. The uncle wanted the oldest, Duncan, returned to him sooner. Malcolm had refused. Mar, who kept small Donald, waited amiably on the king's will.

Malcolm took time to visit many of his properties, including the grand fortress at Dun Edin across the wide firth, as well as his other royal properties throughout Scotland. But Margaret could not travel and felt disappointed, for she was impatient to see more of the land and to meet Scots beyond Dunfermline and Fife.

"After the child is born," Malcolm promised, "we will go on prog-ress for you to see our other residences and the whole of the land. I want the Scots to meet their new queen."

She felt tired but well, and kept pace with prayers and household duties. As chatelaine of the king's households, she had much to do. But one day she felt such a headache upon standing that she collapsed to the floor. A day's rest cured it, and she resumed her routines, reassuring others that she was strong, and telling herself that she must keep to her prayers and duties equally.

Malcolm went south and returned with a physician, a surly Saxon who thought much of his abilities. He had been ousted from Northum-bria with thousands of others, and hoped for a place in the royal house-hold. But when Master Bartholomew questioned Margaret closely in pri-vate and asked to see a cup of her urine, she refused. When he informed her that her strict habits would harm her babe, she was both offended and alarmed. She would never compromise her child's welfare, but feared slacking off of her obligations and the regular penances and light fasts that kept her, so she hoped, cleansed in soul and body.

"I will not see him again," she told Malcolm. "I have no need. I have my women, and I have my priests." Within days, she learned that the physician had boarded a knorr for Flanders, with a note of praise from Malcolm and a bag of coins on his belt.

"No physicians, then," Malcolm told her, "but you must give up fasts. Even Brother Micheil and Father Otto have mentioned this to me. You are too thin for a woman bearing a child."

"I eat sparingly but well," she said in defense. "And I tend to my prayers and fasts as I see fit."

But she noticed that Malcolm sometimes served her with his own hand an extra portion or a sweetmeat at the table. She could never bring herself to taste another sweetmeat after her father's passing, but she nib-bled other foods to please Malcolm. Her stomach had always been a little finicky and discontented after eating certain foods. But sometimes she simply felt the need for more penance—her temper had grown short of late and she could not tolerate that, even in herself—and so she sometimes fed the dogs under the table rather than eat the food herself.

Eva, seeing this, whispered to her to stop. "The dogs have had enough," she said. "You have not."

"A little edge of hunger keeps me vigilant," Margaret confided. "It reminds me that some do not eat as well as we do here. Besides, my figure is too full, too lush and earthy of late."

"It is as it should be," Eva said. "Take care."

But Margaret felt compelled—she could not eat more, could not indulge herself, and needed to keep to her strict regimen. Something within her demanded it.

With her kinswomen and her ladies, she left Dunfermline now and then to visit nearby sites, agreeing to travel by cart just to get beyond the confines of fortress and glen. Accompanied by Brother Micheil or Malcolm's housecarls, she visited chapels and hilltop crosses and sites that boasted of long-ago saints. With or without their holy history, the places were remarkable to her for their natural beauty, and she looked forward to seeing more of what had become her adopted homeland, though her advancing pregnancy curtailed her travel soon enough.

Yet she felt in good health, and gradually tried to eat more, certainly sleeping more than was her habit. Carrying a child suited her, made her calmer; even her mother commented kindly on it. When she developed a taste for hot, crisp oatcakes and cooked carrots, the increased appetite embarrassed her.

"Wanting carrots means you are carrying a boy, and the reason is obvious," Dame Agnes said one day, grinning while Margaret blushed.

By late autumn, her girth was awkward, and by Advent she and her women were completing the little garments and linens they had been stitching for months. Over Yuletide, she began to meet potential wet nurses invited by Dame Agnes and a very helpful Wilfrid. After speaking to a few local women whose infants were nearly due or whose babes had recently died, Margaret decided on a granddaughter of Mother Annot, Mirren, whose daughter had died unexpectedly in her cradle. Margaret empathized with the young woman's heartbreak and liked her quiet grace, a good quality to pass on to her own infant through a nurse's milk. She asked Mirren to keep her milk full for the royal infant to come.

Old Annot offered to act as midwife, having delivered many babes in more than fifty years, and Margaret granted her a generous fee, glad to have a familiar attendant for the birth. In her spare English, Annot said it was an honor. She and Mirren moved to a room in the tower, and the wait went on.

ON THE EVE of the Epiphany, at the end of Christmastide, her labor began. Margaret felt heavy, dull aches of such pressure that she could not always catch her breath. Pacing the room, she anticipated the birth, relishing it as one of the real tests of courage and power she could face as a woman. She knew the great risks, yet felt strangely unafraid, even excited. Heaven and hell would both challenge her that day, and she wanted to triumph, wanted to tap the stronger spirit that she knew resided within her.

So she welcomed the struggle, endured it in silence but for murmured prayers. She obeyed Annot's advice, translated deftly by Eva, who remained calm and by her side throughout. Margaret fell to her hands and knees on the bed as an unyielding power ripped through her body like a gale through a glen. When Annot and Kata pulled her upward to sit, squatting and striving, she pushed until she felt the child slip slick from her, and gasped. Annot caught it, wiped the squalling and red-faced little thing quickly, and held it up as Kata held out the swaddling.

"A son, a fine little son," Kata said in German, then English. "Listen to his strong cry!"

Margaret sat up, exhausted and exhilarated, while her mother wiped her face, smoothed back her damp hair. Kata held a cup to her lips, filled with a cool, sweet drink of herbs and water that Annot had prepared for her. "Your labor was very quick, only a few hours. It was easy!"

Margaret laughed; the storm in her body had more than tested her, and had not seemed so easy. She reached for the child, then cradled him close. Eva was there, speaking quietly in Gaelic with Annot, Mirren, and Finola, whose eyes had been wide and frightened through the labor. After a moment, Eva came forward to admire the child.

"Mother Annot says you may have many babes," Eva said. "She says it was indeed easy for you, and each labor may be quicker than the last. Remember that for your next one."

"Next one!" Margaret said. Eva turned as the midwife spoke again.

"Aye, she says you and the king make strong, beautiful children together. There will be more," Eva said. While the other women in the room laughed, Margaret held her little son close, carefully, the fragile, warm bundle suddenly dearer to her than anything on earth or in heaven.

"Malcolm," she said then. "Is he here?"

"Returning soon," Eva said. "Two housecarls rode out to fetch him from the hunt. He has been gone two days, but promised he would cut it short for this occasion."

Margaret leaned back against a slope of pillows and gazed at her son in candlelight. The hour was late, not yet dawn on the day of the Epiphany, and here he was like a miracle, her firstborn, quickly born and healthy. He quavered a thin cry, stretched, and opened his little mouth like a bird, and she fell completely in love in that instant. She kissed his brow and let him nuzzle her breast.

Lady Agatha came toward her, shaking her head. "Let the wet nurse take him if he is hungry," she said. "You must not suckle. You will become overly fond of the babe."

"There is nothing wrong in that," Margaret said.

"Babes die," her mother said bluntly. "They sicken and die. A good mother cannot become too fond of the little creatures God puts into her hands. Let the nurse see to his welfare."

"Mama," Margaret said then. "Did you . . . lose a babe of your own? You have never said."

Lady Agatha sighed. "Two others. One was a boy, pretty as Edgar, the other a girl, dark as Cristina. But it is past and forgotten. I did not give them my heart. Nor should you give this one your heart until he is much older and you know he can survive."

"But I love him already," Margaret said, pressing him close to her.

"Babes are fragile creatures. This one seems vigorous, but wait to be sure. If he thrives, your obligation is to teach him courtesy, prayers, and other lessons. His father will train him to be a warrior, and his tutors will tend to his princely education. But while he is small, let his nurses care for him—let them bear the sorrow if he does not survive."

Shocked, Margaret stared at her mother and cuddled her son. Finally, quickly, she understood why Lady Agatha had been so distant with her children. Yet Margaret could never imagine withholding love from her own child, even to spare herself grief if he did not thrive.

"He is a healthy babe," she said. "And his birth on the holy feast day of the Epiphany, which is the true birthdate of Christ in our own Hungary, gives him even more protection." The holy day had been a favorite in her childhood, celebrated with gifts of gold and pungent frankincense, and by the chalking of the names of the magi over the doors of homes for protection.

"*Christus mansionem benedicat,*" Margaret said, uttering a traditional Epiphany blessing. "May Christ bless this house. He will be fine, Mama," she told her mother. Lady Agatha sighed.

Margaret kissed the baby's warm little head. For the first time since she had come to Scotland, she felt at home, truly blessed.

MALCOLM ARRIVED THAT EVENING, bringing Duncan and Donald with him into the room. Margaret sat with her child in her arms, letting his tiny fingers curl around her thumb. She stroked his soft cheek and smiled up at Malcolm.

"He is blond like his mother," Malcolm said. "He is healthy, and his lungs seem to be strong, after all that wailing we heard as we came in here. Good."

"What is his name?" Duncan asked in English. Margaret smiled at him in quick approval, for she had asked the boys to speak English as often as they could.

"He has none yet. What shall we call him?" Malcolm asked the boys. "You are Duncan for my father—and you are Donald for my brother. My grandfather was called Crinan. Should we name your brother for him?"

"Oh, not that," Margaret said quickly, determined to avoid such a foreign name for her child. "I have been thinking about names for weeks now. I would like to call him Edward for my father."

"A Saxon name?" Malcolm frowned. "But he is a prince of Scotland."

"He has royal Saxon blood, too," she reminded him. "The name also belonged to my uncle and my great-grandfather. Such a strong name would be recognized by the Saxons, the French, and many others. What would best serve a Scottish prince in future—a good Saxon name, or a Gaelic one, however old and proud, that foreign leaders simply cannot pronounce or remember?"

Malcolm seemed thoughtful, then nodded. "I suppose there is wisdom in that."

"And it would mean a good deal to me," she whispered, looking down at her little son.

"Aye then. For you," Malcolm said. "He will be christened Edward mac Malcolm."

Margaret smiled and propped the babe higher in her arms. "He looks a bit like you," she said.

"No shame in that." Malcolm reached out to touch the child's rounded head. "But he is fair beautiful like his Saxon kin, and that is good. Edward," he said. "He is the first Scottish prince to carry such a name."

"No shame in that," she said softly.

WHEN SHE HEARD from Finola that Edgar had returned without notice one afternoon, Margaret left her reading and hurried down the turning steps with several of her ladies, including Eva and Juliana. A maidservant had told them that Edgar and his companions—he had brought strangers and priests, the girl said—had gone to the great hall for refreshment. Margaret found them seated at a long trestle table as she entered the hall.

A servant was ladling soup into bowls, and the men had cups of new ale, so strong that most jugs had to be liberally diluted with water as they sat quietly talking. She did not recognize all of them, but Edgar often brought men to Dunfermline on business with the king. Wilfrid was there, too, and when he saw the queen and her ladies enter, he murmured to Edgar. They stood.

The hem of her gown swept over fresh rushes as she hurried across the room. One of the king's gray hounds loped to its feet and came to her, and Eva stooped to pat the dog's head, holding back, for Edgar and his men were not well known to her. Lady Juliana hurried, too, no doubt hoping to hear some news of her father, Cospatric. Moments later, Cristina entered the room as well, looking for her brother.

Immediately Margaret noticed two newcomers with the men. Both were Benedictine monks, judging by their black hooded robes, hempen belts, and tonsured heads, and likely Saxon. One seemed familiar, a long and lanky man with flaxen hair, though she could not recall who he was. The other was a stranger, stocky and dark. Both stopped their conversation and stood.

Grateful to see Edgar safe, for any journey south was inherently dangerous now, Margaret embraced him. "You have been gone but two months," she said, "yet you seem taller!"

"And you are lighter of your burden," he noted with a smile. "Congratulations. I am eager to see my nephew—but Dame Agnes told me right off he was sleeping and I must wait." He grinned, his jaw bearded with gold, the angles of his face harder, losing the softer contours of youth. He was grimy with travel, garments rumpled, but he looked handsome, growing into a mature man, Margaret thought proudly.

"Margaret—Cristina, there is news," he said, kissing his other sister, too. "I rode into Northumbria to meet with some Saxon landholders there, and back again. Took us weeks, and what adventures! Later for that. I met an old friend along the way." His eyes sparkled.

"Sir, did you see my father?" Juliana asked, stepping forward.

He shook his head. "We heard news of him. He and Walde have been meeting with William in York, and seem tight. But I hope they know that they cannot trust him—he will ask more of them than they can ever guess, and they will regret giving their obeisance, even to retain their English properties. Nay, I did not meet with them—but I found another old friend." He turned, beckoned. "Brother," he said. "You remember my sisters."

"Of course!" The taller of the two monks came forward. Margaret narrowed her eyes, curious, trying to remember him. Up close he looked gaunt, his ice blue eyes shadowed beneath, his cheeks pale. He was a golden man in a way, with pale lashes and brows, and his tonsure was ringed by thick, smooth golden hair. Even his thin, whiskered cheeks sparkled with a fine, pale beard. His features were long, as the man was long and lanky. In one hand he gripped a gnarled stick, and he leaned on it, limping, as he came toward them. Otherwise he had a strong build and appeared rather younger, close up, than he had first seemed.

"Queen Margaret," he said quietly. "Princess Cristina. How good to see you again."

Beside her, Cristina gasped and laid a hand to her ample bosom. Then Margaret startled. He was thin and much changed but she knew him. "Tor!" she said. "Thorgaut the Dane!"

He smiled. "I am glad to see God has kept you both well."

"Tor!" Cristina rushed toward him. "You were a king's guard when last we saw you!" She smiled, extended her hands, took his though he had not offered them readily. "And now you are . . . a monk!"

"It is good to see you, princess." He laughed a little—Margaret remembered then that Cristina had always been able to draw a laugh out of somber Tor, even when he was a king's guard—and then he turned to Margaret. "And you, Lady. We heard news of your arrival

here, and your marriage. And now a little son. My sincere congratulations." He bowed his head.

"Thank you. How good that you are here." She was so moved to
see an old friend safe, but she could not display her feelings as Cristina could. Not only was she queen, but her own reserved nature
held her back. Let Cristina effuse in welcome, she thought, watching Tor flush as Cristina clasped his hands. He might prefer that to a
queen's necessary coolness.

She smiled, waiting while he spoke to her sister. Years ago, Tor
had been one of King Edward's housecarls, assigned to guard the
Aethelings and to train young Edgar in arms. He had become a friend
to all of them, guarding them on every outing, spending time in their
quarters, sharing suppers and chess games with them. Several years
older, he had been a good friend to both Edgar and Margaret. She
would never have admitted it aloud, but as a young girl she had
been infatuated with the handsome young guard. Now her cheeks
grew hot as she remembered how dreamily she would stare after him,
grasping for reasons to speak to him. Margaret felt relieved, now, that
he had never learned her feelings.

"The last news we had of you was that you had escaped Lincoln
for Denmark," she said then.

"We were told you fled your prison in Lincoln's castle," Cristina
said. "I feared for your life once I heard that. I could hardly sleep at
night for worrying. Oh, it is so good to see you!"

Margaret wondered at her sister's display but said nothing. She
only continued to smile, folding her hands, though her heart beat like
a bird's wings within her chest. Despite the tonsure and the gaunt-
ness that aged him, despite the pall of somberness around him, Tor
was handsome still, a strong and vital man with a deep and rich voice
that could thrum through her.

But she could not think of him in that way, for she was a queen, a
wife, a mother, now. And he had declared himself a man of God and
of peace. He was to be admired and revered.

"I left Lincoln and sailed for Denmark, and returned to England again. The rest is done, and in the past." Tor did not seem inclined to add details, but Edgar turned and clapped the monk's shoulder in an easy manner.

"Left Lincoln!" Edgar said. "Tor escaped a Norman dungeon with his guards on his heels all the way to the coast. It is quite the tale, if he will tell the whole of it."

Tor's cheeks stained pink. "I did what anyone would have done given the chance when they let me out briefly. I walked away when the guards were not looking."

"He hit them over the head while they played dice," the other monk said, coming forward. "He scaled a stone wall and stole a horse to ride to the coast, with the guards after him. My lady queen," he said, bowing his head. "Princess, and ladies," he went on, acknowledging the others. "I am Brother Aldwyn, if you please, of Durham priory."

"Welcome, Brother," Margaret said. "Please sit. Do not let us keep you from your meal. You must be tired after your journey." Before she sat with them, Margaret waved away the servant and poured fresh ale for her brother and the other men in more formal welcome.

"Tell us how you came to be a Benedictine," Cristina said.

"Had I not been captured in Lincoln, I might have remained a knight and so would have come north with your family," he said. "But life took me along an unexpected path. When I was a boy, years before I entered King Edward's service, my family had intended me for the Church, and so I was educated in a monastery. Some boys want more adventure, so I left and came to court. But once I came to Durham after Denmark, I rediscovered my monastic calling." He shrugged. "The Lord sent me there."

"So you felt spiritually guided?" Margaret was fascinated. Secretly she longed for the sort of holy calling that came to mystics and monastics more than queens.

"I came to Durham by accident, Lady. As I returned from Denmark, our ship was wrecked along the coast. I was the only survivor. The monks of Durham took me in, and I recovered in their care."

"We are so glad you are safe!" Margaret said. "We were ship-wrecked as well, and so came to Scotland."

"The North Sea can be treacherous," he replied. "Yet we are guided by such turns of fate. I have found a purposeful existence now, for which I give thanks each day."

Margaret caught her breath, for Tor had echoed her own thoughts and feelings. She, too, wanted greater peace, and despite all in her life now, she still felt as if there was some larger purpose for her. She wondered if it would present itself as it had for Tor. Still, she reminded herself, she had a son now, and motherhood was purpose enough for the time being.

"I have found a calling," he continued. "Otherwise there is little left for me in England. My family and friends are gone or scattered. I would have joined the rebellion with my kinsmen, but I cannot fight now." He gestured toward his leg. "I was injured in the shipwreck. But perhaps all this was part of a larger plan. I tell myself that I was brought to Durham for a greater reason."

Margaret sat forward. "What reason is that?"

"I do not know. One day I hope it will become clear."

She nodded. "We all have a greater purpose in life, Brother, but few know what that is."

"Very true, Lady." He watched her, somber. "But I believe you have found your way."

"I try to do my best in all things," she murmured.

"What news of your cousin Hereward, Brother Tor?" Cristina asked, interrupting them.

"He still drives the Normans mad, from what I hear. I pray for his safety every day."

"Now that you have found us, Tor," Cristina said, "you must remain with us. We could certainly use another Benedictine confes-sor in our household."

"Thank you, but that is not possible." He shook his head. "Brother Aldwyn and I must return soon. The abbot at Durham sent us north to do some work at Melrose near the border. The ruined abbey there once housed Saint Cuthbert himself, who later came to Durham as abbot, and became our dedicatory saint. It was in Melrose that we met Prince Edgar and his party."

"Interesting! What work are you doing in Melrose?" Margaret asked.

"We are supervising the restoration of the old Benedictine houses at Melrose and Jarrow. Although they are in Scotland, they still belong to the diocese of York. Long ago they were flourishing priories, but fell into ruin when conflict ran high between the Saxons and the Scots."

"Lately several more brothers have settled at Melrose," Aldwyn said. "Now we number fourteen. We will maintain a farm there, and Brother Tor has set up a scriptorium as well. He has a gift for copying manuscripts and for original writing, too. He is composing a biography of Saint Cuthbert, among other projects."

"A scribe, as well as an author and historian! That is excellent. I am very fond of books, too." Pleased to find yet another trait in common with Brother Tor, Margaret resisted an urge to touch his arm where he sat beside her. "I would like to talk more of books and learning with you, if you could only stay longer."

"We must return, Lady. The abbot of Durham awaits our report on what we have accomplished these past months. But we came north with Prince Edgar for a brief visit, hoping for an audience with King Malcolm on certain matters that may interest him. We could stay a day or two, if we are welcome."

"Certainly," Margaret said eagerly. "And you are welcome here any time." She remembered an easy friendship with Tor years back, yet now he seemed cool and remote, perhaps due to his status as a monk. Or did her status as queen cause the distance between them? Surely it could not be her marriage. Tor had never thought of her in that way, for she had been a young girl when she had secretly doted on him—and now he was a monk.

"Brother Tor, we will make sure you meet with the king before you go," Edgar said then.

"My husband rode out for a judgment court, but he will be back by evening," Margaret explained.

"I see," Tor said. Then, while the others chuckled over something Brother Aldwyn was saying, he leaned slightly toward Margaret. "May I say, Lady Margaret, that it is good to see you again. Queenship and motherhood suit you, and you have done well. God was wise indeed to send you to Scotland."

Margaret felt her cheeks heat again, but she knew that Tor was right. She was in Scotland for reasons beyond her grasp, and she must accept that. "I would like to think that someday I might find peace and purpose here, where I have been set, just as you did."

"You have found it," he said quietly.

"Sometimes I feel . . . as if I must seek more. I have achieved little so far." She glanced away, aware that something was amiss within. Only she knew her sins, the flaws in her character that she could never expunge and could not easily confess. If Tor was her confessor, she thought then, she might feel free to speak of those feelings someday. He was a friend, even after so long.

"You are graced with so much now. Perhaps God is done testing your spirit, after the last few years," he replied.

"Brother, I long to be challenged," she whispered. "I yearn to be tested and proven."

He leaned closer. "If you feel so, then prove yourself through good works and devotion as queen and mother and as a pious woman. Let that ease whatever troubles you."

She paused. "Brother Tor, would you . . . confess me and hear my sins?" She said it impulsively, with a surge of hope, and a twinge low in her body that felt, for a moment, like the deepest excitement of lovemaking—she caught her breath against it. But she wanted to confide in this man, who would sincerely understand the bliss and forgiveness she sought in prayer and had not yet found completely.

"Margaret, I am not your confessor," he whispered.

"But I wish you were," she whispered breathlessly, blushing hot. Her confessors were Father Otto, Brother Micheil, even Bishop Fothad when he visited the king, but she could not open her private heart to them. Somehow she felt Tor could fully accept her thoughts as well as her sins.

"It is not my calling," he said, and his eyes, so pale a blue, sparked brilliantly. "Though for your sake I, too, could wish it."

"MELROSE! THAT PLACE was abandoned a century ago at least," Malcolm said. He leaned forward at the table during supper, hand gripping a small knife, point upward. He spoke sharply, though he addressed the two monks who were his guests. "I was not told of that decision—and that place is in *my* territory." He pounded his fist in emphasis. "What the devil are you doing down there, Brothers?"

Eva listened with interest, seated beside Margaret as her companion that night. She, too, was eager to learn more about Tor's activities along the border, particularly if it was news for Moray. Silence fell over the table as the others—a few gathered with Malcolm and Margaret, their closest courtiers, and the guests—waited for Brother Tor to reply.

"Sire," Tor began, "we came from Durham months ago to restore the place and prepare it to house monks again. With such turmoil in northern England now, the abbot and the bishop of York see the need to establish monastic centers away from the conflict. As of this month, we have over a dozen monks at Melrose, with more arriving. We hope to do good work there for the community and the region."

"I gave no permission for monks to live there!" Malcolm burst out.

"Sire, if I may remind you," Brother Aldwyn said calmly, "the monastery is part of the wide-flung parish of Durham and the bishopric of York, rather than the Scottish church. Our permission came from the bishop of York as well as Archbishop Lanfranc in Canterbury."

"Neither of them consulted me," Malcolm groused. "Margaret, did you hear aught of this from Lanfranc? You have had a letter or two from him lately."

"We have had a brief correspondence about spiritual matters only, sire. He promised to send one or two of his own Benedictines here to join Father Otto in our household, but he did not mention Melrose or York. But it seems that Brother Tor and Brother Aldwyn are doing very good work, sire."

"Huh!" Malcolm turned his knife to spear a bit of mutton from his bowl. As at other times, Eva saw that he listened to, and considered, Margaret's opinions. That the queen had a firm, gentle influence over the king seemed clear. "Why Melrose? If Benedictines are settling on Scottish land, I would know about it."

"We assumed that you knew, sire, for we met with Sir Robert concerning the scriptorium," Tor said. "Our apologies if the exact news of our situation did not reach you."

"Saint Cuthbert was a monk at Melrose before he moved on to Durham and Lindisfarne Abbey, did you know, sire?" Margaret asked.

"Cuthbert?" Malcolm frowned. "He is not a warrior-saint, so he is of little use to Scotland. Cuthbert does not like Scots much. The Saxons pray to him for protection from us." He laughed curtly.

"Perhaps his holy intercession has made a difference," Brother Tor suggested. "You are now assisting the Saxon cause, and have married into the Saxon royal family."

"I decided that, not Cuthbert," Malcolm grumbled.

"Honoring Cuthbert invites his blessing," Margaret said. "I think it is an admirable plan."

When Malcolm glanced at his wife, Eva noticed that he did not seem pleased. "Brother Thorgaut, now that you have settled on my lands without my permission," the king said, "I suppose you will want further income to finish the work there. Is that why you have come here?"

Listening, Eva blinked. The king could be even more direct than her grandmother at times.

"We did hope for generosity, sire, as Melrose is in Scotland. The

bishop of York sent a letter explaining the work we are to do at Melrose," Tor said.

"I had no letter. But not all messages from England make it over
the border into Scotland." The king took another bite of food. Malcolm seemed calmer, though still displeased.

Eva spooned up some of the peppery stew of mutton and vegetables and ate. But she noticed that the queen only nibbled some
cooked barley. She knew that Margaret had gone to Father Otto that
morning to request extra penances, feeling remorseful after snapping
at her women for giggling while they worked. But Margaret had
seemed even more out of sorts after the two monks had arrived, refusing her midday meal in favor of more prayers.

"Lady," Eva murmured. "Please try some of the stew." Margaret
shook her head.

Eva saw how closely Margaret listened to Brother Tor. The queen
blushed as if she had a fever, while Eva hoped that Malcolm would
not make note of it—though Eva thought the queen's distraction
rather obvious.

Sipping wine from a silver cup, she studied Tor herself and wondered what truly brought him to Dunfermline. He was an intriguing
man—nearly as tall as Malcolm, his tonsured hair thick blond, his
cheekbones broad, and striking blue eyes set deep. He looked like
some of the Vikings in her grandmother's service, yet too thin, with
an air of reserve and authority all at once. He did not quail before the
contentious king, and when he looked at Queen Margaret, the hard
lines in his face and the coldness in his eyes softened. The fair skin
of his high cheekbones went visibly pink, too. Eva had the sudden
desire to warn both the queen and monk to beware.

"The book," Malcolm said. "Tell me more about it. You came here
to discuss it."

Book? Startled and attentive, Eva sat forward.

Robert De Lauder turned toward the king. "Sire, you will recall that
months past I told you of a monk in the south who was skilled at com-

posing histories and scribing manuscripts, who had agreed to compose your history. Brother Thorgaut is that man. How fortunate that he was finally able to travel here so that you could meet him yourself."

"What book?" Eva whispered to Margaret. "Has the king commissioned a book?" The queen nodded and set a finger to her lips for silence.

"So how is my history coming along?" Malcolm asked.

"The book progresses well, sire," Tor said. "We are very busy at Melrose, repairing old buildings and preparing for our first vegetable crops this spring. But I have found time to work on your manuscript pages. I am also writing the story of Cuthbert, though I give your history precedence, of course. Lately I have been listing your ancestry, according to the information Sir Robert gave me when we discussed the commission. I am not a Scot, so some of the record is unknown to me, though I have a copy of an Irish chronicle that lists some Scottish events for generations back. Your book is a privilege to compose." He smiled slightly.

"See that you do justice to it," Malcolm said.

Brother Tor nodded. "I hope that while I am here we can discuss some of the details."

"Good. Be sure to include my victories and achievements," Malcolm replied. "This must be a *vita* as well as a history relevant to my line and my reign."

"Indeed, it begins with the early kings of Scotland and will end with King Duncan and yourself."

"What of my father?" Eva asked suddenly, so that the others turned to look at her. "What of King Lulach and my step-grandfather, the great Macbeth? They must be included as well."

"The king supplied details of their lives, my lady," Tor told her.

"You should ask me about the truth of their reigns," she said. "I am a bard as well as of the royal family."

Tor nodded. "I would be glad to discuss some details with you."

Malcolm slapped the flat of his hand on the table. "Lady Eva misspeaks," he rumbled. "This is my history, not hers. You and I will discuss this later, Brother Monk."

"Sire." Tor tilted his head.

"I hope you will represent all the worthy kings and warriors in this book fairly, Brother Tor," Eva said. "It would be a waste of good ink to spill falsehoods on those pages."

Margaret gasped. Malcolm glowered. Eva watched them evenly, feeling her heart beat hard and fast as she waited for reprisal. But in this company, with the Benedictines to impress, the king only shot her an arrow glance and turned to Tor.

"The facts of Scottish kingship are well known and there are good chronicles to consult," he said, while the monk nodded. Tempted to speak again, Eva thought better of it, hoping she had made her point about the accuracy of his work.

"I am interested in your book about Saint Cuthbert," Margaret said gently into a moment of awkward silence. "I look forward to seeing your history of my husband's life, too."

"I would be pleased to share it with you," Tor said.

"Nothing should be written of my kinsmen unless I am consulted," Eva persisted. "I have committed the genealogy of Scotland's royalty to memory."

"Excellent," Tor said, leaning toward her. "Perhaps you know—"

"Lady Eva, give us a song," Malcolm said brusquely.

Eva knew what he meant: *Give us a song and cease this talk.* But she had finally found the source of the ill-conceived manuscript meant to ruin the reputation of her kinfolk.

"Brother Tor—" she began.

"Lady Eva." A warning colored Malcolm's tone. He wanted to prevent her from talking to Tor. He knew, she thought in a panic. He feared she might mean to destroy his false record.

Bowing her head, she rose from the table and went to her harp, which perched on a low stool, another stool beside it. Settling into place, she used the little harp key strung on a cord around her neck.

When the metal strings were in pitch, she lifted her hands, stroked her long nails delicately up and down to bring out an array of harmonies, and then began to play.

STILL SLEEPY AT DAWN, Eva entered the anteroom chapel behind Margaret, who had woken her only minutes before, whispering that she wanted to pray before the ebony and gold cross in the little chapel. Through the parted door curtains, Eva saw the cross gleaming in the light of the candles flickering on the altar as Margaret went ahead, hands folded.

Eva was in awe, a little, of the beautiful, mysterious black cross. Margaret had said that it had been adored for centuries in her birth land because the glass vial at the heart of the cross held a sliver of wood— a tiny relic, Margaret had explained, that represented for many the power of trials, strength, and faith.

Speaking of Hungary and her childhood, Margaret had hinted of hardships and loneliness, of her terror of the sea and the devastating loss of her father. "But where the black cross finds its home," Margaret had said, "there do I also."

Now Eva had understood a little better why the young queen felt so compelled to pray at odd hours. To be sure, accompanying her was not always easy, for Eva tended to keep late hours practicing on her harp; the music lulled the maids, Wynne and Matilda, to sleep while Eva played on.

As she pushed aside the curtain behind Margaret, she realized that someone else was in the chapel. Clad in dark robes, he knelt in the dark shadows. Eva stopped short when Margaret halted.

Brother Tor prayed before the altar, head bent. Margaret motioned in silence that they should leave, and Eva nodded agreement. Watching a monk at his private prayers felt like an intrusion.

But he turned, saw them, and beckoned them forward. Margaret knelt next to him, candlelight rippling over her veiled head and blue-cloaked shoulders as she pressed her hands together. Eva sank down beside her, bowing her head but looking sideways at Tor, who murmured in Latin. He rocked a little on his knees as he prayed, and his sleeve touched Margaret's. Just behind them, Eva saw their shoulders press for a long moment until they leaned away.

Bathed in stillness, Eva breathed slowly and heard Margaret murmur Latin verses in whispers. The queen begin to sway a bit, as she sometimes did when her devotions became fervent. Once again the queen leaned toward Tor, and he toward her, the two of them rapt in their prayers, both staring up at the black cross suffused in candle glow. They looked twinned somehow, Eva thought: a golden, peaceful pair, like two bright candles themselves.

For a few moments, inspired by the purity and strength of the two people kneeling in front of her, Eva heard in her mind not the prayers she should be reciting silently but a poignant harp melody and phrases of a song:

> *Thou shell of my heart*
> *Thou face of my sun*
> *Thou harp of my music*
> *Thou crown of my senses.*

She nearly hummed it aloud, and caught herself. Odd to think of a love song rather than a prayer when kneeling in a chapel with the queen and a monk. Yet in that moment Eva realized how suited they were, a matched pair.

Tor ended the peacefulness when he stood, and Margaret did the same, gathering her skirts. Eva got to her feet and followed them to the corridor. There, Tor turned, smiled.

"Brother Aldwyn and I will depart shortly," he murmured, his gaze on the queen. "The horses are waiting in the courtyard. I am glad to have seen you and your kinfolk again. And pleased to have met you, Lady Eva," he added, almost an afterthought, as if he had just noticed her standing near.

"Brother Tor," Eva said. "I had hoped for a chance to speak with you about the king's book."

"There is no time for that now. Perhaps you and the queen can travel south to Melrose and we can talk at length about the book."

"Not with such tension along the border," Margaret said. "The king would not allow it. But we can hope that you will visit us again."

"Lady, that would be most pleasant," Tor said politely. Then Eva saw him step back suddenly, as if he was aware how close he stood to the queen, how intently he watched her. "Truly I do not know if we will meet again. But you will always have friends in Durham and Melrose."

Margaret smiled up at him. "Perhaps you will consider joining our household as one of our confessors. I would treasure your opinion and your advice here."

Eva lifted her brows at that. If the monk had been invited to take up residence in Dunfermline, he would bring that unfinished manu-script with him—and Eva would have the chance to look at it for her grandmother's benefit. "Indeed, Brother Tor," she chimed in, "your presence here would be most welcome."

"It would not be wise, Margaret," he said, ignoring Eva. "You are queen—" Then he stopped. "You already have excellent spiritual advisors. And you have found the most important mission of your life in your marriage, your family, the good work you can do. I have no place here. My work is elsewhere."

"It could be done here," Margaret urged. "Your bishop would agree to a new assignment if I request it and the Scottish king approves, too. I will write to Lanfranc—"

"Do not," he said quickly. "But I am honored by the suggestion. Farewell." His gaze was so focused on Margaret that he scarcely looked at Eva. Turning, he hurried away.

Margaret sighed, watching him unguarded. Eva realized suddenly how lonely the queen must feel—an intelligent, educated, pious woman married to a blustery warrior could sense a kinship of spirit with a man like Brother Tor. Surely that was all that passed between them as they prayed and leaned together, and as their gazes met and met again.

"Eva, why are you standing there? We must summon the ladies to their prayers," Margaret said briskly. "They are doubtless still in bed this morning." Drawing her skirts into her hands, she walked away.

✢

Chapter Twelve

Then she went out and ordered her harp to be fetched.

—APOLLONIUS OF TYRE, ANGLO-SAXON,
ELEVENTH CENTURY

T oday, my lady," Brother Godwin said after the door of Margaret's solar was opened to him, "the king says you are to be crowned queen before supper."

Astonished, Margaret realized that Godwin was in earnest. The young Benedictine was new to the household, having arrived shortly after Brother Tor's visit. He and another monk had been sent north by Archbishop Lanfranc, who had learned that Margaret wished for more Benedictines to come to Scotland to help spread Roman teachings there. Lanfranc had written glowing letters to Margaret from Canterbury, so warm that she felt his almost fatherly approval and support, and she welcomed the monks Godwin and Brand, who had arrived with another letter from Lanfranc. Although Malcolm had cautioned her to beware any French archbishop appointed by King William, Margaret was pleased with Brand's competent clerical assistance and Godwin's youthful spirits, and she thought that both young men added much to her household.

"Malcolm is convinced that they were sent here as William's spies," she had told Eva only a few days earlier. The Scottish princess had blinked at her with wide gray-blue eyes, her expression echoing Margaret's own disbelief. "I could never imagine such a betrayal in my house!"

"They do seem sincere," Eva had responded quietly.

"I trust them as well as I trust you, with my very secrets," Margaret had said, smiling as she helped Eva, who had dropped a basket of yarn skeins.

Just now, Godwin stood inside the doorway, flushed with the excitement of his announcement. "Crowned, Lady," he repeated. "Malcolm has just returned from his travels and has brought with him Fothad of Saint Andrews. There will be a ceremony today, a traditional Scottish crowning."

Margaret, still stunned, finally found her breath. "I had no idea," she managed. "Today?"

"It is an honor," Eva said. "Few of the queens of Scotland have actually been crowned."

"But I am a foreign queen, and so I never expected this."

"Malcolm worries that the Scottish people still resent your foreign birth, despite your deliberately good deeds," Cristina said. "He must think a crowning will help."

"Surely by now the Scots accept Margaret more than at first," Lady Agatha said. "She has given Scotland a strong little prince."

"Another prince," Cristina corrected. "Who knows if small Edward will ever gain the throne in the future, though he ought to have the right over his Scottish half brothers, whose bloodlines are not nearly as good as his."

Knowing her sister's penchant for stirring trouble, Margaret ignored that. "Malcolm did say he wished to mark his gratitude for our new son," Margaret said. "I thought he would found a monastery or a church.

This had never occurred to me. But what should I wear?" she added then. "I have had no time to consider the ceremony! Malcolm has been gone a fortnight—and returns ready to do this!"

"The king says, Lady," Godwin said making himself heard as the ladies spoke, "that while you cannot be full queen here due to your foreign blood, you should and will wear a crown. Bishop Fothad will explain all to you before the ceremony."

"I must have my own priests there as well," Margaret replied. "Father Otto and Brother Brand, and you, Brother Godwin." She was glad to have three Benedictines in her household, a step toward the religious strengthening that she felt would be good for Scotland now. Lanfranc's kind letter—*Truly,* he wrote to her, *He has spoken with thy mouth . . . Learn from me because I am gentle and of humble heart*—had flattered her overmuch, she thought. But she was grateful that the archbishop had understood her best intentions.

I would consider it a great honor if you would advise me as my most kind and benevolent father in the Church, she had written in reply. *Heaven has seen fit to place me in Scotland, and so I will do my very best for the Scottish people.* Lanfranc, as the highest authority of the Church in Britain, was therefore greatly interested in establishing the tenets of the Roman Church in Scotland. And he agreed with her that news of the goodwill and good works of the king and queen of Scotland should reach the wider world. Malcolm needed an improved reputation outside the bounds of his country—within it, too, she knew.

Brother Brand was a surly fellow who had earned Cristina's loyalty straightaway by agreeing with her on every point, hearing her confessions and giving her so little penance that she felt vindicated in her opinions, which pleased her no end. Brother Godwin, fair-haired and freckled, sometimes forgot his Latin and had a huge appetite. He also had a knack for ball playing and would scamper around the bailey with Duncan, Donald, and the children of servants and nobles in packs, scooting a feather-stuffed leather ball around, keeping the young ones out of mischief. And he sometimes made Margaret laugh, too, which few could do. She took her confessions to him rather than to lecturing Otto, and though Godwin did not always have the wisdom to counsel a queen, he was a frank and loyal friend.

But she wished more and more that Tor had stayed at court. He would have been her choice for a personal confessor—she felt a natural harmony between them, both spiritual agreement and the ease of friends. In the past weeks she had received two letters from him telling of his work in the border area at Melrose. He wrote of the satisfaction of renewing a Benedictine house in an area where the farm could help some of those who were without food, with so many poor wandering out of England into Scotland. Her heart ached to hear again of the plight of so many—and she felt a swelling of pride, too, that Tor felt moved to help them.

She had written to him quickly, eagerly, in her own hand rather than asking Brand to write it out for her. Praising Tor's efforts, she knew that his humility would not accept the compliment for himself, but she wanted him to hear it from her. Then she had waited with almost girlish anticipation for a return letter, brought at last by a king's messenger, who also carried a report from Tor to Malcolm and De Lauder, detailing his work on Malcolm's commissioned manuscript.

Margaret had shown part of her letter to Eva, for in a postscript Tor had asked that Eva write out a list of the kings who had preceeded Malcolm. Eva had agreed and had set to writing the names out—Margaret was pleased to see that the girl had a good, clear hand and could compose in Latin as well as Gaelic.

Tor's latest letter was still tucked in the little purse of necessaries at her belt, and now Margaret wished that he could be there for her crowning. She looked forward to writing to him about the event.

"We had best hurry," she told her ladies as Godwin left the room. "I have had hardly enough warning to change into a fresh gown! Finola, quickly," she told the little Scottish maidservant, "my sky blue silk gown would be lovely for this, the one with the silver thread embroidery. Please shake the creases from it and freshen it with a warmed stone. I will be there soon."

Once changed, thankful for Finola's efficiency, for the girl had also smoothed a gauzy white undergown and had laid out black silk slippers and stockings, Margaret slipped two wide silver bracelets on her wrists, and went to the great hall with her ladies and kinswomen to find others already gathering. Malcolm waited with a few members of his Scots council, whose Gaelic names Margaret found so difficult to pronounce, though Eva was helping her with such things lately. Fothad stood with two Celtic priests, one who had accompanied him and Brother Micheil, along with the Benedictines of the queen's household.

Tantalizing smells of supper filled the air, though she knew Dame Agnes had little time to prepare a proper coronation feast. But no matter: the king wanted this and so it would be done. The fire basket crackled with flames as Margaret took a seat on a leather-slung stool on the dais, her pale blue silk gown pooling at her feet. Folding her hands, she sensed her pounding heart.

Fothad explained what would be required: she must only sit, wait, repeat a vow, and provide her head in graceful manner, doing all with the sincere and pure intention befitting her station. Malcolm stood waiting, arms folded, legs wide in the tough stance common to him.

Hands pressed in prayer, Margaret bowed her head while the Scottish bishop spoke blessings over her in Gaelic. Then he gave a benediction in Latin and asked her to repeat a vow to act as a fair and good queen to her king and his people. Father Otto spoke prayers, which she said with him. Then Malcolm beckoned, and Margaret expected to see the crown carried forward by one of the priests.

Instead, Eva stepped out between the priests and walked toward her, while Brother Micheil carried a pillow with a narrow golden circlet on it. Margaret sat straighter, astonished to see Eva. The girl wore a pale gown, her black hair shining loose, her eyes vivid. She emanated purity and power, and seemed to strangely belong. When she began to recite in Gaelic, her voice melodious and rhythmic, Malcolm nodded approval. Margaret realized that Eva recited a list of the names of the King's predecessors—some of whom were the girl's own deposed and murdered kinsmen.

Minutes later, the list complete, Eva turned to Margaret and pronounced her a queen, all in the Gaelic tongue, and then lifted the small chaplet of beaten gold and set it on Margaret's head, which was bare of its usual veil. The sharp-pointed leaves along the golden base pricked her scalp. Eva lifted her hands and stood back.

"Queen Margaret," she said. "Lady of Scotland."

Malcolm stepped forward to take Margaret's hand and brought her to her feet. Those watching clapped and smiled, though Margaret saw that some of the Scots nobles stared, arms folded. The occasion did not please all of them, apparently. But she smiled as suited her role.

As soon as she had a chance, she turned toward Eva. "Thank you," she said. "How did you come to be involved, rather than the priests? Is it because you are a bard? I do not understand."

"It is a hereditary right through my mother's Macduff kin, and through my grandmother, too, who is also of that line. And bards are part of the ceremony to ensure that previous kings are named and honored. The one who is the current crowner of Scottish royalty could not be here, so it fell to me to do this for you."

Margaret touched the golden fillet on her head. "Who should have done? Your uncle?"

"Lady Gruadh," Eva said. "She has the right to crown Scottish royalty."

Margaret paused, staring at Eva.

Malcolm took her arm then. "Come, Margaret. Supper is served. I am hungry."

❦

DEEP WINTER SNOW kept them inside Dunfermline for days, with the household growing so restless that many gathered in the silvery snow light to eat at midday. Hector the Saxon told of a hero long gone; though the story was vivid and exciting, he seemed to drone on.

Malcolm and his comrades spoke of battles and victories. Eva, restless, too, and thinking often of home again, grew attentive when she heard the name Macbeth put about a good deal. The men recounted tales for dark-haired Donald, curious and rambunctious, and Duncan, his father in miniature, though calmer and almost stony at times.

Malcolm asked Eva to play her harp while Hector took a draught of ale to soothe his throat. She played a string of melodies, some of Margaret's favorites, for the queen was there, too, looking pale and weary. Snow and cold did not suit the queen, who looked very thin lately; she thrived better with sunlight and warmth, though Eva never heard her complain.

Malcolm had enough to drink that afternoon that he must have forgotten Eva was there, for he suddenly boomed her father's name, laughing, in conversation. Hearing that, she looked his way, still plucking through the fingerings of a song.

"Lulach the Fool!" he shouted. "*Baobach,* the dimwitted—hah! He made a monk's decision—peace over revenge. I grant he was young, but he was a fool to meet me thinking of peace—" He stopped when Margaret laid a hand on his sleeve and murmured.

Eva played on as if she had not noticed. But she had her grandmother's temper. If her father had plotted like a monk, she would plot like a Viking, with thoughts of revenge. What she could say, what she should do, whirled in her head.

A moment later Edgar came toward her with a cup of wine in his hand. "Pay the king no mind," he said. "It is just warrior boasting, and nothing to worry over."

"I know what is worth my worry, what to let pass, and what to keep in mind," Eva said tersely.

"Be careful. That spark in your eyes is neither worry nor peace." He tilted his head as he regarded her. Then he set the cup on the floor for her and returned to the table.

"Lady Eva, give us another song," Malcolm called out.

She settled the harp against her shoulder anew, lifted her hands to the strings, then paused deliberately. Not many there knew her parentage, or that the king had just dealt her and hers a direct slight. Most knew only that she was one of the queen's women, with a talent for music and a face worth gazing upon, so only a few would understand the song she was about to give the king. But Malcolm would comprehend it—that was what mattered.

She plucked the path of strings. Had her harp been a weapon, it could not have fit the grip of her anger any better. Lifting her head, she began to sing in Gaelic.

> Bring to me a harp for my king
> A magical knot-carved one
> Upon whose strings I shed my grief
> For the loss of my father so young
>
> A fair young man, fierce and bright
> He held a champion's seat
> The men of Moray rode at his back
> And he like a strong young tree
>
> Fair-haired Lulach fathered me
> Let me praise Gilcomgan's son
> A bright and worthy branch
> Cut down by Duncan's blood

Silence filled the room when she finished. Then Malcolm pounded his fist on the table and roared like a boar's bluster. "Her father was a fool! More fool the daughter for this. Get her out of here!" He gestured to two housecarls, who stepped forward.

Eva stood, tilting her harp to rest on its base, then turned to Edgar, who was now striding toward her. "Look after my harp," she said quickly. "I must leave it here. Likely he will forbid me to play."

"What did you do?" he asked. "I did not understand your song, though clearly Malcolm did. He is furious."

"I sang of my father, King Lulach."

"Ah. That would rile him. Is it so, what they say of Lulach? Aye, then. Perhaps the king feels guilt over it."

"I hope so," she said curtly.

"Your temper will not serve you well here, though I cannot blame you. Leave her be," he added as the guards took Eva's arms. But Edgar was not their lord and they were obliged to follow the king's orders, though they seemed uneasy with it. Allowing them to guide her forward, Eva glanced back at the prince, who rested a hand on her harp and watched her go.

Chatter buzzed through the hall. The king looked like thunder, and Margaret looked puzzled, questioning her husband. Eva realized that the queen had not understood the Gaelic either, and would be bewildered, as were others from the Saxon court. A few there would recognize Eva's reference to her father's death—the rest would see only her defiance.

"Hold!" The man's voice was loud enough for most to hear, and Eva turned as her uncle, Kenneth Macduff, entered the room. "Hold, I say!"

Eva caught her breath as he approached the dais, shaking the snow from his cloak. She wondered if he had heard enough of her song to know what had transpired. Macduff walked past her to stand before Malcolm.

"Let the girl go," he said. "She is hot-tempered. That song was just the mewling of a kitten."

"Raised by a lioness," Malcolm returned.

"Declawed," her uncle said dismissively of Gruadh. "As for Lady Eva, the best bards have fire in the soul. For her music alone she should be forgiven."

"For her kinfolk she should be condemned," Malcolm said.

"She is kin to me," Macduff pointed out, tapping his chest.

"Then get her out of my hall," Malcolm barked.

Macduff went toward Eva. "Girl, could you not have played a pretty song?"

"If you heard the song, did you hear the king's remarks before that?"

"I did. But what you did was dangerous."

"I sang in honor of my father."

"And now your king may decide that you never sing again." He indicated the dais, where Malcolm spoke with Hector. "Be wary, girl. Damn that weasel," he said in Gaelic, taking her arm and turning. "What right does the Sassenach bard have to speak in this matter?"

"Sire, certain punishments are reserved just for bards," Hector was saying to Malcolm. "If this girl is well trained, she will know that."

Malcolm nodded. "True, I could require that she clip her pretty fingernails."

Eva caught her breath. An old punishment recorded in Irish law was the cutting of a bard's nails so that a wire-strung harp could not be played for weeks, but she had not known the sentence to be invoked outside of the old tales. She moved toward the king, past her uncle and the guards.

"Sire, you may choose to punish me by tradition," Eva said, facing Malcolm. "But I can play a gut-strung harp regardless of my nails." She held up her hands, palms flat. "I would have to lose my very fingers to keep from playing the harp. In fact, tales tell of a harper without arms, who played with his feet." Spiteful and angry, she tread even closer to danger if Malcolm was furious enough to follow through.

"You have your grandmother's manners, I see. Remove her from here," Malcolm told her uncle, who walked toward her. "She is forbidden to play music in this hall until I say otherwise."

Relieved then to be excused, Eva went with her uncle, joined by the two housecarls that Malcolm motioned toward them. Voices murmured all around, and when her guards stopped at the door, bowing their heads deferentially, Eva turned to see Margaret walking toward them.

"Lady Eva will come with me," the queen said. A mere look from her and the guards stepped back. "Eva, I wish to retire to my room," she said. "I told the king that you may come with me. I do not understand why he is so insulted, but I know you can explain it to me. Sir Kenneth, thank you," she told Macduff. "It was kindly done to defend Eva as you did."

"Lady," Macduff said. "I give my wayward niece into your cus-tody. Eva, take care."

As her uncle returned to speak with the king, Eva walked beside Margaret. "Thank you," she said as a few of the ladies who had attended supper joined them a few steps behind.

"Why is Malcolm so upset? I did not understand the Gaelic," Mar-garet reminded her.

"I sang a song of praise for my father."

"What is wrong in that? Even if it was a hymn in the Scottish tongue rather Latin, the king would not be so bothered. Was it blas-phemous?"

Eva laughed. "Not that Father! My own father—King Lulach. Malcolm did not like it."

"Ah," Margaret said. "I heard what he said about your father. Responding to that was bravely done in a way, but foolish, too."

"I could not remain silent when my father's memory was insulted by the one who saw to his murder—so it is said, though never proven. If my rudeness shocks you, Lady, perhaps you will not wish me to serve you. I should be sent home to Moray," she said quickly.

"I want you to stay with me. And Malcolm will not release you yet. Eva," she said thoughtfully, "I do understand how you feel about your father. My own was unfairly killed when I was a girl."

"Oh my dear," Eva said impulsively. "I did not know."

Margaret shook her head. "Tell me this. The king threatened to have your fingernails trimmed in punishment, and forbade you to play—but why?"

"The Gaelic verses told the truth of my father's death."

"Ah. I know so little of the language. I have been thinking—Eva, you must teach me more Gaelic."

"I am happy to do that." And it might keep her out of a dungeon, she quickly realized.

"If I could converse a little with the Celtic priests, I could better convince them to respect Rome. Please come inside," she said as they reached the door of her solar.

Once seated, Margaret took up a piece of embroidery, and Eva did the same. Lady Juliana and her stepmother entered the room after them, and a few minutes later, Eva looked up with surprise to see Edgar standing in the threshold. He held Eva's harp in his hands, having carried it up the stairs. Margaret beckoned him inside, and he set the instrument on a table.

As Eva thanked him, he smiled. "Malcolm suggested that I toss the harp out a window," he said, as Eva gasped. "But the harp did nothing to deserve it."

Eva laughed a little. "The king would rather toss me from a window."

"That may be. But I would have stopped him. I would have caught you," he added in a low tone, a little shyly. Then he looked around with reluctance, as if newly aware that they were not alone. The other women smiled with amusement, though Margaret frowned without comment. Edgar inclined his head in polite farewell and departed, cheeks showing pink through his light golden beard.

Drawing the needle through the cloth in the silence that followed, Eva felt at odds, sewing while her harp sat by, and she forbidden to play it.

"Eva, please, a little music." Margaret spoke as if she knew her thoughts.

"I am not permitted."

"The king need not know what he need not know." Margaret smiled quickly and impishly, as if enjoying her rare defiance. "Malcolm said do not play in the hall, but this is my solar. Music will relax us after such a trying evening. We retire to bed so early in the winter, and a harp melody before sleep would be soothing."

Eva moved another stool beside the low one that held the harp, and lifted her hands to the strings to begin a tune that was gentle but uplifting, and then went seamlessly on to another. Juliana and Edith began to yawn as Eva played a tune of the sort called the music of sleeping. The queen sent them on, and they bade good night, leaving Eva with Margaret.

She glided her fingers into another melody, while Margaret sat reading her Gospel in silence. The leather covers flopped open, worn at the edges from years of handling, and the queen traced graceful fingers over text and images that she knew well. After a while, the door of the solar opened and Mirren entered, carrying Margaret's little son wrapped in trailing swaddling clothes. Taking the child on her shoulder with kind words of affection, Margaret dismissed Mirren and began to walk holding Edward, soon humming softly to the music as she patted his back.

Plucking the strings together as the song ended, Eva lifted her hands. Margaret turned.

"Play the song about your father for me, in English."

Eva nodded and closed her eyes to think through the translation, knowing that her bardic training would help her as she sang. The words tumbled forth, the greater challenge in finding the rhythm. Margaret listened, swaying gently as she held her son. Her translucent veil cast a shadow over her pensive features in the candlelight.

When Eva finished, the queen's eyes glistened with tears. "You loved your father very much. I, too, loved and respected my father."

Eva had met Lulach but once and so had not truly known him, but she was deeply proud of him even so. And she envied, a little, Margaret's affection for her own father. "Lulach was a good king, unfairly slain," she said.

"My father would have been king of England, and a strong ruler. But he was . . . poisoned one night. I—I had a hand in it," she said in a rush. "Oh—forgive me, I did not mean to say it . . ." Margaret looked pale, stricken.

"A hand in that? You could never do anyone harm," Eva reassured her. "I heard of your father, the heir to King Edward, when I was a girl. I remember my grandmother speaking of him at supper one night. She said he was a good man who had been killed due to others' ambitions."

"His enemies were ready when we arrived in England. I was eleven, and I made a terrible error that night. My father might be alive now if not for what I did. All our lives would have been different. William might never have won England."

Leaning the harp away, Eva stood. "A child's deed did not cause the war. It is not possible."

Margaret lifted a shoulder. "What if it were so?"

"Your memory is that of a child, Lady," Eva said. "You cannot be to blame for his death."

"No matter," Margaret said quickly. "I spoke too freely. We will not discuss it again. But your music was calming, and you . . . have proven a friend."

"I am honored, Lady," Eva responded, drawing her brows together as she wondered at Margaret's revelation. The queen held herself accountable for some sin; that was clear from her constant praying, and perhaps this supposed deed was it. Eva sighed, aware that if she had blamed herself for Lulach's death a fortnight after he risked visiting her in Fife, that burden would have been unbearable. She felt a little frisson of sympathy for Margaret, who must have tormented herself for years with inner accusations. Eva wanted to offer comfort, touch the woman's shoulder or embrace her. Instead she traced her fingers over the harp strings, releasing soothing whispers of sound.

"I admired you so much tonight, Eva," Margaret said. "Your song about your father took courage. I do not have such bold spirit in me. But now I know that you think of your murdered father as I do mine. In a way, that makes us sisters." She kissed her infant's head. "The little one needs to go to sleep now, and his nurse waits outside. And I need to go to the house chapel again before I retire tonight. Good night, Eva."

She went to the door to pull it open, supporting her infant in one arm. The nurse was there, reaching out for the child. As Margaret descended the steps toward the chapel, the sound of her footsteps cascaded as if she ran.

WHEREVER THE QUEEN WENT, Eva went, too. As the king's hostage, and still forbidden to play harp for the court, she had little else to do but watch the dynamic, demanding king and his somber, charitable, beautiful wife. She garnered what observations she could to please her grandmother, and yearned to go home, lonely despite the friendships she had made. Margaret was good to her, Juliana was a joy, and Edgar made her heart beat fast and oddly—but he was often away. Even when he was there and greeted her, lingering to chat, his Saxon and Scots comrades would pull him away for debates, chess, or dice.

What troubled her even more than her disgrace, Eva realized one day, was that her music was suffering since Malcolm had limited her playing. She had believed, however foolishly, that she would have the privileges of a court bard in Dunfermline. Instead, she was housed like a servant and watched like a prisoner, and now for the most part silenced.

She knew that Hector profited by her eclipse, making a show of playing after supper, even adding more Irish melodies to his performances. "Hector is an evil man, to gloat so over your fall from favor," Wynne told her. "Do not let that bother you. We know who is the more gifted!"

The Saxon poet knew no Gaelic and had not mastered the old tunes as Eva had done, so that sometimes she wanted to stand and walk out of the hall when he struck the beginning chords of an Irish tune, for he did not always capture its spirit. But the king's stern gaze discouraged her. She would not cross him again until there was more to gain from it.

One evening as Hector was beating the life out of one of the Irish tunes, Ranald mac Niall and Angus of Mar joined Eva at the table and spoke to her kindly, saying they missed her music. And Angus shook his head.

"If that poet were a Scot," he remarked, "he would know the code of honor that binds *seanachaidhean* to each other in loyalty. He would help you regain favor with the king."

"He does have an exalted position in this court," Ranald agreed.

"But we have influence with the king as well. We will speak to him about this."

"No one need help me," Eva said. Her fingers itched so to play that she curled them into fists in her lap. "I made the choice to sing of Lulach, and I will bear the consequences."

"Ah, you are the granddaughter of Macbeth and Gruadh," Angus murmured, smiling.

As Hector finished the Irish tune and began to tell a story from the oldest Irish cycle, Eva sighed. She wanted to play, and needed to practice. Both were essential to her art, and that routine was as important to her as prayers were to the queen. The intricate notes and fingering patterns of music could vanish from the mind without due practice, and callused fingers could lose toughness and strength.

Nor could her work of remembering be neglected for long. Bards did not capture music and verses on parchment but stored them in memory, to be refreshed and elaborated on during solitary hours of review and creation. She had little freedom or solitude, and at times she felt desperately that she must practice or wither; play and sing, or go mad.

❧

MARGARET CLIMBED INTO BED, wondering if Malcolm would suggest some robust intimacy before sleep—if so, she would tell him what she now suspected, that she was carrying a new child. Feeling weary and sick that day, she had eaten little and had spent hours with Dame Agnes in the musty storerooms beneath the main tower, going through crates, sacks, and barrels as they inspected the stored goods that had lasted through the spring. Then she had soaked in a bath to take away the dust of the day, and had ordered a warm tub left for the king, the water freshened with herbs. Now, seated on the bed in her shift, her hair over her shoulder like rippling gold, she drew her fingers through the tangles. When Malcolm entered the room, his hair in dark ringlets from the bath, she stood.

"Sire, I will take to bed early tonight. I am tired," she said.

He slipped a hand to her cheek. "I have just been to see our little Edward," he said. "He is a fine boy. I would not mind if there was another child soon." He glanced down at her figure, which she knew was already thickening.

Margaret felt herself blush. "There will be . . . by year's end, I think."

"Good. I did wonder, though ladies keep such things to themselves. And you keep too many secrets, Margaret. Unnecessarily so."

"I will try to do better in future," she promised. Some of those secrets, she thought, she would never reveal. For an instant, she thought of her letters to and from Brother Tor, for she sensed that Malcolm would be displeased to know that his queen corresponded with a mere monk who had angered him by settling in Scottish territory without permission. But it was friendship, only that. All her deeds were known and counted in heaven, and that was enough, she assured herself.

Malcolm leaned down to kiss her, drawing her into his arms. He rarely kissed her outside of their encounters in bed, and now she expected his usual advance to follow—a hand to her breast or the hard press of his body—but he only turned and left the room.

At sunrise, she heard the sounds of men departing in the courtyard—hooves on packed earth, the clatter of armor and weapons, voices calling out. She rose from bed and drew aside a shuttered window, peering out as riders cantered through the gate. Malcolm rode in the lead under the fluttering blue banner stitched with a boar's image, which he favored.

She sank to her knees to pray, her stomach queasy again. Thin sunlight glowed over her hands and tousled hair as she gave thanks for the well-being of her family and begged forgiveness for her sins, each of them, as she did every day. Then she begged intercession from the warrior saints George, Mercurius, and Julian for her husband. Malcolm did not pray often enough, and she had rarely seen him earnest at what prayers he made.

Since the first weeks of her marriage, she had begun fervent, secret appeals on his behalf, and now she feared to abandon her effort if it kept him safe. Perhaps her faith could be stronger, she told herself.

Perhaps prayer, once expressed, took on a life of its own in God's ear and did not bear repeating, yet she did not know for sure. If she relaxed her diligence, dangerous forces might slip through her net of prayer, like icy cold through chinks in a wall, and let grief back into her life. Beginning to feel glimmers of happiness, she feared that it would not stay.

Chapter Thirteen

The busy cuckoo calls,
welcome noble summer . . .
The harp of the wood plays melody,
its music brings perfect peace

—IRISH, TENTH CENTURY

Eva drew her lightweight cloak snug despite the warmth of the summer morning. Tucked inside the silk lining was a parchment for Lady Gruadh, which she would soon give to the one who would send it on to Moray. By midday, she would be at Saint Serf's monastery—and then her only challenge would be to find some moments alone with Abbot Drostan so that she could discreetly hand him the letter.

She had not sent a message to her grandmother in a while, and so this one contained the news of the last several months—the birth of the queen's first son and the news that she was expecting already; and the arrival of Brother Tor, the author of the manuscript Lady Gruadh wanted to possess. If her letter was discovered, Eva would face serious questions, but the folded page was safe inside her cloak. She smiled and raised her face to the sunlight, happy to be outside and traveling again—the queen's condition and sedate activities had kept her ladies confined, too—and Eva looked forward to seeing Abbot Drostan.

She rode with the other women in a van fitted with cushions and a canopy with linen curtains now open to allow sunlight and wide views of the green hills and summer meadows of Fife. Seated between Margaret and Cristina, she felt every bump as the wooden vehicle moved along a rutted road north toward Loch Leven. The queen's condition prevented her from riding, but she had been determined to make the journey that day. Soon enough they reached a wide, cobbled stretch of old Roman road, and the way became easier. While the other ladies crowded in the van—including Cristina, Juliana, and Gudrun, with Wynne and Finola, too—chatting together, Margaret turned the pages of her little Gospel, mouthing the words. Eva rode facing outward, savoring the air and the beauty of Fife, where she had spent her childhood years.

Brother Micheil had offered to escort the queen and her ladies to Loch Leven, an island monastery well north of Dunfermline. The party was guarded by several housecarls riding alongside the wagon, and Prince Edgar had decided at the last moment to go, too. Eva saw him now, riding beside Micheil, in pleasant conversation.

"Eva, tell us again the name of the place we are visiting," Cristina said. "Why must we ride out to see yet another Scottish church? They are all alike—nice little chapels, yet some have pagan features. It might be sinful to pray in such places!"

Eva was glad Brother Micheil had not heard that. "But Saint Serf's monastery is not pagan in its origins. The first priory on Loch Leven was built long ago when Saint Serf—Saint Servanus, who was a pope of Rome—traveled far north to settle in Scotland, once he saw the beauty of that place."

"A pope!" Christina said, while Margaret looked up, her attention caught.

"A pope," Eva said. "We are not so far removed from Rome as you may think."

"Ladies," Brother Micheil said as he caught up to them. He gestured. "Rome would indeed approve, for this road is part of the pilgrimage road that leads to Saint Andrews, and is part of the larger route that begins in Spain. The devout come from all places to follow this Scottish road, and they visit our other holy sites along the way, including Loch Leven. The pilgrimage routes are the drove roads in Scotland, too, so they can be crowded on market days. We are fortunate to have it to ourselves today."

The road cut between golden moors and rumpled hills beneath a bright sky, leading onward. As the day grew warmer, the escort stopped in small villages once or twice for refreshment. Later, as they continued, Brother Micheil rode beside the wagon and named native saints who had once lived nearby, here and there.

"I would like to see the cells and caves where the holy ones lived and prayed," Margaret said. "It is a boon for Scotland to have a pilgrimage route in Fife. One day soon I would like to walk it myself, at least through Scotland."

"Next year, Margaret," Edgar said, riding close to the wagon, "when you are fit for it, after the babe."

As they traveled, Margaret asked Eva to correct her pronunciation of the Gaelic names of the Celtic saints, though Eva admitted to knowing little about their lives. Margaret shook her head. "I do worry about the state of your soul, Eva," she said. "You should know your saints!"

"If there are songs about saints, I know those." Eva laughed.

Margaret smiled, then turned to speak to her sister. Eva saw Edgar riding beside the van again, mounted on a pale stallion with a braided mane, a tall Saxon-bred horse. She thought the human rider equally beautiful.

"It is a good day for a tour," he said. "My sister seems pleased."

"Aye. She has been confined overmuch lately."

He nodded. "Malcolm has insisted that she remain hidden for her own protection."

"Protection against the Normans?"

"Aye. There is always the danger that they could come north. King William still demands the return of the royal Saxon fugitives. But he has gone to France for now, so Malcolm gave permission for Margaret to travel if inclined. Fortunately Saint Andrews is too far for a day's journey," he added. "I fear she would go there on her knees, even in her state."

"She will enjoy Saint Serf's. Loch Leven is a very peaceful place. I lived in Fife as a child with my kinsmen, before I was sent to my Moray kin."

"Ah. Your Fife uncle helped convince my sister to marry the king." He looked sideways at her as he rode beside the wagon.

Eva gazed at him in surprise. "What coaxing would a princess need to marry a warrior-king? The only ones who might hesitate would be from Moray," she suggested wryly.

He laughed. Eva liked the warm sound. "My sister refused at first, too, saying she would rather live in a convent than be queen." He spoke in a low tone so that only she would hear. "But heaven's will brought us to Scotland. And from here I must win back a kingdom, if it can be done." With that, he urged the horse to canter ahead.

She sighed. Her heartbeat quickened whenever Edgar was near, however inexplicably. True, he was a fine and heroic young warrior, as in songs and tales; he was charming and attractive, and near her age, even younger. But no Saxon prince would be interested in a deposed Moray princess, and neither would her kin welcome him. She tilted her head to watch as he brought his horse in line with the accompanying guards. Edgar's Saxon cause was impossible, but it was noble as well, and she admired his conviction. Besides, as he was Margaret's brother, Eva had reason enough to like him.

He reminded her of someone—of her father, she realized. Like Lulach, he was blond and handsome, fresh and ready despite a hopeless fight. Should Edgar, too, beware Malcolm, though the king was his supporter and brother by law? Eva drew back inside the wagon, resting against the cushions in silence.

Within the hour, they came to the shores of the great loch. Low hills, like peaked green and blue draperies, spread out beneath the sky, and the surface of the water was mirror-calm. A narrow dock bridged to the rocky shore, where a ferry waited, a small birlinn manned by a robust man and a young boy. As the housecarls assisted Eva and the others out of the wagon, Edgar went forward to pay the man a few silver coins.

Seeing Margaret hesitate as they approached the boat, Eva took her arm, for the queen looked suddenly pale. "Are you ill, Lady?"

"A boat," Margaret said faintly. "I had not thought of a boat."

"It is only a short way." Surely Margaret's stomach was bothering her again, Eva thought. Edgar took his sister's other arm, and together they helped the queen into the boat. As Eva sat beside her, Margaret leaned slightly toward her.

"I made a private vow when we first came to Scotland," she whispered, "to never again ride over water. I must amend it for small water crossings, but I like my feet on land."

"I understand." Eva smiled slightly, touched that Margaret had again confided in her. For a moment, she felt a little stir of guilt. The letter in her pocket did not prove her faith as a friend, though it met her obligation as a granddaughter. But these small trusts—these she surely would keep.

The loch had several islands, and the ferryman rowed toward the largest, where Eva saw the flat-topped hill, monastery, and encircling stone wall. She had been here as a child, but hardly remembered except that it had been winter.

"Pilgrims, are you?" The ferryman spoke English and seemed unimpressed to have royal passengers. "We have not seen many pilgrims this year. The Culdees here keep to themselves, but the faithful visit and worship. Still, we do not see as many as we once did."

"Why so, sir?" the queen asked.

"Some cannot afford to pay, and we cannot take them over for free.

Years ago I ferried over the great firth between Dun Edin and Fife, but I brought my family north for safety, and we keep a farm here now. The wars in England have emptied Scottish purses, too. There are fewer trade ships, so fewer merchants with goods and fewer customers to buy them."

"It is very true, what you say, sir," Edgar agreed. "We are doing our best to improve it."

"See that you do. People have made the pilgrimage across Scotland to Saint Andrews for generations, hoping to save their souls," the ferryman said. "Not as many complete the trip now. But it would help the Scottish treasury if more pilgrims would come here."

"The treasury!" Margaret said. "It would surely help their souls."

"My lady, not all pilgrims go on foot as penitents," he said. "Many pay for ferry service and stay in inns along the way, and they visit our markets and buy pilgrim badges and relics. They donate to church coffers, too. We can blame the wars in England for the change."

"Ah, so Scotland gains from pilgrim visits," Margaret said, nodding her understanding.

"Indeed, pilgrimages are gold for Scotland. But if travelers cannot afford passage over water, it is a very long walk to go all the way around. Here we are," he said, as he halted the boat in the shallows along the pebbled shore. Nearby rose the monastery walls, stark and beautiful.

"It is lovely, but so isolated," Margaret said, gazing at the flat-topped slope. "However do the monks support themselves?"

"They raise sheep. See the flocks grazing on the hill," the ferryman pointed out. "There is good income for Scottish wool exported elsewhere. The monastery also owns farmland near the loch. The kings of Scotland have always been generous to Saint Serf's," he said meaningfully as his charges stood, preparing to disembark. Edgar, taking the hint, paid him with several coins.

Two housecarls who had ridden in the boat—the rest had remained onshore with the horses and wagon—began to carry the ladies through the shallows. Margaret kept Eva back, turning again to the ferryman. "I presume my husband, the king, supports the monastery?"

"I believe so," the man answered. "Most of the land was acquired years back, when this place was favored by Macbeth and Queen Gruadh. They granted lands to the monastery, farms that supply income in rentals and market profits. I am a tenant of Saint Serf's," he added proudly.

Margaret stood as the guards returned. "Macbeth and Gruadh endowed land here?"

"Aye, Lady. She was born a princess of Fife, and inherited lands when her father died, though much of that was taken from her by the Macduffs. This land south of the loch"—he gestured—"was hers to grant, and she endowed it here. Abbot Drostan was fostered by Queen Gruadh's own father, so he knows that lady well. One of the few men she trusts, he is."

"Ah!" Margaret turned to Eva. "So you know this abbot, Lady Eva? You never said."

"We met when I was small, but I do not remember him well. He does know my grandmother, but with the long distances between here and Moray, they rarely meet." She did not add that Drostan and Gruadh kept regular correspondence via messengers. "My mother was born near here as well," she added. "Her father was mormaer of Fife after Lady Gruadh's father, my great-grandfather Bodhe, was killed . . . by King Malcolm's own great-grandfather." Honesty had more value than reticence, she decided, especially with this queen, who appreciated forthrightness.

"I see," Margaret said quietly. "So your life, and the legacy of your family, is bound to Fife and to this monastery as well."

"In some ways. But Moray is my home."

"And where your loyalty lies?" Margaret looked thoughtful. Then she smiled at the ferryman. "Thank you, sir. Will you be back for us soon?" He nodded.

The guards carried Margaret ashore, and then Edgar stepped down into the water, offering to lift Eva. She accepted, riding in his arms as he waded through the water, her arms locked about his neck. He set her down on the rocky shore, and as she thanked him her heart beat hard—she thought of the feel of his arms long after he had walked ahead up the hill with Brother Micheil to announce the arrival of the queen's party. Eva came after, offering Margaret an arm, for the queen seemed pale and weak.

Two monks welcomed them at the gate and brought them inside the walls. The monastery spread out over the hilltop, with several buildings, including a refectory, a dormitory, a chapel, and outbuildings, most of them made of fieldstone, all with unobstructed views of the loch and open to the winds but for the protection of the surrounding stone wall.

One of the brothers explained that the abbot was in the scriptorium, for Saint Serf's was a center for the copying of manuscripts and had an extensive library, which Margaret remarked she would like to see. As they walked, Eva saw a man hurrying toward them, wearing the white robes of the Céli Dé, as did all the monks of Saint Serf's. His hair, in a frontal tonsure, was dark and long at the back, silvered throughout. She stopped and smiled, recognizing him, even after years.

He smiled as well, extending his hands as he neared the party. "Welcome," he said. "I am Drostan, abbot here." He spoke warmly, addressing Margaret and her siblings more than the others, only looking toward Eva once, as if he did not recognize her. Likely he did not, she thought, knowing she needed to find a chance to speak to him privately. She touched the letter hidden in her cloak, its stiff crackle reminding her that it was secure there. Yet it was like having a hot coal in her pocket—she desperately wanted to be rid of it.

"Abbot, you will remember Lady Eva of Moray," Margaret said.

"Indeed! Eva, you have the look of your mother and some of your grandmother's beauty as well." He smiled, taking her hands in his.

"Father, so good to see you." Eva could say nothing specific with the others listening, but hoped to discuss her grandmother with him later. He squeezed her fingers and let go.

Explaining that the manuscripts copied at Saint Serf's brought income and helped establish a fine reputation for the monastery, Drostan led the group into the scriptorium. Four monks were seated at slant-top desks, writing or copying out words on scraped vellum pages with quill pens that made light scratching sounds in the quiet room. Full inkwells, black and red, sat on desk corners, and loose parchment sheets curled as the monks leaned over their work. Learning that the queen was in their midst, the monks scrambled to their feet, flustered as they greeted her. Seeing how young they were, Eva suppressed a smile.

The manuscripts on which they labored were beautiful pages from the gospels and a page copied from Adomnán's laws. The certain manuscript Eva sought was well out of her reach here, she knew, for it was in Brother Tor's possession in the south. Soon she would have to tell Lady Gruadh that she might never see the thing, despite her grandmother's insistence.

The group moved on to the library, where Margaret admired several of the books chained to the shelves, and Eva thought the queen might want to stay the afternoon there, so fond was she of the books. But Drostan persuaded them to go to the refectory, where he had ordered refreshments brought. There they were offered ale, barley cakes, and fresh strawberries.

"From our farms. Please eat," Drostan said, shaking his head when invited to join them. "Our meals here are taken sparingly, but you have traveled a long way today. And though we often eat in silence here, we few are the only ones at the table now, so we will break the rule." He smiled.

"Though this is not a Benedictine abbey, you follow some of its precepts, Abbot," Brother Micheil said. "The Saxons among us will be pleased."

"You do have a godly and productive existence here, Father

Abbot," Margaret said. "It is a tranquil life, devoting oneself to prayer and good works."

"There are infinite ways to do that," he replied. "Not all souls are suited to the monastic life, men or women. And others have callings that keep them, quite rightly, in the greater world."

Margaret sighed. "Aye. Have you been to Dunfermline, Abbot? Would you visit us there? Often both Culdees and Benedictines meet to discuss the state of the Scottish church in particular. Your wisdom and experience would be welcome."

"I am honored, Lady, though I will leave larger questions to others to debate. Years back, I came often to Dunfermline, when I served another of Scotland's kings."

"Macbeth?" she asked quickly.

"Aye, and his queen. Now I am content to oversee this monas-tery." As he spoke, the bronze bell in the chapel tower sounded out, echoing over isle and loch, calling them to prayers.

Later, in the chapel, Eva prayed alongside Margaret and the oth-ers, including several monks, for a long while. When Drostan slipped away before the rest, Eva did the same, trusting that no one would give her absence much thought. As she went out into the yard, she saw one or two monks tending to a kitchen garden, carrying baskets of vegetables, while another walked with the abbot toward the refectory. Seeing her, Drostan spoke to his companion, and came toward her.

"Eva, walk with me a moment," he said in easy Gaelic, having spoken English until then.

She fell into step beside him as he led her toward the garden, where she saw wide, verdant rows of staked and spreading vege-tables: full, broad bean plants, peas with wild, lacy tendrils, lush, delicate lettuces, sturdy leeks, and onion. She drew a deep breath of the green and garlicky scents there. Drostan led her along a path-way thick-edged with strawberry plants dividing luxuriant herb and flower beds—daisies, marigolds, hollyhocks, and lavender, and beyond those, neat clumps of rosemary, basil, and a host of herbs. The garden was enclosed by a wattle fence to keep out the goats and the chickens, which favored the tender peas. At the back against the stone wall she saw apple trees, their fruit green and forming as yet.

Drostan spread out an arm. "The yield has been good this summer, and so I have asked the brothers to fill baskets for your party to take back to Dunfermline."

"Will you consider coming to Dunfermline, sir, some other time?"

"I will not." He strolled in silence for a moment. "Lady Rue was here a fortnight ago."

Eva looked up in surprise. "She rarely leaves Moray."

"She felt concerned, having had so few messages from you. We dissuaded her from riding toward Dunfermline to see you. The risk would have been too great for both of you."

"Was she so frantic to know what goes on at court? I have a new letter for her—will you send it on?" Eva reached inside her cloak, sliding a hand into the pocket in the silk lining.

"Of course." He took the letter and slipped it inside his white sleeve before tucking his hands within the generous folds. "Eva, your grandmother wants to know that you are safe, above all. She also wants to hear whatever might be of interest at court. She expects frequent letters from you."

Feeling chided, she sighed. "I understand that. But little at court would truly interest her," she explained. "I wish I had known she was here."

"We can arrange another visit, if you like," he murmured.

"I am a hostage, and close watch is kept over me. I could not get safely away unless Queen Margaret returned here, too. Father Drostan, I would ask you something," she said impulsively. At his nod, she continued. "You know, I think, what my grandmother expects of me."

"She told me something of her request. I think you have the spirit for it."

"But is it right to do this? When I came to Dunfermline, I wanted to carry out what Lady Gruadh asked, even though it goes against what is proper for a bard."

"Honor has always been part of the best bardic traditions."

"Just so," Eva said. "What the lady asks of me is a betrayal of what I have been taught, yet she is my grandmother and a former queen, and I owe her loyalty. And no one doubts that Malcolm slew my father, so I owe loyalty to Lulach's memory as well."

"I will not condone revenge, but I understand this difficult choice."

"Now made more difficult," she rushed on. "I have come to know the queen so well—and so my earlier promise feels like a betrayal of her, too."

"Ah. So you wonder which course is right."

She nodded glumly, head bowed. "When I first came to court, it seemed clear that Margaret and Malcolm could be harmful to Scotland and that my kinfolk were right and just. But now . . . I do not know. If I spy and send reports to Moray, even if I am not caught out, it is a betrayal of Margaret's trust in me, as well as a betrayal of my trade."

"And if you do not, you betray your grandmother's trust." Drostan sighed. "I cannot sort this tangle for you, Eva girl. You must decide what seems right."

"What seems right is tending to my music—but it also seems right to love both my grandmother and my new friend the queen. But what seems most wrong, Father," she added, "is for Malcolm to ruin Macbeth's memory with his false history. If I can help change that, surely I must, even if my grandmother has set me an impossible task."

"You are answering your own questions," he said, smiling a little. "Come, they will be looking for you soon. Here," he said, tearing off a thick handful of petaled lavender fronds. "Give these to the queen if you wish to explain your stroll through the gardens with me."

"I will say that I needed your spiritual advice." Eva breathed in the fragrant oils on her fingertips. "Lavender is good for headache and fosters a tranquil spirit. Margaret will appreciate that."

"Lavender also invites the protection of the angels, which you may sorely need the longer you remain in the royal court," he said.

Chapter Fourteen

❧

May the taste of honey be
On every word you say
To commons and to nobles
This day and each day

—Traditional Scottish charm

Malcolm kept his end of the bargain. He took Edgar's cause as his own, raiding into England to defend the Saxon claim, knocking spear butts into Norman helmets, burning Norman-held lands, as if enough war and recklessness would gain back England. But the Norman foe was not dissuaded by attacks or rebellion, and more effort was needed, much more. Margaret heard Malcolm and others debating and passionately arguing it at night when the men were there; often enough they raided south, with scant word of their whereabouts or well-being.

Margaret had honored her part of the marriage bargain, bearing a healthy son before they had been wed a year and breeding again soon after. Small Edward stayed in the care of his wet nurse and the maidservants, but Margaret visited him each morning after prayers and in the evenings, and whenever her heart and her arms missed him. He thrived. She was proud and grateful, and glad that her mother saw him flourish and relaxed her doubts.

Duncan and Donald stayed on, dividing their hours between tutors at the table and wooden swords in the practice field, and played with the children of nobles and servants, while Lady Edith and Cospatric's son, Dolfin, became like a brother to Malcolm's sons. Margaret found time each day to read to the boys herself, and she pointed out to Malcolm how well they got on with each other.

"A child's affection is without guile," she told him when he complained about too many young ones underfoot, chasing about the great hall and the bailey or fussing during supper. "The one who nurtures them is nurtured in return. And we learn good charity from little ones. We benefit by keeping them close." She eagerly awaited the birth of her second babe, now tumbling and lively within, and wished for more babes in the future, if heaven willed it so.

Sometimes she fed little Edward herself, asking Dame Agnes to bring boiled gruel thinned with goat's milk for him. Other mornings, Mirren brought Edward, Dolfin, and other small children to the hall and Margaret would cuddle them one at a time on her lap and feed them from her own porridge bowl, though her women scolded her for not eating enough herself.

"If I forget to eat sometimes, it is fine," she said. "The company of children is food for my soul, and better for me than a little salty porridge." They did not agree with her, but she carried on as if they did.

The children did not provide an escape from other matters that clouded the days. Reports of King William's continued wrath and Malcolm's retaliations made it clear that her marriage had invited more violence upon the Saxon people. Messages reported ravages in the north country, homes and fields burned and destroyed, skirmishes and brutalities, evictions, rapes, murders: the annihilation of a people and a future. The Scots herded thousands more north to be taken in as slaves;

no matter their previous rank. It was better than dying in a ditch, as Malcolm had once hinted.

Yet Margaret could not help but feel that the destruction was partly her fault, and that awareness sickened her deeply. Her mother said she was ill because she was brewing a babe within, but bad news from England too often gave her knotty nerves and a rocky stomach. She could neither sleep nor eat, thinking of Saxons hungry and suffering, their children without shoes or cloaks, without porridge, without mothers to reach for them. Her own family had so much, and the contrast made her prayers more fervent. But she did not know how, as Queen of Scots, to help the Saxons.

❦

MACDUFF CAME TO COURT past harvest time and greeted Eva with a brief kiss and tentative affection—he told her she looked well and, holding her hands, asked after her harp playing.

Unexpectedly she teared up, touched that he'd thought of it. "I have not been permitted since you were here last," she said, and her uncle frowned.

"I will speak to Malcolm of it. We have much to discuss with or without that," he said when she protested.

He met with the king and stayed for days as they joined with others in heated debates behind closed doors. When Angus of Mar and other Scottish leaders arrived, the king took the discussions out on horseback or on foot with hawks and hounds. Their daily hunts were so profitable that meals were generously supplemented with fresh roast venison and stewed hare, and grouse as well. Although Eva enjoyed the fresh dishes, the queen pushed most of her servings away, citing either a tender stomach or the need to fast.

The last night that Macduff was there, planning to leave before dawn, he leaned toward Malcolm. "I would like to hear my niece play for the company," he said. "We spoke of this."

Malcolm was silent for a moment, and Eva held her breath. "Very well," he finally said, and she heard the begrudging in it. "Eva, have your harp brought down."

She gestured to Wynne, seated nearby, and the girl went up to their shared bedchamber to fetch the harp. Eva had kept to her room that day, practicing a few melodies, and so she knew the instrument was tuned. She settled the harp against her left shoulder, thought for a moment, then glanced toward the king. He looked tense, his face drawn. She bowed her head.

"Here is a song," she said, "that I composed in praise of my mother, Lady Leven of Fife, who was kinswoman to good Macduff. She first taught me to find the music hidden in the harp strings."

> *Her love promised her a mirror*
> *So her beauty she could see,*
> *A veil of silk and a silver ring*
> *And a harp-tree for melodies*

Eva sang all the verses, some of them sad with longing, and played the delicate tune that so reminded her of her mother's grace. When she finished there was silence, and a few people dashed away tears, including the queen. Malcolm, looking grim, said nothing. He could not gainsay a song made for her dead mother, though Eva knew he would note the implication that her mother had loved Lulach, whose song had caused such trouble for Eva several months ago.

Before she left the hall that night, having lingered to bid her uncle farewell, Eva was surprised when Kenneth Macduff offered her a purse of coins. "Your song for Leven was beautifully done, and took courage. You are a bold girl."

She shook her head at his gift. "Please, I cannot accept this. A bard should not trade music for coin."

"This is not for your music. It is from me in trade for years of neglecting you."

"You gave me a dog and a pony," she reminded him, half smiling.

"I did. Use this for your keep here, or for your dowry." He pressed the soft leather bag, heavy and full, into her hands. "I will grant you the rents from a parcel of land in Fife. You will be a wealthy woman and will marry well. There are fine young warriors here in the king's court."

"And not one of them would marry a daughter of Moray, for fear the kinship would ruin his good name." She guessed this would be so for Edgar the Saxon, too. No matter, she told herself, lifting her chin. But no one could quicken her heart or make poetry spin in her head as Edgar could.

"I will discuss the matter of your marriage match with the king," Macduff said.

"Discuss it with my grandmother."

"I would rather negotiate with a trained bear," he replied. "Now give this sack to the king to hold for you, rather than keep it under your bed."

"He might not give it back. I will entrust it to the queen."

"That one? She might give it away."

"Then you keep it for me." Eva thrust the bag back into his hands. "I trust you. I do," she said in a rush, knowing it was true, as if the years of mistrusting and resenting him for dumping her out of his household seemed to vanish in that moment. She was older, wiser—so was he. Forgiveness flowed in her unexpectedly, and for a moment she wondered if it was some magic from her mother's song; she had not sung it in years, and it filled her heart.

Macduff seemed caught for words, and leaned down to kiss her brow.

IN ALL THE TIME she had been in Dunfermline, Margaret had never set foot inside Malcolm's treasury, the locked room adjacent to the king's bedchamber. Discovering from De Lauder that Malcolm was there one day, she made an impulsive decision and boldly climbed the stairs to knock and announce herself. After a moment he came to the door and turned the iron key from within so that she could enter.

The room was small, dank, lit by the bright flicker of an oil lamp and the rainy light that came through the oiled parchment of a very small window. The space was crammed with chests and fitted with a table and stool, and Malcolm resumed his seat to hunch over the parch-ment sheets and rolled documents scattered there. He opened one and Margaret saw a long list written in a cramped hand, perhaps his own or that of a cleric. Rain drummed against the shutters. Poor weather was often the only reason the king stayed indoors.

She turned. Arranged against the walls were large, locked chests and several small, metal caskets banded and engraved, with hinged, peaked tops—the sort used for containing relics, jewelry, or personal items. Two reliquaries were open, and Margaret saw the gleam of gold and silver: coins, jewels, and chains, literal handfuls, inside. Imagining what treasure the larger chests might hold, she tipped her head, con-templating. So much wealth sitting here, simply counted and stored; it would be better used for those in need, she thought, folding her arms.

"The chests are not all stuffed with coins and jewels, if you think so," Malcolm said, as if he knew her thoughts. "They hold other items—vessels and dishes, relics of ancient kings, some swords and daggers. And hundreds of documents—deeds, writs, lists, in rolls or as books."

She looked about. The walls were hung with embroidered panels, the floor covered in a thick woven tapestry, so that the room seemed hushed, dark, cushioned, protecting its secrets. "Nonetheless, the King of Scots appears to be wealthier than some would think," she said.

"There is wealth here, I grant. Not so much as once was, but less than in the future, if we are fortunate. Did you come here to tell me something?"

She folded her hands. Seeing proof of his wealth excited her sud-denly, gave her a sense of hope as the idea dawned. For weeks, she had been thinking about ways to do more charitable acts, partly because it was expected of her rank and position, and partly to lighten her own sins.

"Dear husband," she said with careful flattery, "I think often of the poor and suffering. Do you?" She did not let her gaze wander toward the gold and silver. Though she had immediately decided some of it must be shared, she dared not be too obvious.

"If this is one of your frequent confessions, not that you have much wickedness in you," he said, "I am not a priest. Or is it the woebegone mood of a woman with child?"

"It is only a thought. Daily we hear of stragglers and survivors coming out of England. Some have found safety in Scottish households, but others still need our help."

"Then pray for them. It is the best you can do. Or does your tender heart long to spend the crown's gold on more than silver spoons and curtain cloth?" He perused his account rolls.

"Some of this treasure is mine, too, from my dowry," she reminded him, indicating the chests. "And what I speak of is not tenderheartedness but simple strategy, sire. We must show Scotland's charitable throne. Almsgiving will help make good your name in places far flung from Scotland. Our generosity would be smiled upon in heaven, too, on Judgment Day."

Malcolm cocked a brow. "I suspect you would give all we have to the poor, just to earn that."

She ignored that. "We could do even more if the court was in Dun Edin," she said.

"You, my dear, are safer in Dunfermline."

"I have been here ever since my family and I arrived, while you travel about place to place. I hear that many Saxon fugitives go to the town of Dun Edin. Most do not come this far north. We have been protected from the war here in Dunfermline."

"For good reason," he said. "King William may yet bring Normans into Scotland, and he still demands your return to England, even now."

"I thought the threat of invasion was gone. We heard he went back to France, leaving his generals in charge in England."

"Lessened but not gone. He is in France for now but will return, and he may yet try to come into Scotland with his swords and fire arrows. I will not endanger you or our children."

"Dun Edin is one of the strongest fortresses in all Britain, I hear, and you are improving it further with stone walls and additions. It is secure. How can I be an effective queen if I am restricted to one place?"

He paused. "I did plan to go to Dun Edin for a while, but first I mean to visit Saint Andrews to confer with Bishop Fothad and tour some of my northern properties. I might take you with me," he said, glancing up from his columns of items and numbers, "when you are unburdened of your child."

"Soon enough," she said, resting a hand on her high, rounded abdomen. "The babe kicks freely but no longer turns. The time is approaching. Take me on progress once he or she is born."

"I suppose you could sail to Saint Andrews with me. We could go from there to Dun Edin. Perhaps you are right. It is time the Scots saw more of their queen."

"Sail?" Suddenly the plan was much less appealing. She had taken ferries here and there for necessary local travel, but she held firm to her vow not to sail in a longship on the sea—besides, her stomach quailed at the very thought. Beyond the window, a hearty boom of thunder reminded her of storms and sinking ships. "But I do not want to sail."

"It is the fastest way to travel from here to Saint Andrews, and from there to Dun Edin."

"Surely there is a landward way."

"There is, if you go on pilgrimage, but that takes time, which I do not have."

Or patience, she thought. "I do not want to travel to Saint Andrews by ship."

"Margaret, it takes too long to cross the whole length of Fife on land, with a full entourage."

"When I arrived in Scotland, I vowed that if God brought us safe through those storms and to land, then I would keep away from the sea, and aid others in their own sea journeys."

"Woman," he said, "that is a foolish vow. We must often travel by water in Scotland."

"I did not think of that at the time," she admitted. "Still, I made the vow and will keep it."

"Stubborn!" He turned another page in the accounts. "At least you will not be sailing back to Hungary." He seemed amused. "The faster route to Dun Edin is also by ship. What of that? Will you stay away?"

Margaret shook her head, always serious; truly she did not know how to be otherwise. "But Scotland has a pilgrim's route available to all. Saint Andrews houses the relics of the very first apostle. I must go on foot out of respect and devotion."

"If a queen walks a long pilgrimage, she will be said to be burdened by sin and guilt. Do you want that rumored of you?"

"Piety is admirable. I will walk the last miles only."

"I suppose that will suffice."

"And I will only travel over land to Dun Edin," she added, suspecting she had lost ground.

He made an impatient gesture and she knew that he was done listening to her, intent on his documents, peering at a list of taxes recently paid. "After you are lighter of the child and recovered, we will make the journey. Margaret," he added as she turned for the door. "Order spare cloaks and shoes made, in case you feel a need to give them away on your travels. And do not think about my treasure chests," he warned, as she glanced at those again.

"Of course not, sire," she said, smiling.

WITHIN THREE WEEKS, Margaret rose from her bed at the sound of bells, before it was light, to kneel at a little altar set in a corner of the bedchamber for her use. But her back ached as she prayed, and had ached all night. She had gone up and down stairs too much lately, she thought. But soon she felt the undeniable constriction of her womb, again and again within several minutes. Her time had come, and would soon be in earnest.

Hearing that word, Malcolm left to dispatch a rider to fetch Mother Annot, who had been the midwife for the last babe and had been granted a cottage and plot of land closer to Dunfermline, giving her comfortable quarters while she waited out the weeks with the queen. Margaret sent Finola to wake her ladies and her kinswomen, but their chatter and company soon tired her and she sent some of them away, allowing her mother and Eva to remain, asking the latter to fetch her harp. If she could hear the music of sleeping, the soft melodies she loved best, Margaret reasoned that the birth might go easier.

The waters burst just after Mother Annot arrived. Eva kept to a stool in the corner, playing, and Margaret labored quietly, intensely. At times she felt as if she floated on the delicate, soothing sounds, as if the harp strings were plucked by the angels of heaven itself, and as the pressures in her body grew more insistent, stranding Margaret in a storm she could not escape, she clung to the music as if to prayer.

Hours passed, deep into the day, while she fought, surrendered, lost to all but the grinding demands of her body, the only relief the airy music lifting around her. Pushing, and pushing again, she threw herself fiercely into it by late afternoon, and finally felt the deep release as the child was born, but twelve hours from when she had first felt the twinges.

"A beautiful boy," Kata said, taking the bundle from the midwife. "Another fine prince!"

Laughing, exhausted, Margaret took the new little one into her arms to gaze at his tiny face—flushed deep pink, eyes squinting and mouth already pursing, he had a wizened yet familiar look. He was fair and delicate—and she realized that he looked like her, as if she gazed into a tiny mirror and saw herself, years ago. Her heart nearly burst with the expanse of love she felt in that moment, for him and for herself, small like this once. She nuzzled him against her bare breast, holding up a hand to Lady Agatha when she began to protest, still believing that caution and fear were better than risk and love.

"Tell Malcolm," Margaret said, though someone had already been sent to find him in the great hall or in the bailey—he had sworn not to go far. "Tell him that his Edward must soon give up his cradle for a new brother." Tears sprang to her eyes then, for she thought, too, of Edward, growing too fast from babe to child—but she would never say that aloud, or risk her mother's snappish disapproval, even now, for being too attached to her children.

Eva came forward, smiling as she looked at the babe. "He is a very pretty babe, and strong," she added as his tiny fingers curled around her thumb. "What will you call him?"

"Edmund," Margaret said decisively. "I decided that if it was a boy, he would be Edmund for my grandfather, who was called Edmund Ironside. He was a king and a warrior."

"But Edward has a Saxon name. Should not this one be named for his Scots lineage?"

"They are sons of a Saxon princess, descended of West Saxon kings, as well as of a Scottish king," Margaret said, and looked up as Malcolm entered the room. "Come see our new prince, sire."

As he came forward gingerly, the child set up a lusty squalling. "Ah, this one is a warrior," Malcolm said, smiling. "Were you just talking of a name to suit him?"

"Edmund." Margaret drew back the swaddling to better show his face.

"Crinan is a proud name," he suggested. "My grandfather was called so. I wanted it for our first son."

"Prince Edmund," she said firmly, "will benefit from carrying the name of his Saxon great-grandfather, who was known to the wider world for his courage. Ironside, they called him. Our new son must be Edmund. I will not be gainsaid on this."

"Aye then," Malcolm murmured. "The mother of such lusty princes shall have whatever she likes of me."

"Gold?" she asked eagerly. "A special almsgiving in honor of the new prince?"

"I will think about it," he said, and kissed her hand.

Chapter Fifteen

Sagacious in spirit, elf-lovely lady

— ANGLO-SAXON,
EIGHTH CENTURY

T wo healthy sons!" Gruadh walked with Drostan and Ruari,
gesturing, the March winds sweeping at her linen veils, whipping at her dark green gown and her cloak of pale plaid wool. Together
with the men, she crossed a sloping meadow toward Elgin, having
walked to chapel that morning and now back again. Whenever Drostan
came to Elgin, which was not often, Gruadh made an effort to show
pious ways—sincere enough, though there would be no competing
with the southern queen. "How soon before she breeds another son?
Fertile as a hare, she is, though she acts all but a saint. And her Scottish princes have Saxon names! Where is Malcolm in this?"

"According to Eva's latest note, which came last week with a messenger, the babes are healthy and Malcolm is improving into a fine Saxon
king," Drostan said.

"As for the sons, if the queen's babes are thriving, we can only be glad of it," Ruari said.

"I do not begrudge any woman joy in her sons," Gruadh said. "But I am weary of reports of her beauty and intelligence, her charity and mercy. She gives away her own cloaks and shoes. She prays like a nun. Her hospitality is a marvel, with foreign foods on golden plates, foreign wines in precious goblets. She dresses Malcolm like a French king and teaches him courteous ways. He is content with pretty, praying Margaret and the wee Margaretsons, as Eva says the princes are called by some."

"When they are grown warriors, they will be the sons of Malcolm." Ruari was pragmatic.

"She has no Scots blood in her, this queen, and dilutes the royal Gaelic line in her sons. Drostan, you say she wishes to change the Celtic church, and has invited Benedictines north. The black-robes will reform us all, quick-like. Bless Eva for sending news at last," she said, patting the leather purse at her belt, where she had tucked the parchment Drostan had delivered that day. "For all it is a catalog of praises. I want truth."

"There is much to praise in Margaret, and that is truth," Drostan said calmly.

"Even Eva hints at the queen's perfection and saintliness. It is much to bear," Gruadh said.

"She has shaped the court to be more English, I vow, or French," Ruari admitted, "but it is good for the Scottish court to learn the ways of the larger world. More ambassadors will be willing to visit. We will have more allies—and more support, should we need it against William one day."

"And we will be less Gaelic." Gruadh had seen something of that in her visions, but she would not say it aloud. Drostan did not want to hear of the old methods, and Ruari paid them no mind.

"The Gaels will always honor and protect the traditions of this land," Ruari said. "Nothing that can happen in the south will change that."

"The Englishing of Scotland," she remarked. "We knew it would come. Macbeth knew it, too, years gone."

"And did not fear it," Ruari said gently. "He welcomed what was good for Scotland."

"That is the crux of it." Gruadh paused on the hillside to gaze across the moorland toward Dun Elgin, which crowned the steep-sided hill that supported and protected it. "What suits lower Scotland does not always suit upper Scotland. As Malcolm adopts more Saxon ways, he stirs more thoughts of rebellion in Moray and elsewhere. We in Moray would be better off without this king if he continues to favor Saxons and lets the Normans in."

"There are many in Moray and elsewhere who would see the back of Malcolm," Ruari said. "But if King William pushes north into Scotland, I believe Malcolm would resist with all he can muster, and if luck goes with him it would be enough."

"He has more luck than might," Drostan remarked. "He is not as strong a leader as he thinks."

"Nor does he have the whole of Scotland at his back, and never did," Ruari agreed. "He has sided with the wrong party too often in the past, even before the Normans—he supported the wrong Saxon leaders, and the Danes who supported only themselves. Now he backs a prince no older than Nechtan and no match for William. Only a warrior with passion and talent and thousands of troops at his beck could win against William the Norman. Edgar is not that man."

"To be fair, that can be said of young Nechtan, too." Drostan looked at Gruadh.

"But if William comes into Scotland, we cannot trust Malcolm," Gruadh said. "Rather, we must protect Moray however we can. And if Malcolm holds William at bay but continues to make Scotland into a Saxon land, I think we find a way to put Nechtan on the throne for the good of all the Gaels. He is young, but he is still the rightful blood leader of Moray as well as Scotland. And he can be ready."

"The lad has a scholar's mind," Drostan said. "He dreams of a monk's life. You know that."

She did. And she knew that Nechtan was not the warrior his kins-men had been—but now that Moray teetered on the sharp sword edge of rebellion, his bloodline was too significant. "He has a clever mind for strategy, and he understands the need."

"I believe that William would first demand Malcolm's homage to him as king of England before he would attack," said Drostan. "If Malcolm were to refuse that, there could be war on Scottish soil."

"Either way, those who once supported Macbeth have long memo-ries," Gruadh said. "If we must rebel against Malcolm, we would have the strength of other mormaers behind us. It is this push to let in Saxon ways or Norman forces that could bring Malcolm down in the end."

"But rebellion may not be necessary," Ruari said calmly. "We need only show strength and threat if Malcolm makes a foolish move to endanger Scotland. That would bring others away from Malcolm and behind us."

"Before it comes to that," Gruadh said, "we would have to bring Eva north again."

"Having a hostage makes the king feel safe, so he does not train his wolf's eye this way," Drostan pointed out.

"True," Ruari agreed. "And Malcolm will never let her go if he sniffs even a hint of rebellion from us."

THE KING WAS IN A TEMPER, Eva heard it said, because they must proceed to Saint Andrews by cart, horse, and foot rather than hasten south to Dun Edin. The journey could be rushed in a day if needed, but he had promised the queen that she could make part of the pilgrimage. Margaret held him to that, even though the Saxon lords and Edgar the Aetheling, too, had ridden south a fortnight earlier to Dun Edin, then farther into England. Rumors flew of a new, fierce rebellion forming, and Malcolm seemed anxious to reach his southern capital.

But moving the household to a new royal center meant going slowly regardless, although Malcolm was used to riding quickly. The things of the household, such as garments, bedding, dishes, furnishings, and so on, had to be packed and taken along. Eva knew that part of his treasury had been taken, too, for Malcolm did not know how many months they would stay in Dun Edin. Those things had already gone by merchant ship across the firth to Leith harbor and from there to the fortress of Dun Edin. The king's party would head northeast through Fife, a lighter escort but for the cart loaded with some precious things, including Margaret's best garments, and an exquisite gold cross that she planned to give to the bishop of Saint Andrews.

Having wrapped her harp in leather and fur, Eva kept it slung on her horse's saddle or tucked in the van when she traveled with the queen. Although she liked most of them, she did not relish sitting with the queen's kinswomen, who found much to complain about. Another van carried the nurses, children, and maidservants. Duncan and Donald proudly rode with the king and his guards, that group in more of a hurry than the queen's party.

Before leaving Dunfermline, Eva had sent a messenger to Loch Leven with a note for Abbot Drostan intended for Lady Gruadh. She narrated for her grandmother mundane details of packing for Saint Andrews and Dun Edin, but chiefly Eva wanted her to know that the court was moving south. She kept to the facts, sensing that if she seemed excited about the adventure or happy to travel with her friends, the queen, Juliana, and others—let alone any interest in Edgar—then a phalanx of Moray men might be dispatched to snatch her home, hostage or none.

THEY FOLLOWED THE COASTAL route toward Saint Andrews, for the pilgrimage roads were wide and cobbled there. Eva rode a white pony some of the time, enjoying the wide sky overhead, the vast expanse of the sea to the right, and the blue hills of Fife to her left. A few pilgrims walked the same wide road, intent on their missions, easily identified by the scallop shells and clay or metal badges they wore pinned to their cloaks and wide-brimmed hats.

At times the queen ordered the escort to stop so that she could kneel and pray with the pilgrims. Moved by the plight of the poorest ones, she freely gave away her own things: her blue cloak to one woman, shoes to another, linen shifts, pretty gowns, embroidered purses, and silver coins to others. Inspired by the queen's charity, the other ladies relinquished some of their things, too, giving veils, gloves, stockings. When Margaret looked pointedly at Eva, who stood by, she took the nod and gave her hair comb to a curly-haired child who needed not only that but a bath. Later, Margaret slipped into Eva's hand a beautifully carved ivory comb, and would not take it back.

Saint Andrews lay at the opposite, easternmost end of Fife, and they plodded toward it like a bunch of noble pilgrims, replete with cushioned vans, good saddles, and baskets of hearty food for when they halted in the shade. The king chafed at the pace and rode back impatiently to hurry them along, but Margaret took her time, stubbornly insisting on meeting pilgrims as well as stopping at chapels and tall stone crosses along the way for a prayer. By nightfall, quite late in the summer months, they were welcomed into the home of a thane whose wooden fortress perched on a hill behind a palisade. Malcolm had sent riders ahead to ask for shelter.

On the second day, they made faster progress in sunshine and sea breezes, and met a large group of pilgrims, for they were drawing closer to Saint Andrews. As Margaret stopped to kneel with them for prayers, Eva realized that she had never seen Margaret quite so happy except when she played with her little sons. When some of the pilgrims pointed out a cairn of stones along the road as the place where a Scottish saint had once rested on pilgrimage, she seemed exhilarated.

Had Margaret been free to live a saint's life herself, Eva was sure she would have done so, and would have been worthy. Within Margaret's heart was the seed of an extraordinary life not lived. She had a true acolyte's ability to commune in ecstasy with God. Margaret still yearned for that, Eva thought, watching her, feeling humbled by her genuine, heartfelt devotion to all the daily demands and promised rewards of her faith. Margaret craved something, Eva saw, in her piety, an appetite that grew more fervent, even as her earthly appetite seemed to diminish.

Within a few miles of the town of Saint Andrews and the little church at Kilrymont where the relics of the apostle Andrew were actually kept, Eva saw another crowd of pilgrims ahead, and the royal escort slowed. Though she respected the pilgrimages of others without interest in doing the same herself, she took more delight in the adventure than she had expected.

Margaret then asked the driver of her van to stop. She climbed out despite the protests of her women, lifted her skirts slightly, and began to walk. The king turned to ride toward her, stretching out an arm, offering to lift her up to his saddle if she was weary of the wheeled vehicle. She shook her head.

"I am within miles of the relics of an apostle," she told him, within Eva's hearing. "There are only two other places with such treasures—the traces of Saint Peter in Rome and Saint James in Santiago. I may never see either of those places, but I am here now, and humbled. I will walk."

Without waiting for Malcolm to answer, Margaret lifted her skirt hems out of the road dust and tramped ahead at a brisk pace to catch up to the other pilgrims.

Malcolm turned in his saddle, saw Eva, and beckoned. "You, Lady Eva," he said. "Go with the queen. She speaks little Gaelic, and her manners are too fine—no matter how humble she thinks she is, she will give herself away, and there will be the devil to pay with a crowd. She only wants the peace of this place. Walk with her."

Nodding, she dismounted and handed her horse's reins to one of the guards. When the king called out after her, she turned.

"Aeife," he said, "tell a maidservant to bring Margaret a straw hat and a flask of water. She will be sick from sun, fair as she is. I vow she has not eaten much today."

"Sire," she said. "I will do it myself."

"Thank you," he answered. "I am indebted to you. She wants to do this on her own, but I—" He stopped.

"But you are concerned for her well-being, as any good husband," she finished. He nodded.

Eva fetched two hats and water flasks from Wynne inside the van, and hurried to join the queen. Margaret seemed in a fever to get to the church of the apostle, and they walked for nearly two hours, the escort following slowly and discreetly behind. Margaret stumbled to her knees more than once, for she had eaten and sipped very little that day. The king rode close once or twice, and Eva thought he might simply snatch up the queen and lift her to his horse.

But she saw, too, though Malcolm had little tolerance for the pace of the journey and very little interest in pilgrimages, he showed much patience for his queen.

"WE LEFT THE BISHOP in quite a contented mood," Margaret confided happily to Eva as they waited for Malcolm and the rest of the escort outside the little church at Kilrymont. "He has a coffer of gold from the king and a special gift from me—that gold cross, all bejeweled, once belonged to my great-uncle, King Stephen of Hungary, who may be named a saint by Rome someday. It is not the cross Bishop Fothad hoped for, but he says it will do."

Eva nodded at the smiling queen. She had passed an hour in prayer with Margaret, kneeling before a stone sarcophagus and an altar that housed a metal reliquary inset with crystal so that relics within were partly visible: part of an arm, a foot bone, and a few toenails of Saint Andrew were enough to create miracles, according to some, having been brought all the way to Scotland by Saint Regulus, or Rule. A great church in honor of Andrew and Rule would soon be constructed now that heaven, via the king and queen of Scotland, had helped to fund it.

When the escort appeared without Malcolm, De Lauder, who had ridden along with them, informed the queen and Eva that Malcolm waited for them along the road southward. Then he led them a short way to the coast, where Malcolm waited, pacing on board a longship.

Eva stood by awkwardly as Margaret protested, despite hours and days of prayer and penance. And the king's inherent impatience, long suppressed, erupted.

"We will not travel by land, which would take weeks at your

pace," he nearly shouted, "but by good Norse-built ships—fast, effi-
cient, and *safe*, Margaret. Your gear is on board already," he went
on, "including your gowns and your crosses, your women, my
housecarls, the servants, the dogs, the horses—and our sons in their
nurses' arms!"

"But you know I have vowed never to travel by sea!" The queen,
standing up to her husband, looked slight beside him, and in such
a fury that her cheeks went deep rose and her hands fisted. "I must
travel by land."

"Alone?" he demanded.

"Eva would come with me," Margaret countered. Malcolm flicked
his gaze toward Eva, who stood wary and silent.

"Margaret, this ship will follow the coast, and will not head out to
sea. At Dun Edin, we will cross like the damned ferry that goes back
and forth there. Your vow is for ocean travel."

"I cannot divide my vow into particulars, in sight of holy Saint
Andrew himself!"

"He cannot see this. Only his toenails are in that church," Malcolm said, as Margaret gasped. "I am done with girlish oaths said in
haste. We must reach Leith harbor and Dun Edin today."

Within the quarter hour, they sailed, and though Margaret refused
to speak to her husband, she was soon too ill to speak at all, for her
stomach plagued her. By turns, Eva helped to hold her head and her
hand and wipe her brow.

"Leave me be," Margaret said, wan and slumped on a bench, the
sea air whipping at her veils and cloak. "I told the king I must not
sail. See, it is punishment for breaking a holy vow. And it is the
child."

"The what!" Malcolm said, turning around, for he stood nearby.

"The child," Margaret said, and leaned over to retch into the
bucket Eva held for her.

"*Jesu.*" Malcolm smiled. "That is a remarkable woman. I never
thought to have so many sons to carry my name."

"The people are calling your princes the Margaretsons," Eva said, unable to resist. He grunted at that.

Later, as the longboat sheared across the water with Leith harbor in sight, Malcolm approached Eva where she stood by the prow, the wind heavy in her face, blowing her unbound black hair as free and loose as whips. She tamed it back with a hand as he stood beside her.

"How does Margaret fare now?" he asked.

"She will recover once we are on land."

"This is my doing," he said, looking at the shoreline crowded with docks and ships, and buildings higher on the hill. "I insisted on tricking her into the boat, and now she is ill. Is there any danger to the child? It is early days yet."

"I am sure all will be well." Eva spoke carefully, flatly.

"Margaret takes her oaths, her prayers and penances, all to heart," he muttered. "She rises in the middle of the night to pray like a nun, fasts even while carrying a child, though she has a dispensation for that. She gives away her clothing and thinks only of the poor, the suffering, as if she were somehow at fault for what is wrong in the world."

"She is a good and kind soul, though demanding of herself."

"Aye," he said quickly. "And too many around her agree with her, pander to her, let her do these things to herself. Her own mother and sister complain that nothing is good enough and induce her to more prayers and confessions, as if she were doing them wrong." He frowned deep, looking down at her. "But you, Aeife—you are her friend."

"I am a king's hostage," she reminded him. "But I love your queen well."

"I will not forget this." He turned and walked away.

❀

TWILIGHT SHONE PURPLE over the rippled water of Leith port, where dozens of vessels moored at a large stone quay. Merchant knorrs,

the great wide, low ships loaded with goods, floated on the waves farther out in the bay. Above the harbor, Margaret could see the high
crested rock and fortress of Dun Edin just a league away. She gasped at
the majestic sight, and felt almost as impatient as Malcolm to be gathered
and going, though she felt nervous, too, about to enter the king's largest
royal center.

Housecarls from Dun Edin came to meet them with extra horses and
carts, but Margaret insisted on riding a horse into the city. She did con-
cede to using a small saddle so that she could hook a knee over the low
pommel, a gentler way to ride preferred by some ladies.

Wearing a clean white veil and a gown of pale blue, she draped a
lightweight cream-colored cloak elegantly over her shoulders, and sat
tall. Feeling dizzy and weak after a half day's sickness on the water,
she was determined to enter Dun Edin—which Malcolm sometimes
called Edinburgh in the Saxon manner—in a dignified way as the
newly arrived queen.

As they left the harbor, she noticed a cluster of people walking
away from the shore toward the road that curved north and east
around the firth. Seeing their walking sticks and telltale scallops and
badges, she recognized them as pilgrims. Twisting in the saddle to
watch them, she saw one of the Dun Edin housecarls riding beside
her.

"Pilgrims, Lady," the young man said. "They must have been
turned away from the ferry boat that crosses between here and Fife.
They will walk instead, and sleep along the road. We see it often
here. Few can afford the ferry passage or the price of an inn."

Margaret listened, watching the people trudge onward. She saw
two women helping an older man who was hunched over, progressing slowly with the use of a stick. She turned to the Dun Edin guard
and drew out her purse to hand him a few coins.

"Here, sir. Go to those people and give them the fee for the ferry.
And give them enough for a meal and a night in an inn as well, as it is
already evening." Smiling, accepting the silver, he rode off. Margaret
turned to find Malcolm watching.

"We will run out of coins at the rate you give them out, Lady," he said.

"Aye, but we will garner a wealth of good will," she answered.

"I have married me a wise queen," Malcolm remarked to De Lauder, who laughed.

Chapter Sixteen

They think you a generous king, sire.

— BISHOP TURGOT, *Life of Saint Margaret,*
TWELFTH CENTURY, QUOTING
QUEEN MARGARET

The cliff-sided hill on which the citadel stood overlooked the sea in one direction, hills to the other. Dun Edin itself, a stone and timber fortress, was sometimes called by its older name, Castellum Puellarum or the Castle of the Maidens; legend claimed that some ancient Pictish king had kept his several daughters guarded there, Malcolm told Margaret.

The place looked formidable on its high perch, with an outer palisade of stone and one side melded with the massive rock into a sheer drop. Inside, Margaret saw scaffolding in places where Malcolm had ordered wooden buildings rebuilt with stone. She had seen the stone castles built by Normans, and she felt proud that the King of Scots was learning from the enemy to transform his own fortress into an impregnable stone castellum.

As the royal escort advanced slowly up the long hill that fronted the castle, Margaret saw crowds of people gathering to cheer and shout, and she lifted a hand to wave tentatively. Even in the growing darkness, she could see that many of them wore tattered clothing and were barefoot and unwashed, and some held out their hands to beg. Children and adults clustered along the sloped street where a straggling chain of houses, shops, and vendor stalls leaned. The street ran muddy with rain and sewage. Some of the people slept in the streets, for she saw pallets, blankets, and sagging tentlike shelters in corners and side lanes. Dogs wandered the streets, and children walked with them. The stench in the air was so strong that she wrinkled her nose against it.

A few people ran forward to tug at the hem of her cloak and gown, frightening her and startling the horse, and the housecarls chased them off. Suddenly the crowd looked more like souls of hell begging for succor and release than happy people welcoming their queen. She realized then that most of them implored her in English rather than Gaelic or the Scots tongue.

Margaret turned to Wilfrid, now riding at her left side. "These are not Scots—but Saxons!"

"Aye, fugitives who have nowhere to go," he said. "Thousands of Saxon slaves were taken into Scottish homes over the last two years. Countless more have come north since, looking for hospitality . . . and for hope as well."

"Hope?" Margaret looked at him.

"They know that the royal Saxon family fled north and found welcome in Scotland and that many fugitives have found homes here, mostly as slaves and servants, but it is a life. Now other refugees pray that the royal Saxons in Scotland will make sure their people are cared for, especially with you as queen here. Who else do they have now?"

STANDING BY THE WINDOW in the great hall of the keep that thrust high on the rock of Dun Edin, Margaret leaned against the frame, shuttered open, to gaze out over the town. The hour was well past matins and gone so dark that she saw torches and bonfires flare here and there in the town, beneath a sky sparkling with stars. Beyond she could see the black gleam of the port.

"Come to bed," Malcolm said gruffly from there. "The hour is late."

Margaret sighed and drew her indoor cloak closer over a loose shift. She had rested a little and had risen for midnight prayers, asking for help for all the troubled souls who lived in the king's town without shelter, food, or necessities. Unable to sleep now, she rested her hands on the slight swell of her belly. Only recently she had known that she had conceived again, and after her arrival in the town, the thought of her own little ones kept her awake.

"I keep thinking of the children," she said. "So many small ones in need, though my own sons sleep content in their cradles and the newest one is safe in my womb. Too many have no cradle, or even a mother, to hold them while they sleep at night. Too many will lack food when they wake in the morning."

Malcolm sighed and sat up in the bed. "Margaret, we cannot feed them all."

She turned. "Can we not?"

"It is too much for anyone to undertake. Pray for them. It is all you can do. It is enough."

"I suppose so. I am tired, and will take to bed. The bells will ring out soon enough—I heard them from some church nearby—and the next hour of prayer will come all too soon."

"You have the ears of a hound, to hear the bells so far. Sleep through next time," he said. "We have been journeying for days, and your health is more important than prayers. Have you eaten this evening?" he added.

"Of course," she said, having only tasted her supper. "I cannot sleep through and miss a prayer appointment. Nor can I ignore the plight of so many outside our gates. I want a place in God's good heaven one day, my lord."

"Huh," the king replied. "We see the poor at our gates nearly every day here, with the crowds in the streets of this town and nearby areas. My steward sees that they are given the scraps that we have to spare."

"Almsgiving with scraps of food?"

"Aye. So we can sleep soundly at night. Do not fret over it."

Nodding in silence, she went to the bed and slid in between the bed linens. Malcolm, weary, rolled over and soon began to snore. The bed was unfamiliar and larger than theirs at Dunfermline, but its deep, comfortable feather mattress lured her quickly to sleep.

Before she drifted off, she reminded herself that a queen must look after the people in her husband's kingdom as if they were guests in her own house. And, remembering Wilfrid's remark, she felt responsible, as a Saxon, for refugees from her outlawed brother's kingdom, too. But she ached deepest of all for the children in need of even the simplest comforts.

Indeed, she would do something, but she was not certain what.

❦

THE TALL, GRACEFUL QUEEN led the rest of her ladies like a pale swan with cygnets following. Eva walked behind Margaret through the darkest hour before dawn as they all headed down the wooden steps of the timber-built tower that crowned the rock on its northernmost side. Ahead of Eva and the others, Margaret went steadily downward, her long, loose hair rippling like golden mist down her back under a veil of translucent silk, her gown a creamy glow in the light of oil lamps carried by Wynne and Matilda.

They followed the queen out the entrance and down those steps, and across the bailey to a small square wooden building. Inside Eva saw a tiny chapel with a simple altar, a carved ivory cross hung above it. For a while they knelt in prayer, and then Father Otto, who had come with them to Dun Edin, entered to conduct Mass, though the place was crowded. When they departed the chapel, Eva stepped outside into the fresh, sweet air just as the sun rose over the sea. She paused to watch the light bloom, while Margaret joined her.

"That is a peaceful little chapel," Margaret said. "But old. Perhaps as the king is rebuilding, he will consider replacing it with stone. I will suggest it."

In the great hall, a separate one-story building adjacent to the tower, breakfast waited on a table for the queen and her ladies. Margaret had requested that her custom at Dunfermline of hosting a simple meal after morning prayers be continued. They were greeted by Sir Parlan, Dun Edin's steward, a red-bearded man with a limp, the injury acquired when he had saved Malcolm's life in a skirmish; the deed had elevated him from housecarl to steward. His daughter, Ella, helped her father to oversee the daily needs of the household.

Now, Eva saw a trestle table filled with platters of steaming oat-cakes, an iron kettle of porridge, a platter piled with sliced wheels of cheese. Pouring a cup of golden ale, already diluted with water for morning consumption, she gave it to Margaret and poured another for herself.

"Will you eat, Lady?" she asked. "There is a great deal of food here."

"It truly is a generous amount," Margaret said, and accepted an oat-cake from Kata, who spread it thick with butter. But when Kata handed her porridge in a small rock crystal bowl, along with a small golden spoon, Margaret shook her head.

"Eat some for the child then," Kata urged.

"Oh, very well," Margaret said, and swallowed a spoonful.

Eva nibbled some cheese, noticing that the queen seemed distracted, looking at the table. When Wilfrid entered the room, Margaret hurried toward him, the crystal bowl and spoon still in her hands. She spoke earnestly to him, and beckoned Parlan into their discussion. Bowing his head in assent, Wilfrid escorted her to the door, while Parlan summoned the servants to speak to them.

"What is it?" Eva asked Juliana, who came to stand beside her.

"The queen's almoner says there are several people at the gate asking for charity. Parlan said their alms are generally whatever is left after meals, but the queen says that is not enough, on her first day here in

Dun Edin. There is Wynne—she was just speaking with Parlan."
Juliana turned toward Eva's maidservant, who came near.

"The queen says the poor are to have whatever is here," Wynne
told them. "She says our souls will be cleansed by giving, and we can
wait for the next meal." Looking sour, she began to gather up food
with Matilda's assistance. They wrapped oatcakes in linen cloths and
stacked empty porridge bowls, and Wynne took hold of the wooden
handle of the small black kettle that held hot porridge.

"We can help," Eva said, and Juliana joined her to pick up
wrapped cheeses and gather cups and a jug of watered ale.

Outside in the cool air and sunlight, Eva and the others crossed
the bailey and proceeded down the slope toward the entrance gates.
Nearly two dozen people had already been allowed inside, she saw,
and more waited for the housecarls to admit them.

Margaret stood with Wilfrid as the strangers, mostly women and
children with a few older men, came forward. They were shabby,
grimy, yet proud—Eva saw not a beggar among them, but heads
high as they looked around, protecting their children in their arms or
beside them. The queen walked closer, graceful and elegant, her long
gown of pale green wool and a cream-colored cloak sweeping the
cobbles. Within the group, she looked beautiful and ethereal as she
held out her little bowl and spoon and bent to offer a taste of porridge
to a small girl. When the girl's mother thanked the queen, Eva heard
English rather than Gaelic.

Margaret looked toward Wynne and Matilda. "Give them alms of
food," she said quietly. "Lady Eva, please help them." Silently Eva
came forward, as did Juliana.

In the midst of the crowd, a small curly-haired child of about a
year cried piteously in the arms of an older girl, who jostled her
while holding the hand of a toddler who sniffled as she looked up
at the women doling out food. Breaking off a bit of cheese, Eva
stooped to give it to the little girl, then offered some to the crying
child. He buried his face in the oldest girl's shoulder, who took it

to feed it to him. "Thank you, my lady," she said in good Saxon English.

"I had not expected to see so many poor in Dun Edin," Juliana said soberly as she and Eva poured ale into cups that were quickly shared and passed to others.

Lady Agatha and Princess Cristina joined them, watching as others gave out the food and drink. Eva came near to pick up some oatcakes from Wynne. "Lady Eva," Cristina said, "if your people in the north still think poorly of Malcolm Canmore, send this word to them—the king helps many here."

"This day's deeds belong to the queen more than the king," Eva said.

"Margaret knows the value of charity," Lady Agatha said proudly. "She honors the old custom of royal almsgiving to the needy."

"My sister knows the advantage of showing generosity at the king's door," Cristina added.

Certainly Margaret was clever as well as charitable, Eva thought as she handed broken pieces of oatcakes to some of the people. The queen walked among the crowd, her veiled head easily visible as she greeted those at the gate. Malcolm and Scotland would indeed benefit from this, Eva was sure.

Nearby, the fussy baby still wept in the older girl's arms, and the toddler now wailed, too. Eva watch as Margaret offered her spoon to the baby, who mouthed it hungrily and opened his mouth for more. Margaret obliged.

"Dearling," she told him gently, "you may have as much as you like." While she fed him, Eva offered a bit of oatcake to the toddler, who took it, sniffling. Then Margaret smiled at the older girl who held the baby. "What is your name, girl?" she asked.

"I am Gertruda. My little sister is Inga, and this is our brother Alfred." She hefted the baby.

"Ah, Alfred," Margaret said solemnly to him. "My great-great-grandfather had that good name. Alfred the Great, they call him. Where did you come from, Gertruda?"

"We lived with our parents near York," she answered. "But they are gone, and our home is burned. I brought Inga and Alfred north hoping I could find work as a servant, but we have been turned away because the little ones are an extra burden. We came to Dun Edin because I was told we could find alms at the gates here. But we have never had alms so fine, and this not even a feast day!" She smiled, winsome, skin freckled, brown hair framing her narrow face.

"Was it Normans that took your parents and your home?" Margaret asked.

The girl looked down, nodded. "My mother told me to bar the door when they came to our house in the night, but I was not quick enough, and they came inside because the bar was not there. They . . . killed my parents . . . I hid in the clothes chest with the little ones."

"Dear God," Margaret said.

"Then we ran," she said. "And we met people who were also fleeing, and they took us north with them. A priest said I must seek forgiveness for this wicked punishment, so I pray each day."

Margaret gasped and handed the empty bowl to Eva. "None of this is your doing, Gertruda. Do not think it." She touched the girl's shoulder.

"I know," Gertruda said, but her lip quivered. "But we are doing fine, Alfred and Inga and me, and a priest in the town says he will find a priory to take us in."

"Gertruda," Margaret said. "You see that man over there, with the white beard? He is my almoner. Go to him and tell him that the queen says you are to stay in the queen's household. You are good to your brother and sister," she said, "and you would be good to my little ones. We need another maidservant in the nursery, where these two little ones will be welcome, too. Go, now." She turned the girl toward Wilfrid, who watched them now. "Talk to my steward."

As the girl walked up the hill, Margaret glanced at Eva. "I could not let them leave," she said. "I could not have slept in my bed, wondering where they slept."

"Mirren will be glad of the help. And the girl speaks refined English. She will be a help to your sons, since so much Gaelic is spoken around them."

"I had not thought of that. Good!" Margaret seemed relieved. "Oh, there is Malcolm."

The king, Eva noticed, now stood high along the slope, fists at his waist, brow furrowed as he surveyed the activity at the gate. Then he and a few of his guards walked downhill, where he met Margaret, greeting her softly, taking her hand to escort her with him. He paused, placing a hand on her arm, leaning down to listen to her.

Now as they stood together, Malcolm nodding solemnly, as if taking a lesson from an advisor. His queen's act of almsgiving would be perceived as his charity, too. He only benefitted from her deeds, both on earth and in heaven, and so he would have to approve.

※

MOST NIGHTS, MARGARET ROSE with the distant bells of Dun Edin to pray before dawn, but now she too often dozed over her needlework in daylight while Eva played harp melodies. One of her ladies would take the work gently from her hands and let her sleep. Some of her fatigue was due to the new little one stirring in her womb, and with this third child, her state became obvious more quickly. She laced her gowns more loosely and let out, once more, the deep side seams.

Other days, Eva would play lively tunes when the nurses, including sweet-tempered Gertruda, would bring the children to the queen's chamber, where the ladies would read to them and show them the paintings in the queen's books. Flaxen-haired Edward patiently listened, while redheaded Edmund was a rascal more likely to tear a page than sit quietly in a lap. Lady Agatha said such a child must be whipped as he grew older if he would not behave. Margaret would never give such an order, but instead encouraged Gertruda to play with Edmund, who did well with calm and affectionate attention.

Within a fortnight of the royal household's arrival in Dun Edin, Malcolm and Edgar gathered a host of men from Lothian and elsewhere to ride south, armor glinting and weapons spiking the sky. So far they always returned safely from such forays, and Margaret had learned to accept the comings and goings of the warriors in her household. But often she would stop to gaze from a window as she passed, searching in the distance for riders returning.

Only messengers came and went, bringing reports she did not want to hear—skirmishes along the border, Normans beating Saxons, burnings and tyranny continuing. The messengers brought little word of Edgar or Malcolm, and no direct word to ease her mind.

Chapter Seventeen

My little queen is a thief . . . a pious little robber.

—BISHOP TURGOT, *Life of Saint Margaret*,
TWELFTH CENTURY, QUOTING
MALCOLM CANMORE

Knights arrived at the gates one September evening, setting up such a ruckus to be admitted that Margaret awoke from early sleep, hearing the shouts. She bounded from bed and went to the window, panicking when the torchlight showed men running across the bailey, ordering the gates opened, calling for arms, for assistance. Malcolm had left De Lauder in charge of the royal residence, with Edgar and the rest south in England.

Wriggling into a loose-cut tunic over a shift, then grabbing a cloak, for the air was chilly, she shoved her feet into slippers, left her hair loose and uncovered, and hurried down the steps. In the bailey men dismounted from horses and grooms led weary animals to the stables to be rubbed and watered.

Ranald and other housecarls gathered about the men who had newly arrived, and in the light of torches through the darkness, she saw Edgar on horseback, his hair gleaming golden as he shoved back his chain mail hood. He slid from his horse and spoke to the king's men, then walked with them toward other men dismounting, a group having arrived at once. Her heart beat fast with the relief of seeing her brother well, on his feet and safe. She turned to Finola nearby.

"Quickly," she told her, "send a servant to wake Cook, and find Parlan and Ella. Tell them that I would like food and drink to be served in the hall for these men, no matter the hour."

Wilfrid saw Margaret and came toward her. "My lady, Prince Edgar is here and well, and brings news . . . dire news from England."

She clutched the cloak at her throat. "Malcolm?" she asked low.

Wilfrid shook his head. "The king is safe, last we heard."

"Margaret!" Her brother approached, stooping to kiss her cheek, for he had yet grown taller, even more so than their father had been. "Malcolm is unharmed." He blew out a breath. "But there is other news."

"Tell me." She could see that he was weary to the bone, and recovering from an arm injury, his forearm and wrist wrapped thickly. Some of the other men had bandaged injuries, too. She did not recognize all of his followers, particularly in the darkness and torchlight, but she saw a black-robed monk and caught her breath. "Brother Tor!"

"Aye, we went to Melrose and saw him, and he decided to ride back with me; he has matters to discuss with Malcolm. But the king is not yet here," he said. "He will be soon, though."

"Thank God. Tell me what has happened," she repeated, while she saw Tor speaking with Ranald and Wilfrid, then turning to greet Brother Godwin as the younger monk hastened across the courtyard to see if his help was needed. Margaret turned back to Edgar.

"We moved south a considerable distance into England this time," he said. "And so we were nearby when a rebellion erupted on the Isle of Ely, led by Wilfrid and Tor's kinsman, Hereward of Lincoln, the rebel who has driven William near mad with frustration. A host of Saxons held out there against a Norman siege for days in a swampy area of the fenlands."

"Were you with them?" she asked, pressing a hand to her chest. "Were you injured there?"

"This? A sword cut to the forearm, and healing," he said. "We were not in the fens exactly, but nearby, engaging a few Norman knights to distract them from attacking the rebels in the swamps. Edwin and Morcar were with the rebels, though. They have stayed in Northumbria and gained back some of their lands from William, though they fought against his men without his knowledge. So they joined Hereward when he and his men pushed north, secretively, through the forests. They set up a siege in the swamps near Ely."

"Was it successful?"

He sucked in a breath. "King William heard of the resistance and brought fresh troops north. They went into the fens to drive the rebels out—burned them out, to be sure."

"In a swamp? How could they manage? Surely the rebels stayed safe from flames there."

"There are tall rushes and foul liquids in the fens that burn like wick and oil," he said. "Nonetheless, William's efforts did not work. So"—he paused, half laughed, shoved a grimy hand through his hair—"he hired a local witch and paid her to curse and defeat the Saxon rebels with her black arts."

"Witch! Dear saints!" Margaret covered her mouth. The thought that there could be people of such evil skill and intention truly alarmed her.

"Aye. He paid the old hag good silver and had her brought to the swamp. His engineers constructed wooden ramps that they laid flat to bridge areas of the fens, and they even built a wooden scaffold tower high enough that they could see for a distance. The old woman climbed the thing and shrieked vile curses at the Saxons. We could hear her screaming," he said.

"What then?" Margaret asked, as others gathered near her—Eva, she saw then, clutching her plaid close about her shoulders, her hair wild and loose, and Juliana, gentle and wide-eyed.

"She showed her bare arse—pardon me, my ladies—and spewed

her curses. The Saxons paid her no mind, laughed at her, and plotted their next attack from their stronghold in the fens."

"What was the outcome?" Eva asked, standing beside Margaret, shoulder to shoulder now.

Edgar looked down at her. "Eva," he said. "Lady Eva, it is good to see you." He sounded tired, relieved, staring at her for a long moment as if dazed.

"You are hurt," Eva said softly, and Edgar shrugged as if to say it was nothing at all.

"The outcome," Margaret reminded him.

Edgar sighed heavily. "We did our best to distract William's troops as they came and went in that swamp, but it was like nipping at a great furious beast. They shook us off and prevented us from getting help to the Saxons within the fens. Then the Normans loosed a thousand fire arrows and the swamps seemed to explode . . . I saw the witch fall from her post and flee along with others, Norman and Saxon. But her curses must have taken hold. Hereward's lot were defeated."

"Were there many lost?" Margaret asked. "Thank God you are safe. What of your cousin?" This she said to Wilfrid and Tor, who now came near again. "Brother Tor, I am remiss. Welcome. It is good to see you here." She gazed up and smiled.

"Lady, my thanks," Tor said. "Our cousin escaped, we heard later. Edgar and his men were able to get away as the Normans turned out of the fens. They made their way into the border hills and from there to Scotland. They came to our small monastery at Melrose to have their wounds tended, and because they knew they had friends there."

"Some of the others did not fare as well. Morcar," Edgar said, "was captured. William took him down to London in chains. We may never hear of him again, unless a ransom or trade can be arranged with Malcolm. I do not have the means to rescue my own," he added bitterly.

"We will talk to Malcolm," Margaret said crisply. "Our friend will not be abandoned."

Edgar paused. "As for Edwin . . . he was one of those killed."

"Dear God," Margaret breathed. Morcar's brother, Edwin of Mercia, who always smiled, who made an effort to consider the fairness in every matter, gone. "Killed at Ely?"

"He got away, but we heard he was attacked by his own men soon after. William had bought off their loyalty. The king is ruthless. How can we sustain a rebellion when the enemy uses gold as a weapon?"

"Aye. Dear Edwin, I will pray for his soul, and Morcar's safety," Margaret said. "But who is left to run with you, Edgar, in the resistance?"

"Cospatric has changed sides again," Edgar said. "Lady Juliana, your father is at Melrose—we brought him there after he was wounded helping us in a skirmish. I believe he regrets the terms of the bargain he made with William to save his lands, and he has thrown in his lot with the Saxons and Scots again."

"Thank the saints for that. But what of my father's injuries—is he well?" Juliana asked.

"He will recover," Brother Tor said quietly. "He took an arrow to the chest, but Edgar and his men acted quickly in bringing him to Melrose, where we have a small hospital. Medicine and prayer are helping him. If I may speak with you and your stepmother, I bear private messages from your father." Juliana nodded gratefully and hurried to fetch Lady Edith.

Margaret watched Edgar carefully. She could see that he was tired, and that he seemed to hide something more from her—perhaps just the depth of his despair over this cause, she thought. "What of Malcolm? Tell me what you know."

"He was in Northumbria and Cumbria last we heard, but I do not know where he is now."

"I see." Knowing the danger her husband faced, all she could do was pray for him. Thanking Edgar, she linked her arm gently in his, and with Eva at his other side, walked with him to the great hall, where soup steamed in bowls and servants waited ready. Aware that her brother and the others needed no more questions but should eat and rest, Margaret slipped out of the room. She did not approach Brother Tor, though she dearly wanted his thoughts. But that could wait, as Juliana then brought Lady Edith into the hall and Tor showed them a folded parchment, likely a letter from Cospatric. The three sat down together.

Margaret noticed that her brother chose to sit with Eva a little apart from the others. While he ate soup, they murmured together, heads close. Margaret paused by the door, unexpectedly touched by the sight of her brother, her friend, and the degree of kindness that now seemed evident between them. How had she not seen this before? And then she wondered if either of them realized it, and what good could come of it—little, truly, for anyone.

She had much on her mind and in her heart, and ought to take it to her prayers, she thought, and so she hastened across the yard toward the peace and privacy of the little timber chapel.

DAYS LATER, MALCOLM RETURNED, grim and drawn, with little to say about the events in England. He met with Edgar, with his council of lords and thanes and priests, and he stayed awake at night, pacing. But he told Margaret little of what weighed on his mind, only that William thrashed in a temper ever since his return from France—some of which Margaret had heard from Edgar. Otherwise, Malcolm praised the state of the royal household, where Margaret had set servants to refreshing and refurbishing Dun Edin just as she had ordered at Dunfermline. And he gave her a somewhat distracted approval when she told him that almsgiving was now a regular occurrence at Dun Edin.

"Every Thursday morning, sire, when you are here," she said one day, "I think we should go to the gates and portion out alms as food, clothing, or coin."

"As you wish," he said. They stood in the treasure room in Dun Edin, a chamber hidden in the storerooms beneath the tower, bolted by lock and key and accessible only by stairs leading from the king's chamber. Malcolm had brought her there to go over an accounting sheet of her own dowry things brought from Dunfermline, including a box containing sacristy vessels that she wanted to donate for use in the citadel's chapel.

"I will go out more often than that," she said, "if there are people at the gate."

"Thursdays will do. Send servants on the other days."

"And on holy days we will bring basins and wash the feet of the poor." Malcolm looked up sharply at this, and she smiled. "We shall do the same at Dunfermline when we return there. For your reputation as a good and godly king, sire, it is surely important."

"For my sins, Margaret," he muttered, "what you will."

"WHERE IS MY BOOK?" Margaret asked irritably. "I cannot find my book of the Gospels." She turned over the cushions on a bench near where her ladies sat sewing in the great hall, growing impatient, having looked for the book in several places that morning. "It is not in my chamber on the little table where I usually keep it. Has anyone seen it?"

"I saw it last week," Cristina replied, "when you were reading to the king from its pages. Why does he not read to himself? He must have been properly educated."

"Aye, he was tutored as a boy in Scotland, and at his uncle's home in Northumbria, too," Margaret said. "He is adept at languages and skilled in arithmetic, but he is not much of a scholar, I will grant." She sighed. "His attention was more on warrior training, and though he studied the histories of the Greeks and Romans for battle strategies, his tutor read those to him. He had little reason and, I imagine, little patience for much reading." She flipped over another cushion and looked inside a sewing basket. "Where is that book?"

"Read another one," Cristina suggested. "You left Aldhelm's *De Laude Virginitatis* in your sewing basket with your other things. I saw it there yesterday."

"So the king cannot read the books he owns?" Eva asked. "Or the book he commissioned?"

"He reads Latin for documents, a little Gaelic for the same. I have been tutoring him, and he is progressing nicely," Margaret replied. "I was so sure I left the book on a little table in my chamber, wrapped in a cloth. Shall I read from the Aldhelm?" she asked, pulling the volume from the basket.

"That one is so dull," Juliana said. "Your copy of the Gospels is one of the prettiest books I have seen, and it is all extracts, and not so much to read all at once. Surely it is somewhere; it could hardly fly away."

Margaret stood, still distracted. "I will go upstairs and look again. I am weary of this weather," she added, as rain poured over the tin roof of the great hall. Margaret, quite frankly, was tired of the sound, bored with sewing, even bored with reading and conversation. Her back ached, she was hungrier than she would admit, and she felt rest-less. That morning she had not even gone outside to help with the alms-giving at the gate, for fear of slipping on the wet slope.

She was quickly growing large with this child, her tunics stretching tight even with the lacings open, and three months to go as yet. She had succumbed to Kata's urgings to eat more, and this was the result, she thought. But there was no excuse for gluttony, even in a breeding state; she must be an example in all ways, and should not be lax in her discipline.

Leaving the solar, she climbed the stairs to the bedchamber to search for the missing book. At night she still shared the great curtained bed with Malcolm, despite her mother's advice to banish him until she was lighter of her child. But he let her be, and she let him stay. His warm bulk beside her at night was a comfort. Accustomed to his presence there, she missed him when he was gone and was grateful each time he returned.

Determining again that the manuscript was not there, she heard a soft knock and turned to see Eva in the open door. She waved her into the room. "I cannot find it," she said. "I fear my head is fuzzy with my condition." She gave a weak laugh.

"Let me help you look for it," Eva said, then glanced out the small window where the shutter gapped slightly open. "Such a big crowd on the High Street today. Is it market day?"

Margaret shook her head. "They came here for alms, and Malcolm allowed the servants to give away only some scraps from last night's supper today, though I told Parlan to take a few old blankets and cut them up to share. My husband claims we simply cannot feed and clothe everyone who comes to our door. But if I had gone down to the gates today, I would have let them all inside. It is raining," she said. "It is cold."

"The king's argument is sound," Eva said gently. "There is not always enough to share."

"He can afford more than he will admit," Margaret confided. "His treasury has silver and gold enough to feed and clothe all of Scotland, I vow." She stopped. "Shut the door, if you please. I want to show you something."

Eva did, and Margaret beckoned to her. "The king has a chamber here—and another like it in Dunfermline." She opened a cupboard and a box within, and removed a few small iron keys on a metal chain. Then she lifted a flaming candlestick in its ceramic dish, and went to a curtained corner of the room to reveal some narrow steps. She led Eva down these to an oaken door, heavily latched. Unlocking that, she pushed it aside so that she and Eva could enter.

Like the treasure room at Dunfermline, this one was stacked with chests and boxes. Margaret set down the candlestick and used another key to open one of the larger chests. With Eva's help, she tipped back the hinged lid.

She stood back, smiling a little as Eva gasped. The gleam of gold and silver coins was an astonishing sight, and proof of the wealth of king and crown. Eva sank to her knees and ran a hand over the coins—some were English silver pennies and deniers stamped with an image meant to show the queen's deceased uncle King Edward; some were gold pieces, others stamped Flemish and French coins. Many of the edges had been clipped, evidence that the coins had circulated long before reaching Scotland.

"Malcolm means to have these melted down and imprinted as new Scots coins with his own image," Margaret said, "though for now,

Scotland still relies on foreign coinage even within its own borders. There is more than enough here to help the people in Dun Edin, and all of Scotland."

"There seems to be. Margaret," Eva said with a rare, impulsive use of her baptismal name, "is this yours to dispense?"

"Where do you think my dowry coins are? Here in Malcolm's treasury chests. If I want to help the Scottish people with some of this, the king himself cannot say me nay," she said thoughtfully, looking down at the glittering mass of coins. "I could do that."

"He would object. The crown needs the treasury for buildings, for roads—"

"For wars," Margaret said.

"Surely he is practical about expenses. Though it does look like an enormous amount."

"I do not know how much is here, but a little will not be missed. We could buy more woolen blankets in the marketplace, perhaps some candles, and more foodstuffs to give out . . ." She made a quick decision, her heart pounding. "Hand me that pouch, there." She gestured toward a few empty leather pouches piled on top of a small chest.

"Where is the king?" Eva asked as she grabbed a pouch.

"He left earlier with a hunting party. They were chafing to be gone and rushed through the gate even before the almsgiving." Margaret began to fill the pouch with coins, the chinking of silver and gold loud in the small room. She handed the full pouch to Eva then scooped up more coins as Eva fetched a second pouch. When that was filled, too, Margaret shut the lid and locked it, holding one leather bag while Eva held the other.

"There," Margaret said. "If I cannot spend this in the lawn market for supplies, I will give the coins away myself. Come," she whispered, as Eva took up the candle. Turning, Margaret gasped.

Malcolm stood outside the doorway, and with him were Brother Tor and Edgar, too, having come down the steps. Margaret froze, as did Eva, as the three men walked into the room.

"Look here," Malcolm boomed. "I have caught me two little thieves in my own house."

"Aye, and what will you do with them?" Edgar asked, folding his arms.

"Arrest and punishment for robbers," Malcolm said.

"At the very least they must return what they have stolen," Tor remarked, holding the curled handle of an oil lamp that set the room aglow.

"My lord," Margaret said, lacking patience for flippancy. "I thought you were hunting."

"The rains were too hard. We came back."

"Let us pass, please, sirs," Eva said, holding her head high, her sack of gold close.

None of the men moved. Malcolm folded his arms, leaning squarely in the doorway. "And where are you going with those? What, exactly, is in those bags?"

"My dowry coins," Margaret said. "In part." She could not lie.

"For what purpose? Silks for a new cloak? Gold thread for needle-work? Do you crave new shoes and rings, by God, when Scotland has expenses to pay?" His voice rose.

"I crave to share with the poor to ease their many needs." Margaret hugged the bag to her.

"Good God, woman, we do alms every morning and feed count-less souls at our gates," Malcolm burst out. He looked at the other men. "Thieves in the king's own household should have immediate punishment, I think."

"Sire, allow me to apologize for not informing you sooner," Mar-garet said. "But this is, after all, my dowry fortune, and I may do with part of it as I see fit." She had seen his temper flare for a moment, but now he looked amused again, his green-brown eyes sparkling, lips quirked. Edgar, too, smiled openly, but Brother Tor was utterly somber.

"Robbery is sinful," Tor said, "but sire, this is the queen."

"Ah, I have it," Malcolm said. "Come with me." He took Margaret's arm and lifted the pouch from her hands, dropping it on top of one of the chests. Edgar took Eva's arm, too, relieving her of the bag of coins. Margaret saw the girl glare up at Edgar.

"Let go," Eva said.

"Share the queen's thievery, share her fate," he said.

"And what would that be?" Eva demanded.

"Truly, I do not know," Edgar muttered. "Malcolm, what's to be done with them now?"

"I want to show you something," Malcolm said. "So you will remember that stealing king's gold is disgraceful."

"It is charitable, especially if it is hoarded when it could benefit others," Margaret argued as he led her into the corridor. Edgar followed with Eva, and Malcolm turned to direct the monk to lock the room again with the key that Margaret relinquished.

"Watch the steps, now." Malcolm guided her upstairs carefully, through the bedchamber, and out and down a corridor. A servant, passing them in the hallway carrying an armload of linens, stopped to stare.

"That gold can be put to good use," Margaret said as they went. "We can do more than give alms at the gate. Thousands of Saxons wander this land. We can help them."

"Let William feed and clothe them all. He created their destitution, not I." Malcolm led her along another set of stairs to exit the tower.

"But you brought them to Scotland," she pointed out.

He did not answer as they crossed the bailey to enter a building used as garrison quarters and storage, though Margaret had never gone inside it, having no reason to do so. Her husband guided her down some steps that seemed to go deep into the very earth, the musty dankness and darkness encroaching. They turned along a low-ceilinged, stone-walled corridor that cut a channel through the living rock that supported the fortress. Arches of stone formed small niches that were barred shut with iron grates. She saw several cells lining the tunneled passage like small caves.

"Dungeons!" she said.

"Aye, for thieves and the like," Malcolm said.

As they walked past, Margaret noticed with surprise that there were men in those cramped, dark spaces. They came to the grates to peer at the visitors, and as she passed, Margaret saw in the light of Tor's oil lamp that each man had a glimmer of keen intelligence and even sadness in his eyes, so that meeting their gazes pulled at her heart.

"Who are they?" she whispered to Malcolm.

"Normans," he said. "A few Saxons who side with Normans. Knights whose ransoms will bring more gold to Scottish coffers. A good thing, given this day's events," he added.

"How long have they been kept in here?" she asked, peering past him.

"I brought them from the south weeks ago. No need for you to know at the time. It need not concern you, as the matter is well in hand. Letters have gone out for their fees."

"But Malcolm—"

"Guardsman," he called. "Open that last door for us."

Two housecarls stood at the end of the grim corridor, both look-ing bewildered as the king approached with the queen in tow. One opened the iron grate of the last cell with a key and scraped the door back on its hinges. Malcolm led Margaret over the threshold, with Edgar and Eva just behind, and Tor following with the lamplight. Inside, Malcolm waved a hand.

"Ladies," he said. "Would you want to stay in this place?"

The little chamber was like a cave carved from the rock, with steeply curving walls and a floor scattered with straw. The only furnishings were a flat pallet with a folded blanket, a triple-legged wooden stool, and a chamber pot.

"We would provide more blankets," Edgar said.

"Do not take such delight in this," Eva snapped at him. Margaret smiled to herself in spite of her mounting irritation and, undeniably, a little frisson of worry.

"Well?" Malcolm asked. "What do you think of the king's chamber for thieves?"

"It is of course a horrible place," Margaret answered impatiently. "Those men should not be here either, for they have committed no real crime. And why bring us down here? Your jest is hardly amusing."

"Brother Tor, tell the ladies what you think of this place, and their crime."

"Of course the queen and her lady do not want to be here," Tor said calmly. "Yet this cell poses a metaphorical quandary as well. Would you visit such a dark and sinful place in your soul through questionable moral deeds? I believe that both of you are innocent souls, of course," he said, "but the king's message in bringing you here is very clear. Even if you meant to do a generous and merciful thing, you trod a wrongful path, and this is where it could lead."

"Thievery is thievery," Malcolm summarized.

"What we did was out of charity, not sinful urges," Eva said.

But for a moment, Margaret felt her gut constrict with doubt. She had thought Malcolm was merely amused at her indescretion, and bored on a rainy day. But Tor, whose judgment she valued, looked stern and disapproving. "Do you believe we sinned in this?" she asked the monk.

"I believe your pure soul was led astray by base instincts that mankind must fight," he said.

"It was my idea, not the queen's," Eva said quickly.

"It was mine," Margaret said. "And my portion to use as I please."

"I suppose that is true," Malcolm admitted.

"Enough," Edgar said. "The jest is done. We all know the queen's deed, and Lady Eva's, was charitably meant, if hastily done."

"I will confess and be cleansed, nonetheless," Margaret said.

Malcolm sighed and took her arm again. "This was simply a small lesson in manners, as you have often tried to teach me."

"I do not teach manners quite like you do," Margaret said indignantly.

"In future, do not take a man's gold without his permission—even if you obey one of your saintly urges." He led her back through the door and along the corridor, while the housecarls and the prisoners, too, gaped after them.

"What about the coins?" Margaret asked. "Give them to me for my own purposes."

"Very well. If you distribute silver coins at the gate tomorrow, do so sparingly, please," he said. "And send your steward to the market with orders to purchase what you will to give for alms this month. Within reason," he warned.

"I will see to it directly after prayers," Margaret said as they stepped out into the light of the bailey, with the rain clearing to clouds.

Chapter Eighteen

❦

*She ordered that nine little orphans utterly
destitute should be brought in to her at the first
hour of the day, and that soft foods such as children
at that tender age like should be prepared for
them . . . she did not think it beneath her to take
them upon her knee.*

—Bishop Turgot, *Life of Saint Margaret,*
TWELFTH CENTURY

I t is a simple request," Margaret said. "Why such fuss?" She had
only suggested to Wilfrid and Parlan that a group of orphaned
children be brought to the great hall each morning to be fed. "The children should come from the town and nearby region."

"But, Lady—" Wilfrid began.

"Cook only has to stew some fruit and grind the porridge fine
before cooking it, and Ella can find dishes, spoons, and cups small
enough for little hands and lips. Some of my own dishes will do;
they are of a delicate shape and size."

"But dear Lady, we cannot allow these children to handle such
precious things," Parlan protested, standing with Wilfrid. "Wood
and pottery suit children best."

"We should set out the best dishes for this, to welcome them and show that we honor them. Sir Wilfrid, I think we should have one hundred little ones here, orphans, too. Bring them to the hall each morning. Let us begin this very week." She felt excited, inspired by her new plan.

"One hundred a day?" her steward exclaimed. "Lady, finding them and escorting them here would take up a great deal of time."

"Perhaps one hundred is too many," she conceded. "Fifty a day, then, and a hundred on holy days. More at Yuletide would be fitting. I will feed them all myself."

"Beg pardon, but that might take all of a week, not just a morning, and would require the time and efforts of many here. You have many duties, and this could be a burden. And if I may say so, I am a steward and a warrior, not a herder of . . . lambs," Wilfrid finished.

"Ah," she said, thoughtful. "Thirty, then, every day."

Still he seemed dissatisfied. "Who will shepherd the imps at the gate?" Wilfrid asked. "Who will watch them and keep them from running, climbing, hurting themselves and others?"

"Godwin," she said, inspired. "And Gertruda. They each have a sweet way with children."

"What of the parents and kinfolk of these children? Do we turn them away hungry only to feed their broods?" Wilfrid asked.

"We must have something for them as well, then," she said. "Parlan, go remind Cook to grind the oats fine and cook them with a little milk. And have him stew apples with cinnamon and nutmeg, for the children may enjoy that. Both dishes should be ready at sunrise each day."

"As you wish, Lady," Parlan said, and she could see he was no happier than Wilfrid.

She was determined to have the small children brought in to her each morning after her prayers and before her own breakfast. She had devised a new penance for herself, though she would not reveal that. "I wish to honor the little children more," she said. "And this is a way."

"Then spend more time with your own," Wilfrid said honestly.

"Your little Edward follows you everywhere he can, and Edmund is always happy to see you. And there will be another soon to take up your time and concern."

She blushed at that. "But it tugs my heartstrings so to see the little ones in need at our gates. They are sometimes too small to eat what is given in alms, and so they do not get much just for themselves."

"Then invite a symbolic number of children," he suggested. "Keep the groups small but for holy days and celebrations. Six children," he suggested.

"Twelve, the number of the apostles."

"Nine," Wilfrid countered. "Surely that has some significance."

"Ah, nine choirs of angels. Perfect," she said. "And a hundred children on holy days. I will not be gainsaid on that one. See it done," she added, when he began to protest the larger number.

Looking around, she saw her husband crossing the room then. Malcolm must have heard the commotion and some muttering as Parlan went past him. She explained her plan. "Admirable," Malcolm said. "But do this only if you promise to eat with them."

"Just after they do," she promised, while he pursed his mouth to one side, seeming no more content than her stewards.

Two days later, Margaret emerged from prayers leading her ladies like ducklings, while Eva followed her, head high, looking more a princess by nature than even Cristina. In the great hall, nine children of various ages surrounded Wilfrid and Godwin, until Gertruda shooed them toward a table. Margaret sat down and took the smaller ones into her lap, one at a time, and fed them with a golden spoon dipped into a crystal bowl. The older ones were each given their own spoon and bowl, and as they ate they laughed, beaming like sunshine.

The next day, more children were brought in, and so it continued until feeding the children was routine at Dun Edin, while almsgiving continued at the front gates. Wilfrid and other housecarls easily found little ones to bring to the queen, and word spread that kindness and alms could be found at the king's residence.

While Margaret's ladies stitched little shirts and stockings from cloth scraps, Godwin revealed sleight-of-hand tricks with silver pennies to amuse the children gathered in the hall. He even taught Brother Tor, though his solemn attempt at such tricks made Margaret laugh.

Nine children became twelve, twelve became thirty, then fifty, and on All Saints Day on the first of November, one hundred children were led into the great hall. Margaret fed as many as she could manage with her own hands, her own spoon, and she encouraged her own Edward to help, no matter how small he was, along with truculent Duncan and willing Donald.

"Their father will make them warriors," she told Tor, "but it falls to me to make them merciful princes."

"As much use as warrior skills, if not more," he replied.

Her secret ambition was to invite a thousand children to the royal fortress one day, though she suspected that Wilfrid, Tor, and Malcolm would have none of it. The feeling of charity, whether to children or people at the gates, or some other form, was heady—she wanted more of it, could not get enough; it was like water for her thirsty soul.

WINTER SKIMMED BY like a vague dream, Advent to Lent, days filled with her duties, her prayers, caring for her small sons, seeing to her charity gestures. Exhausted at times, Margaret pushed on as the liturgical calendar came round to Septuagesima and the beginning of the Lenten season and the advent of her own devoted fasting. Diligent about cleansing any existing sin, she also tried to consider her condition, allowing herself a little porridge, a withered apple from storage, or a little broth each day.

Malcolm told Parlan to obtain some wheat somewhere to make risen bread for the queen, and though trading ships from England came to Leith less often, Parlan managed to make wheaten bread loaves, though from the crude dark grain mixed with rye that monks favored. Malcolm himself sliced and buttered it thick and handed it to her at the table. She dared not refuse.

Eva played harp for her when she took to her bed now and then, and one day, head spinning, Margaret saw a tiny being seated on a stool; it smiled and told her to eat and worry no more. Then a second shadow that she thought was surely angelic, for it was quiet but stern, told her that pain defeated sin and not to listen to temptation. She felt faint, and did not know which vision to obey.

One evening Eva brought her a warm, thick liquid concoction she had made from oats, warm milk, spices, and the Scots drink called *uisge beatha,* strong spirits made from fermented barley. Eva stayed until the queen swallowed much of it, and Margaret slept deep that night, even through her prayer hours. Still, she became bird-thin and as pale as linen—yet she felt clean, pure, ethereal.

One day Brother Tor took her aside. "You have fasted sufficiently," he said. "Now go to broths and fruit, and then eat something substantial each day, every day. Until the birth, do not go to chapel during the night, and do not return to fasting. Praying in your little chapel or by your bed is more than enough proof of your devotion."

"You sound like a physician, not a priest," she said.

"I am a physician for your soul," he answered. "Margaret, please do as I ask."

Looking up, she saw in that solemn blue gaze a tender concern, and when he touched her shoulder briefly, the gesture of a counseling priest, she felt such comfort that her knees oddly weakened. She leaned toward him, sensing that he understood, knew, accepted her for all her flaws.

"Brother Tor," she said, "sometimes I want to fast until all the sin is burned clean from me. Once I begin, it becomes like a fever demon and I must continue even against my will."

"You have such a pure soul," he whispered. "There is no need to clarify yourself, especially now."

She nodded, and then fled, blushing hot, feeling the correction more than the praise. His good opinion of her was so important—too important, she told herself, and mentally assigned herself three additional Pater Nosters to recite that evening, for she had let pride best her again.

A few days later, Malcolm brought her a bowl of soup with his own hands and sat by her bed while she ate a little. When she set it aside, he handed her a parcel wrapped in cloth and string. Peeling away the cloth, she saw a book—quite a magnificent one, bound not in leather as were most of her books, but with boards encased in engraved silver studded with a border of small jewels and a golden cross fastened at its center. Gasping with delight, thrilled with its beauty as well as Malcolm's surprising thoughtfulness, she carefully opened the tiny brass locks attached to the leather buckles that fastened the covers tightly shut. Inside, another cover was of new, fragrant leather lined in thick white satin, and she saw that the pages were separated by individual squares of white silk. Turning a few pages, she caught her breath in astonishment.

"But—this is my own copy of the Gospels! The book that went missing! How did you—"

"A little thievery of my own," he said. "I took the book one day after you set it down. We had been reading, you and I, and you were very patient with me." He smiled a little. "The leather cover was so worn, it was splitting apart. I thought a new cover would please you. A goldsmith in the town did the work, and finished it just this week."

"Thank you," she said, tears stinging her eyes. "I do not deserve such a fine gift."

"Of course you do." He sounded almost annoyed. "Do not say otherwise. I hope you will continue to teach me to read these words as well as you can."

She turned a page. "*Incipit evangelium* . . . Now you read the rest. It is your book, too, now."

"This is the Gospel . . . according to, uh, Mark," he read. "Look at that fancy fellow, with his red beard and quill like a sword," he said of the painting that faced the opening page. "And that foolish little chair, as if he is sitting on top of a building."

"He is. That is the very Church itself. Now read this bit." She pointed.

"*Ecce mitto angelum . . .*" he began, tracing the words with a fingertip.

❧

A SOFT KNOCK at the door woke Eva in the middle of the night, and Matilda got up to open it. "The queen wants you," she whispered. "She waits outside."

"To chapel again?" Eva groaned but rose from bed, dressed, and twisted her hair into a long rope, tying it with a ribbon as she went to the door.

Margaret waited in the corridor, wearing a black hooded cloak so voluminous that at first Eva did not recognize her in the shadowed passageway. She held a flickering oil lamp of brass in one hand and a similar cloak draped over her arm, which she offered to Eva in silence. Puzzled, Eva slid the cloak over her shoulders, wondering at the queen's secretive mood. The entire household knew about the queen's eccentric habit of praying and strolling about at all hours. Yawning, she followed Margaret down the steps and around the side of the main keep.

"But the chapel is that way," Eva said.

"Hush!" Margaret took her arm and pulled her across the shadowed, moonlit bailey.

The air was so cold that Eva's breath frosted in a cloud. She followed Margaret, who led her to the building that housed the garrison and the dungeons.

"Why are we going—" Eva began. Margaret touched a hand to her arm.

"The guards are not here just now," she replied in a whisper. "Malcolm has kept them up late, meeting with his advisors and most of the housecarls over some talk of securing the fortress against invasion from the south. Even the dungeon guards were summoned there. They will not be gone long. And I have the key." She opened her palm to show a glint of iron.

"What is this about?" Eva asked.

Margaret seemed curiously excited, her eyes sparkling in the moon-light as if she had a fever. "I want to free the prisoners."

"What?"

"Hush! Follow me." She proceeded down a few steps to the cor-ridor leading the dungeon. The flame of the oil lamp formed a small pool of light just ahead of them as they went.

"This is foolish," Eva hissed as the queen drew her forward. "Who are these men, and what are their offenses? You should not be going near them on your own."

"Four Saxons and two Normans, all taken captive in England," Margaret answered. "Malcolm says he is only holding them for ran-som. They have committed no crimes and their families and proper-ties are in harm's way in the south. But so far William has given no reply to the ransom request, and their Saxon kin have no fortunes left to buy their freedom."

"This is not your concern, truly."

"Can I ignore good men lingering in prison in my own household? Malcolm admits they are honorable men, and this is only a custom of war—but it seems sinfully wrong to keep them here and away from their families. You keep watch while I let them out," Margaret said.

She led the way along the dark channel and went to the first cell, where she spoke to the men inside in French, which Eva understood only slightly. Then came answering murmurs, and the chink and clank of key and lock. The door creaked open and two tall, shadowy figures emerged.

The queen moved to the next cell, and again Eva heard her speak low, again in French. As the door opened, four men emerged this time. Eva heard rapidly murmured English then.

"Hurry," Margaret said, "you must all flee. There is little time before the guards return."

"Lady, you have taken a great risk," someone said. "We thank you."

Margaret's hood slipped back as she looked up, her golden hair, without a veil, flowing free. She looked young, vibrant, and calm as she turned toward Eva with a smile. Exhilaration shone in her like a light.

"You are enjoying this," Eva said. "I think you love the adventure even more than you love the justice of this."

"Of course not." But Margaret looked pleased. "Quickly, we must reach the gate before these men are seen. Come ahead," she said, as the prisoners followed them.

"Wait!" Eva stretched up an arm, seeing some long cloaks hanging on wall pegs near the outer end of the corridor. One of the men reached over her head to take the cloaks down.

"Excellent thought—take these," he told the others, handing them out.

"But that is stealing." Margaret looked doubtful.

"Will we quibble sin this night? Replace them later," Eva said. "What about the sentries?"

"I will tell the guards that I am sending some servants out with urgent messages."

"Your sins are multiplying," Eva said.

"As are yours," Margaret said. "Later we will go to the chapel and pray."

"Instead of the entrance gate, we should use the postern gate at the back," one of the men whispered. "We can get away without being seen."

"But there is a steep drop there," Eva said.

"We can follow the ledge behind the palisade, and there is a way down the cliff if we go carefully," the man replied. "I have heard the guards talking about it."

"Rope," Margaret said quickly. "At the back of the yard is a byre. There will be rope there."

"Thank you." He bowed solemnly. "Queen Margaret, your charity will never be forgotten." He took her hand and kissed it.

Each man gave the queen a grateful farewell and turned to Eva to thank her also, all in a rush, a few seconds or more. Then they were gone, cloaks whirling away in the darkness.

"So," Margaret said with satisfaction, folding her hands before her. "It was right to help them. Though I do not know how to explain this to Malcolm," she added.

"You will find a way," Eva said, feeling admiration—Margaret was made of more than prayers and pious sin-fretting, and more than sweet and charitable goodness. "That was very courageous, my lady. Best we go to chapel now." She took Margaret's arm. "We should be seen there rather than near the dungeons."

Margaret laughed. "You are a true friend."

Eva said nothing. If she fulfilled her promise to her grandmother, she would be no friend.

MALCOLM'S ROAR could be heard throughout the tower, even in the great hall where Eva sat with the queen and others, having just fed a few small children who had been brought up from the front gates. When the king burst through the curtained entrance of the great hall moments later, Eva jumped up, but was hardly surprised to see that the king was not taking the news well. The queen, sitting with a child on her lap, looked up calmly as Malcolm stomped toward her.

"Margaret," he said in an angry, warning tone. "Where are my prisoners?"

"Hush, sire," she said. "You will frighten the little ones."

"A word with you," he growled as he stood over her, a fist at his waist, his face red. "*Now.*"

The child in Margaret's lap began to cry, staring up at Malcolm. Handing the little girl to Eva, Margaret stood and walked away with the king. He led her to a far corner and began to talk in a low, angry rumble accompanied by swift jabbing gestures toward the doorway and outside.

Eva jiggled the child on her lap and dipped a spoon into the porridge as she watched the queen and king. Margaret smiled at her husband and set a hand on his arm as if to calm him. Then she rested a hand on her stomach. Under the long, layered draping of the queen's garments, the burgeoning curve of her body was obvious, and Margaret used that.

When Malcolm subsided quickly, Eva smiled to herself, silently applauding the queen's cleverness. The king took his wife's hand, then leaned down and kissed her cheek. He left the hall, and Margaret returned to sit once more.

She smiled at Eva. "He saw that the key in our bedchamber had been moved, and he realized I had taken it. I confessed that the prisoners' escape was all my doing. He thinks he will lose a good deal of income from this, and that is why he is angry. He says that I am coming into my own ever since I learned thievery." Margaret grimaced slightly.

Eva laughed. "And I am your accomplice."

"MY LADY!" Robert De Lauder approached Margaret as she and her mother and sister walked across the bailey on another morning. "The king rode out early, but left this word for you. He implores you to order your servants to pack whatever is necessary. The household must leave very soon."

"What is wrong?" Margaret set a hand to her throat, heart surging with fear.

"Dun Edin is no longer safe for you. Malcolm wants you to depart for the north before nightfall."

"But we would need days to pack!" Astonished, she stared at him, and felt fear growing as she recalled fleeing other places. "Is it the Normans?"

"Malcolm had a message from the south—a carrier rode into the bailey at first light. William is gathering troops and preparing to cross into Scottish territory. Cospatric sent word that Saxon boats are being constructed at Berwick, and once they are ready, it will take William no time to reach Scotland with thousands of warriors.

When that will be we cannot say, but Malcolm wants you to leave Dun Edin immediately."

Margaret crossed herself, head and heart. "God protect us. What of Malcolm?"

"He and Edgar, too, will remain here for now. Brother Tor will accompany you to Dunfermline."

"Is that place even safe, if William has ships?"

"You may need to move farther north," De Lauder replied somberly.

With a child due soon that might prove impossible, she thought. "I will order the servants to begin packing."

"Only what is most essential. Other things can be sent later. The ship departs Leith this afternoon. The king bids me tell you that you will be aboard, or he will throw you on the boat himself and tie you to the mast. *Pardonnez-moi, ma reine,*" he finished.

MALCOLM HIMSELF CARRIED his wife in his arms through the shallows to the longship, and though Eva could see Margaret was not happy about it, the queen did not protest. Edgar lifted Eva, too, and she rode lightly in his arms, clasping her hands about his neck. He was stronger than his lankiness suggested, and when he set her down he thanked her gallantly for the privilege.

"Sir, I am honored to be carried by a prince who should be a king," she had said, playing the little game of courtliness that he had begun. She preferred honesty over flattery, but smiled at the flirtation. He blushed red to the ears and wished her a good voyage.

"I will see you in Dunfermline later, as soon as we can join you there," he said, and his long fingers lingered over hers, tightened, then let go. He leaped down into the water and waded back.

"Husband," Margaret said as the king set her down beside Eva. "This ferry reminds me—there are so many people in need of transportation to complete their pilgrimages. I want to sponsor a ferry that would cross the firth to Dunfermline and Fife for no fee for pilgrims."

"Not now, Margaret," he said. "We will talk of this later."

"If I must travel over water, then you must hear me out. Quickly, now—"

"Your ferryman would have plenty of customers for his free ferry but no supper on his table."

"I would pay his yearly fee from my own coffers. I have dowry funds and rental incomes, and even a portion of that would keep a ferryman and his family. We could also provide a hostel on the other side of the firth for pilgrims, so they can rest before continuing their journey."

"Such a bargain would attract more than just pilgrims. Everyone would want to ride free."

"We would provide the ferry for free to pilgrims and others—and charge only the bishops. They can afford it, and their fees could help pay for the pilgrims."

He laughed. "Clever Margaret. I will ask Sir Robert to look into the arrangements when he can. I must leave you now—but I will see you soon, I promise."

Eva saw them exchange a quick, tender embrace, and Malcolm looked her way as he left.

"Lady Eva," he spoke, "take good care of her." She nodded.

Later, as Eva watched the frothy, white-capped waves of the firth stream past, she savored the freedom of salt wind on her face as the longboat slipped along, surging and cresting in a whippy wind. The queen's kin and retainers were crammed between crates and chests and the ride was bumpy that day, but took only an hour or so.

Margaret sat in silence, pale face lifted to the wind, her hands fisted. When they landed, she was quick to request that two house-carls carry her, sling-like, to shore. When Eva joined her, Margaret looked very pale, and Eva took her arm in sudden concern.

"I have not been very good about keeping the vow I made," Margaret said.

"But your new ferry will do a great deal of good. That will out-last any vow."

"May it counter my shortcomings," Margaret said.

Walking with her toward the cart that would carry the queen the rest of the way to the royal tower, Eva sighed to herself. No matter the good Margaret did, it was never enough in the queen's regard. "Lady," she said then, "I think I shall compose a praise poem for you."

"A new melody would be lovely to hear," Margaret said, "but there is no reason for a queen's poem. Write one for the king instead—that is the tradition for a court bard, is it not?"

"Only if the king is one the bard admires. Otherwise, it is best to keep silent."

"Eva, that grudge will outlast you," Margaret said.

It might indeed, Eva thought.

Chapter Nineteen

Thou shell of my heart
Thou face of my sun
Thou harp of my music
Thou crown of my senses.

—SCOTTISH GAELIC CHARM,
FROM ALEXANDER CARMICHAEL,
Carmina Gadèlica

W ithin days, the queen became quiet, pale, and drawn,
though she had been confident and glowing recently at
Dun Edin. Eva assumed she had exhausted herself while supervising
the unpacking of the household and the settling of the children at Dunfermline.

"You have Dame Agnes for that, and Gertruda and Mirren for the
children," Eva reminded her. "Trust them to see to all, and rest."

But Margaret rarely rested body or mind for long; her devotional
routine alone could make a lesser soul quail. Concerned, Eva rose even
earlier each day to accompany Margaret to prayers, and she played
music while Margaret went to bed each night. But a week after their
return, seeing the queen walk slowly and stiffly, then pause with a
hand pressed to her back, Eva knew.

"Margaret, has this endured all day?" she asked. "You said no word of it."

"It is too soon for the birth," Margaret said, looking weary. "I hoped it would stop."

Taking her arm and guiding her to the bedchamber, Eva sent Finola to find the housekeeper and the queen's mother, then sent a housecarl for Mother Annot, hoping she would arrive soon.

"Please, fetch your harp," Margaret told Eva when she returned to find the queen tucked in the bed wearing a linen shift, while Dame Agnes went about the room untying any knot she found in garments, shoes, curtain ties, to ease the babe's arrival. "The music will help to play this little one out of me, though it is too soon for him to come—this will not take long, I think."

Not long at all, Eva discovered. Dame Agnes barely had time to tuck rowan branches at the threshold and stow a knife under the bed to cut the pain when the midwife appeared and Margaret strived to push. Fingers shaking, Eva played a tranquil song as Margaret's third son slipped, small and slightly blue, into the world.

His hold on life seemed fragile, though Mother Annot stroked and swaddled and cradled him in her strong, gentle hands, and baptized him quickly with a vial of holy water she kept, like all good midwives, in her satchel. Then she placed him in Margaret's arms, and turned to Eva.

"This one may not survive," she whispered in Gaelic. "Too early, too small. I will sing a charm for his healing." As she began, Eva plucked the strings of the harp softly so that the woman's prayerful chant would seem just another song.

Margaret drew down her shift and began to suckle him, her breasts heavy. She looked up at her mother. "No wet nurse has been found yet, for we lingered in Dun Edin too long, and this little one came early. I will be his nurse—and he will thrive," she added fiercely. "I will see to it."

Expecting Lady Agatha to continue to pray fretfully in Latin and German over her black prayer beads, Eva was surprised to see the woman set to work helping Mother Annot to change the bedding and create a small, safe nest for the babe on the queen's bed. Eva admitted Brother Tor, who had been pacing outside, into the chamber to baptize the child again and offer a prayer and a word of comfort to Margaret, holding her hand until Lady Agatha shooed him away.

Margaret gave herself to the child from the first hour, going without rest herself unless the child slept. Mother Annot stayed, with her mystical charms and her practical sense, as did Lady Agatha, and they hardly left the queen's bedchamber for a fortnight or more. Eva stayed, too: the softest harp music lulled the babe to healing sleep, and she played day and night. Margaret slept, too, now and then.

Though christened, the child had no true name beyond the first one Mother Annot gave him: Leanabh, or Baby. Margaret would not name him formally, and Eva realized that his mother still feared he would be lost.

❋

WEEKS PASSED, SIX AND MORE, while the babe slept, fussed, fed weakly. Then he spent two hours awake, alert and peaceful, and again the next day, and so on; his color grew pinker, his suckling and grip stronger. Margaret began to feel sure in her heart that he did indeed thrive, despite what she had told her mother, for the fears had been great within her, and the need to pray profound. Grateful, needing solitude, she left him with her women and for the first time in weeks walked out into the April sunshine. She sought Brother Tor for confession and blessing and the comfort of his unquestioning spirit; and she asked Father Otto to conduct Mass in the anteroom chapel.

Within days, she ventured into the glen, Eva at her side, along with a few of her ladies, to attend Mass for her churching in the hillside chapel. Afterward, as she lingered alone, she wept as she prayed, glad for the child's health as well as the day's freedom. But the ache in her breasts soon urged her to return to her little one, and that very night she asked Mother Annot to find a wet nurse. Her small nursling would be fine now, she reasoned—but she had neglected her duties as queen and had all but abandoned the strict routine of fasting and prayer that simply, utterly, sustained her in all ways.

Weeks passed before riders came with Malcolm's blue silk banner, sewn with an image of a boar in white—the insigne of the king, who followed their advance. Seeing that blue flashing in the distance, Margaret hurried down to the courtyard just as the larger party entered the gates. Malcolm, dismounting his horse, looked up.

She felt a burst in her heart, some need and emotion that she had contained all this time, and she bunched her skirt in her hands as she ran toward him. He looked well and robust, so much so that she sobbed out, lifted her arms, touched his face, let him kiss her even though others stood watching.

"My son, the little one—I had your message but could not come away until now. Where is he?" Malcolm clasped her hand in his, and Margaret turned to lead him toward the tower and the great hall, where the cradle sat in a warm shaft of sunlight. The child, wrapped in blankets, was small and golden-delicate, as fair and pretty as Edward and Edmund, who played nearby with their half brothers, Duncan and Donald, who had remained in the king's household. Lifting the infant into her arms, Margaret showed him to Malcolm.

"We call him Leanabh," she said.

"What! 'Baby' is no name for a warrior-prince. At least it is Gaelic," he muttered.

"Now that you are here, we will have an official christening. I want to call him Edgar. It is English," she added in apology, "but—"

"It is a worthy name and I would be proud to give it to our son," he replied solemnly.

Margaret's breath caught in her throat. Malcolm's quick approval worried her. "My brother—is he well? Has something happened?" Edgar had accompanied them to Dunfermline but had ridden south since to join Malcolm, and there had been no word from him.

"He is well enough," he answered grimly, "for a prince who will never reclaim his kingdom. William marches north again with vigor and temper. It is only a matter of time before he comes here."

✣

JUNE BROUGHT WARMTH and the soft fragrance of flowers as Eva walked out with Margaret and Brother Tor one morning. The queen was eager to see the site of the new church she had convinced Malcolm to build with funding decided from a portion of the queen's gold, the income from Margaret's rental lands. Though construction would take years, Margaret was excited by each small step. Ground had been broken, plans were drawn, and stonecutting rang out in the air.

"After the birth of small Edgar, Malcolm finally agreed to this," she told Tor as they walked. "He was so thankful for the child's health that he promised me my church out of gratitude."

Eva strolled behind, listening but not much interested. The new stone church was Margaret's dear project, all she talked about lately. More and more, as another year slipped past, Eva wanted only to return to Moray. She let her gaze drift northeast, where in clear weather she could just see the crests of the faraway mountains that bordered that province.

She had not sent word to her grandmother for months, after dispatching a note to announce the birth of the third prince, followed by another to report Malcolm's fears that William might yet come north. But Lady Gruadh would not want to hear about flourishing babes or the building of churches. Eva had mentioned the releasing of the prisoners and the stealing of the king's gold—she thought it might make Gruadh laugh, and perhaps approve of Margaret more, knowing that the young queen was capable of mischief as well as tedious piety.

"Three sons to hold his kingdom would make any king proud and thankful," Tor now told Margaret. "He would agree to anything you asked of him."

Masons, an architect, and laborers had already begun the work, as De Lauder had been quick to find an accomplished master designer in a displaced Saxon doing masonry work at Dun Edin. Before leaving England, the architect had assisted in the designing of a new cathedral at Durham, its construction still under way. The design he had recently suggested for Dunfermline would echo and rival Durham's powerful design of stout, carved columns springing upward into vaulted ceilings, and clerestory windows filtering light downward to lessen the stone's visual weight.

Now, as Margaret and Tor looked over ink drawings with the master designer, Eva stood listening to the natural rhythms of hammer and chisel upon the stone in the newly designated churchyard at the top of the narrow glen. The builders had estimated a year to frame and enclose the structure, and many years beyond that to finish the walls and roof and see to the elaborate carvings and interior details. Would she still be a captive in the royal household then?

When they bid the mason good day and walked ahead, Eva followed, unnoticed as Margaret, cheeks flushed pink, talked of her church with Tor. "You must consider staying here in Dunfermline," she told him. "Surely your bishop would agree to a request from my husband."

"My lady, you have permanent priests and monks in your household already. And I have my own work to do at Melrose. The king's manuscript is nearly done, and there are others I will do. Malcolm wants another history of Scotland, and I am completing a life of Saint Cuthbert as well."

Eva's attention was caught. "So Malcolm's manuscript is at Melrose? Will you finish it soon?" she asked.

"I will, but I cannot risk keeping it there, with the Normans so close to the borderlands. I travel with it and have it with me here. I sometimes find time to work on the pages."

"Excellent!" Margaret said. "I am eager to read it as soon as it is properly bound. To read it before then might damage the pages. There is a skilled binder in Dun Edin. We will send it to him."

"Brother Tor, what will you do with the finished book?" Eva asked.

"That is for the king to decide, Lady Eva," he answered. "He may keep it with his other books, chained to a shelf, or he may donate it to a religious house, since it is a valuable history."

"Our new church here at Dunfermline would be an excellent place for it one day," the queen said.

"May I see the book sooner than later, Brother Tor?" Eva asked.

"I look forward to your opinion later, Lady Eva." Tor smiled. "You supplied the accurate list of names, though I have yet to complete the final pages. I am still scribing the information."

"Ah," Eva said, disappointed. She desperately wanted to see the book—what if Lady Gruadh had been wrong? Tor's manuscript might correctly describe reigns and battles and outcomes. But if it was indeed a concoction of lies meant to ruin others to make Malcolm seem the better king, she would have to act, even steal it, if need be.

The thought stunned her so that she stopped along the path. Tor had been kind to her, praising her music, even one day stopping to thank her for befriending the queen. To take the work he had created with such dedication would feel like a worse betrayal than simple thievery.

But if she did nothing, Malcolm would have the manuscript, and order it copied to share its contents further. That would betray her kin and the whole of her lineage. First she must see the manuscript. Then she would know better what to do.

"I would be happy to look at it as soon as you would like," she said, and Tor nodded.

"Brother Tor," Margaret said then, turning toward the monk. "I would dearly like to found a house of Benedictines here at Dunfermline, especially with the new church under way."

"I thought the church might be dedicated for Scottish use. It is Malcolm's choice."

"Benedictine makes sense if Scotland is to improve its standing in the world. Would you agree to supervise a Benedictine house here? I will write to Lanfranc in Canterbury myself about it."

"It would be a great honor, but the king—"

Margaret smiled like a cat at the cream. "He will agree, if it is what I want."

"What of Father Otto, Brother Brand, and Brother Godwin?"

"They will be here to help you. Surely Melrose can be left to the direction of Brother Aldwyn, who is doing a fine job there. Come up to Dunfermline, if it can be arranged."

"Lady," he said solemnly, "if you so desire it, we will ask for permission."

Margaret rested a hand on his arm briefly. "Your presence would be a boon to me, Tor. You would truly counsel me, correct me, assign me penances. You know my shortcomings almost as well as Eva does," she said, smiling over her shoulder.

"Lady, you have no shortcomings," Tor spoke quietly.

Something flashed between them, soft gaze and deep spark, and Eva saw for an instant an aware, silent exchange that friends share—even lovers. The queen and the monk had a rare spiritual bond, Eva thought. Friends early in life, they accepted each other now as fervently pious and dedicated to their ideals. Tor and Margaret had found a perfect mate of the spirit, a keen communion of minds. Neither would cross the unassailable boundary between them—neither would dare even think it.

Surely that was so, Eva told herself, watching them smile, hesitate, then walk on.

Chapter Twenty

*King [William] will not cease from attacking
them . . . he will discover that he had better make
peace with them than continually attacking them
and prevailing nothing.*

— De Gestis Herwardi Saxonis, ANGLO-SAXON,
TWELFTH CENTURY

W illiam," said Edgar breathlessly, standing in Dunfermline's dusty, summer-baked yard, "has sent his troops marching into Lothian to burn fields while he has gone to Berwick, where his ships are waiting." Grim, weary, he looked at Margaret and De Lauder, who stood at her side. "He could reach the shores of Fife in a day or two."

Margaret clenched her hands, her heart beating fast. She had dreaded this, prayed against it, yet it was here. "What of Malcolm?"

"He is in Dun Edin, mustering troops and ships. They are trading messages by fast rider. William threatens to cut a swath through Scotland unless Malcolm surrenders and offers recompense."

"For what?" Margaret asked sharply.

"William is furious about the continuing Saxon rebellion, and still holds me accountable for that—Malcolm, too. And he wants the Saxon royal family returned to his custody, including you, Margaret. He claims you could not marry without his permission." Anger sparked in his eyes.

She raised her chin. "I did not need his approval. When will Malcolm be here?"

"He will soon depart Leith before William's ships even sail out of Berwick. He sent me ahead with the news."

"We will wait for my husband, then decide what to do."

Edgar shook his head. "Malcolm wants you gone from here quickly. Robert," he said to De Lauder, "you are to escort the queen and her party north to Loch Leven. Malcolm sent a messenger to the abbot."

"Drostan would welcome us," Eva said, walking forward. "But why must we go there?"

Seeing her friend, Margaret tucked an arm into Eva's. But she sensed tension thrumming in the slender girl, and noticed that Eva trained her gaze solely on Edgar.

"You will have sanctuary on the holy island," Edgar said. "There is mortal danger if William comes here. He would take us all captive if he could." He wiped a hand over his brow where sweat dripped, and glanced over his shoulder as his horse, glossy after a fast morning's ride from the coast, was led away by a groom. "You must go, while I stay here and wait for Malcolm."

Edgar looked exhausted, Margaret thought, his face so drawn that he looked years older. She touched his arm. "All will be well. Should it come to battle, Malcolm will prevail on his own ground."

"Not everyone has such faith in him." Edgar's solemn gaze flashed toward Eva. "We cannot know what will happen."

"We can only try to ensure the safety of the queen and the princes, so long as we move quickly," De Lauder said.

Margaret sighed, but felt a calm acceptance begin to fill her. "So be it. Dame Agnes"—she turned toward the housekeeper who waited nearby—"we must ready the children and the household to leave this afternoon. Edgar, surely you need some refreshment."

"I will see to it," Eva said, and Edgar nodded gratefully.

Commotion soon filled tower and bailey as Dame Agnes called out orders like a general and servants packed and toted what would be taken along, while the nurses readied the children and gathered their things. In the midst of the activity, Margaret sought out the little chapel beside the great hall. She wanted to pull a weaving of prayer like a blanket over herself, her loved ones, the whole of the situation. Entering the room, she saw Brother Tor there, kneeling. He glanced up as she sank to her knees beside him.

"The Normans are on their way here," she said, clasping her hands, bowing her head. "Tor, I am frightened. When they came to Winchester and took us away—and you were taken, too, in Lincoln—"

"Years ago," he whispered. "Now William must acknowledge that you are queen. If he treats you otherwise, show him who you truly are."

She drew a quick breath. "Come with us to Loch Leven."

"Aye," he murmured.

Relieved, she began to whisper a round of Pater Nosters. When her shoulder pressed Tor's, for they knelt that close in the small space, she did not lean away. His solidity and wisdom were comforting, and she needed that now.

❦

LATE AFTERNOON SUN TURNED the meadows golden as an envoy of mounted guards, carts, and two vans conveyed the queen, her children and kinswomen, her ladies and servants, northward. As Eva rode on horseback, she was aware of the silent, wary mood among them all. Edgar had remained in Dunfermline, and suddenly Eva missed him keenly—his calmness and vitality, his humor and compassion, would have been welcome today. Except for a few moments in the bailey and later in the hall, they had said little earlier, though he seemed glad for her company. His gaze had sought hers and lingered, and in a dim corridor he had taken her hand—but De Lauder and Ranald mac Niall had come out of the hall then, and Edgar had stepped away quickly.

She wanted to ask Margaret if Edgar had expressed any feelings toward her, but she could hardly do that now even though Margaret sat in the cart beside her. The queen held her oldest son, Edward, in her lap, while she turned the pages of her Gospel with the elaborate silver cover as Edward looked at the pictures. Lady Agatha held baby Edgar wrapped in swaddling, while Edmund slept in Gertruda's lap. The mood inside the van was somber even among the children, and the ladies were especially quiet.

In the distance, rounded hills couched Loch Leven like a jewel. Eva was anxious to meet Drostan again, for she had written another letter for her grandmother, this one tucked in the seam pocket of the blue tunic gown that she wore beneath her plaid of five muted colors. Her harp was wrapped and carried safe in another cart, though she expected that its strings would be silenced for quite a while.

If only she were free to deliver the note herself to Lady Gruadh, she thought. A quick pang of loneliness pulled at her. After a few years away, she wanted desperately to go home to Moray, yet could not leave the king's custody until he released her. At Saint Serf's she might find a chance to get away, even escape. If the Normans came north as expected, Malcolm would not care about his hostage. He would have far greater troubles.

But then the queen, who was reading aloud to Edward, looked up and smiled at her. Eva felt the heart-tug of the trusting friendship that bound her further to the court. If she left, she would worry about Margaret—her health, her state of mind, the way she demanded perfection of herself. Without Eva, the queen would have no accomplice for her small rebellions and adventures. She might succumb to her strict disciplines of prayer and fasting, listening more to the somber priests, with no more music to lighten her spirit and carry her through.

Under a deep violet evening, after being welcomed at the island monastery and shown to the guesthouses, Eva left chapel after prayers with Margaret and some of the others. While they went toward their beds, she saw Drostan beckon to her, and turned to walk with him in the darkness.

"I have a note for my grandmother," she said. "Will you send it on to her?"

"We may do better," he replied. "She wanted to be told if you came here again, so I sent word to her. She will be here within the week."

"Here!" Eva stared at him. "But—"

"You will meet in secret." He turned in the shadows and was gone, leaving Eva to walk back to the guesthouse alone, her thoughts spinning. He had not taken the note she had offered. That night she did not sleep, pacing and fretting, and by the first glimpse of morning light, she was again at prayers with Margaret.

"You are very quiet," the queen remarked later.

"I cannot play my harp here," Eva said, shrugging. "It sets me ill at ease."

Days passed, near a week, while Eva counted hours and endured the peace in the monastery, which made her more anxious than relaxed. Near one spot by the outer wall, she could see the widest view of island, loch, and mountains, while warm summer winds pushed at her. Day after day, rounds of prayers and chores continued, beginning with matins and lauds, then terce and sext, and so on. Eva often went with Margaret, pretending to be intent on her prayers. Late one afternoon, she heard whispering among the two monks who kept the gate, and saw Brother Tor and the housecarls hurrying there.

"The ferryman is crossing the water," one of the monks called out, and Eva started in surprise. Would Gruadh arrive so openly? She began to hurry toward the gate.

"Malcolm has arrived," Tor said, turning to Eva. "Fetch the queen, quickly."

Eva whirled and ran, her heart pounding in dread.

"WILLIAM HAS COME into Scotland at last," Malcolm told Margaret grimly. They strolled the lush green gardens in private while some of her household stood waiting in the yard for whatever word the king had brought. Eva seemed most nervous of all, so pale and tense that Margaret had taken a moment to reassure her that although Edgar was not with the king—her brother had ridden ahead, Malcolm had reported—he was safe. Still Eva did not seem comforted. Something more bothered her and though Margaret did not know what it was, she knew that every step northward was a step closer to Moray. Perhaps that weighed on Eva's mind.

"What matters most is that you are well, and here now," she told her husband.

"William marched through Lothian, burning crops at first, but met no fight to fuel his temper. So he sent his troops over land toward Fife, and met his ships to sail the firth. So far, the Scots have shown him little resistance."

She set a hand to her chest. "What does that mean? Have we surrendered in defeat?"

"We have not met in battle, nor will we. The people decided this—they surprised him at every turn with hospitality, greeting his men, offering food, cattle, oats. Cleverly done, as it took the wrath and purpose out of him. Yesterday he sent a new message, proposing to meet with me, and soon."

"Surely not here, where we have sanctuary and peace!" Margaret cried out.

He shook his head. "I suggested Abernethy, an afternoon's ride north of here. Kenneth Macduff is lord there. Margaret, I will do this," he said fiercely, taking her arm as she began to speak. "I will not let Scotland fall into ruin and tyranny. I will not have Normans here as in England—and so I must meet with him."

"Will you sign a truce? What other reason to meet, but war or peace."

"I will pay him homage."

Margaret felt her temper flare. "But you are not his vassal!"

"He and his troops will not leave Scotland otherwise. No King of Scots has ever been a subject of England, and I will continue that, I swear it."

"How, if you will kneel as his subject?"

"It will be an homage for my properties in Northumbria, not for Scotland," he said. "This I will insist upon. Other than that, I will grant his requests within reason, and promise to leave the borders be. Once he is gone and we see the back of him," he said, "I will do as I please. I am no vassal, nor a fool. I will protect Scotland and gain land and coin by this, or be damned for it."

"What more does he ask?" She feared for the safety of her sons.

He looked away. "We will soon know. This is the best we can do. This, or war."

"Then you must go," she said quietly. "When do you meet?"

"In two days," he said. "You must be there with me, you and the rest. It is one of his requests. He comes by ship, so we must leave immediately, to be there before him."

"As his hosts?" She laughed, though it was hollow.

"Order the packing done again," he said. "I cannot say when we might return here."

❧

"SUCH A CURIOUS STRUCTURE," Edgar remarked, standing beside Eva as he gazed up the length of the seventy-five-foot bell tower in the market square of Abernethy. The bronze bell at the top had just sounded out, resonant in the morning fog.

"Why is it called the Irish tower?"

"It follows an old Irish style. I remember climbing the steps inside with my mother when I was small." Now Eva and Edgar waited, together with the rest of Malcolm's party, for King William to arrive.

"Why here, for the meeting, I wonder?" Edgar mused aloud. "Your uncle holds this place, and he is a powerful leader—quite pleased to be host to this, too," he added of Kenneth Macduff, who stood now with Malcolm and the rest of the Scottish party.

"That bell tower has a meaning that Malcolm and the Scots recognize," Eva said, "but William will not—the ancient pride of Scotland, with its Irish and Celtic roots, resides here in Abernethy. A meeting of kings here says that our future will never be Norman."

Edgar smiled. "Excellent," he murmured.

When the Norman party arrived, all grand horses and men in fine gear and armor, Edgar moved toward his sister and Malcolm, and Eva stood near them with Lady Juliana. The foreign king, once he dismounted, was shorter than Malcolm, yet powerful, broad-chested, bowlegged, swarthy. He spoke English with an abominable accent, but Malcolm managed French well, so they spoke directly, while Malcolm translated the Gaelic of the priests who stood with him. William seemed impatient throughout the greetings and blessings, and Eva heard him remind Malcolm in rough English, then smooth French, that they could delay no longer.

Without more ceremony, Malcolm soon knelt before William and bowed his head. Though never Malcolm's supporter, Eva felt a twinge of sympathy for him, seeing that great-headed man, powerful and dynamic, subjugated. She felt helpless, frustrated for him.

In a rumbling voice, Malcolm repeated and promised what William asked, while a cleric produced parchment documents to be signed and sealed. Then the avowing followed, when the terms were formally announced. As William spoke, Malcolm replied in French, but did not translate for the Scots this time.

Eva leaned toward Lady Juliana, who had excellent French. "What are they saying?"

The young woman paused, listened. "William grants Malcolm twelve manors in England," she replied, "while Malcolm promises to respect the borders between England and Scotland."

Eva knew he would not, though he took the oath regardless.

"William will pay Malcolm a yearly fee of fifty gold marks,"

Juliana said, "which is just cheap of him. Ah, but Malcolm must guarantee that all Scots will give up their ancient, wicked practice of eating human flesh."

"Their what?" Eva said, so loudly that others glanced at her.

"It is a widespread rumor of the savage Scots," Juliana whispered. "Hush," she said then, for with William's next words, Malcolm looked up sharply, displeased.

Juliana leaned toward her. "Malcolm must give up his firstborn son for a royal hostage."

Eva looked over at Margaret and saw her blanch and grip Edgar's arm. Surely Margaret had known this was possible, for Eva herself was a hostage—Edgar had been one as well. Now Edgar reached out to guide young Duncan forward, but Margaret was the one who stepped into the cleared circle to present him to King William and Malcolm.

Just then, Margaret turned and beckoned for all her sons to come with her. Eva caught her breath, seeing Margaret take little Edgar from his nurse to carry him, silk swaddling trailing, while Lady Agatha and Princess Cristina came forward with chubby Edmund and Edward, the older boy's blond hair shining like sunlight. Together with young Donald they all moved forward. Murmurs ran through the crowd as Margaret and her beautiful family approached.

Eva felt a sob constrict in her chest. When Edgar came toward her and took her arm, she stood in silence beside him to watch.

The queen faced William and spoke in fluent, elegant French. Though Eva did not understand that exchange, she saw that William was touched by it. He looked at the children and reached out to shake little Edward's hand solemnly, and he spoke to Duncan in French, as the boy squared his shoulders. Malcolm then placed a hand on his eldest son's shoulder.

Edgar leaned to whisper a translation to Eva. "Margaret says she values kin above all but God, and she trusts that William does, too. She would sacrifice her own soul before she would let any harm come to her sons. She appeals to him as a father—William has two sons," he murmured, "and she asks for his promise to protect Duncan with his life."

"Out of honor, he cannot refuse a woman and a queen," Juliana said.

"William says," Edgar went on, "that he has rarely met a woman of such beauty and character, and for her sake, he will be merciful—and alter his final request."

"Final request?" Eva asked, grabbing his arm, feeling his tension. He was silent.

Then William turned and beckoned Edgar. "The Saxon prince," William called out.

Eva sucked in a breath as Edgar walked forward and stood before William, looking proud, handsome, ready to accept his fate.

"William will take Duncan for his father's good behavior," Juliana went on, translating as William resumed in French. "But now he says that Edgar the Outlaw should be tried for treason and executed. But out of respect for Queen Margaret, he asks only"—she paused, while Edgar stood still as a statue and Eva held her breath—"that he be banished from all of Britain for life. He must sail now, today, so William knows he is gone."

"Oh, no," Eva whispered, stunned. "No!"

Inclining her head serenely, Margaret turned, her gown swirling as she handed the infant in her arms to her sister. Stepping past, Margaret faltered for a moment, and Malcolm moved toward her. She shook off his hand and walked toward the little church by the bell tower.

Eva turned to follow as the ceremony ended—she did not stay for the rest, concerned for Margaret, though her thoughts were also with Edgar. And within moments he was striding beside her. In the shadow of the church entrance, Edgar took her arm and pulled her toward him.

"Eva," he said, "listen to me. I will return."

"But it is banishment for life." She pressed her hands against his chest.

"I will return and find you. Will you wait?" He leaned his head down, pressed his brow to hers.

"I hope you will come back for your family's sake. But you will not remember me for very long," she said. "Besides, I will go north soon, I hope. I cannot stay forever in the king's court."

"Will you not wait for me?" His face was close, breath warm, surrounding shadows deep.

"Whether or not I do, Edgar, I do not belong here." Suddenly, keenly, she felt how very true that was. And just as quickly, she realized that she did not belong with him, either, despite the lovely hope she had fostered for a while. Being in his arms somehow dissolved her illusions—he was a friend and no more. She felt affection for him, felt sadness and loyalty, but no deeper than that, much as she might want it. "I am not a boon to you."

"You are. Think of me each day, as I will of you," he murmured, and stroked her black hair, grabbed a fistful of thick braid to guide her head closer to his own. He kissed her then, so quick and tender that Eva nearly sobbed out for the sharp yearning, unmet. What she wanted was there in the kiss, and yet not. She wanted passion, strength, freedom—perhaps he did, too. But she did not feel it there between them now—only desperation, masked as need.

"I will think of you and pray for your well-being each day. Farewell, my friend," she said, hand lingering on his arm.

He seemed to understand, taking her hand to kiss it. "See to my sister," he said. "She loves you, trusts you." Then he stepped out into the sunlight and turned to meet William's knights, who waited for him.

❊

DEEPLY WEARY, HAVING WEPT and prayed through the night, Margaret watched as Edgar's things were brought aboard a sleek Danish-built vessel. Her brother was bound for Flanders with notes of introduction from William and Malcolm to the Count of Hainault, and Margaret could only pray that he would be welcomed. Given the strength of trade exchanges—Flemish cloth relied on Scottish wool and flax—surely diplomatic courtesy would follow.

In the space of an afternoon, her world had gone askew. Her stepson would be a hostage in England; her brother, sister, and mother would leave, too. William's desire to remove the Saxon royal family from Scotland would succeed—and only by virtue of her marriage, and William's greater respect for her earned that day, would Margaret remain. Since Lady Agatha was of no importance to him, William made no request regarding her, though he banished Edgar and demanded that Cristina, being a princess of marriageable age, go to Wilton Abbey in England.

Cristina now walked along the shore, looking both furious and helpless. William had granted English properties to Cristina and Edgar to supply their income, but they were not permitted to inhabit those places. Once the demands were set, Lady Agatha, sad and angry, had decided to go with Cristina and return to the abbey where she had once been banished herself.

The women's few things, brought from Dunfermline, were now loaded on the ship, which was leaving soon. Cristina turned to Margaret, eyes red with weeping. "Send the rest of our possessions, if you will," she said. "Our garments and books, our precious crosses and such."

Most material goods at Wilton would go into storage, Margaret knew, but she nodded. In a daze, feeling caught in a dreadful dream, she embraced Cristina. "You will do well there," she said, trying to smile. "I vow you will be abbess one day, for you are not shy! And if I have a daughter someday, I will send her to Wilton for her education."

"See that you do," Cristina said, and turned away to hide a sob. Lady Agatha, having given each of her little grandsons a kiss, now came toward her daughters. She embraced Margaret in a quick, stiff manner and stood back, head high, chin trembling.

"You are a fine queen, Margaret, a devout woman, a good mother," she said. "Do not forget us, I beg you." Tears pooled as she walked down the beach toward the water's edge.

Though a deep ache within threatened to bring her to her knees, Margaret had learned from her mother to persevere, to endure. She stood still, utterly controlled.

As her kinswomen were carried through the shallows to the ship, Margaret turned to press coins in small purses into the hands of Kata and Hildy, who had chosen to go as well. Hugging them, she could hardly see for tears when they, too, boarded the longship. Not knowing if she would ever see any of them again, she dared not think about it. Hurt ran too deep that day.

She saw Edgar standing on the pebbled shore with Eva, taking her hands in his, speaking to her, their heads close together. When Eva nodded and stepped away to hurry past Margaret, the girl's silverblue eyes were impossibly sad.

Edgar walked toward Margaret. "I told Malcolm to gather his gold and his men, for I will be back. We can still ride into England to help the Saxons. I will not give up, Margaret." He wrapped his arms around her, and she returned the embrace. Then he moved away to wade out to the Saxon-built ship afloat in the lapping surf.

As the oarsmen drew the longboat into deeper waters, Margaret fought such grief that she could scarcely breathe, as if the pain in her chest were physical. But then she turned to see Malcolm standing beside Tor, a little distance away.

They had let her say her farewells alone, and she blessed them for it, and realized for an instant how much she loved both men, how deeply—and how differently. Smiling through tears, she went toward them.

Chapter Twenty-one

❧

Wounds inflicted by a friend are better than a flattering enemy's kisses.

—Bishop Turgot, *Life of Saint Margaret,* twelfth century, quoting Queen Margaret

I t is nearly gloaming, Lady." Eva looked over at Margaret from her perch on horseback. "Will you read your book in this light?"

"I memorized every page long ago." Margaret smiled, though she looked weary as she rode in the van with the group traveling from Abernethy back to Loch Leven, where they would stay before moving on. "But I will put it away for now." After buckling the book's cover shut, she wrapped it in supple leather to protect the silver casing from scratches. "If you please, put this in your saddlebag. It is heavy to hold, and we are crowded in the wagon." Although Lady Agatha and Lady Cristina and the others were no longer with them, the van was full enough with the children, maidservants, and the other women.

As Eva took the book, which was heavy indeed, another horse neared hers, and she turned to see Brother Tor on a gray palfrey. "I will take that, Lady Eva. I have room for it in my satchel." He indicated a leather bag strapped to the front of his saddle.

Eva had a sudden thought. "Do you have the king's book with you?" Given all that had happened recently, she had nearly forgotten the offending pages.

"Aye, as unbound leaves—rolled tightly, and safe enough. Would you look at a page or two now to give me your opinion? We are riding slowly enough for that." His tone was wry.

"Certainly," she replied calmly, her heart thumping. Though the light was fading, she would not refuse this chance. Tor took the silver-covered book from her hands and slipped it inside the leather bag, then removed a cylindrical shape, wrapped in leather and tied with thongs. He opened it to remove some sheets. "Please look at these pages quickly."

Here, handed to her without ceremony, were the very pages her grandmother wanted. Eva slowed and stopped her horse, and Tor did the same, mounted beside her.

Transfixed, Eva uncurled the pages, which were of good size, though they would be folded and sewn into quartos when the volume was bound, so that the final pages would be much smaller than what she held. Tor's script in black ink was neat and small. She saw lists of names and dated item entries, as in some annals she had seen. She recognized the names Duncan, Malcolm, Macbeth, Lulach— even Gruadh.

Eva stared. Ahead, the escort reached the banks of a flowing burn, so that the vans and carts must be guided carefully across first, while the horses—Eva's and Tor's included—came last. She paid little attention as they went ahead. Silent, intent, she studied the pages in her hands.

On Lammas Day in 1040, she read, *King Duncan was unjustly slain by the hand of the usurper Macbeth . . .*

Eva glanced up at Tor, caught her breath, then read on. *Pressed by his wife, Gruadh, daughter of Bodhe, to do harm to others to gain the throne for himself, Macbeth was a poor king. Righteously Malcolm pursued him, and when his uncle Siward was killed cruelly by Macbeth, the kingdom was divided north and south. Malcolm killed Macbeth in the year 1057 on the anniversary of his father's murder.*

Included was an annotated list of battles that her Moray kin had mentioned. She saw her own father's name, too: *The luckless King Lulach ruled for seven months until Malcolm had him slain in March of the year 1058.*

Eva breathed heavily, resisting the urge to weep or to nurse her growing anger over such unjust comment. She rolled the parchment pages again and looked at Tor. "Some of this is correct," she said in a tight voice. "Some of it is very wrong."

"I thought you might say so," he replied.

"Will you have your name on what is a wrong accounting?"

"King Malcolm dictated what he wanted in his history. He was adamant about part of it." He held out his hand for the parchment.

Hesitating, Eva did not want to give it back. Here in her hands were the pages her grandmother wanted stolen and destroyed. But even then, the monk could write another one. "Should false history be preserved and taught to future generations?"

"Lady Eva, no event can be preserved as it was. Every recounting depends on a memory, and changes with every telling. Every bard and storyteller alters the old tales and songs over time. So it is with history."

"Bards are trained for their memories. Mine is good and fair. Malcolm's is not."

"This is not an annal based on reports, but an accounting by a king. It is an important work."

"Aye, that does ill to good people. My kin."

"I was not there," he said. "Were you? Though I understand your desire to protect your kin."

"He has long held a grudge against my own. I could ruin this page," she said suddenly, holding it. "It would be done."

"I could write it again," he said. "My obligation is to my patron."

"Truth and history are better patrons!"

Tor held out his hand in silence, beckoned. Sighing, Eva handed the pages to him at last. He slipped the roll back into his satchel. She felt furious with him, with Malcolm—with herself, for not destroying the parchment then and there, regardless of the consequences.

"Your lady grandmother," Tor said then, "could commission a history, too, as she likes."

"Which would survive? Hers, or one belonging to a King of Scots?"

The line of horses was moving now, and Eva urged hers ahead toward the water, glad to get away from Tor, from all of them. Tears dripped down her cheeks now, and she dashed them away. All of her waiting, her patient effort, wasted in but a few moments, for she could do nothing about the pages, giving them back like a coward. By the time the party returned to Loch Leven, her grandmother might already be there, and Eva could not bear to tell her the truth.

Her horse crossed steadily, and just as he reached the bank, Eva heard shouting and a heavy splash behind her. She whirled to see Tor's horse stumble in the water, sink down to its knees. The monk, a trained warrior, eased his horse upright again, speaking calmly, his hand firm on the reins. Yet the fall had twisted the leather satchel, which slid into the water, opening, its contents spilling out. The queen's silver book, the monk's roll, floated then sank out of sight.

Crying out, surging her horse onto the bank, Eva leaped down and turned to wade into the water, lunging for the satchel and its contents. She wanted to save Margaret's silver book—and she would not miss the chance to snatch Tor's pages as well if she could retrieve them. Wet to her skin, sinking to her knees on rocks in the cold, rushing water, she groped about, gasping, reaching, missing. Tor had jumped down into the water, too, as did two housecarls, all of them grabbing for the pages that floated, separated, spun in the current. They splashed about, too, looking for the book, which seemed to vanish in the sparkling moving water.

Then Eva saw a silvery flash like a trout under the water and she lunged, her hand finding the book's hard metal casing. She brought it up, water sluicing from the cover, and handed it to Tor, who took it and mopped at it with his black woolen sleeve.

Seeing one of the loose pages float by, Eva grabbed at that, then saw two and three more. Like the men near her, she, too, reached for the pages, shaking water from them as she caught them like fish, as a dozen and more parchments swirled and flowed over rock and through fast-moving currents. Tor waded downstream, snatching at pages, too, black robes floating around his legs.

Just as she turned to go toward the bank, Eva saw two more pages skim past, and she picked these up—and recognized the very pages she had been holding only minutes ago, the two she had separated from the roll. Quickly folding these, she crammed them into the deep pocket of her wet tunic gown with the letter for her grandmother, still there. Picking up her soaked skirts, she waded toward the bank.

One of the men reached out a hand to pull her up, wrapping a dry cloak around her shoulders. She turned to look for her horse, but the man guided her toward the queen's van, where he helped her inside. She was shivering as Juliana and Wynne shifted to make room for her, and Margaret reached over to drape a blanket over her lap. Tor stood by the wagon and handed Margaret her silver-cased book.

"I am sorry. I fear it is ruined," he said.

Margaret accepted the book, gently drying it with part of her cloak. The leather cover was partly around it, and she peeled that away to undo the latches as water slid from the silver cover. Carefully she turned the pages.

Eva leaned closer, astonished, for water had only beaded on the parchment sheets. The scraped and polished skins had survived the soaking, the pages only a little damp. Fanning the book open, Margaret dabbed at the wet areas. "It is not much harmed," she said. "I thought it would be ruined!"

"That's quite miraculous," Juliana said, looking over the queen's shoulder.

Tor examined it when Margaret handed it to him. "The silver casing saved it, I think, along with the fine quality of the vellum," he said pragmatically. "The leather wrapping and silk sheets between the pages also helped to protect it against the water."

"Miracle or not, Eva saved it." Margaret set an arm around her shoulders. "I am in your debt," she went on, pressing her cheek against Eva's.

Aware that two wet pages were stolen and secret in her pocket, Eva said nothing.

"HAVE YOU HAD word from Lady Gruadh?" Eva whispered when she saw Abbot Drostan at Saint Serf's that evening. They stood in a corner of the refectory as the others ate at a table in the monks' dining hall.

"She is nearby," he said. "She will not come to the island with the king and queen here, but she wishes to see you. I sent a message to her—she knows you have news for her."

"I do," Eva whispered, thinking of the pages folded in her pocket. Returning to Loch Leven that evening, she had found a few moments in the guesthouse to dry the parchment sheets more thoroughly. The ink was smeared but legible, and the contents clear. Holding those pages might ease Lady Gruadh's heart some, Eva thought. That much she could do toward fulfilling her promise to her grandmother.

Then she meant to go to Margaret and tell her that she could not stay, even if she had to escape, like the prisoners who had slipped away from Dun Edin with Margaret's help. More and more, she felt compelled, even desperate, to return to Moray and the life that suited her best, though her heart near broke to think of deserting or disappointing either of her two queens now. Years had passed, and Lady Gruadh had been unable to win her back from Malcolm's custody—and with Edgar departing Britain, she felt one more tie to Malcolm's court slipping free. The need for home burned in her heart, and yet her loyalty to Margaret had grown as strong as her love for her own kin in the north.

"We had word that the Moray party was headed this way just as you left to go with the royal party to Abernethy," Drostan said. "Lady Gruadh is staying nearby, and waits for you."

"When can I see her?" Eva glanced over her shoulder, hoping others would assume that she was listening to her spiritual advisor and leave her be.

"You will find her by the falls just west of here," he replied quietly. "There is a forest among the hills three miles to the west. A waterfall there can be seen from a distance. The property came to Lady Gruadh with her first marriage dowry, and she granted it to Loch Leven when she was Macbeth's queen. We give her use of it whenever she likes. Her message to me said that she would wait by the falls for three mornings, hoping to see you before she returns to Moray."

Eva smoothed a hand over the cloak that Margaret had given her in place of her still damp plaid. Securely hidden in the lining pocket were the two pages that had floated free in the water. Brother Tor had asked her if she had seen the same pages she had been reading after the spill into the water that day. She had made no commitment, and he had concluded that the parchments were swept away and destroyed. "I will write them again," he had told Eva.

"If you do remake them," she had replied, "please consider first what is true and what is false. What would you want future generations to say of Thorgaut's history?"

Thoughtful, frowning, he had not replied, and had resumed his monkish sober expression. Little could ever be read, she knew, in those elongated, handsome features.

FOLLOWING PRAYERS the next morning, Eva announced that she would ride out to see her kinfolk in Fife. "I was born near here," she reminded Margaret, "and I have kin nearby." She hoped Margaret would assume she referred to her uncle.

"I will ride with you today," Margaret replied, to Eva's sudden dismay. "It is a pretty morning for a ride, and the abbot mentioned that a little cave in the area was once the cell of an early Scottish saint. It is only a few miles from the shore. I suppose it is worth taking the ferry over the water," she said with a little grimace, "to visit such a holy place."

She could neither refuse nor leave without the queen, Eva thought, so she waited while Margaret changed to sturdy shoes for the ride into the hills. They left with an escort of several housecarls—even worse, Eva thought, for her secret plans—and Margaret mentioned that she had told the king of their day's journey. Now Eva fully dreaded the day.

A capable horsewoman, Margaret nonetheless set a leisurely pace, pausing to take in the stunning views as they headed west toward the hills. Eva was in an agony of impatience. Somehow she would have to slip away to meet Lady Gruadh to quickly hand over the parchments, without time even for a true reunion.

When they found the saint's cell at last, it was a small turf-covered cave in the side of a hill, unimpressive but for its history. Sitting her horse while Margaret ventured inside, Eva felt a knot of anxiousness in her gut—the morning was dwindling, and her grandmother might not wait.

Impulsively, she took up her horse's reins and turned to a housecarl who sat nearest. Her horse sidestepped, picking up her nervous state. "I have kin who live near here," she said. "I want to visit them for a little, while the queen is still at her devotions. You know she could be another hour at her prayers," she added, hoping the guard would agree. "I will be back soon."

"One of us should go with you," he said, looking doubtful.

Eva hesitated. As a royal hostage she needed permission from the king or the queen to go off on her own. The risk she took was great, for secretly meeting her Moray kin could be treason. "I will be fine," she told the guard. "Meet me in an hour or so, a few miles north of here. There is a waterfall in a grove between two hills. I will meet you there."

"I know the place," the man called as she turned her horse and left.

"REBELLION WILL COME—we do not know when," Lady Gruadh said. Eva listened as they walked among the trees, arms about each other—though her grandmother was not often affection-ate, she had a warmth and a strength that Eva craved to absorb in this brief reunion. The sound of the nearby falls and the rush of the summer winds softened their words as they spoke. "My men lately rode about to tally the men in Moray and other provinces who would be willing to march southward, if needed. The numbers reach into the thousands."

"Men discontent with Malcolm Canmore?" Eva asked. "But it is true that he has changed some of his ways for the better, with Margaret's influence."

"Let her remake him all she likes," Gruadh said. "He has displeased many in the north by paying homage to William at Abernethy for the price of a few English farms. At least he has booted out the queen's brother. That is a hapless one whose cause has come to naught."

"Edgar put his heart into leading the revolts," Eva insisted. "He is earnest, a good man. He reminds me a little of my father."

Gruadh paused. "Then he is a caring young man? A good king, if given the chance?"

"He is. And he has been unfairly treated by fate, and by William."

"Ah. Do you have feelings for him, and he for you?" Gruadh looked at her sharply.

Eva sighed. "I thought I did . . . but we are not suited. I do care for him, and I wish . . ."

"Marriage to a Moray princess would not further his cause," Gruadh said gently.

"I know," Eva said. "He has gone over the sea," she added low. "I will not see him again. That is done." She breathed against the regret.

Gruadh hugged her close for a moment and kissed her head.

"As for Malcolm," Eva said, "at least he took the oath in the shadow of the Irish tower."

"Just so. But he has had little luck in military matters, for all his storming about. Better he harasses the borderlands and leaves the rest of Scotland to those who are more interested in building its wealth, protecting its traditions."

"So you still think Nechtan should rule Scotland someday."

"Some of us think it the best solution, but the lad remains unconvinced. He is young yet, and will come round. Tell me more about the queen—so she prays at all hours, and deprives herself with fasting? I cannot understand it. Her little ones are healthy, her husband treats her well—why does she torment herself?"

"She tries her utmost in all things," Eva said. "She cares so much. Too much. And she has come to love Scotland."

"Despite her Saxon ways, she is a better queen than I expected of her. So Malcolm will build her a new church in Dunfermline in honor of the sons she has borne? Good. I always thought that little chapel needed replacing," she said. "The roof leaked."

They paused beside the falls, the water rushing downward, fine spray misting their hair, their faces. The morning, toward noon, grew warm. Eva leaned against her grandmother. "I have missed you," she said.

"And we miss your brightness in our household." Gruadh pushed damp tendrils of hair from Eva's brow. "I will write to Malcolm once again and tell him it is time to set you free. He has refused every request I have made in your absence—I doubt you were even told, and I did not want to trouble you. And as far as he knows I have behaved myself quite well."

"I doubt he believes that. Oh! I brought something for you." Eva reached into her pocket and drew out the tightly rolled, now dry parchment sheets. "These tell of Macbeth and Lulach—"

"Let me see!" Gruadh reached for the sheets, hands trembling as she untied the ribbon that held them curled.

❀

"GONE? SHE MIGHT have waited," Margaret said. Emerging from the cool interior of the ancient saint's cave, she felt expansive and peaceful. But she was puzzled to learn that Eva had ridden off on her own. "I would have gone with her to see her kin. I thought it was our plan."

"She went toward a waterfall not far from here, a very pretty place indeed. We can find her there. This way," the guard said, as Margaret turned her horse to follow him, the other housecarls falling into line behind her.

They followed a path that led west toward a grouping of round-shouldered hills. Soon the track met the bank of a wide, calm river, the way winding over a moorland and curving around the base of one hill after another. The path grew thick with trees clustered along the river's edge, and water churned over rocks and boulders as the sloping ground climbed. Awed by the rugged landscape, Margaret paced her horse slowly and looked around, fascinated. She had rarely seen this face of Scotland—secretive, dynamic, powerful.

Ahead, she heard the rush and fury of a waterfall and craned her head to search for it through the trees. So far she had seen only a few homes tucked here and there against the steep hillsides. Roe and white-tailed deer flitted past, sheep grazed placidly, and in places wild goats clung to sheer, steep rock. Pine trees arrowed upward out of the hillsides, and everywhere the air was cool, brisk, and damp.

One of the guards led the party toward an overhang above the river, where the land sloped sharply downward and water poured over some high boulders in a narrow pass. Dismounting, he reached up to assist Margaret, who was eager to get down to see the falls.

"Come this way. We may see some salmon here," he said, guiding her toward the overhang. "Careful, Lady," he warned.

Reaching a cluster of boulders, Margaret leaned against a sizable rock to peer down at the turbulent, foaming white falls beneath. After a while, she saw the flash of a salmon as it surged upward, then another and one more, so quickly that she was not sure, at first, what she had seen.

"Beautiful—oh!" she said, straightening. Below, amid the cover of trees, figures moved about. She glimpsed Eva's glossy dark braids, her pale skin, and finely shaped profile. "Look! Lady Eva and some-one else—likely her relative. Let us meet them down there." Picking up her skirts, she went carefully down the rocky slope, while the guard, now and then, reached out to assist her.

Coming closer, she saw that Eva's companion was a tall woman in a dark cloak. Behind them were a few plaid-draped Highland war-riors, clearly an escort keeping their distance. The woman, whose head was draped in a white veil, moved gracefully as she walked with Eva among the trees. They spoke intently, and paused while the older woman gestured.

Though Margaret called out, Eva did not seem to hear her over the noise of the falls. A moment later she saw Eva hand over to the other woman what looked like a sheaf of parchments. They opened the pages, heads together. Suddenly wary, Margaret slowed, still unseen.

Close enough now to hear them speak in Gaelic, Margaret saw the taller woman roll the pages up and shove them into a deep pocket in her cloak. Just then, Eva turned to see Margaret standing higher along the slope, and she blanched, grew still. Her companion looked up as well, and tilted her head curiously. She spoke to Eva, who nodded.

This was Macbeth's queen. Margaret realized it, heart and soul.

Slim and elegant despite being two generations older than Eva, Gruadh had an uncommon beauty—timeless, balanced, exquisite. She showed willfulness, too, and daring in the way she stared at Margaret. She resembled Eva in her long-lidded silver-blue eyes, so vibrant that they seemed mystical, capable of seeing into one's soul.

Pausing, her confidence wavering under that sure stare, Marga-ret drew a deep breath and walked toward them, motioning for her guard to stay back. The Highland guards who stood upon the hill also stayed still, though alert and watching.

"Lady," Margaret said in English. "Queen Gruadh."

The older woman nodded once. "Queen Margaret." Her English was softly accented.

"I am glad to have found you together," Margaret said. "I hoped to meet you one day, Lady Gruadh. I have heard much praise of you."

"And much that is not praiseworthy, I imagine," Gruadh replied. "May I offer my congratulations on your three fine sons, and my compliments on your efforts as queen. You have proven yourself . . . worthy of the throne." Her beautiful face was taut, proud.

"My thanks," Margaret said, sensing sincerity and grace of character in the remarks. "Sometimes I wish, Lady Gruadh, that I had your wisdom and experience as queen. I wonder what you might have done in some of the situations I have faced."

"I would not have set those prisoners free," Gruadh said bluntly. "I would have wanted the ransom income. But I do not fault you for your kind heart."

So Eva must have told her grandmother about that night, and Margaret wondered when. "I have heard, Lady Gruadh," she went on, "that you have worn armor to lead armies against your husband's enemies. That is admirable and remarkable."

"The enemy was your own husband, Lady," Gruadh replied. "I was trained to the warrior life as a girl, and so I did what had to be done."

"You fought for the welfare of your people, just as I fight for the welfare of their souls."

"Then we are alike in some things," Gruadh said. "I am the last of all the Celtic queens who fought beside their kings. You . . . are the first of the new queens in Scotland. Queens of the heart and the book, queens who can be strong in their own way. The wider world comes to Scotland," she said then, "through you."

A chill went through her, as if a prophetess had spoken. "Why do you say so?" Margaret asked.

Gruadh stared at her for a moment. "Your sons and their sons will rule Scotland for generations to come. I feel it is so. The claim of my

kin, pure as it is, is only another branch now. Fate is proving a powerful opponent."

Margaret felt a surge of sympathy. "Lady, I never intended—"

"I know that now," Gruadh said. Then she looked past Margaret and turned quickly. "Eva, help the queen—hurry! It is not
safe here!" She pushed Eva toward Margaret, just as an arrow thun-
ked into the ground near where Gruadh's Highland men had been
standing—they had all vanished into the cover of the trees, along
with their lady.

Eva pulled Margaret behind a tree as more arrows suddenly spit
downward, slamming into earth, into tree trunks. Margaret saw
movement between the trees and rocks as the hidden Highlanders
now returned a volley of arrows that sailed well past Margaret and
Eva, where they hunkered down together. Some of Margaret's guards
now ran toward them, and even more arrows shattered into the lush
leafy canopy of the woodland, arching overhead from opposite direc-
tions now.

Hearing shouts, Margaret turned her head and saw Malcolm striding through the bracken like a great boar, roaring, red-faced. His men
loosed a flurry of arrows and a spear went sailing past, too, launched
from Malcolm's own hand to split the earth where one of Gruadh's
men appeared for just a moment. One of the guards pushed Margaret to the ground, shielding her behind him as as arrows soared all
around.

The arrow volleys seemed to last an interminable time—Margaret
hated the sounds, the shouts, the shrieks as some were injured. She
pushed the guard away and saw Eva stand. Calling for her to get
down, Margaret reached out. But Eva ran ahead and bent down to
pick up a piece of parchment, which Margaret had seen fall when
Lady Gruadh had pushed her granddaughter and the queen toward
safety.

"Ha! So they have run off now, the cowards!" Malcolm shouted
as his men rushed past Margaret and Eva to pursue the Highlanders

into the trees. "You, Eva! Come here! It was you who led the queen into this ambush, and betrayed us to the rebels of Moray! You aided them!"

"Husband, she tried to save me——" Margaret began.

"Are you sure? She would not have expected us to ambush them here—this was a trap to harm you," Malcolm said. "When I knew you had come this way, I remembered that Gruadh owns lands in this area. I feared she might try some rebellion, and so it was. Eva—you and your grandmother meant for the queen to die this day! This is treason and worse."

"I never intended harm to the queen," Eva said firmly.

Margaret came closer, her heart still pounding hard. She had never experienced anything like the chaotic fear of the last few moments. Always protected, never witnessing a skirmish or ambush, she had not known how fear and panic could overtake thought. She brushed her skirt clean and clasped her shaking hands.

"Sire, surely Eva speaks the truth——" she began.

"Aye? What is this, then?" Malcolm snatched the parchment from Eva's hand and looked at them. "Here is certain treason! She has stolen pages from the book I commissioned of Brother Tor. These pages are the account of my war with Macbeth. Why do you have these?"

"I meant to destroy them," Eva said. "That history is wrong, deceitfully and cruelly so."

"This is part of her grandmother's plot!" Malcolm grabbed Eva's arm with such fury that Margaret winced just watching. "Hostage you are," he told Eva, "and hostage you shall remain. You will be tried for treason and witchcraft, for consorting with the witch of the north and endangering the queen's life. Take her!"

Guards came forward then and took Eva between them, walking her up the slope toward the waiting horses. She went quietly. Malcolm turned toward Margaret.

"Woman," he said, "your friend has betrayed you."

His words struck her to the heart. Stunned, Margaret allowed him to escort her up the slope. She had never imagined such betrayal could exist in her own household from a friend she had come to love. Her prayers and meditations, not even heaven itself, had warned her of this.

"Malcolm, that cannot be?"

"Trust my judgment in this," he replied. "I know too well what a viper Lady Gruadh can be—and now we see her granddaughter is the same. I should have known," he went on. "I should have suspected when Eva sang of her father. I only blame myself. You might have been lost to me this day." He took her hand.

Chapter Twenty-two

⚜

Bring to me the harp of my king
That on it I may shed my grief

—IRISH, THIRTEENTH CENTURY

Having betrayed her two queens, one to the other, herself to each, she was a hostage in earnest now. Malcolm had ordered her brought to the sole dungeon at Dunfermline, a dingy place deep in the stone foundation of the tower, where no noble prisoner had been held but for those who lingered a day or two during the king's annual moot courts. She was reminded of the dungeon she had visited in Dun Edin with Margaret, where Malcolm and Tor had threatened to leave them—that had been teasing, then. This was grim and real, and she was alone.

Margaret came to see her once and went away angry and haughty, the gentle face of the friend gone. Eva mourned the relationship she had never expected to find or to value so much. Lady Gruadh had warned her that no one in Malcolm's court would wish her well. That was proving true now, with even Margaret turned against her.

The guards told her that her trial would be within the week, and had hinted that her execution might well follow. Another said the king alone would decide what was just. But Eva knew that they all believed she had committed treason by deliberately leading Margaret into danger. That she had not known, had not intended any of it, did not seem to matter.

The queen's ladies visited her briefly with little to say, though they left linens and food. Lady Juliana lingered, though she, too, looked at Eva with a questioning gaze. "I know your loyalty to your kin was stronger than your loyalty to the queen," Juliana said. "If my father, Cospatric, had needed my help, though it harmed another, I think I might have chosen him."

Eva had been grateful for her attempt to understand, but Juliana had left and had not returned. At night, Eva dreamed of Edgar, and then wished she had explored more of her heart with him—she did care about him, and thought him her friend. But if he heard of her plight, he, too, might no longer trust her.

Most surprising to her was Tor's visit one evening, when he sat with her and took her hands, spoke to her of redemption and priestly matters, and then questioned her closely on her reasons for taking the loose pages from his manuscript.

"The account is wrong," she said. "I tried to tell you before. My step-grandfather was a just and fair king, my grandmother a good queen."

"Tell me more," he said, and she did. He listened in silence as she recounted the tale of her grandparents' reign and the bitter conflicts between Malcolm and Macbeth, and later Malcolm and Gruadh. When she was done, Tor made little comment, only knelt with her and prayed, absolved her sins, and left.

Her trial came on a bitter cold autumn day, when she was brought across the bailey to the tower, the familiar hall that had felt like home to her once, yet no longer. She stood before Malcolm, faced him with as much bravery as she could muster, and heard the list of her crimes read aloud by De Lauder, another friend turned cold. He sat with Malcolm, Brother Tor, Ranald mac Niall, and others, all of them stone solemn, after the litany of her betrayals had been read.

She had intended no harm beyond taking the manuscript pages, and she had been unwise in some of it. Perhaps she should admit to foolishness, she thought, and to loyalties that ripped her in two. She wondered what a fair penalty would be for that.

"We will have done with this quickly," Malcolm said then. The hall was crowded, the silence dense with a noise of its own—a hum of anticipation, of curiosity, accusation. "I welcomed you here in my household, in agreement with your kinswoman. You once showed your defiance by singing praises of your father in my presence. Treason then, and I let it go. But now you have committed the worst sort of betrayal, that of the snake in the nest of those who have loved you."

"I have shared my music and befriended your queen, as you yourself asked of me," Eva said. She saw Margaret cross the dais, having entered the hall after the king had begun proceedings. Eva wondered if Margaret's hesitation to watch this came from sympathy or bitterness. Now she sat in a chair a little apart from the king, observing rather than judging. She wore pale blue and cream, her long braids golden as the crown set upon her veil, her face pure. She looked angelic—but her eyes held anger and hurt. Eva knew that the queen might berate herself for being uncharitable and unforgiving, but she knew her temper, too. Loyalty was all to Margaret, and that trust had been broken.

Yet Eva, too, felt abandoned and hurt. Margaret had betrayed her by believing Eva capable of such heartlessness. Margaret followed rules, loved discipline and strict routine and the lessons of her faith. So perhaps it was not surprising that she had accepted what the king, as authority, had said of Eva.

So be it, Eva thought. She would endure on her own whatever came.

Malcolm conferred with the mormaers gathered near him, along with Brother Tor, Father Otto, and Brother Micheil. Margaret sat calmly and silently, waiting, as did Eva.

"Aeife inghean Lulach," Malcolm said when he turned back. "The decision to be made here is not of your guilt, as that wrong-doing is clear. The question is what to do now. Given the charges, your crimes might merit a burning."

Eva felt suddenly faint. Margaret, too, had hinted at that when she had visited Eva in the dungeon. Yet witches were not burned in Scotland as they might be in England, as Eva had pointed out to the queen.

"It is unworthy of you, King of Scots," Eva said, "to apply Saxon law in Scotland."

"We learn from Saxon law, and it behooves us to adopt some of that wisdom in our laws. You may have done more than treason. It is possible that magic may be involved."

"Magic!" She nearly laughed. "I have no knowledge of that."

"They do say of Eva the bard," Father Otto said, "that her harp music is magical in itself."

"And you believe that means witchcraft?" she asked, incredulous.

"You have been defiant and devious, exerting influence over the queen," Malcolm said. "In your company, she was involved in thievery and deceit. Now I believe it was you who stole gold from my treasury while the queen stood by. You released prisoners to deprive me of income, and let her be blamed. And you took the pages that Brother Tor created for my book."

Whatever they thought of her, she would not give up Margaret. "I never intended harm to the queen, nor would I commit treason or witchcraft. I think kindly of Queen Margaret."

"Few in Moray support the queen. It was a mistake to welcome you into our household."

Eva lifted her chin at that added blow; she cared that much for Margaret, the children, most of the others. And she felt Margaret's continued silence keenly. The queen could have spoken in her defense and did not. Hurting, Eva could not, just then, look at her.

Yet as she watched the others, she felt new understanding, even sympathy, blossom in her heart for them. She had done what her grandmother had asked out of love and loyalty, and she knew that, because of loyalty to his patron the king, Tor had written down what Malcolm wanted. And Margaret, too, must feel the hurt of a broken trust.

As for Malcolm, who had murdered her father—Eva understood with better clarity that he had done only what he thought was right. Canny, ambitious, he kept Scotland's welfare in mind as well as his own. Each of them had acted from loyalty and belief in rightfulness, and each saw the truth differently, like the many facets of a jewel.

Eva stood straighter, hands folded. She would not bow her head. She was royalty, her blood as pure or more so than the rest. "I have erred," she said, "but not against you or the queen."

Malcolm grunted at that admission as if surprised. He leaned to listen as some of his men conferred with him. While they spoke, Eva heard a commotion behind her as the doors to the great hall were opened. When others in the room turned to look, Eva did so as well.

Lady Gruadh entered the room, escorted by a few of her men, though they were held back at the door by Malcolm's housecarls. The lady proceeded on her own. Eva stared—she never expected her kinswoman to appear here; Gruadh took her life in her hands to face Malcolm.

Moving deep into the room, Gruadh paused beside Eva, her green gown and black cloak swinging gently. Eva could smell the fresh air of spring around her. The lady raised her head, draped in pale silk, her face strong and beautiful, eyes snapping like crackling blue ice.

"Malcolm," she said.

"Gruadh," he returned warily. "Come to defend your duckling?"

"She is capable on her own, but I will not abandon her to you. I came here to tell you that you are making a terrible mistake. Another," she added.

"She betrayed the queen and myself."

"How is it betrayal to meet with kinfolk after a long separation, or wrong to bring me pages with the names of my husband and son, which I had a right to see? Pages that never should have been written."

"Destroy them if you like," Malcolm said. He picked the parchments up from a table where they sat in evidence, crinkled them, tossed them at her feet. Gruadh did not move. "I will have them written again, and again. Ruin as many pages as you can find. You will never know how many copies exist. Whatever tales I choose to put forth about Macbeth, and about you, witch," he said, sitting forward, voice lowered, "will survive. You cannot stop that."

"Some of us know what happened. Truth is an obligation in a king."

He bristled. "I have my own truth."

Tor cleared his throat. "Sire," he said. "In these past several weeks, I have rewritten the ruined pages." He looked at Eva directly and nodded once, as if to convey an unspoken message. "I will make more than one copy as well for safekeeping."

Eva caught her breath. Had Brother Tor revised the pages to reflect the very truths Malcolm meant to avoid, the fair account of the lives of Macbeth and Lulach? If so, he would make sure that the truth survived, protected somewhere, no-matter what version Malcolm himself saw. Eva wanted to tell her grandmother her thoughts, but that was impossible with Malcolm glowering over them.

The king stood. "Good," he told Tor. "Now let us be done with this. Lady Eva—"

"You cannot burn her, so do not think to declare it," Gruadh said bluntly.

"If a law needs to be instituted, I can do that."

"You have no authority to execute her under any circumstances."

"I am king here! And you are not on my council, to advise me so."

"Nor would I want to be," she snapped. "As king, you ought to know that Scotland is bound in part by the ancient Irish laws set down by holy Adomnán, who recorded the Brehon laws for Ireland that are still used now, even in your own reign," Gruadh pointed out. "And that law states that no woman born of noble or royal rank can be executed, no matter her crime. She can only be reprimanded or banished. Thus goes the law that every King of Scots must follow."

Malcolm looked stormy. "So you remember those old laws, do you."

"Of course. I was queen here. And those old laws are still in force, if forgotten in your reign."

"Not forgotten," he said. "But not always needed these days. Very well. Then I will banish her out of Scotland entirely."

"Sire," Margaret said, standing then, breaking her silence. She glided across the dais. "Hear me, husband. This is wrong."

"How so?" He turned to look at her. Eva noticed, as always, that his tone gentled a little.

"Lady Eva never committed treason. Nor did she betray me, either, on the day we met the Moray party. I followed her there myself that day, and so I was not lured into danger. And you sent arrows out first, if you recall," she pointed out.

"To stop the Moray folk from harming you!"

"No one threatened her," Gruadh said. "Trust that."

"Can I ever trust you, lady?" Malcolm sounded resigned.

"You could have, years back, before you betrayed my husband and then my son. When you were a small boy in court and took my hand as I minded you, we liked each other well. I am a loyal friend to those in whom I have faith."

"What of my claims, Gruadh?" he asked. "What of my rights? I am always your enemy. Never a fair enough king interested in justice for his people and forced to defend what should belong to him and his. Never seeking the right thing, eh?"

"This is not your trial," Gruadh said, "nor mine. Our concern is this one." She placed a hand on Eva's shoulder, the grip strong, warm, a comfort. Eva stood beside her, silent.

"That concern we all share," Margaret said, stepping closer. "Regarding theft, sire, I told you at the time that any wrongdoing was mine in taking the gold and releasing the prisoners. Eva tried to stop me but I acted rashly."

"You would never—" the king began.

"I did. As for the manuscript pages, they fell into the river when my book went into the water, which some now call a miracle. What does it matter about a few pages? Other pieces of Brother Tor's book were lost that day, and he must remake those, too."

Malcolm frowned. "It is a setback and a delay. And more cost to me."

"But he can add the truth that belongs in that history. As Lady Gruadh said, truth is our obligation, is it not?"

Malcolm stared at her as if speechless. Margaret smiled and stepped down from the dais to walk toward Gruadh and Eva. Bending, she picked up the fallen pages and handed them to the older woman, who accepted them. Then Margaret stood between Eva and Gruadh.

"Much of this is my fault, too," she then said to Malcolm. "Will you accuse me as well?"

"There is no need for this," he replied sternly.

"I was wrong to mistrust my good friend Eva. And I believe that you yourself misunderstood, sire, and did what you thought was just. Lady Eva is innocent and Lady Gruadh is brave to come here for a reconciliation, considering her grievance with you."

Malcolm glowered. "Reconciliation!"

"What!" Lady Gruadh said sharply. Eva stared from one to the other, uncertain what might come of this.

Margaret linked arms with Eva and Gruadh. "A little peace between us all is needed. Surely you agree, sire."

Malcolm narrowed his eyes, displeased, Eva thought—yet he would not gainsay his queen before the court.

"Since Lady Gruadh is here, she and I will talk," he said. "In private."

"I want my guard with me if we are to speak," Gruadh said.

"Best I call my guard, too, if I am to be alone with you," he returned. "We will talk of Moray and peace in Scotland, with the Normans at our gates."

"Politics," she said. "Not forgiveness."

"As you wish," the king muttered. "Come to my chamber when you are done coddling your granddaughter. Bring as many guards as you like. Margaret," he said, turning toward the queen. "The girl-bard is yours to rescue, like your orphans and beggars. She will not be the first prisoner you have set free."

"Sire," Margaret said, "it would be a gesture of peace to release her from your custody as a royal hostage. And perhaps you and Lady Gruadh will agree to a truce."

Eva looked at her grandmother, who remained expressionless. Gruadh was too proud to cave easily to any arrangement with Malcolm, but she would not jeopardize the moment.

"I have said what I will say." Malcolm turned to stride heavily across the dais, beckoning to his men, many of whom followed. Some remained, including Tor.

Sighing out in relief, her knees near buckling beneath her, Eva leaned against Gruadh, her other arm still linked with the queen's. They formed a circle for a moment, heads bowed together.

Margaret laughed, a sound of joy and relief. Then she stepped back. "I must go ask Brother Tor to confess me, for I did not tell all the truth about those pages."

"Nor I—for I did take them," Eva admitted. "And I am sorry for the trouble it caused."

Gruadh turned to Margaret. "Lady, you saved Eva out of loyalty and kindness. I think there is much to admire about the foreign queen after all. We are surely in your debt."

Margaret shook her head, embracing them both, and Eva felt her heart leap when she saw the two queens leaning together, whispering. Then Margaret stepped away and looked toward Brother Tor, who nodded and followed her from the hall.

"She will be up all night in prayer," Eva said. "She will take herself to task for this."

"It is not her doing."

"She will think so nonetheless. Grandmother," she said, "perhaps I should stay here."

"In Malcolm's court, rather than come home? If Malcolm lets me go," she added.

"He will. He dare not hold you here and risk an uprising in the north. Margaret needs me for now—and I need to make peace with Malcolm myself before I go home."

Gruadh sighed. "Just so. Eva, girl—a greater, kinder heart than mine showed you that need. Bravery I taught you, and boldness. But Margaret understands giving and compassion. Forgiveness, too. Stay, then, if you wish," she added. "Will you wait for her brother to return?"

"Edgar will never come back. I feel it so. Not for me, at least."

Gruadh took her hand. "We cannot know some things until we see them unfold."

"I had best fetch my harp," Eva said as she walked with her grandmother from the hall. "I will play for Margaret later. The music soothes her spirit."

"She searches for peace, that one, yet never finds it, though it flows all around her to others. She cares so much, but must take care of herself as well. Tell her so, Eva," Gruadh said.

"I am thinking of a praise song," Eva mused, "just for the young queen, verses to tell of her good soul, with a sweet, quiet melody to suit her. And another song," she added, "to praise my own heritage. I am the daughter and granddaughter of kings, and granddaughter and friend to the Queens of Scots. What do you think?"

"I am thinking they do need you here in this court. There is an enchantment in your music to soothe them all—though you must not let them know it," she added.

"And if that fails, I will show them the pride and common sense of the north."

"Now, that is something we can safely boast! Though I will admit, your foreign queen has a certain magic of her own. She teaches others to be better than they were. Even me, a little."

"Best keep that to ourselves," Eva said, as Gruadh smiled. "Do you want me to go with you to face Malcolm?"

"He and I have much to say, but we must say it alone. I do not forgive easily, and I will make that clear. But I will tell him that I am grateful."

"For what?"

Gruadh did not reply, but tucked her arm in Eva's to draw her close as they walked.

AUTHOR'S NOTE

*There is perhaps no more beautiful character
recorded in history.*
—W. F. Skene, *Celtic Scotland,* 1895,
on Queen Margaret

A medieval fairy tale: a princess, the eldest child of an exiled prince
and an exotic noblewoman, raised in a pious royal court, sails with her
family to the land of her father's birth and the throne promised there.
The father dies within a week of arriving, possibly poisoned, and his
widow raises their children alone—two princesses and a small prince
who is to inherit the throne. When the aging king dies a decade later,
his enemies invade and the royal family must flee. Sailing over rag-
ing seas, they are shipwrecked along a northern coast belonging to a
barbarian people.

That king, known to be a brute warrior, offers the fugitives sanctuary; he soon falls in love with the eldest princess, requesting her hand
in marriage. Devout, educated, a beautiful young creature of a virtuous

and charitable character, the princess intends to become a nun. But for the good of all she is persuaded to marry the warrior-king.

Their marriage of near opposites produces eight healthy children—six boys and two girls—and the queen works tirelessly to bring charity, refined culture, and religious reform to her adopted nation, earning the love and trust of the people. The king and queen adore each other: she teaches him to read and turns his plain fortress into a palace; he translates for her when she lectures his foreign priests on theology; she feeds orphans with her own golden spoon and establishes a free ferry for pilgrims; she steals the king's gold to give it to the poor and releases his ransomed prisoners, for which he affectionately calls her a little thief. He orders a cover of precious metal and gems made for her favorite old book; she gives away her garments; he adores her, and she loves him, their children, and her faith more than life. Their enduring affection for each other is widely admired.

Twenty-two years later, the king is killed in battle alongside his eldest son, and the queen dies of heartbreak within days. Their royal dynasty lasts generations, the queen is declared a saint by her descendants, the king is immortalized in literature, and their memory is still revered.

Fairy tales and romance, indeed—yet this is Margaret and Malcolm's story in a nutshell, handed along by generations of historians and supported by medieval documents. Historians know a good deal about them by now, but their romantic story remains a solid foundation beneath both new and accumulating facts.

Margaret of Scotland has long fascinated historians as one of the most complex women in medieval history. What adds to her uniqueness is a rare detailed biography written by her personal confessor, along with annals and records by other chroniclers and historians both in her lifetime and after. More is known about Margaret than about most medieval queens. Her biographer, confessor, and friend, Bishop Turgot, was an Anglo-Dane who escaped Norman captivity in Lincoln to join the exiled Saxon royals in Scotland; he later became Bishop of Saint Andrews (at the time called Kilrymont or

Cill Rimhinn), and he was also prior of Durham. Margaret regarded Turgot as a close friend, and he was another who adored her. Several years after her death he wrote about her life for her daughter, Edith, known as Queen Matilda after she married Henry I of England.

Despite stilted medieval language and ideals, Turgot's *Vita S. Margaretae,* which has survived in medieval copies, was based on his personal memories and brings Margaret to life as an intense young woman of piety, conscience, charity, compassion, and intelligence. "There was gravity in her very joy and something stately in her anger," he wrote. She gave birth to eight healthy babies who thrived to adulthood (Edward, Edmund, Edgar, Aethelred, Alexander, David, Edith, and Mary—four kings of Scots, an abbot, and a queen of England among them) at a time when too many infants were lost early; that Margaret survived eight births was remarkable as well. As a mother, Margaret was attentive and affectionate, teaching her children lessons and manners but recommending that her beloved brood be whipped "when they were naughty, as frolicsome children will be," Turgot tells us.

And she had a feisty side, pilfering her husband's treasury and springing his prisoners loose, and disguising herself as a boy to enter a church forbidden to women. After losing her temper, she would ask for more penances, and she pressed Turgot to rebuke her if he saw fault in her behavior. When he said he could find no flaw, she gently chided him for negligence.

A certain mythology has developed around Margaret, in part due to the information gathered for her sainthood 150 years after her death. She kept an altar in a hidden cave near Dunfermline where she prayed and meditated; she fed and clothed the poor and provided for pilgrims; she lost her silver-cased Gospel while crossing a river, but by some miracle its delicate painted pages were unharmed (even more miraculously, the manuscript survived the ages and is now preserved in the Bodleian Library, Oxford).

So much of Margaret's life is known—almost too much to pack into a novel that covers just a portion of her life—and only some of it can be real, the rest exaggeration. Certainly her medieval chroniclers applied to her the ideals of perfection that measured most medieval queens and noblewomen, based on the model of the Virgin Mary (the Marian cult was already developing in the eleventh century). Yet any woman with eight young children and several households to run was simply too busy to spend hours praying each day, which may be closer to the truth than some of the tales about her.

Turgot's Margaret conveys as genuine, her charitable deeds believable, such as giving away the clothing on her back to the poor on outings (her courtiers did the same, embarrassed into it by her example), feeding orphans from her own dish, and creating Scotland's "queen's ferry," free to pilgrims (bishops could pay or walk). She prayed, admonished, and celebrated with fanatical intensity, fasted frequently, and lost sleep to devotions, benefitting her soul and ruining her health.

Modern historians accept that Margaret was that good and more, but they point out her other side, too: a complex, highly educated woman obsessively driven by demanding socioreligious standards, regarding herself as an unworthy sinner (she loved bright colors, fine clothing, fancy tableware). She was proud and determined, elegant and compassionate, but the darker side of her character is seen in the demands she made of herself, including apparent anorexia in excessive response to the tenets of her faith.

Raised in cosmopolitan courts, she knew that her roughshod Scottish husband's reputation needed polishing. Margaret crafted Malcolm's transformation from warrior-barbarian to worldly medieval king most deliberately. "By her care and labor the king himself, laying aside the barbarity of his manners, became more gentle and civilized," wrote Simeon of Durham, a probable acquaintance of Turgot.

Almost singlehandedly, Margaret brought Celtic Scotland into the medieval age—encouraging trade, raising standards in the royal households with fine dress and luxury goods, and bringing Roman rite and Benedictine guidance more cohesively into Scotland, a land previously content with the Celtic church. She argued theology with

Celtic priests—one session lasted three days as she debated Lenten observance and other differences—and she founded Benedictine churches. In a sense, she was a missionary who worried about Scottish souls.

Her increasing physical frailty is mentioned by Turgot, and her death in her mid-forties, said to be from heartbreak after the deaths of Malcolm and their son Edward, may have been due to a heart damaged by habitual fasting; even her priests, said Turgot, would beg her to eat something when she stubbornly deprived herself.

Given all that, I knew that a novel about Margaret could become a doorstop of a thousand pages unless it explored only part of her life. Enchanted by her history and curious to know more, I began the research while I wrote *Lady Macbeth*. For Margaret, I focused the story on her arrival in Scotland, her courtship with Malcolm, and the first few years of their marriage, babies and miracles and all. In the young queen, I wanted to show the elements that would create the mature queen of the historical record.

But a female protagonist who has one pregnancy after another, who fasts despite that and prays intensely, is best seen, at times, from another perspective—so Eva the Bard entered the story. Eva is purely fictional, but her bardic craft and courtly position fit Scottish medieval society. Male bards were certainly more common, but female bards and harpers were recorded consistently in Scottish history—from early myths, to the songwriters and poets of the eighteenth and nineteenth centuries, and beyond to current Celtic music.

Though it is unknown if King Lulach, son of Lady Macbeth, actually had an illegitimate daughter, it is possible. Neither do we know if Queen Gruadh (Gruoch in the historical record) survived her husband to see the reign of Malcolm and Margaret—but again, anything is possible. By the dates alone, Gruadh had a good chance of still being alive when Margaret was a young queen, and, I think, would have bitterly resented Malcolm Canmore.

Regarding Margaret's birth family, her father, Edward the Exile, was whisked out of England as a toddler to escape the wrath of Cnut, new to the English throne; harbored in Kiev and later Hungary, he married Agatha, who was perhaps of Hungarian, German, or Russian blood; for the novel, I favored the strong theory of Agatha as a princess of Kievan and Swedish descent. She was indeed widowed suddenly in 1057 when Edward the Exile dropped dead virtually at her feet in London. Stranded with her children in the court of Edward the Confessor, she escaped with them following the Norman Conquest, and all were shipwrecked in Scotland.

Edgar the Aetheling apparently never married (at least a wife is not recorded). King William probably exiled him as a condition of the agreement with Malcolm at Abernethy; Edgar went to Flanders, returned to Scotland two years later, and was offered property and a title in France. Probably eager for his success, Malcolm and Margaret fitted him out with a ship loaded with the finest belongings. It sank. Edgar, who has been described as "hapless," survived another shipwreck and made his way back to Scotland.

Next he went to England to do homage for William's forgiveness and was granted modest English properties, providing he gave up his claims. Edgar next went to Italy, perhaps hoping for adventure and profit, but soon he was back in England, losing his lands under rough King William Rufus. He returned to Scotland prior to the deaths of Malcolm and Margaret. Hapless indeed—yet a man of high ideals, if lacking the talent to see them through. In a sense, Edgar was the Bonnie Prince Charlie of his day.

However, he successfully championed the claims of his nephews, the Margaretsons, as they were called, against Malcolm's eldest, Duncan, for the Scottish throne. Eventually four of Malcolm and Margaret's sons succeeded to the throne of Scotland, establishing a Canmore dynasty. Traces of their blood continue to this day in British royalty.

Cristina, who was given lands in England by William, became abbess of Romsey Abbey and later oversaw the education of Margaret's young daughters, Edith and Mary; some accounts have her treating Edith so cruelly that the girl wrote to her father to fetch her home.

King Malcolm Canmore, or Malcolm III of Scotland, will be known to some readers through Shakespeare's *Macbeth* or through historical accounts of the Norman era in Britain. He was undoubtedly a rough, cunning warlord of a king who was civilized, in a sense, by his younger, sophisticated, and devout queen. More about Malcolm can be learned through reading my novel *Lady Macbeth,* as I have in many ways continued a story—that of the tensions between Malcolm, Macbeth, and Macbeth's wife—that begin there.

Part of the contribution of historical fiction, I think, is the ability to conjure a historical era and bring to life historical persons such as these who otherwise might exist only in dry nonfiction accounts. I hope that *Queen Hereafter* conjures for you the reputable and sainted Queen Margaret of Scotland as a real, vulnerable, likable young woman, placed—with the help of a lady bard and a trouble-stirring former queen—within the context of the Scottish society that no doubt the actual Margaret must have struggled to comprehend.

For the sake of fiction, I played a little with some dates, folding and tucking here and there so that events would move more quickly and make sense within the plot. Some well-known incidents and threads in Margaret's life, though integral to the historical queen, hit the cutting room floor in this fictional account for very practical reasons. Other events were altered slightly, such as the existence of Margaret's chapel in Edinburgh; true, the actual stone chapel was built under her son King David of Scotland, but it is possible that a wooden chapel existed there first. Also, fictional characters were added to support the main players, but the core of the story is, I hope, close to what could have happened in the early years of Margaret's marriage.

If these two Queens of Scots, Gruadh and Margaret, ever met (we will never know), each might have seen in the other her near opposite: one was the product of an archaic Celtic warrior society more Dark Ages than anything else; the other was a true medieval woman (modern in her own terms), greatly devout with a worldly sophistication.

The story of Margaret and Malcolm is a fairy tale of a beauty and a beast, two people who changed the course of Scottish history. The story is told that centuries after her death, Margaret's coffin was removed during renovations from its original tomb in the church at Dunfermline to be placed in the new apse. The workers carrying the coffin found it so heavy that they set it down and could not budge it again—then they realized that next to them was the tomb of Malcolm Canmore.

Only when Malcolm's coffin was moved to the new apse first could the queen's coffin then be easily lifted and installed in its new position. Legend says that the queen's spirit, out of love and respect for her husband, prevented her coffin from preceding his into the new space.

Tiny, beautiful lights, it is claimed, sometimes float around her tomb in Dunfermline, proving that she still watches over Scotland. To this day, her presence is recalled in various places—her simple, serene chapel in Edinburgh Castle; St. Margaret's Loch and St. Margaret's Well; the water crossing she founded at Queensferry in Fife; the boulder where she sat to rest near Malcolm's tower in Dunfermline and the little cave tucked under a hill there; and the cove where it is said she first set foot in Scotland, which is called Saint Margaret's Hope.

ACKNOWLEDGMENTS

I am grateful for the encouragement and support of many friends and colleagues, including Julie Booth, Joanne Zaslow, Anita Havas, Joanne Szadkowski. And endless thanks are due Mary Jo Putney and Patricia Rice as willing sources of opinion, inspiration, and friendship.

Also, I am very thankful to Benjamin Hudson, Ph.D., who discussed with me the many historical complexities that surround Malcolm and Margaret (and shared his inspiring theory that good girl Margaret and bad boy Malcolm are like the song "Leader of the Pack"). In addition, Malcolm Furgol deserves a nod for his stalwart defense of the merits of Margaret and his namesake, helping to convince me to write the book. Special thanks are due Mary Grady for graciously tutoring me in Celtic harp and sharing her wisdom in lessons that despite our crazy schedules did indeed sink in (I can pluck out some tunes!). I must thank Celtic harper Ann Heymann once again—the conversations we had when I wrote another book about a medieval harper, along with Ann's dazzling CD recordings, were inspiring for this novel, too. And thanks go to Richard Green for carefully correcting the Latin so that my characters would sound like educated royals rather than idjits playing around with an online translator; and lastly, thanks to Tommy D. for the harp!

My editor, Heather Lazare, has gentle patience and a guiding hand, and my agent, Karen Solem, is always there through thick and thin—and the Crown art department produced a gorgeous cover right out of the gate. Finally, my wonderful guys, David, Josh, Jeremy, and Sean, have put up with a lot, accepting the books as practically family members . . .

Thank you all.